LAST SEEN

LAST SEEN

KENT HARRINGTON

Copyright © 2021 by Kent Harrington
Cover and jacket design by Mimi Bark

ISBN 978-1-951709-23-5
eISBN: 978-1-951709-53-2
Library of Congress Control Number: available upon request

First hardcover edition May 2021 by Polis Books, LLC
44 Brookview Lane
Aberdeen, NJ 07747
www.PolisBooks.com

Around noon he asked for a pad of paper and scribbled…

"LSD, try it intermuscular 100mm."
—Aldous Huxley

PREFACE

His pistol held in front of him in a two-handed combat grip, Detective Michael O'Higgins climbed the bullet-chinked stairs in San Francisco's Mission District, where he and his partner had just fought for their lives— all because of a clerical error.

The front door was wide open. The detective walked into CJNG's1 meth and fentanyl transshipment house on Alabama Street, the squawk of the approaching ambulances in the distance. Adrenalin-hammered, everything felt both physically intense and effortless, as if he'd swallowed the perfect drug.

Clearing the house, room by room, he discovered a severed head in a clean blue plastic bucket in a small airless bedroom, a yellowing bed sheet for a curtain. Unspeakable things had gone on in the place, beyond anything he'd seen before. He stared down in horror and realized it was a woman. The dead woman's expression was placid, surreal, terrible proof that Mexico's failed-state savagery had come to California. Everything he feared and hated in life grabbed him at once, and with it, a profound despair he'd not felt before—even in war. It was as if he'd fallen into hell's center ring.

Walking back into the living room, he kicked a magazine-emptied AK-47 away from the dying gangster, as the man's neck wound bled heavily. The weapon spun across the hardwood floor, bouncing off a bullet-pocked black vinyl couch that had been shot up in the gunfight.

O'Higgins turned toward the man, intending to finish the job.

The asshole who had tried to kill them was looking up at O'Higgins in shock. He was slumped—in full tactical gear, with the latest bullet-proof vest— against an old '50s Frigidaire, a military-style haircut, his face sweaty. O'Higgins could have tried to help him, but didn't move. He felt no compassion. He could see the man was dying—a lucky shot. The bullet he'd fired from the street had torn an artery, entering just above the protective vest's collar. Blood pressure zeroed out, the gunman had collapsed in the kitchen, his legs going out from under him, all his special equipment useless. Infinity lay in front of him.

O'Higgins wanted to ask who the woman in the bedroom was. What did you do to her? But he didn't. Instead he bent down and picked up a pistol lying on the floor—a brand new Sig Sauer, just out of the man's reach. He put it in his coat pocket.

He and the man looked at each other, the victor and the vanquished. The gunman said something in Spanish and reached up as if he wanted a hand up or was just waving goodbye to his shitty world. He had that confused look of the mortally wounded. The detective had seen it in Iraq. It was a slow-motion gesture, as if the dying might, in the last seconds of life, find some way to save themselves, some magic trick.

There is a shadow of death, O'Higgins thought. He put the barrel of his Glock against the man's forehead.

"Why?" he said.

The asshole died before he could pull the trigger. The man's head rolled forward.

O'Higgins stared down at him, the front of the bulky vest blood saturated.

O'Higgins had stood and taken the hail-Mary shot as soon as the firing from the house stopped. He'd guessed correctly that the gunman was reloading. Marvin was lying at his feet, bleeding from his wound. The two had taken cover behind a VW Micro bus at one in the afternoon on a winter-cold Thursday, the VW hammered by withering automatic fire. The gunfight had lasted only a few minutes... enough time for chaos's masterpiece to play out in the city named after a Catholic saint, long forgotten.

O'Higgins was glad the man was dead. He was glad he had caught the man reloading. The moment he'd lined him up in his sight—a silhouette in the window— a muscle memory now. Years of training and combat experience had paid off again.

O'Higgins turned around and walked out of the shot-up house that smelled of weed, gunfire and raw meth. He passed two young EMT guys on the shoddy wooden stairs, not bothering to tell them the shooter was dead—or that others had fled out the back while he'd poured gunfire down on them from the window. The Mexicans had thought, incorrectly, that the two detectives had come to rob them, probably because his partner was black.

It had all been an accident. They'd been given the wrong address. O'Higgins wanted to tell the ambulance guys that, too, but didn't. The whole life and death struggle had been based on a mistake of the simplest type: someone on Bryant Street had transposed a set of numbers in an address. A simple mistake that might cost Marvin Lee, a family man, his life. It had been that way in the war, too—one strange incongruous event leading to chaos and sudden death.

Latins and white fresh-faced New Economy types—in their twenties, the kind who were changing the Mission District—were taking photos with their ever-present phones, gawking at the swarm of cops. Clusters of callow civilians stared at O'Higgins as he walked past them and toward the unmarked Ford. One corner of his shirttail was pulled out and torn where he'd made a bandage to stuff into Marvin's gaping leg wound.

It hadn't even been thirty minutes since they'd gotten out of the car, thinking it was just a normal day on the job. The street was quiet, fog-embraced, cold.

O'Higgins slid in behind the wheel of the Ford, his hands cut from the broken glass whose small white shards carpeted the street around them. He started the Ford, ignoring his cuts, and drove toward the hospital—

the police radio on, tense voices talking about the mayhem on Alabama Street.

San Francisco, in all its past glory, inhaling and exhaling, fog and sun, no notice taken of anyone. Cities don't take any notice of human suffering and never will, the detective thought.

They never found out who the woman was, or anything about why she'd been treated in such a brutal way. Her cruel death was emblematic of the ugly new world he was charged with policing.

He called Marvin's wife…

Chapter 1
Paris

The train carrying Emma Barre and her parents, her father Adrien and her mother Cecile, was approaching the Gare Du Nord in central Paris. The family had left Lyon early that August morning with tickets for a flight to San Francisco.

The Barre family had only the week before celebrated Emma's birthday with a big party at her grandmother's house. Their daughter had been born in late July in a hospital in Strasbourg seventeen years before, almost to the day. Having postponed having a family, the couple were joyous when they'd brought Emma home from the hospital all those years before. They'd thought family life might be denied them, but they'd been proven wrong. The Sturm und Drang of their daughter's teenage years, difficult, seemed to have passed like a summer storm. The family understood they were on the verge of a new era, as Emma would be entering university soon. The strong bond among the three was obvious to anyone who saw them that morning.

Perhaps because Emma was deaf, the connection seemed more intense and immediate.

The Barres were going to San Francisco before Emma entered one of the best universities in France on a full academic scholarship. Her mother and father couldn't have been prouder, or more invested in Emma's future, which seemed secure. A degree from this first-tier university opened the door to the highest positions in French government and industry.

The Barres had come from working-class stock and were aware that social divisions in the country were getting worse, not better. Lyon had seen Yellow Vest movement in the streets. Much of the fighting between the police and the Yellow Vest demonstrators went unreported and had been extremely violent. Just that week the army had been called out with shoot-to-kill orders, shocking the Barres. The demonstrators lost eyes and hands in the melee, filling hospitals.

France seemed on the verge of a second revolution.

The movement had touched a nerve in both of Emma's parents, who couldn't help but identify with the working-class protestors, but they never spoke about it with their daughter. She was too sensitive, and too young. Emma, they believed, belonged to a different France, untrammeled by history.

Emma's father, the son of a truck driver, had excelled in his career and was one of the most important and respected physicists in Europe. Her mother taught modern French history at the university in Lyon. Because Emma was the daughter of two very bright people, it was expected that she, too, would do well academically. But it had not been expected that she would be a genius in the classic sense, like Mendelssohn or Curie— effortless sparkling intelligence that was ultimately mysterious, and couldn't be measured. Doctors had told her parents that despite Emma's handicap—she'd been born deaf— the toddler was testing off the charts. She had learned to walk at two months, and was reading at age four. She was precocious, but not unduly intense as many bright children are. Her intelligence could be overwhelming for the adults charged with her education. Emma was a relaxed, well-adjusted, pretty teenage girl who seemed to be enjoying life at a certain academic pitch.

Sitting next to her mother on the train that morning, she lost herself in France's summer landscape, golden wheat fields and silent mountains in a "psychic landscape" that she could appreciate. As they finally pulled into

Paris, passing a shoddy area before arriving at the famous train station—the same station the Germans used for deportations to the East during the War—she debated whether to tell her parents that she planned to free-climb an E7-rated route at Céüse. The weekend before, she had tested herself on a difficult cliff at Yzeron near her home, without a climbing rope. At any point she could have died.

Her parents believed her desire to rock climb was a passing teenage phase that would run its course. But it had turned into something else: an odd means of expression. And if Emma was being honest, a way of spitting in the face of the Fates for the injustice of being deprived one of the key human senses. The loss of her hearing had been unexplainable and rude, and made her always feel like an outsider. The idea that she could fall to her death while free climbing was an odd blandishment to the sport. A psychiatrist might suggest Emma had a death wish at the bottom of her unconscious, in that center-of-the-center place present in all of us, regardless of IQ, which propels some to excel and others to waste a life dithering in negativity.

Nothing on her beautiful young face betrayed that dark longing shared by creative people and mountain climbers—to climb to some unreachable spot seen from afar and survive the balancing act between life and death.

Emma's deafness made her instruction in the sport that much more difficult, as none of her teachers at the climbing gym in Lyon—all young men—knew how to sign. They had used a variety of techniques to get around her disability and pass on what they knew. The instructors were kind to Emma and a little smitten: she had a talent for the sport, and was enthusiastic and of course beautiful. She'd read everything she could on the subject of free climbing. That too had helped give her the tools she needed to learn the art. Her body began to change as a result of the arduous training, from that of a reed-thin girl to that of a young woman. Men took even more notice of her, as her physical strength became obvious but uniquely feminine.

Their flight on Air France took off on time, packed with happy tourists setting out on adventures. Emma had decided not to tell her parents she intended to climb one of the difficult routes at Céüse as soon as she got back to France. She'd heard someone had just died on the route she planned to take, so it seemed cruel and unnecessary to tell her parents at the start of their vacation.

Instead, as the plane taxied, she'd opened her Kindle and started to read about her chosen route. Like life itself, she thought, it would be simply be a series of key handholds, exact shifts, and good weather.

Chapter 2
San Francisco

Dusk with its army of sidewalk shadows had taken Columbus Avenue as the two detectives pulled out into the afternoon traffic. The wide street was chock-a-block with what the cops called "taxpayers" heading toward the Embarcadero, or the myriad restaurants and bars along Columbus. It was happy hour in San Francisco, the new Paris, a youthful dream city desperate to hold onto its storied past.

That intense history still vibrated on the busy streets where Chinatown met North Beach.

It had been, until very lately, a European city trapped inside Anglo-Saxon America, sitting precariously on the edge of the western world. But it was changing, becoming every day more like New York or LA, robbed of its sophisticated not-like-anywhere-else identity. The drug epidemic and the New Economy had created two cities—one wretched and one opulent, both schizoid and extreme. There was a real sense that things had gone too far, that no one could stop it—whatever "it" was.

"He's got her," O'Higgins said.

"No shit," Marvin said. "No shit… You figure that out all by yourself? I'm going to kill that motherfucker. I swear to God."

They pulled by the Transamerica Building. They'd listened to the police radio, the Central Station channel, and heard about the missing tourist girl.

"We got to find him, first," O'Higgins said. A text pinged his phone. It was his daughter, asking him to send money to her PayPal account. She'd gone away to school at NYU. He missed her terribly, but hadn't told her that. Later that night he would send her 500 dollars he didn't have, borrowing it from his IRA. The first year's school tuition had cleaned out his savings. He had no idea how he was going to pay for her sophomore year.

The two homicide detectives—one a hulking white man, Michael O'Higgins, the other a good-looking, tall African American, Marvin Lee—met the missing French girl's parents in the lobby of the Marriott Hotel on the corner of Columbus and Bay Streets. It was noisy. Tourists came and went from an ugly stucco-chipped porte-cochere outside. Ubers—sporting their weird Germanic black logo—were letting tired fog-belted families out and immediately loading others, pulling U-turns on Columbus, honking, bulling their way back into commuter traffic. Their sullen drivers were the meshing gears of mass tourism—a rough mural of confusion. It was all part of San Francisco's new status as a must-visit Mecca.

The missing girl's father's name was Adrien, and his wife's Cecile. The family name was Barre. They were French nationals from Lyon. O'Higgins and Lee learned later that the father was an important French physicist, in charge of the EU's fusion project among other things. He was hoping to harness the smashed-into-one subatomic power source for the first time, and make fusion capable of creating electrical energy, cheap. But at first Barre seemed just like all the other hapless European tourists visiting the city. Except he was terrified, because his beautiful seventeen-year-old daughter, Emma, had disappeared.

"Do you speak English?" Marvin asked. It was the first in the series of blunt questions they'd had to ask since the first tourist girl had disappeared. One had been Italian, two had been English. All three had been raped and murdered.

16

"Yes," the man said. They shook hands, very formal, all around. The father was holding his passport in his left hand, as if that was going to help matters. He wore gold wire-rim glasses that underscored his intelligence and marked him as an intellectual. The glasses were what you noticed first, then his fire-blue eyes and his pale skin.

He lifted the passport. "Yes. French citizens—we're from Lyon." The Frenchman's expression contained both panic and fear. It was a look O'Higgins had seen in soldiers often enough. But this was a different kind of war—no rules at all.

"France?" Marvin said.

Marvin had sobered up and was dead serious, the slightly high and volatile Det. Marvin Lee of the car banished. Both had been drinking since the shootout that had nearly killed them six months before. They'd slid into a place in the Tenderloin—the Outsider— before responding to the call, having a "refreshment" in a dank bar on Geary Street that catered to black street-level dealers and pimps. The criminal clientele shut up when they walked in, sensing they were cops from the way they acted—so unafraid.

The two men had drunk in silence. The bar's jukebox played an especially ugly rap tune. O'Higgins had been a million miles away, remembering his mother covering a book for him in sixth grade using a brown paper bag, cutting the paper carefully. She'd come from Ireland, born into a poor rural family of tenant farmers. The fancy store-bought covers his classmates sported would never be his, despite the fact that his father, a successful criminal lawyer, could afford them.

"It's high time you learned some Gaelic," she'd said that day. From then on when they were together, she had started teaching him her ancient language. He'd loved it. Tree became *crann*… car became *cairr*, market was *margadh*. He was the only one of her four children she was teaching Gaelic. He never understood why, until he'd learned that he was adopted. Had she been making up for his biological mother? Had she spoken Gaelic? He thought so now, sitting at the bar, the ugly music blotted out by his escape into his past. His biological mother had been Irish… he was sure of it somehow. He wondered what she'd looked like, how she'd come to have him, and how his parents had ended up with him.

They'd finished their drinks and left, not high but not quite sober either.

"We're here on vacation," Barre said in his heavily accented English.

O'Higgins nodded. He couldn't bring himself to look the man in the eye. It was impossible. He felt sick, a hopeless dread spreading over him. He saw the naked hog-tied English girl left out on a cold country road near Bodega Bay, so alone and pathetic as they'd walked toward her. She was the first tourist girl they'd lost. She, too, had come to the city on vacation.

They'd lost another two young women since, all teenage girls visiting the city, all raped and murdered by the same man, whom the press had dubbed the "Seven Hills Killer." A young editor thought it would sell newspapers, and he was right. The tabloid-inspired name had stuck, sending the well-oiled and profitable serial-killer industry into full gear.

"Your daughter, do you have her passport?" O'Higgins asked.

"Yes." It was the mother who answered. She was smoking. She was blond and had short hair—pretty, about forty and petite but very pale, too. She vibed Frenchwoman dynamo. "Yes, here." She held it up.

O'Higgins took the missing girl's passport. He glanced at the photo. She was, as he'd expected, an attractive girl with a full mane of auburn hair. She favored her father, he thought. She was going to be a beautiful woman, no question. He took the passport.

"Our daughter Emma is deaf," the father said. "We have other photos. On our phones, of course. I can send them now? Print them out?" The father looked toward the hotel's busy front desk as if he would run there and get them copies.

"Deaf?" Marvin said, struck by the idea that their killer had taken a deaf girl. Something about that horrified him. He nearly jumped. His handsome face was drawn since he'd been wounded. Still handsome, but forever marked—etched—by the violent near-death day.

18

"Yes," the mother said, noticing the sudden change in the atmosphere.

The four of them didn't speak. O'Higgins held the passport, terrified that the girl might already be dead.

"She's been deaf from birth," the father said. "She signs, of course, and she can speak." He broke into French, looking for the right words. "Congenital ..." He looked at his wife for help. The physicist, who could explain the squeezing of matter that was a black hole, didn't fully comprehend yet that their precious daughter was truly missing, having been squeezed into a different kind of special, horrible moment in time and space.

"Yes, please," Marvin said. "Send me some very recent ones, please—ones you've taken here." He handed the man his card.

The father took it and handed it to his wife. Barre said something in French. His wife pulled her phone out of her back pocket and sat down nearby to search for recent photos of their daughter.

"What happened?" O'Higgins said, watching the mother.

"We were at Pier 36. My wife had gone into The Alcatraz Store. Emma didn't like that kind of thing. She hates the idea of prison," the father said. "I got a call from my work—it was important. I stepped away. Emma went into the Hall of Mirrors—maze, I think they call it. She bought a ticket. I watched her—I was on the phone with a colleague, there was a problem with..." he stopped himself. "When Cecile came out of the shop, Emma had vanished. I went into the..." Barre searched for the English word. "Attraction. I thought she'd gotten lost—but she never came out."

The Marriott's lobby was full of guests. It was the end of summer, and the place was a United Nations: Hindus from India, Muslim women from the UAE, wearing hijabs. A gaggle of English teenage girls, black, white, and brown— a school group—in hiking shorts and backpacks paraded by them, led by a stern middle-aged woman, East Indian-looking, who was keeping a sharp eye on the group. O'Higgins watched the girls troop past. Any one of them could be taken, he thought. They were exactly Seven Hills' type.

O'Higgins wanted to stop the schoolgirls' chaperone, warn her that out there, somewhere, was a madman. That the man had texted him throughout his victim's ordeal, sending him random remarks, having seen O'Higgins's name in the Chronicle when the English girl was found. Some texts were pedestrian, some about the presidential election, some about O'Higgins's experience in Iraq. The killer had obviously Googled him and found out O'Higgins had been overseas, an officer in the Marine Corps.

One of O'Higgins's former soldiers had written a bestselling account about the Battle of Fallujah and used his name. He and Seven Hills had become odd acquaintances. It was difficult, but he'd tried to nourish the relationship, answering the killer's random questions in hopes of getting him to say something revealing about himself. But the man was careful, knowing full well what not to say. He wanted to know about the battle. What it was like? Had O'Higgins been frightened? It was as if the man were a normal civilian with the normal questions about combat, all questions O'Higgins had been asked a hundred times in barrooms since he'd come home.

He'd stopped telling people he was a vet to avoid having to talk about his service. "You were on the phone when she disappeared?" Marvin asked.

Barre nodded.

O'Higgins watched the English girls go by, most of them involved with their phones, their accented teenage sing-song voices lovely and loud in the lobby. They were still children, he thought, turning toward Barre. His body felt heavy from the Irish coffee he'd drunk. He didn't want to be addled by alcohol, but he was, if only slightly.

"Have you tried calling her on her cell phone? Texting?" Marvin asked.

"Of course!" the mother said. She'd found the photos and had joined them again. She said something in French, obviously a curse word of some kind. "Of course. Do you want to see?!" She held her phone up, angry, obviously thinking the two detectives were stupid for asking the question.

She too was a high-powered academic, they'd learn, and didn't suffer fools gladly.

"So, she has her own phone? Emma?" O'Higgins asked, ignoring the mother's outburst.

"Yes—yes. Emma has a cell phone. She texts, of course," the mother said. O'Higgins could see she was angry. And he guessed she might be blaming herself, the way he was blaming himself for losing the other girls.

"No answer, then?" Marvin asked.

"Nothing," the father said. He spoke in French to his wife. She looked at her husband and nodded. He'd no doubt told her to calm the hell down, or something to that effect, as she looked down. O'Higgins saw her hands were shaking.

"Can we have your daughter's cell phone number?" O'Higgins asked. They took down the girl's cell number along with the parents' numbers.

"I'm sorry, I have to ask these obvious questions," Marvin said. The woman nodded. "It's the way we work. Step by step." She nodded again.

"They said—another policeman—that there were—that other girls were missing from the same location?" the father said. His face looked drawn and already haggard, and his daughter had been missing less than 24 hours.

It would get worse. O'Higgins knew the road well. And he knew only too well where, for the other girls' families, it had ended. "Has your daughter ever gone off? You know—run away?" he asked.

"Once," the father said.

"Once?" O'Higgins said.

"Yes."

"While she was here?" Marvin said.

"Yes. She left the hotel, with another girl she met here. Another French girl," the father said.

O'Higgins looked at Marvin. "When?"

"The first night we were here," the mother said. "Sunday."

"So, it's possible she and that girl are together?" Marvin said.

"No, her friend went home to France with her parents."

"You're sure?" O'Higgins said.

"Yes. Emma texted her and she was back home already."

"Was the girl staying here at the Marriott?" Marvin said.

"Yes," the father said. "May I have the passport back?"

O'Higgins took a photo of the missing girl's passport's details page with his cell phone and handed it back.

"It's biometric—the passport. It's connected to Emma's handprints," the father said.

"Good." Marvin said. "Well, right now it's been about ten hours since she went missing."

"They said that we had to wait twenty-four hours before we could report this…" The father spoke in French to his wife, then turned back to them. "Make an official report," the father said.

"Yes. That's right," Marvin said. "We heard it on our radio, and we thought we'd speak to you."

"We have had other girls go missing," O'Higgins said, finally. "From about that same location." He didn't want to say that they were homicide detectives, but he knew they would find out as soon as they looked at Marvin's card.

He also didn't say that since his wife died, he'd been unable to be emotionally distant. O'Higgins reached for the mother's hand. He recognized her anger for what it was, a horrible suffering.

She looked at him surprised, not expecting it from someone like him, a bruiser type.

She'd thought he looked stupid when he'd introduced himself, as often happens to physically big men. But she didn't pull away. The woman looked at him, her eyes drilling into him. It was a look he would never forget: femininity laced with intelligence swamped by fear and horror, emotions/colors all intertwined and encased—and at the very bottom, hope.

"We're going to find your daughter. I promise you. We're not going to wait twenty-four hours," O'Higgins said. He gave the mother his cell number and told her to text him her photos and Emma's social media passwords, if she knew them.

"We don't spy on our daughter," the mother said. "We never asked for them."

He stared out the barroom window at the cars lined up in front of the Palace Hotel. Later, after Marvin had gone home to his wife and kids, in a bar across from the famous hotel, O'Higgins looked at the photos of the French girl. He was alone, with no one to go home to.

Since his daughter had gone away to college, he hated going home to San Rafael and an empty house. He would wait until it was good and dark, and he was high enough to take the feeling of an empty house full of ghosts: his wife, before the accident that killed her; himself when he'd made detective; their daughter when she was five, a real sprite. He missed all the optimism and joy that had once been his.

He didn't recognize the number, but had a horrible feeling that it was Seven Hills as soon as the text pinged his phone.

"She's deaf... Want to talk to her?"

"Yes."

"Okay..."

His phone rang. He stood up at the bar, listening. He heard breathing on the other end of the line. O'Higgins heard a particular noise, but he couldn't tell what it was. Perhaps something to cancel out other sounds, but it sounded like an air compressor. He strained for any clue as to what it might be.

"Are you okay? Do you have any idea where you are? Anything you can say?" He spoke to her despite her being deaf, hoping it would somehow comfort her. The thought of her not being able to hear him was horrifying.

He listened carefully, hoping to hear the man's voice. He'd heard it only once. He had spent hours trying to place it, and had played it for experts who could identify accents. They had theories: maybe he was from

Southern California, one expert said. Around Bakersfield? Another said he was from South Africa. He'd given up. It was just a man's voice, nothing special.

He moved for the app on his phone that would allow him to record the call and toggled it on in case the caller spoke again. The bar was noisy.

The sound of Emma Barre's voice stopped him cold.

"Sir, my... name... is Emma Barre... Please... tell my parents I'm okay... Tell my father I love him. He'll worry..."

Later, on the way home, he played the recording in search of clues, his phone on the empty passenger seat as he headed down the freeway.

"Sir, my... name... is Emma Barre... Please... tell my parents I'm okay... Tell my father I love him. He'll worry..."

The girl's voice had an eerie quality. She'd probably learned to speak using oralist techniques, he thought, so she wouldn't have the normal hi-low colors associated with teenage girls. The halting voice touched him. He reached for his phone and played the recording again.

Chapter 3

The old orchards and farmsteads O'Higgins remembered from boyhood had been torn down to make way for the brave new world of big-money wineries. The hoary redwood barns of the past were gone. He remembered coming on them when they'd hunted quail nearby, the mystery of those old hovels almost holy. Their church-like emptiness full of some sweaty Irish American or Italian American story, forever lost. Their crude paint-less rafters stained with bird shit, swallows having nested near chinks in the roof. The birds would whirl as they watched from below, he and his pals. Their shotguns broken open, carried over shoulders, the day almost over. Dead quail in bloody backpacks at their feet. Four years later he was at war, and all that seemed a dream.

O'Higgins looked at his phone when it pinged. He read the text:

Do you love me? Is it true, Michael? Should I believe you? I want to believe you.

He looked away, unable to answer. The hills just north of Calistoga were silent with phalanxes of ascending grapevines, drenched in bright sunshine. Beyond the newly staked vines were traces of burnt ridge tops, metallic blue-looking from the fires that had swept over them the summer before. The Tubbs Fire had nearly burnt down Calistoga.

O'Higgins tried to spot his new girlfriend amongst the crowd standing about on her winery's new deck, but he didn't see her. The text had come from India… his girlfriend had come from San Francisco. They were different women. Different looking as two young women could be.

That late July afternoon he was amongst Robin Sparks' people. The Bay Area's richest, and he was the outsider and felt it. He was just a San Francisco homicide cop. They were titans and billionaires, software playboys with their trophy size-zero girlfriends from LA and New York. His girlfriend was very rich. He liked her well enough, he thought, pocketing his phone and looking for her.

He moved away from the edge of the deck and spotted her. Robin was wearing skinny jeans and a white blouse—very chic, her dirty blond hair long. It was what had attracted him, her style. She didn't look rich, just pretty. She'd just turned thirty, and they'd gone to Mexico to her family's place in Cabo San Lucas to celebrate the month before. He watched her make her way amongst her kind—efficient, gracious, beautiful, welcoming. It was her party, and she knew how to throw one. She owned it.

It was just six and still, before dusk started to settle things. It seemed that God favored these people. He'd given them so much, after all. Gave them these sacred rich places—wineries, California valleys, planes, power, a city at their beck and call. At heart, he realized, they were just like anyone, only better dressed.

It was an odd thought. People are people—criminals, the very rich, the very poor, and everyone in between. The war had taught him that. What it was to be human. It was the one thing you could count on: human beings to be just that. He made his way to the impromptu bar and ordered a glass of wine, his third. He watched the tidy-looking bartender pour it. O'Higgins felt someone jostle him from behind, but didn't bother to turn and see who it was. The bartender slid a full glass of wine toward him. He nodded a thank you.

He shouldn't have sent that drunken text to the woman in India. But he'd done a lot of things lately that he shouldn't have. His daughter's leaving had made his longing for Asha worse. She was on his mind constantly and always with him, even when he was making love to the other woman—

whom he liked well enough. He was ashamed of that, but it was the truth.

Drinking made it easy to lie to himself. He longed for the woman in India, and he was afraid of that longing. To love someone again, like that, was too much to bear. Loving someone that way carries a burden—a big price you must pay, or it was just sex or friendship. Love costs.

"Are you carrying your gun?" a young man asked, interrupting his solitary moment on the edge of being high. He'd come up from behind and signaled the bartender, lifting his index finger.

Michael O'Higgins turned to face him. The young man who'd asked the question received a fresh glass of white wine from the bartender. O'Higgins had met him before. His father ran a hedge fund. He was sockless and wore a cool shirt open at the collar, several buttons undone. He'd never been punched in the face, or ever worried about making the rent or getting sick and not being able to take time off from work because he couldn't afford it. He had it all by the balls and knew it.

"You're the policeman, right?" He said it the way all her fancy friends did: with a slightly mystified tone—or derisive, if O'Higgins was being paranoid, which he had a tendency toward.

"Yeah, that's me," O'Higgins said. "I'm the cop."

The young man touched his glass of wine in a toast O'Higgins wasn't privy to. He caught the detective by surprise, so that he thought he'd spill wine on the new pants he'd been forced to buy for the occasion, yet another new winery opening.

"Well, do you? Permit to carry—I want one but can't get it because California is full of fairies that don't like guns. Democratic fairies. Give us back the German—" the young man said, referring to Schwarzenegger.

The bartender was gay, and heard what he'd said. He gave the young man a quick look.

Okay, the guy's drunk, O' Higgins thought. It had become obvious, suddenly. He'd been thinking about Asha and not picked up on it. He smiled. But it was his flat Irishman's smile, slightly derisive at its core. Street people saw it when they were lying to him. He let the guy blab on…

He'd promised Robin he'd be nice to her guests. And he was, if nothing else, at least true to his word.

Dusk crept up on them later, around seven, seven-thirty. Dirty wine glasses smudged with lipstick and finger food abandoned and set aside on new teak tables... Guests starting to leave... hugs and kisses and the like. Expensive foreign cars—a few must-have Teslas—started. A yeah-baby-we-had-us-some-fun cacophony as the party broke up.

They had stayed amongst the dirty glasses, just the two of them sitting on the edge of the new deck with his bottle of Patron. He drank too much. But even then, despite that, the beauty wasn't lost on him. It was soothing. His girlfriend didn't understand why he wanted to stay on, but she stayed by his side, patient. She was a good person and he thought she might be falling in love with him, that she might care for him. Something was sad about that. But all he could do was drink and watch the sky turn colors, touch things—move in delicate ways. A rumble toward night, the colors dusky, subduing the smooth landscape, the way he liked when he was drinking. Then night—the sun extinguished finally, like a cigarette thrown down a well—doused.

"Did you have fun?" Robin asked as they were leaving. She marched him toward the car, her arm around him protective. It was six months since a gunfight that had almost been the end of him and his partner, and she was sensitive to it. It was on her face, her willing him to relax, be himself; drink, if that was what he needed to do. She'd made sure she didn't bring up his work. He told her once he didn't want to talk about his work and she respected that, although it had been hard for her not to ask.

She'd read about the shootout at one of her family's corporate offices in St. Helena as if she were reading about a stranger. He said it was because she wouldn't understand. It was an unkind thing to say. Maybe it was true, but he regretted saying it. He didn't want to hurt her, or anyone, now. When you've been hurt, you know what it's like.

He didn't love her, so why should she be hurt if some asshole shot him dead? It was a twisted drunken logic that he formed on the way to the parking lot. He decided it made sense to him, as he slid into her new German car. He liked how solid it felt. He liked it that she was rich and owned beautiful things. He liked her, especially the way she would touch him when they were making love. Reach up and touch his face. He liked it.

She looked at him and started the car, all its fancy dials springing to life.

He remembered as they pulled out of the dirt parking lot that he wanted to kill someone.

But that was oddly different, and professional—and separate from the soft night.

They drove up the new dirt road guarded by cloaked oak trees, the smell of dust: a weird perfumed mixture of warm earth and Johnson grass from the new tractor-torn road. The darkness plowed by the car's headlights. Before he knew it, they were on Highway 12 and the ride home to the City. They crossed the Golden Gate. The bridge always there for him, since he was a kid— the Golden Gate where they'd tossed his mother's ashes early one morning, everyone in the family on the deck of the boat. He remembered that a wave had sprayed up on the deck, a watery keen. It was as if his mother was, in her Irish way, saying goodbye to them all. Then they'd dusted the ocean with all that was left of her—ashes.

Robin Sparks read Asha's text later, after he'd fallen asleep in her beautiful bedroom at the Harrison. It didn't surprise her. She told herself O'Higgins would fall in love with her if she was patient. She would keep trying. She was a brave woman, not the cliché rich girl people assumed. She had real grit and intelligence and was capable of a lot—including real love.

He misunderstood her, and she had allowed it. She wanted him to love her and would keep at it, she told herself. Somehow prove to him that she wasn't to be summed up as simply his girlfriend. She didn't care about the girl in India, she thought, putting down his phone. She'd unlocked his iPhone by simply holding it up to his sleeping face, an indiscretion she wasn't proud of.

She looked down at him. He was not really handsome, at least not in any conventional way. She wondered about him the way women do about their men—his silences especially. His were palpable. And then she read the text again… she couldn't help herself, she was jealous.

Do you love me? Is it true, Michael? Should I believe you? I want to believe you.

Chapter 4

Sheer frustration, and anger too, were at the dream's source—unstoppable male anger. Volcanic. Red. Dangerous. Odd scraps of twisted frustration and regret welded together at the bottom of his psyche, like unidentifiable hulks left on the ocean floor after a fierce naval battle.

It always started, this dream, with gunfire from the shootout that had almost taken their lives. The BOOM-BOOM-BOOM of returning gunfire... The way his pistol wanted to twist wild as he fired, with no clear sight picture at first. Just the nondescript house above them. The way he brought the barrel under control, no time for a two-handed grip, everything happening in a time without time. The gun-feel, part instinctual muscle memory, part training. Oily polymer grip. Brass spit out and rolling, primer punched. Kill someone... The target found, a broken-out window above them... familiar muzzle flashes... They're trying to kill us... Marvin falling ... the special heart-choking hysteria. He'd reached down, grabbed Marvin by the collar of his jacket and started dragging him down the long flight of wooden stairs that had been quiet and unremarkable seconds ago, as they'd drudged toward the front door to interview a witness.

The hidden shooter's AK-47 ripped a dotted line down the wooden stairs a few inches from his feet—chinks appeared, surreal. The sounds of combat—full auto attack. Crazy jacked-up Mexicans yelling from inside the house. Mayhem. The adrenalin dump creating tunnel vision.... But in his dream, he could see clearly in a panoramic technicolor, everything vivid, every detail muscular.

He hustled Marvin down the stairs, dragging him toward a bright yellow VW microbus, grabbing for his one spare magazine. Marvin gasped for air, going into shock, arterial bleeding. The look in his eyes. The VW's door panel being slammed by rounds, like a strange horrible insane clock ringing an alarm: clang-thud, clang thud, clang thud, clang-thud. Him hoping they were putting the engine block between them and the shooter. The odd feel of the asphalt on his open palm, rough. His other hand doing the work. Marvin silently handing him his own weapon, offering it up, his black hand wet with blood, like a detail in a Goya painting.

Then all of the sounds and fury would fade away down to the singular sound of an old-school record needle being set down, scratching. He could see them both huddling against the yellow ancient VW micro bus that was shielding them. As if he were looking down, suspended over the street. Then the Nina Simone song would start up… the recurring dream's familiar soundtrack.

It was a dream, so nothing was tethered to the outside world's linear time/place logic. Yet it made perfect dream sense, a special simplicity that was in turn a complex brain-language that he understood despite its strange meter. It had to be… In fact, the dream was his life force— asleep or awake, it was present. The two were one thing. In a sense you dream your life, and life dreams you. You're not in your body, your body is in you, a girlfriend once told him.

When everything goes wrong …. Don't let me be misunderstood.

Nina Simone's cover playing on their car radio… powerful black female filling up the car… a woman's voice—somehow all women. Marvin driving. Simone talking to them—to him. The full weight of west Marin in winter, old-school saturated color slides… surreal and moving: storm-wretched blue-grey sky, penciled-in green hills their lines smudged by fog, oak trees, bits of dead tree's dark limbs… reaching out… an ancient hubcap stuck by the half-sun in a tide pool, oddly brilliant and singular.

A sullen permanent feeling of rootedness. California along the Marin coast … gloomy, sublime, but also somehow ancient and unforgiving. A preternatural dreamscape.

The car would always pull off Highway One at the same spot. A dirt road descending toward the Pacific Ocean… Nina Simone's voice not letting up, singing for humanity. She was rooted in her art, at precisely the moment the car's tires left the asphalt and the pitted dirt road started to rock the car from side to side gently, but meaningful—life transition. End of the beginning. A you've-left-civilization-feeling. Now they were alone with the events to come.

Life's dirt road.

Baby, I'm just human… don't you know I have faults like anyone…

"This is Joy Road…. back there?" Marvin would say over the music.

He would nod to confirm, as he had had to confirm an order in Iraq. "Load them up," part of a memory of war. "Load up the dead! Load up the living!" Load up the guns and the misery and the Hurt Locker masculinity, so much bullshit. Sold to get young men to lose their minds in cradle of nationalistic blather. Didn't Prince Harry wear a uniform? A black one? Whose uniform? Chic? Or something else, their defiant message: We own you. We've always owned you. Aristocrats hugging page after page of soft-sell agitprop about a worthless class—his mother had said that to her American friends, who were astonished by the remark.

"That's what the map said," O'Higgins the dreamer would always answer.

"Maps? Maps lie, man. You know that. Jesus, Mike! You were a soldier. You should know that. Shit, white boy, what's wrong with you, man?"

In this, *the* recurring dream, a dream he didn't welcome, he'd conflated various important events in only the way the human mind can: a psyche attached to a supercomputer, minting its odd beautiful logic energized by facts dwelling in his subconscious—electric: this second part of the dream, including the dialogue, was always the same and was agonizingly, coherently incoherent.

Because it recurred every night, it was more frightening, more intense and more real each time … sweating… building to some insane crescendo— a real mind-fuck. It was as if his subconscious wanted to fill in new parts, adding details, each time pressing in another piece of this huge dream-puzzle into place. Each piece tiny but important to the whole, his psyche as mosaic. The repetitions were a kind of profitable OCD where he metaphorically washed his hands in the terrible events, in the sound of Nina Simone's more than just poignant and beautiful lyrics… until his mind skin was red. But they continued. Always forward. Always driving forward, toward the horror.

In the exact middle of the dream, signaled by their leaving the asphalt road, he and Marvin Lee, his partner, rode in silence. But they had a sense that they were very close to their cold destination. Their dirty Ford slowed, Marvin at the wheel clenching his left fist, just the sound of the car's tires popping as they rolled over dirt, loose gravel, piles of bright green cow shit. He noticed Marvin was bleeding from a wound in his leg. Seeing the wound from the ambush had become routine. Yes. There it is; he's bleeding out… Okay death, you bitch… you dirty bitch. Who takes and never gives. Tell God your plans and see him laugh.

The dairy's black and white cows would cross the dirt road in front of him, their stringy-looking tails stained with dry shit. The car would have to slow for them. The windshield caught a thick cream-like Tule fog that turned to a mushy rain, leaving tracks on the windshield—bits of hope? The loose fingers of water collecting and moving hyper real, bits of mercury. And beyond that the view would turn suddenly opaque— white-out conditions. No sense or non-sense. Life was full of moments when language didn't work because it couldn't. The human voice/mind completely trammeled. The view obscured. Confusion's kingdom.

He would look down at his phone and the coordinates their nemesis had sent for them to find and collect the body. He would watch the longitude and latitude, the digits change/spin like a slot machine's lemons and cherries, as if the killer was making up his mind about the exact location.

Then he would look up from his phone and they would be clear of the Tule fog, and he could see the ugly rutted dirt road heading due west across a dairy farm with its signature naked hills, smooth and distinctly female in their contours. They were beautiful, so beautiful he wanted to cry, but it was important he didn't. Marines don't cry, no matter what— or do they? Maybe they should, he'd think. Hadn't his doctor said that once: To cry was to purge, and to purge was the secret to sanity? Rear view mirror stuff. Like My Lai—96 tears shed by dead mud-covered young mothers from Vietnam to Syria. Massacre. Children incinerated... Can't the dead cry too? After all, don't they have that last right? Anyway, who would care. The dead have no friends.

"This is Joy Road—back there?" Marvin would ask again.

And he would nod to confirm. "That's what the map said," he would answer. "Maps? Maps lie, man. You know that. Jesus, Mike!"

He would turn and look at Marvin for emphasis. But he'd be gone, and he, O'Higgins, would be behind the steering wheel and Asha Chaundhry would be in the passenger seat, riding next to him, holding her phone and looking down at its map... stoned, naked. Like the women depicted at Angkor Wat.

"Are you sure you want to do this?" Asha would ask. Then she would look at him and smile. "Don't you miss me at all? Don't you want to make love to me? Don't you want to hold me? Don't I make you happy, Mike?"

"Of course, I do..." he'd say. Then he would try and stop the car, but he couldn't. He would press down on the brake with all his might, but it was of no avail. The car would go on nonetheless. Unstoppable... The dream was always forward, always forward toward the horror and his inevitable history.

He would roll down the car's window, the car automatically driven, uber-cool Übermenschen vehicle. How bracing it was, how clean it all smelled. He hung his arm out, fifty yards from the body, the shame of their failure sucking the air out of everything. He hates women... He hated women. He hates women…They hate women… Why? Didn't he have a mother?

In his dream, the killer's motivations were obvious and seemed important, as if O'Higgins were discovering something new and seminal about the case. Then he would see the girl by the side of the road. The young English girl—only nineteen—whom he knew, even in the dream, was dead. They would find her horribly naked. But now instead she was on her phone, calling for help. He would drive by the girl… And suddenly Marvin would be in the driver's seat again and he would be talking to the English girl on his phone, telling her it was all a terrible mistake and that they were on the way, and not to worry—but he knew it was a lie, because he'd been on this road before. He knew how this story ended.

"That was her. She's all right," Marvin would say, turning to look at him, relieved. "See, it's her." And they would see her again, standing smartly dressed and normal, seemingly full of life and holding her phone up taking a selfie, beautiful, whole. Her expression happy. All women and one woman.

Then the car stopped. Everything was dreadfully clear. They could see the English girl's naked hogtied body on the road. The way the flesh was puckered, her arms and legs trussed by the killer with wire-ties. Her face held up brutally, looking out onto the ocean. Its surface clean and uncaring, just a shrug of waves hitting a deserted California beach. Just another obscenity on life's shared road. Okay. That's the way it is here… Baby I'm just human. That's when he'd scream, his scream sudden and always surprising—not masculine or feminine, a scream that contained all parts of the human continuum.

The car would stop. He and Marvin would get out. In the dream he would stare first at the girl's fog-wet brown hair, then beyond … a stand of eucalyptus trees, part of a copse that marked this moment between fields and sea. The tops of the trees raggedy and feeble-looking and super real. The trees had borne witness to the tragedy, and, as if willing the girl to get up and live, were waving their limbs in a grey fog-spackled wind, sending the horrifying message: Too late. You're too late. You are all too late. Remember the Somme, remember My Lai… remember, remember… the Butcher of the Balkans… all of the butchers and all the butchered.

Murder of one is the murder of all. It echoes like the ocean in a shell. Murder of one is the murder of all.

He woke up in Robin Sparks' plush bed. The luxe six-million-dollar penthouse apartment at the Harrison had been featured in magazines. He could hear her in the kitchen. He sat up. He was hungover and he had to remember what day it was, where he'd been, and most importantly what he might have said. It all came back. The party, the drive home… he slid out of bed and took a shower.

He heard the bathroom door open. Robin, in a blue silk robe, handed him a cup of coffee, black the way he liked it.

"You talk in your sleep," she said. "Scary stuff."

"Thanks." He turned off the shower. She was looking at him. The water was dripping off his body.

"Breakfast?" she said finally.

He'd said something in his dream that had frightened her. He could see it in her eyes. He was sure of it. Only God knew what it was.

"Sure," he said.

She tossed him a towel. "Runny eggs?" she asked, knowing he must be hung over.

"Very funny," he said.

While he was dressing, he stared at himself in the full-length mirror reflecting the huge bedroom. He'd drawn the curtains and he could see San Francisco's white cityscape reflected behind him. It was reassuring. He'd grown up here. It was, this city, a kind of father and mother. He realized he had to see someone about his drinking. It was getting in the way, and he had to stop. He felt like shit and he was finally tired of that.

He walked to the bed-side table and picked up his phone, flipping off the D.N.D. Texts and notifications that populated the screen, too many to count. They were working at least twelve different homicide cases. None of them mattered as much as finding the French girl, he thought. He couldn't fail Emma Barre, or he might not come back from that.

He went downstairs and they ate breakfast together. Robin had her laptop open and was monitoring the stock market. It was something she'd learned from her grandfather, who had cobbled together an empire based on vegetable production in the Central Valley. Later, his son had branched out into real estate development and become a billionaire.

"Richer or poorer today?" he asked, then regretted it. He wondered what his mother would think of the beautiful woman sitting across from him. She had the Irish dislike for the super-rich.

"Are you always this surly in the morning?" she asked. "Sorry. It's Mr. Patron."

"Who is Asha?" Robin asked, still studying the laptop's screen.

He saw a stock chart with comparison graphs. She'd once explained her chart program, which made him realize how intelligent she was and how out of his league he was. It had been Greek to him, cross currency rates and the like.

"Just a friend," he said. "She lives in India."

"Right. Is she pretty? She sounds beautiful. It's a pretty name. Anyway, I don't care if she is or not—as long as she stays in India." Robin looked up from her screen. "India is a long, long way away."

"Yeah, it is." He stood up. "Got to go."

"The French girl—the one you are looking for," Robin said.

"Yeah?"

"I get it, why you—I just get it. It makes you angry, right?"

"Yeah," he said. "What do you see in me, anyway? You know I don't belong. Yesterday at the party—it was obvious. I can barely pay my daughter's college fees."

"I'm not sure. A man who is doing his best, I guess. That's what I see."

"Is that enough? Doesn't it bother you that I'm not that smart or rich?"

"Why are you trying to wreck this, Mike?" she said. "I hope you have a good reason." She went back to her screen.

Chapter 5

"It's a lesion—on the brain," the young doctor said, looking poised but tired. "You have her medical power of attorney?"

"Yes," Cassie lied.

The bags under the doctor's eyes were magnified by his expensive-looking horn-rimmed glasses. They were standing in the cold, antiseptic, chaotic hallway of San Francisco General Hospital filled with the city's indigent population.

"They discovered it in the MRI," he said. "Near her hippocampus—necrotic tissue. We missed it the last time she was here." The doctor was exhausted, and his voice seemed to lean on the words lesion and brain to get his point across.

"She was here, before?" Marvin Lee's wife, Cassandra, asked.

"Yes. She was admitted six months ago," the doctor said, looking down at his clipboard. "She was here for a week in—" He checked to make sure. "Late February."

So, her friend had been in town months before she'd called her. She wasn't surprised. But it hurt, nonetheless. Her whole body clenched. *Why hadn't she called me?*

The doctor was about her age—late twenties, blond. He had a well-scrubbed look of the middle class that Cassandra associated with authority and manners and intelligence. Her people were poor whites, with shantytown, rotten-tooth expressions that deflected the insecurities heaped on them by the mainstream media. Her people's clothes were Walmart quality, the subject of fun on websites called "Walmart People" or "Can You Believe This." She'd caught her older daughter looking at one of those sites and left the room, too humiliated and too angry to deal with it. She'd wanted to tell her daughter that those people were her people. That they were not objects of derision, but had mothers and fathers, families that struggled for every bit of self-respect they could tear away from the system that hated everything about them.

It was the first time she'd wanted to run from the house as if she'd been caught out about her past. Instead she'd gone into her bedroom and closed the door. She had a secret, somehow encapsulated by the poor whites and blacks, American Indians, shown at their worst most pathetic moments at the checkout counter of life.

She'd lied to her family, to her husband, to everyone about where she came from. It had been tearing her apart from the moment Lana had gotten in touch, saying that she was in San Francisco, and it was an emergency, could she spot her a hundred dollars? "I got to get well, honey child." It was that still-sweet tone of voice that had killed her and made her feel guilty that she—Cassandra Osborn-Lee—had somehow survived their shared past and had walked into the middle class without setting off any alarms.

Her people were, if not obsequious to authority figures like the well-heeled young doctor, then certainly respectful to a fault, knowing that authority would always win, and their objections put down, or worse, simply ignored. No one listened to the poor until they voted for Trump, she thought. Sometimes her people blew up, became white volcanos, after drinking too much, or when on drugs, which were cheap and plentiful in Las Vegas.

It was then, while under the influence, that all her people's hostility came out in blind rages, handcuffed and put in a squad car and driven off to be fingerprinted and sold to a private prison industry—finally becoming profitable to the very people who hated them so much for their addictions, their inability to learn in their shitty schools, or to know their place. But those people were happy to drive through her neighborhood looking for blowjobs from sixteen-year-old girls, her mother one of them.

Despite all she'd been through, what she'd learned about the world, the early imprints of poverty always took hold of her social interactions and she'd put on her Catholic-school manners again. Her trucker stepfather had worked overtime to put her in a good Catholic school for a few years. His brother, a felon on a visit from Washington state, had abused her when she was nine. It was the moment that any hope for a normal life had ended.

Her school-girl manners were an act, but they always sold—especially to men, because of the way she looked. She was beautiful: the girl with a *Sports Illustrated* swimsuit-hard body,

Caribbean twilight blue eyes, and a girl-next-door face that belied the sunburnt Las Vegas ghetto, where she'd been born to a teenage prostitute with a learning disability and a coke habit.

Her looks, instead, hinted at some beach in Mexico or the Côte d'Azur, where she'd actually become just that: a Côte d'Azur girl, in real life. The girl the paparazzi shot as she walked up the gangplank of some billionaire's floating big-money eyrie. She was the girl in that cool beer commercial shown during the Super Bowl, with the tight ass and the friendly come-hither smile, sitting alone on a white-sand beach watching a male-fantasy ass-hugging sunset.

The doctor thought she was breathtaking and was trying to hide it. He was an ass man, and she had one that men had paid a lot of money to see in the flesh. He would think about her for weeks afterwards when he masturbated between shifts.

"What's that mean, exactly—lesion?" she said.

Cassandra Lee no longer looked poor. She was well dressed, although casually; she'd come straight from her yoga class. She'd climbed out of poverty the hard way, been schooled on the streets and dueled with the Rich People sexually and otherwise. She recognized the look men had when they were about to hit on her. She saw it now behind the young doctor's clinical attitude, spilling out at the male ego's far outer edge near his man-thing that could command him at any given second. Men, she'd learned, were ruled by it. Something about his mouth, the lips tightening slightly when he spoke to her, spelled raw unvarnished male desire.

"Well, think of it as an infection. The brain is an organ, and it can become infected. It's part of the AIDS constellation," he mansplained.

"So—you can prescribe something? So, she can think clearly?" Cassandra Lee wanted to say, snap out of it. It was what her people said when someone got sick and the worry started about how, the fuck, they were going to pay for it.

"Yes, but AIDS dementia is not easy to treat. Your friend has been irresponsible about taking her medications. It's not unusual in these cases. I'm sorry—how do you know—?" He had to think about Lana's name. It was embarrassing, and he glanced back toward Lana's room at the end of the institutional hallway. Looking for help, but the door with its sign giving the patient's names was too far away to make out. And so, he gave up—not that important to him, in the end. "Know her?"

"Lana. Lana Taylor. She's twenty-nine years old. She was born in Boston," Cassie said.

Talking to herself, suddenly. She's my sister.

"Sorry. It's been a long day. Twelve hours. I'm a resident—killer hours." He glanced at his watch. "Lana, of course. I remember now. She's very nice." The last bit he'd thrown in as an easy penance for forgetting a patient's name.

"She's an addict," Cassie said. She didn't give a shit about the rich people's killer hours making money, so they could buy houses in the good side of everything. But she nodded as if she understood his high-class problems.

"Yes. I saw it was on her chart. Opioids."

"Heroin," Cassie said. She was angry at the doctor for not knowing her friend's name. It was a street anger she could never fully expunge, no matter how far from the streets she'd gotten. It was the anger she'd needed on the streets to survive, and later, too. Life anger.

"Right," the doctor said.

"So?"

"We'll keep her here overnight, but I'm afraid that there's no—it's not something we can treat, here. I'm sorry," he said.

"So, you mean she has to go back out there?" Cassandra said. She wanted to tell him that this was where their relationship had started, on the streets of Hollywood fifteen years before.

She wanted to tell the doctor that the black girl he saw in the room, so miserable and old-looking and street-broken, had been so beautiful once. Breathtaking.

She tried to parse that out with the strange words the doctor had hid behind, perhaps to keep his own space clear of all the tragedy he dealt with, day in, and day out, in a public American Hospital. She could see the busy street that ran in front of the hospital through the old-school multi-paned wired windows. Those streets were waiting for another victim.

It was dreary outside, foggy— summer in San Francisco. No indication it was the city every millennial in the world pined for. New York was your father's destination. San Francisco was the NOW PLACE for NOW PEOPLE. Cellphone clutchers about to nail it … "Hundo P."

"Yes. I'm afraid so. There's a social worker who will come around. They'll send someone to check on her at home. They can help sort out any work issues."

"Home," Cassie said. "I asked, but she can't remember." Having to say it to the doctor, who looked in such possession of his faculties, made it feel that much more horrible.

She didn't like the doctor in his white coat, his stethoscope shoved in his pocket, his expensive looking horn-rimmed glasses telling it all. It was his fault; all the men like him who had used her friend and then walked away. Lana was nothing more than a cipher to him. It was no different from when they'd been in the youth hostels and do-gooder establishments funded by Hollywood celebrities—mostly young women—who felt better about themselves if they gave some poor kids a "chance in life." Or was it because they too had been used and abused, and understood what that did?

"Look, usually there's more, and then less lucidity. The confusion will come and go. I think the rest alone will make things better. She'll remember things. Come back close to normal. My guess—you've known her a long time?" the doctor asked.

"Yes. A long time. We're sisters." She put on the uptown call-girl face she'd used when she was working. It was ice capped with a fuck-you smile.

"I see." Of course, he didn't understand. Lana was black. For him, that was impossible.

"Yes. Sisters," she repeated for effect.

Her voice had an edge. It was a voice that carried the streets, and in it an implicit indictment. He couldn't possibly have mistaken it for anything else. But an indictment of what? Him personally or something else?

She'd heard her tone slip from good wife and mother into this new-old tone with its leather-strap quality. It scared her. It had started after Lana had come back into her life. Lana was her sister. It was true. She was it. She was family. She was like her daughters and her husband—love itself. Something Cassie felt completely. It was hard and sudden, the realization, like a fall in the playground of Life. You get up and face it: Love. It could be an almost brutish, unexpected-sharp-pain-causing thing. But there it was, she realized. Lana was her sister. She loved the young woman dying of AIDS in the room down the hall. Period. Fuck everyone who didn't, couldn't, understand.

"Cool," the doctor said, looking at her quizzically. "Cool. Well, it's good she has you here. Look, often there are periods of lucidity. They can last for weeks."

"Thank you," she said, not meaning it.

"Do you live in San Francisco?" he asked.

"No," she lied. "No, I live in—up north—Humboldt."

He shook his head. "If you need to call, I'll give you my number." He wrote it on a piece of paper he tore off his clipboard.

"Sorry, I'm married," Cassie said. It sounded strange. Like saying she was a prostitute once to a guy who tried to pick her up on the train to New York. "So, you know it's business if I fuck you," she'd told the guy on the train. "Five hundred bucks." He'd paid the money. They fucked in the bathroom, her face pushed up against the stained mirror. She could watch him… he was embarrassed, but it didn't matter. He wanted his money's worth.

Lana was discharged to a SRO the following day. She was somewhat better. She could remember she had a grandmother who lived in Chicago, and that she was an addict, and that Cassie married a cop called Marvin Lee in San Francisco. Other things from the past seemed to be just out of reach. Like a piece of fruit on a higher limb of a tree, tantalizing her.

Chapter 6

Dr. Schneider's cramped, claustrophobic office seemed to belong to an academic who'd gone too far with her research and been captured by it.

"No windows?" O'Higgins asked. It had been months since he'd seen her.

"Not unless you have tenure." Doctor Maya Schneider smiled. She was more casually dressed than usual, blue jeans and a simple grey sweater, her hair pulled back in a ponytail, no makeup. The casual, somewhat mannish dress didn't dampen her femininity. Her office was messy, piled high with files and medical texts. Three discarded Starbucks cups stood like decorations along the edge of an old Steelcase desk. The office needed a good cleaning, he thought. Nonetheless, all that implied learning was reassuring.

O'Higgins had emailed, saying he needed to talk to her. That something had happened he wanted to discuss with her. She wrote back and asked him if he minded coming by her office at UC Medical Center on Parnassus Street, where she taught part time. He'd agreed, curious why she wanted to meet there and not at her office downtown, where she usually saw patients.

She ushered him in past the books and files piled by the door. He noticed a nicely framed photo on her swamped desk. It was of the doctor and an attractive young Asian woman, taken at an expedition's base camp

46

in the mountains—the Himalayas, perhaps. The two women were kitted out in serious mountain-climbing gear, mugging for the camera, holding hands. It hit him that his doctor was a lesbian, and that all the coquettish calls he'd overheard while sitting in her waiting room on California Street were with a woman and not a man, as he'd assumed.

The doctor picked up a box of books from a chair across from her desk, so he could sit. "Michael—sit down, please. I'm glad you came."

He sat, his feet bumping into her briefcase. He undid his coat and she noticed his sidearm in its holster, her eyes stopping on it as if it were a third person in the room.

She looked at O'Higgins carefully. He'd seen the look before—a staring into him with everything she knew. Piercing, intelligent, clinical. The attitude was of the psychiatric alchemist who could change a mongrel police detective with PTSD into a functioning citizen. And that was exactly what she'd done, for the most part.

"How are you, Michael?"

He launched into it straight away. "I was adopted. My brother, Clifford, told me a few weeks ago."

She gave him a look he'd never seen before: she appeared shocked, or at least backfooted by the news.

"We met for lunch and he sprung it on me—everything I thought I knew about myself. Where I came from was a lie. My mom confessed to Clifford before she died. He dropped it on me just like that ... He'd waited a year to tell me. Wasn't sure he was going to ever tell me, he said."

"That had to be upsetting," Schneider said, her expression registering the gravity of what he'd just told her.

"It was. I had this neat picture of myself, part of a family. It mattered to me. My origin."

"Of course, it would be," she said. "Do your sisters know?"

"No, only Clifford. He hasn't told them yet. He said it was up to me to tell them if I wanted to."

"Are you going to tell them? Do you want to tell them?"

"I don't know." He looked at the doctor, not turning away. "My mother didn't tell me. Why would she do that? It made me angry, and I've been angry enough, lately. Very angry. I thought about killing someone. I had to talk myself out of it." His confession surprised him. He and Marvin, when they were drinking, talked openly of killing Seven Hills if they caught him.

She looked shocked a second time. But it was too late to take the confession back. They stared at each other, his confession hanging in the air.

"Did your mother say anything about your birth parents?"

"Some hippie girl named Infinity, no last name—nothing about the father. My birth mother might have been an Irish Traveler, a friend of my mom's. She used to come around. That's all Clifford was told, but my mom was out of it from the chemotherapy. He isn't sure she was even compos mentis. So, who really knows?"

She hadn't risen to the bait when he talked about killing someone. He'd meant it. It wasn't an idle boast. He and Marvin had decided to execute Seven Hills if they got a chance. After the sentence handed down in the Kathryn Steinle case, they had been afraid that their man might go to trial and get away with murder, as Jose Inez Garcia Zarate had. They had made a pact. O'Higgins had taken to carrying a throw-down pistol he'd picked up after the gunfight on Alabama Street. He intended to use it to incriminate their killer and serve as their defense.

It was the reason they had interviewed the Barre family as soon as they heard Emma had disappeared. They were not treating the Seven Hills case as they had so many others. This time—this case— had become personal, almost as if they were not policemen, but rather the murdered girls' family. When they were sober, they realized killing him would be wrong and took it back—it was immoral, they agreed, and they were the police, not gangsters. Or had they simply lied to each other? He wasn't sure.

On the way over to see Schneider, he'd been anxious. He wanted to bolt because of what he knew was waiting for him: the intense strange intimacy forced by psychiatry. He needed to tell her what he'd learned about the adoption, but hated that need. He saw it as a weakness that other, normal people didn't have. The desire to turn out the contents of his mind, like dirty coins on a countertop, and painstakingly do the math, was, he believed, unnatural. The fact that this type of accounting had saved his life didn't seem to matter.

"I read in the paper—the shootout in the Mission," Schneider said. "Are you okay? I called—did Rebecca give you the message?"

"Thanks. Yes, she told me you called. I'm sorry I didn't call back," he said. He gave her a weak smile.

She shook her head in the sign of universal disbelief. Like most civilians, she couldn't understand what that would be like, but wanted to empathize. It was genuine, her concern, and he appreciated it.

Looking at her, he saw what he remembered: a young, caring doctor. She'd truly cared about him, and that had made all the difference. He'd always felt that about her. At times he'd been attracted to her physically, but that had been a cop-out that allowed him to create a distance between them, inhibiting their therapeutic alliance. It would have been a means of pushing her away.

He didn't want any distance between them. He wanted to take hold of the doctor-patient relationship again, let it pull him out of the mire. He had come to understand that it had been a very serious bond that had saved him from himself. A lifeline. It was something you had to feel, first and foremost. The pull of that relationship that could make you better—trusting someone to dig into you where it hurt. That painful process allowed the patient to see themselves as exactly that: a patient—someone searching for insight that would open a locked door. Some basic truth. Robin had been right: he was trying to sabotage their relationship. Realizing it had scared him.

"What happened to your office on California Street?"

"They're remodeling. I sprung for it," she said.

"So, the practice—it's booming?"

She smiled and nodded. "You were my first patient, did you know? A policeman. I didn't expect that."

"No kidding? I didn't know. Patient Zero. So... LSD. You want me to get stoned, doc?"

Her email mentioned that she was conducting LSD trials, and outlined the study she was heading at UC's medical school: the use of LSD to treat PTSD and addiction. She'd invited him to join the trial the VA was funding.

"Have you done it?" O'Higgins asked. "Taken it?"

"Yes," she said. "I wanted to try it. I did."

"And you think it will make me better? This—LSD treatment?"

"Yes. It can help. Patients with addictions, or anxiety—PTSD. Patients have experienced real breakthroughs," she said. She moved to the edge of her chair and leaned in toward him. She seemed anxious for him to understand what she was offering.

"I knew the shootout—might be difficult for you. You were drinking, you said, the last time we saw each other..."

She didn't mention that he'd stopped seeing her suddenly. He was grateful to her, but had decided it was just a crutch. He wanted to throw it away and walk normally. And now he was back, unable to cure himself.

"Still am. Okay, what do I have to do?"

"You have to agree to take the schedule of treatments. You'll have a guide, here at the hospital, when you—I like to call it, travel. That's a little dramatic, but accurate. It's something you'll have to experience. It's a kind of super dream world that you can control—"

"I get it—take a trip."

"Many patients travel through time and space." She wasn't kidding. He could tell it was serious business to her. She was the drug's acolyte. Timothy Leary was dead, and all the trappings of the '60s drug were to be ignored.

"I don't really understand—I thought it was for hippies and tree huggers. Doesn't it screw with your genes?" It seemed bizarre—even frightening, in fact.

She looked at him and sat back. "All those things were disproven. There have never been any studies showing that LSD is harmful or has long-term side effects. No proven medical histories. It's been used since the fifties—well, until the government shut it down for forty-plus years."

"It's true I've been drinking on the job, and it has gotten worse since the shootout. Marvin, too," he said. "I would like to stop, but it's been—I don't know—I like it. The way it relaxes you. It works. Seems I can't stop. I've tried. But I want to stop. I've had it. It's part of why I wrote you—I can't do it by myself, it seems."

"Don't you risk being high at the wrong time?" she said. He shrugged. "Probably. Yeah."

"It will help with that, if you want to stop. It will help with the anxiety, too... Have you ever looked up into the night sky?"

"Yes, of course." It seemed an odd question. "Who hasn't?"

He remembered doing it with his wife when they first met, on camping trips near Mammoth Lake when they were first dating. They would lie out on their sleeping bags and look up into the starry night sky and talk ... make love under that special eternal no-light. Sweet sleeping-bag orgasms. The smell of her hair, the wonderful silky touch of it, the way she squirmed so delicious so wild and sweet. He'd often remembered those nights. Looked back on them as what he knew was one of the best times in his life only matched by the birth of his daughter.

"Then you know that sense of the infinite we get—from space?" she said. He nodded. "Well, it is the same inside the mind. There is a universe. A kind of infinite space that unites all time. The drug takes you there and it's out there, so to speak, where things happen. We see things that change us—move us forward."

The young doctor he'd met three years ago seemed worldly now. She'd changed. Schneider had become less diffident and was surer of herself, he thought. Sagacious even, nothing left of the desperate-to-make-good young psychiatrist he'd first sat across from years before.

"I don't follow. What's that got to do with my depression? My drinking? The recurring dream that … I've had it now since the shootout."

"You'll just have to trust me," Schneider said. "Do you, Michael?"

"Yes, of course." He was surprised he said it like that. So earnest. "If you think it will help. Why not? …Why did my mother lie to me? She betrayed me—right? Don't mothers owe you some special loyalty? Certainly, the truth."

"She was afraid you might be upset, I would think. She loved you. She was your mother. I don't think she betrayed you. Everything you've ever said about her was positive. She seems to have been a truly great mom."

"I've been upset about it. Angry at her since I heard. That she didn't tell me."

"I understand, but do you really think it changes you? Really? Aren't you the same person?"

He didn't know how to answer her. Yes, he was the same person. And, no, he wasn't the same person. His underpinnings had been wrecked, torn away, by the news.

They spent the rest of the session discussing his adoption. He wasn't satisfied that she wouldn't make more of it. She didn't seem to assign it any special weight, telling him that he was no less his parents' child. He told her about the recurring dream in detail. How he didn't seem to be able to go a night without having it. That it was exhausting him.

"It's typical for PTSD patients to have these kinds of dreams on a regular basis," she said. "I think this experiment can help with that as well. Get you past it." He doubted that some weird psychedelic drug with supposed entheogenic effects—discovered by accident in the 1930s— could be so magically effective.

She wrote something on the back of one of her cards and handed it to him. "Come this Thursday at noon, here at the hospital. Room 40. You'll have to sign a waiver. Remember, it's an experiment, and I can't guarantee it will help you, Michael. But we've had great outcomes with depression and addictions, especially. There are other combat vets in the program. Men and women like yourself. Same problems."

"I thought it was illegal—LSD?"

She smiled. "Not in clinical trials. We have a license from the D.E.A. Don't worry, it's legal, detective."

"So, you have someone with you when you take it?" he asked, feeling silly.

"Yes, a guide," she said.

"I can't tell them at work—it would never fly with my boss."

"All right, don't tell them. There is nothing that says you must, is there? They're micro doses, by the way. We'll keep you here each time. You'll be safe. We won't let you—you know, do anything you'd not want to do normally. It in no way will affect your work."

"Okay, our secret then. I want you to be my guide," he said. It seemed as if all their time together had led to this precise moment: She was going to push him into the unknown.

"I can't promise—but okay, if you like. At least in the beginning. How's work?" she asked. "The missing girls? I've read about the cases in the paper—any progress?"

"We can't catch him. He's very smart." The whole pulse of his life seemed to grab him as he answered her. The anger seemed bottomless and suffocating, and it was why drinking helped. It was only then that he could forget the English girl they'd found. Something about that horrible morning and that place hounded him. He had failed her. The killer had toyed with them, she'd been kept alive… There was surcease when he was high, if only for an hour at a time.

"I'm sorry," Schneider said.

"Yeah, so is everyone. But it doesn't help much, does it?"

"Michael—I know you will catch him." It was a very human and a non-clinical thing to say, and he appreciated it. "Are you sleeping?"

"Not much. When I do, I have the dream."

"Do you want me to refill the Valium?" the doctor asked.

"No. No. I'm good. I'm trying to get on without it."

She nodded, and he left.

He passed Room 40 on the way down the hallway filled with fresh-faced med students. Most were female and Asian. The few white students stood out—the new minority. He tried the door, but it was locked. He peered through the window for a glimpse—of exactly what, he didn't know.

Chapter 7

O'Higgins caught a glimpse of the new Salesforce Building. It was brutal looking, a signal that San Francisco was becoming one of those kinds of cities, cities like São Paulo or Shanghai, where the skyline reflected the beastly mood on the ground: Big Money Dogs were in complete control now. No pretense. Google that. They would and could eat you alive. As if to prove it, they stuck corporate steel dicks in the sky: "You, groundlings, you live in our shadow. Pay your cell phone bill and get to work and come back to your claustrophobic basement apartment at $5,000.00 a month and share that measly space with four other complete strangers who will come and go out of your life — all of you in penurious debt. You are nothing but grease for the gears." It was that kind of city now. Fuck St. Francis. What did he know, anyway?

His phone pinged: a text from Marvin. He grabbed it and glanced at the screen, trying to drive at the same time, cresting a hill on Diamond Heights heading toward Portola.

I'm done here on Gold Mine. Have to be in court— Brick Yard case, I'll call you.

A Russian national had gotten his brains blown out in a condo on Gold Mine Drive and they'd caught the case. He'd left Marvin at the scene and had gone to run a check on the victim, who was unknown to the police. Their victim had been shot around seven in the morning when he'd gone to answer his door. The shotgun blast had almost decapitated him, fired through the opaque front door. The safety glass had littered the floor like glassy pebbles on a beach.

Marvin had Zillowed the address on Gold Mine to see whether it had sold recently. It had, for five million bucks. The victim's face had been obliterated by the blast. Two Russian language newspapers, *Izvestia* and *Vesti*—published in Israel for Russian speakers—lay on the kitchen counter. A gangland hit, probably. The victim was stocky and had huge hands. What was left of his hair was grey.

They found three passports in the man's bedroom: one Russian, one Israeli, and one English. His name—Dmitri Averin—was on all three. Details in each were slightly different: age, height and weight, color of eyes. All three passports were high-end forgeries, they suspected; the passport books real, but stolen, and the photo and details filled in afterwards. The Russian and Chinese mobs were the most sophisticated in the world. O'Higgins and Lee knew it was a dead-end case as soon as they saw the passports.

No one would cooperate. A nervous neighbor, speaking through a cracked open door, said the man spent most of his time abroad. Diamond Heights had become a notorious Russian-Mafia gulag. The Russian mob had come to town and opened "art galleries" in several high-traffic tourist spots—Chinatown, Sausalito, Union Square—money laundering stations for their other real businesses: drugs, prostitution and arms dealing. The condo was full of giant ugly bronze sculptures of Venus and lions, which must have taken a squad of weightlifters to move in. It looked like the same impossible dreck sold in the Russian "antique" stores, which no tourist could throw into a suitcase and take to China or São Paulo.

The condo's hallways were mirrored, the furniture modernist and mostly white. The refrigerator held nothing except vodka and bottled water. Nothing on the walls. It vibed "safe house." It looked like the kitchen had never been used.

They'd searched for the man's cell phone, but the shooter had taken it—another sure sign it was a hit. The victim had probably been in touch with the killers, and was expecting them.

They depended so much on victims' cell phones; not having it would mean weeks of delays in getting a clear picture of who their victim was and who might want to kill him.

They found a briefcase, but all the documents in it were in Russian. Because no San Francisco "taxpayer" had been murdered, the local media didn't pay much attention. They were free to put the investigation, after its initial report, on the back burner.

O'Higgins was on the way to meet the girl's father in the Ferry Building in order to walk the route the Barre family had taken the day Emma had disappeared.

A picture of his girlfriend, Robin Sparks, appeared on the phone as his old-school style ringtone went off. She'd made him put the photo on his phone, taken while they'd been in Mexico for her birthday. She's chosen one of herself in a white string bikini sitting at a tiki bar, high, giggling. It was fetching. She was that girl frat boys longed for—tall, leggy, but he thought she might be trying too hard. He was too old for that kind of photo popping up on his phone.

Marvin had kidded him mercilessly about it, asking him if he had enjoyed spring break, and when was he going back to school?

They were to meet for dinner at Boulevard, and she wanted to know if it was okay for her younger sister to tag along. He texted back a thumbs up emoji.

***

O'Higgins passed the thuggish skateboarders running the wide concrete meridian that separated the Embarcadero from the foot of Market Street. The meridian was a kind of skateboard park cum pedestrian zone. It was the gateway to the Embarcadero, with its string of tourist attractions ending at Pier 39 to the north.

Robin called. He didn't really listen to her talk about her sister, who was visiting from London. She'd married into the peerage and had lots of complaints about her new husband, suspecting he was gay.

He took an illegal turn into a service road that ran along the south side of the Ferry Building and parked where he felt like it.

"Thank you for coming," O'Higgins said.

Emma's father was pale. His thinning scalp was sunburnt—from their days walking the City before his daughter disappeared, O'Higgins imagined. Barre seemed to have aged. He looked haggard, obviously not sleeping, judging from the dark circles under his eyes. It was a look O'Higgins remembered well, one he'd worn himself for months after his wife's death. People had wondered if he was using drugs.

"Did your wife have a safe trip home?" O'Higgins asked. They shook hands. Barre had explained on the phone that his wife's elderly mother had become gravely ill and that she would return as soon as possible.

"Yes. The French government sent us a private plane." Barre gave him a weak smile. O'Higgins started to get just how important Barre must be. He wasn't just any tourist.

They walked through the Ferry Building and a trendy bookstore, going out its rear doors. Barre was taking him on the exact route they'd taken two days before. They came out facing the ferry terminal, across the seagull shit concrete no-man's land. The Larkspur ferry was loading up, mostly tourists heading to Marin, several with groups that were holding "ground flags" to identify their color-coded leaders. No escaping the tourists anywhere.

"Emma wanted to see the Gandhi statue…" Barre said, collecting his thoughts. The ferry's electric gangplank was loud. A slight stench of urine rose off the concrete.

Michael turned and saw the statue of Mahatma Gandhi alone on a huge expanse of no-man's-land, a stretch of bird shit-splattered yard that had always seemed odd to O'Higgins. It was so forlorn, a kind of weird afterthought to the "new" Ferry Building complex so popular with tourists and natives alike. Gandhi's statue was relegated to a place populated with seagulls and a few homeless with their ubiquitous shopping carts stuffed with odd bits of clothing and plastic tarps. The homeless—a large percentage of them drug-addicted— were everywhere in this part of the city, especially.

"So, you got out of the Uber, and—?" O'Higgins said, wanting to get on with it.

"Emma said she wanted to see the statue," Barre said. "She was like any tourist. She would read about something and want to see it. She has an interest in Gandhi. She's become quite the expert."

"I want to go over every second of that morning. Okay. I want to walk the route with you. I want to know exactly what you all talked about. I want to see what you saw. Can we do that?"

The physicist nodded. "Oui, of course." Barre looked at him. It was a measured look as if he were taking the cop's intellectual depth for the first time. He turned and headed immediately toward the bronze statue of Gandhi. The two walked across the no-man's land toward the statue, the smell of diesel exhaust coming from one of the ferry's engines.

Without thinking, O'Higgins grabbed Barre by the arm and turned him.

"I want you to know that we're going to find her. I promise you. I had a text. From the man who is—from the man who has her."

Barre looked at him, startled. It was the look of a man who had already calculated the odds of finding his daughter were diminishing every minute. And the stupid look of hope, of any loved one who is forced to grasp at straws.

"A text?" Barre said. O'Higgins held up his phone.

Please tell my parents that I love them—I'm okay.

"It's a good sign," O'Higgins said.

Barre took O'Higgins' phone with both hands and read the message several times. He handed it back, shaken. His face contorted. "Who is he?

This person who has her."

"We don't know. He has my phone number. He texts. But his phone numbers always change. He uses disposable phones."

"You don't think it's too late. That—" Barre said.

"I know how much this must hurt. I appreciate you coming this morning," O'Higgins said. "I promise you we're doing everything we can to find Emma."

"What's her name—your daughter?" Barre asked. "You said you had a daughter."

"Rebecca."

"I told my wife I wouldn't leave without Emma. And I won't."

O'Higgins nodded, and they walked on toward the statue. A few seagulls milled about on the ground, their wings the same color as the concrete.

"She was excited." Barre said. They had reached the statue. "She said that someday she would go to India. She'd read all about Gandhi."

"Love the sinner, hate the sin," O'Higgins said, not meaning to be insensitive but recalling what his wife used to say to him when he would describe some particularly awful murder. It was a famous Gandhi quote.

Barre looked at him and nodded.

O'Higgins had gotten angry at his wife for saying it at the time—it had seemed both cruel and absurd, a kind of joke. But Gandhi's quote came to him with all its strange power to provoke him.

"Do you believe in non-violence?" Barre asked.

"No. It's absurd. Men aren't built for it," O'Higgins said, and truly believed it.

"Emma used to say that, too. Love the sinner—it something she was always saying after Charlie Hebdo. She was studying about non-violence movements in school. She even stopped eating meat." Barre looked at the statue as he spoke.

O'Higgins recognized the man's stiff posture and realized that he himself was better now. It took seeing Barre to understand how far he'd come since his wife had died. If he could shake the drinking ... he'd be all right, he thought. *I can do it. I want to do it.*

O'Higgins nodded and smiled. His daughter, too, had become a vegetarian at an odd time when her dance teacher told her it would not be physically good for her. She'd ignored her teacher and done it anyway, with no ill effect.

O'Higgins towered over the Frenchman but felt small, powerless and completely insignificant in the face of the facts.

Why did Seven Hills want to hurt these young women? He felt insecure, but hid it. Why had the serial killer become America's emblem? Ted Bundy as a strange brand: Made In America. That morning, two fathers standing in the impossibly fresh air seemed to share some profound truth about humanity. It was failing and everyone knew it. San Francisco itself was the marquee for the New World Order: progress wrapped in an unimaginable dread.

His earlier promise to Emma's parents, no matter how well intended, felt like a mistake. The idea that he wasn't the brave Irish kid he'd thought he was but the son of someone called Infinity hit him as well—another kind of truth. The ground under his feet had begun to shift. *How can I be anything if I don't know who I am?*

"Was there anyone else out here, that you remember?" O'Higgins said.

He was looking at the famous man's statute, the artist having depicted Gandhi on the move with his walking stick in one hand, the future of the whole of India directly in front of him. The likeness a good one, the bronze adding a timeless stamp as if the famous man had actually walked to San Francisco, the first and the ultimate hippie. A plaque gave Gandhi's dates.

"No," Barre said. "We came and stood here. Emma touched—she ran her hands over the walking stick. It—it meant something to her. I understand that now. His life. Gandhi's. I think young people find comfort in the idea of non-violence. I didn't understand it really, until now. It seemed almost silly to me. She is so young, and all that seemed so—" He didn't finish his thought, exhausted from retracing that morning.

"You're sure? Think carefully. How about over there, by those benches?" O'Higgins pointed to iron benches running parallel to the back of the Ferry Building. "No one watched you, no one? No one who might be staring? Someone paying undue attention to Emma?"

He turned and pointed to the hoary dock to their east with benches along the pier, where a few random office worker types ate a late breakfast, all with earbud cords hanging around their shoulders. Servants on the electronic plantation. The view beyond was laced with construction cranes and jagged edges of other piers: a kind of collage of open water, rough dock wood, and metal benches. All of it a foreground to the Ferry Building's iconic tower directly behind them.

"Yes, people were sitting on the benches there, too. But no one I thought odd—or suspicious." Barre's phone rang. He looked at the screen and raised his hand. "I have to answer this. It's my work." He walked away with the call, speaking quietly in French.

O'Higgins turned from the statue and scanned the rear of the Ferry Building. At this hour, it was gearing up for the mobs of tourists and downtown types who would pass through its tony shops and restaurants. Anyone could watch the area with the statue without being noticed.

And had he? Had Emma Barre caught the Devil's eye while standing in front of Gandhi's statue dedicated to non-violence?

He noticed a metal staircase hanging, bolted to a building, across the water at the next pier, directly to the east. It had a perfect view of the statue and was far enough away to be overlooked—a kind of eagle's nest.

Barre walked back. "There was a leak in one of the government's nuclear reactors near Paris. They were asking the new government to issue the first warning to the city government in case a wholesale evacuation was necessary. They wanted my opinion. I told them the leak is routine."

"Jesus," O'Higgins said, realizing what it meant to be one of the most important physicists in France. He'd Googled Barre's name and seen a few references to his work at CERN—The European Organization for Nuclear Research—but no personal information or bio, which he took as a sign the

French spooks were scrubbing Google to keep terrorists at bay.

"We have these leaks on occasion, but the non-scientists in Paris hear the word leak and they start picking up their phones and calling each other in a panic." Barre slipped his phone into his golf jacket. He seemed unphased by the news. "It's nothing out of the ordinary."

"Okay, now where did you go?" O'Higgins said, dragging them both back to the here and now.

"We went to the bookstore, there, and then into the Ferry Building to eat something. We'd not eaten a proper breakfast."

"All right, let's go," O'Higgins said, determined to sound confident.

The two mismatched men—the detective's armed Sancho Panza to Barre's physicist Quixote—walked away from Gandhi. O'Higgins' backup gun started to chafe the skin on his ankle. The Hoppe's oil he used to clean the weapon so carefully—late at night at the work bench in his garage, a fan on to blow the stink of chemicals away from him—was caustic and reacted with the sweat on his skin at his ankle. It had begun to burn slightly. He ignored the pain, a kind of silent flagellation for Emma and for the other girls, the ones he'd failed to save.

Later that night, very late, at home when he took the sweat-wet ankle holster off, he saw the hammerless revolver's short barrel had left a chemical burn mark that would probably scar.

Chapter 8

"You remember me, doll?" the man on the phone asked.

Cassandra Lee was on her way to pick up her oldest daughter at the French School near Hayes Valley. She took the call without looking at her phone, something she rarely did nowadays. Had she seen who it was, she probably would not have taken it. But who knows about things like that, she'd thought later.

His voice sounded exactly the way she remembered it, with its slight Creole accent—just as she'd heard it at The Little Door in LA twelve years earlier, when she'd been only seventeen. It had been a Thursday night in June in the famous al fresco area out back, with its yellow and red-tinged candlelight, walled off from the streets of West Hollywood, a kind of secret garden. The air was fuggy with the smell of citronella they used to keep the bugs down.

The first thing she remembered about Robert Thorpe was that he ordered her a glass of white wine and the waitress brought it even though any fool could see she wasn't twenty-one, not even close. It was that kind of place. The Little Door was a hangout for players of every kind: Hollywood types, high-class gangsters, investment bankers, and even young Saudis from the House of Saud who were above the law and knew it. Thorpe was a big tipper, always leaving fresh hundred-dollar bills, so the waitress would have chopped up a line of blow right out in the open if he'd asked her to.

Cassie answered the call, expecting to hear her daughter's voice. She had been driving up Castro Street heading north towards the light on Market Street. She'd pulled over in front of the Castro Theater, her heart beating fast.

Hearing his voice was like being stung, as she'd once been stung by a jelly fish on her honeymoon with Marvin. It had been a great honeymoon at Playa Del Carmen, two weeks of a lot of lovemaking and drinking, petting dolphins. They'd done all the corny tourist things. She'd been happy ignoring the looks they caught as an interracial couple, and a very attractive one at that. Americans had stared at them, especially on the beach. She wasn't used to being stared at—ogled, yes, since she'd been fifteen—but not looked at like she was born bad without the sense to stay on her side of the color line. The ugly looks from black couples were the harshest, their racism just as amped up as the whites'.

"Yeah?" she said, holding the wheel and looking at nothing and everything out on Market Street. "How did you get my number?"

It's just like that jellyfish. Just keeps on hurting. Marvin had gotten down on his knees and scraped her foot with a credit card to clear the stinger.

"I'm in town," Thorpe said. He didn't answer the question. He was a powerful man with friends everywhere. He could get whatever he wanted, including almost anyone's private number. Big People's private numbers. She'd once called a world-famous actor's personal cell number and heard the surprise in his famous voice. "I have Mr. Thorpe on the line—hold, please," she'd said, ready to giggle with excitement.

Her pimp was also the most vicious person she'd ever known—even in their world, which was built on viciousness and the first law of the jungle: fuck with me and you'll be hurt—or worse.

Not physically—he had people for that—but psychologically. He knew just how to pluck someone's weakness strings. He was never loud or obviously mean—in public. But in private ... that was something else. He called himself a movie producer and he had produced a few movies, or at least caught what was known in the business as the girlfriend credit. He'd bartered for the credits with clients, legit producers, who used Thorpe's service.

He was a world-class pimp, in fact. Many people claimed to be, but he actually was. You wanted to butt-fuck twins who spoke Italian and had gone to the best universities? Call Thorpe; he'd have them on the jet. He'd started as a bartender at the Hotel Capri, where he was often asked if he knew who to call to get laid. His real business began in Cannes, providing what were known as "yacht girls" to the film industry. He'd taken it from there.

"Yeah? So what," she said, not knowing what else to say and not wanting to show she was still leery, if not afraid of him. She thought of ending the call as the traffic passed. She saw a streetcar rolling east down Market Street.

She did what she'd never would have done when she was his most important possession—what the street pimps called a "bottom girl," for one simple reason: at seventeen she was breathtaking, jaw-droppingly gorgeous. She ended the call and punched the accelerator.

Her new white Jeep Cherokee pulled back out onto Castro. She caught the green light and turned onto Market heading east. She passed the streetcar she'd seen, going through a yellow light at Noe and Market. Her heartbeat in her chest like some mad person who wanted to kick a hole through her chest cavity and be free of her.

She sped along Market Street, both hands on the wheel—ten and two. Her phone rang again as she passed the Safeway, its front wall lined with scores of dozing street people. It was no use. Her past was calling her, and there was no escaping it. It was like trying to escape who your father and mother were. You can't. It was part of her and always would be.

She hit the button on her steering wheel, answering the call.

"I think we should talk. You know, about the old days," Thorpe said, as if she'd not hung up on him.

"Why?" she said. "Why would I do that?"

"Because—call it law of the jungle. And I've missed you. Really. You miss people. You're one of them," Thorpe said. "You know, the good old days."

"Where?" She knew what his "law of the jungle" remark meant, and it frightened her into agreeing.

"The Fairmont? Same room. Always the same room. I like the view. You remember the view? Alcatraz. And I love their big towels. Remember the towels?"

"When?" she said, nearly choking on the word. "ASAP," he said. "You've got my number now."

"I've got to—I got shit to do." She was swearing, the way she used to when she was with him. She didn't like it. She was shocked at how she slipped into her former mode. She'd lied to herself about it being behind her. That ability to lie at the drop of a dime. To be tough, more than tough. Calculating in every possible way in bed and out of bed.

She understood men, had a PhD in the subject—what they'd done to her and what she'd done to them. Some lessons you never forget. She'd undress, they'd give her money. They would stare at her nakedness. Sometimes they would ask if they could do things to her that weren't right. And when she was really sick from the dope, she'd nod. She was mostly ashamed of that, of giving up on herself. But sometimes you do give up. She'd been like a prisoner of war who finally succumbs and gives more than their rank and serial number. She'd thrown in the towel psychologically. One day you just throw your hands up in the air and say fuck it.

She remembered when it happened exactly: New York City, at a boutique hotel near the Guggenheim. She'd been there many times. Do it, the whole fucked up thing, to me. I don't care anymore. And then she'd jabbed the needle in her arm in the women's restroom in the lobby and the whole world got warm and she was indifferent to her life's descent from beautiful girl—so familiar to LA's maw— to something left after you've heard no you didn't get the roll, no you won't have any life, no you won't be a mom, no you aren't pretty enough. What young girls who arrived in LA never understood was that there was always a prettier one on the next plane in. It was ironically the same for prostitutes as for actors.

She had tried to book commercials, book some modeling jobs, but mostly it was No. No. No. No. No. No. Like the palm trees lining Los Feliz, that you look up at in dope-awe at five in the morning with their palm fonds glowing in a crepuscular dawn-crawling sky—an allée of failure and snuffed-out dreams. Los Angles didn't kill dreams, it pulverized them.

Fuck him, she thought.

"Four. Why don't you come tomorrow at four? I got a phone meeting at three and you know how people drone on—a reality TV producer. They're the worst. Wear something nice."

"I'm married now. I got two kids. My husband—" she was going to tell him her husband was a cop, but stopped herself. "I got to be home for dinner. I cook dinner for my kids." It sounded stupid to hear herself say it. This guy, the jellyfish, came from a world where all that didn't go on. It was alien to them, like cleaning a toilet bowl, or working with your hands to fix something, or running out of money before the first of the month.

He lived in a big fat hundred-million-dollar bubble. Where the real currency was information. He'd picked her up and made her into a super-whore, took the dope away and put her to work on a world stage. He'd taken her back before she'd squandered her beauty on hundred-dollar tricks. By the end she was getting what girls called the "brick," sixty thousand for a weekend and the "full girlfriend experience."

Marvin had once asked her if she wanted to watch the Starz series of the same name. She'd left the room. She'd already seen the show. "You're joking," she said. "What's this about?"

"Like I said—four." He hung up.

Her iPhone shook. It was a text from her daughter. She read the text like a robot, Thorpe's voice still in her ear. She pulled over.

Where are you?

Running late …Sorry. Be there soon.

Her fingers moved quickly over the phone's keyboard. Without thinking about it, she typed *I love you.*

She looked down at her phone and saw, not the hand of a mother and wife who wrapped birthday presents and cleaned the family dog's bed, who held her husband at night terrified that he might not escape the next random shoot-out, but the hand of what she used to be—a world-class prostitute who had been passed around Hollywood, New York, London and more by the one-percenters who answered to no one, least of all a young girl from Las Vegas who'd come to Hollywood a fresh-faced kid. She'd thought it was the land of plenty, but learned the first hard truth about America: Money talks! and young pussy talks even louder.

Chapter 9

O'Higgins looked out on the city. He could see the Bay Bridge's light show, just below Robin's apartment. The halogen light patterns ran fast—left to right, plunging electrons, then pulsating on and off like some great machine that would spit out an eternal truth as prize. The electric light show was the hallmark of the new city. The Bay Bridge had become, like so much else, a throbbing tourist attraction. The ultimate light show run for free on a summer night. People loved it.

He took a sip of twenty-year-old brandy and turned around. The two-story penthouse Robin Sparks owned had glass walls, ferociously cool, with mid-century furniture, all *Architectural Digest* perfect. The walls were done in dark paneling.

She nodded to him, smiling as she spoke on the phone. She'd gotten a degree in viticulture—her second university degree. He drank wine but didn't pay too much attention to its finer points. As one of his cop friends said, "Booze is booze."

She was wearing a white see-through sheer robe over grey lingerie. She was beautiful.

Looking at her through a glass wall that divided part of the living room, he wondered again what she saw in him and why he wanted to ruin any chance they had. Her friends, the people she'd been to school with at Stanford and the owners of famous wineries—most of them rich kids— thought him a novelty, like rotary dial phones or flying coach. They would ask him questions about being a detective, the usual ones being about serial killers (had he chased any?) or whether he had shot anyone.

He always ignored that last question, especially since the shootout as he thought he'd failed Marvin that day, not acting quick enough. He'd seen the curtain move ominously and ignored it. Because of his nonchalance, Marvin had almost died.

He set his empty glass on a glass table. The apartment's outside deck was wide enough to be a hotel's drinks area. He looked for the bottle, found it, and poured himself another shot.

She walked back into the room and looked at him. She had her phone to her ear.

"What's up?" he said.

"Another fire. Near Calistoga," she said, finally ending her call.

They had been undressing when her phone rang. The look on her face told him that was on hold.

"Serious?"

"I hope not," she said.

"Near your new place?"

"Yes. You don't give a shit, do you?"

It was the first time she'd said anything like that to him. They'd not been dating that long, and nothing had gotten personal. Maybe it was plastered on his face. It was true: the only thing he cared about was putting a round in that fucker's head and finding the French girl alive.

He didn't answer, just stared at her, surprised. "It's okay if you don't," she said.

"I do. Why?"

"The look on your face."

"Sorry. I was just thinking about work."

"What about it?" She tossed her phone on the couch. Something about the way she did it showed she was upset with him.

"There's a young girl out there, and I think she might be dead. That's what I fear. That we're already too late. It's a—what people seem to love—a serial killer. He's got my number. Texts me like were old friends. And all I want is to catch him."

"Who is she? The French girl?"

"A random tourist girl. Her parents brought her to the city on vacation. She's gone missing. That's his MO. He likes tourists, I guess. She's deaf and for some reason that makes it worse, to imagine it."

"I thought you were only involved in homicides?" she said, sitting next to him on the edge of the couch.

He understood that she cared about him, and felt guilty because he realized he might just be using her. It was the first time he'd discussed work with her.

"What kind of fire is it? Grass or what? I do care," he said. "I'm not an asshole."

"I'm sorry. I had a big fight with my sister. It started near Lake Berryessa . . . it's moving fast, toward Angwin. I'm going to drive up. Sorry." She untied her robe. "Sometimes you are an asshole. But I like you anyway."

Her newest winery was just below Angwin, one hundred and fifty acres about to go into production. She'd never said how much she'd invested in the winery, but he could imagine. 50 million? Who knew? His daughter had looked Robin's family up and said they were one of the richest families in California. She never talked about money. She'd grown up that way, in that special world where you don't talk about it.

"I'm going to drive up tonight. I want to be there. I need to be there."

He was swamped by the need to screw. She could tell. It wasn't pretty, that need. It had a desperate quality that went beyond just desire. She recognized it. Was that what she liked about him? His physical need for her sometimes verged on the desperate.

"How are you going to find her, the girl?"

"It's tough. Her phone isn't pinging. And no one saw anything, so we've almost nothing to go on."

"Can I see her?"

He got out his phone and scrolled, looking for her photo. He handed the phone to Robin. "She is pretty."

"Yeah," he said.

"They mentioned you on the *Chronicle's* society page—my date, an SFPD detective." Robin said.

"So what?" He felt guilty, but reached for her and pushed her down on the big sofa.

When he woke up later in her bed, she was gone. He looked up at the ceiling and felt her again, the crush of their bodies … He pushed her arms back… the sound of her little deaths. He didn't care what burnt down or didn't burn down. What he'd cared about was fucking until he was beyond any kind of thought about anything.

He wasn't going to fail Emma Barre. If he did, he would be finished as a cop. He sat up and looked for his phone. It was the first time he'd had the thought, but it started to crystalize like those Chatham emeralds around a string. If he couldn't save her, he'd quit.

The war and the killing there had built a secret place in his mind that was not sane. It was what he'd tried to tell his doctor after his wife died. Somehow, he'd never said it right out loud. He had so much he'd never admitted to anyone or spoken about since he'd come back. It was the one fear/thing he'd never admitted. It was a square dark spot under pressure like a black hole.

Now that he wasn't even sure about who his parents were, or where he came from, he felt completely untethered and free from living up to what he'd thought, until now, was his duty to be a good person, a good son. His mother's son. He didn't feel that duty now.

He crossed the room and found his shirt, his two handguns and his wallet, and got dressed in the big empty expensive apartment on top of the city.

"Fuck it… I will kill this guy." He stared at the East Bay before he left. The sun was coming up, pieces of the Bay Bridge coming to life.

***

"We done this before, man. How many times now?" Marvin asked.

"Humor me," O'Higgins said. He pulled over and they watched the throngs of out-of-towners walking along the Embarcadero.

"They've all been picked up either near Pier 39, or around Crissy Field," O'Higgins said.

"Right," Marvin said.

"Why?" O'Higgins said.

"Because he's got a system. And he wants girls who are foreign—I guess. For one, they'd be disoriented, right?"

O'Higgins looked at his partner and nodded. "What is it? His system?"

"A system for luring the girls. Chats them up. He might be young. An Uber driver—a waiter..." Marvin said, looking out at the passing humanity.

"But it's always crowded," O'Higgins said. He glanced up at Coit Tower, bone white in the bright sunlight. "And why not at night? All four girls disappear in the daytime—in front of everyone, and yet no one sees or remembers anything."

"All in the morning, too, or around noon," Marvin said.

"Before noon. Right," O'Higgins said, both his hands on the Ford's worn steering wheel.

"Maybe he's got a job. He has to get to work—later, after he—after he takes them. They want some action on these other cases, Mike," Marvin said. "I got a call from Toomey."

"Does he work somewhere along here? Or at the Pier?" O'Higgins ignored what he already knew: the other cases were starting to slip. They'd have trouble about it from their new boss, but he didn't care. "Well, come on, Marvin."

He was used to working ideas with Marvin. Before the shootout they'd been quick to develop a line of reasoning. Now—because of the hangovers, or whatever—it was different. Each line of reasoning stopped short of a breakthrough, impeded by anger or frustration.

"It's possible. Yeah. But we have four girls snatched and no one sees

74

anything?" Marvin said. "That just—I don't know."

"Is that so strange? Look out there. Look, seriously." O'Higgins, watching the throngs, realized that they started to all look the same. The Europeans were obvious, a group unto themselves, perhaps because they didn't wear baseball caps or running shoes like the Americans. But the young girls were dressed very much the same way.

"Look at the girls. Go on. What do you notice? Look, for fuck's sake!" His phone rang. "You're scheduled for noon," his psychiatrist said. "I'll be your guide."

"Okay," he said. "Thanks." He ended the call and looked at Marvin, who really was looking hard at the hundreds of people walking by. Thousands were on the Embarcadero at this time of the morning, almost noon, especially in July.

"Okay. They look similar. I get it." Marvin said finally.

"Right. Black, white, or Asian, the young girls dress about the same. Right?"

"Yeah—shorts or blue jeans and backpacks. The white girls all have long hair. Sunglasses…. Most are dressed for summer, somewhere else. Some place warm," Marvin said.

"So, if you were asked about that girl. The one there." He pointed at a European girl with her family. About sixteen, he thought. "Look at her—the one with the brown hair and the sunglasses, the good-looking, tall one."

"I get it. You wouldn't remember, because unless they were really different, they just blend into one teenage girl."

"Right. Out here you don't notice. You walk along with your family, or your boyfriend, and it all starts to look the same."

"If they were black, that would help," Marvin said.

"Right, but all our girls are white, Europeans."

"So what you're saying is that whatever happened to them, they were just another girl in the crowd."

"Righ, look how many teenage girls passed since we've been parked here. Five, ten.

"More. More than that," Marvin said, turning to look at him.

"What didn't we do because they were foreign that we would have done if they were local girls?"

"Social media."

"Bingo. We didn't pay attention to where their friends—what they might have posted about San Francisco. Places to go. Cool places to go. We didn't have their posts. Maybe one of them noticed something, took a photo of someone that we haven't seen. Said something that would help. Some guy who got too chummy."

"Shit. Because they were on vacation—we didn't put that together. That they all went to the same place at the Pier. Maybe where he works?"

"We thought it was random. What if he lures them somehow?"

"How? We have their call records. No one but the immediate family or texts from Europe. None of the girls knew anyone in San Francisco," Marvin said.

"But they all spoke English. Barre does too, apparently. All of them were above average students. All seem to have been good girls that were never a problem. No records. No drugs. No reason to expect them to take up with some random guy in a strange city." O'Higgins pulled out into traffic and they rode down the Embarcadero looking at the crowds. O'Higgins pulled over again in front of Pier 39.

"And then they disappeared," Marvin said. He turned to look at the iconic tourist spot, its various flags and banners blowing in the wind like the entrance to some separate country.

"So, it happens in there—in front of thousands of people," O'Higgins said. "On the pier. Somewhere around here, anyway."

"Do you think maybe she's alive—the Barre girl?" Marvin asked.

"Yes," O'Higgins said. "I want to.'

"Let's keep it that way." Marvin looked at him.

They parked in front of Pier 39 and walked again to the Hall of Mirrors, having the owner shut it down while they wandered its warrens.

The lighting was just as it would have been when Emma walked in. At the end, after mistaking some mirrors as passages, they came to the end exactly where they'd begun. This time sober, they realized almost simultaneously that there had to be a fire escape.

And there was. The manager led them to a door near the very bottom of the attraction. He opened it. The bright sunlight hit them.

"He took her out here," Marvin said.

"Yeah," O'Higgins said. "Yeah. I think so."

"She couldn't scream or yell?"

"I don't know," O'Higgins said. "But yeah, maybe not."

They heard the famous harbor seals barking. They were above the piers where the harbor seals lay en masse, some slipping into the bay and disappearing into a yacht harbor that looked sublime.

Chapter 10

She had refused to speak. It was simply too difficult. She remembered little after entering The Hall of Mirrors with its weird strobe lights. The mirrored hallways reflected random people in the crowd, as everyone tried to make their way through the weird maze. Twice she'd walked into a mirror, her hands out like everyone else. It had been fun. People had pressed against her, all under a splash of colored strobe lights.

The good Samaritan who had helped her when she was overcome seemed nondescript, except for his eyes: pale blue, almost pretty like the eyes of a woman, and seeming to belong to a kinder person. They were certainly not the eyes of a monster. Or was she imagining that? She'd been completely addled—physically overcome, suddenly—while in the Hall of Mirrors. The good Samaritan had walked her out of the attraction, the intense strobe lights making it impossible to see him clearly. When they'd stepped out into the bright sunlight, he'd immediately pulled a cap over her eyes. They'd walked down a quay; that she remembered because she'd thrown up violently. They'd walked past a line of boats. After that she had no recollection of what happened until she'd woken up.

He had duct-taped over her eyes while she'd slept. So now she was both blind and deaf. It seemed an impossible nightmare when she woke and couldn't see.

Someone stood her up roughly.

In a panic, she signed: "I am deaf."

He struck her and knocked her against the wall with a slap. She signed again. "I am deaf. I do not speak English well." She realized that she was going to die and that she would never see her parents again. All those thoughts came to her at once, in a way that had not, until that moment he hit her. It was the man's stupid cruelty that she finally recognized, the depths of it... *If you threw a stone into its well it would fall forever.* A limitless cruelty, without boundaries of any kind, she thought.

She had practiced lip reading English for a year in preparation for her visit to America. She'd so looked forward to it. She pointed to her ears and shook her head. Did he finally understand that she was deaf and couldn't hear? Would he hit her again?

She signed, "What's your name?" She made a pen-in-hand motion, thinking he might understand that.

After a moment he pressed a pencil and paper into her hands. She could smell the sea. She could tell from the motion under foot that she was on some kind of boat.

What is your name? she wrote in English. He took the paper from her shaking hand; she'd been unable to see the paper or pen so had written slowly visualizing the words. She believed she might somehow quell his violence with the question.

He raped her later that day.

Guessing the time of day became important to her. She had to guess at the time. The rape was the strangest experience of her life because she was calm as he climbed on her and found her. Then he raped her, smelling of the beach and fires, and one other smell she couldn't quite put her finger on...

Her sense of smell was extremely developed. She tried to catalog the other odor, but couldn't.

He'd heaved, filling her. She felt nothing. She was far away, in another country, listening to her father. They were walking in the woods near their house. She signed to him about what she was reading: a book about the deportations of women in France during the Second World War. He'd given her a serious look—not of disapproval, but of curiosity. It was her father's questioning look. It was the same when she went out on her skateboard. She was considered a good girl. Her father thought the skateboard riding and rock climbing, and all they represented, didn't fit one of the most intellectually gifted high school students in France. He didn't like either sport.

He signed the words: "Why that book?" He had a way of signing that was vigorous and masculine, smacking of his quick mind.

They'd stopped. It was a beautiful day, the sun warm on their backs. It was September.

She loved to read and had come across the book online: *A Train in Winter*. She'd read it in English on her beat-up Kindle her father had bought her in New York the year before.

"Your grandmother…"

"What?"

"Your grandmother was … Deported."

"Yes… 1944…"

They were signing quickly. September's bright sun shone on her face when they changed direction, its rays coming through the white spruce treetops like a halo. So different from the feeling in the book, which was all about winter—not just because of the book's title, but because it was hard to imagine a place like occupied France in 1942. It was, she'd decided, a winter of the soul, too. The record cold temperatures that year had been so fitting for a Fascist takeover.

How could it be? All of it seemed an impossible nightmare, a horrible fairy tale for her generation, distant history with no way to measure.

Reading the book, she understood that Ravensbrück concentration camp, where so many French women from the Resistance ended up, was not a fairytale, but hell itself. A real hell on earth. Realizing that had upset her in the most profound way, back-footing her emotionally. Demagnetizing the last pieces of her childhood—releasing it.

She developed a fear that the world was not benign and could go *widdershins*, producing a madness in people. Ordinary people of all kinds could go mad and act as if what they were doing wasn't at all wrong or crazy. It was as if she'd walked into the camp's buildings and experimental rooms—seen the near dead, heard them call for their husbands and children. That history had changed her.

Later she would have to go to a "child" psychologist, with a signing translator in the room. The doctor was lost as to why she, a pretty sixteen-year old honor student, was so worried that "it could happen again."

Couldn't it? She'd asked the middle-aged doctor, who had never given that history any thought at all. The doctor's world, Emma understood quickly, was a well-ordered place of psychotropic prescriptions where children could be "treated" for childish neurosis by giving them a pharmacological shove in the right direction. Emma's questions were too basic, too strange, for the psychiatrist to understand. Ontology wasn't for children after all.

"Unlikely that kind of thing could happen again. What makes you think it might?" the doctor asked, devoid of the intellectual commitment the question demanded.

"Is that your professional opinion, or just that of a French citizen?" she'd said curtly. It was then the doctor realized the girl was indeed exceptional, and that the parents' and school authorities had not exaggerated her intelligence. The doctor had sat up straight and looked at her as if he'd been slapped.

She'd asked her father, that day it all started: "Why?" She signed slowly, her face expressing her frustration.

"It was the war," her father signed. It was clear he didn't want to talk about it anymore. They'd moved on down the well-marked trail, with sunlight dancing on it. He turned around and signed more quickly this time. "You're too young for all the misery... It was almost 80 years ago!"

Her father turned and walked up the path quickly, frightened by her intelligence even now, after so many years. Its raw power and its unflinching quality were troubling. She was a genius, yes, but something else about her left people ill at ease. Perhaps it was just the combination of beauty and intelligence that was simply so formidable and impregnable. He had begun to worry about her because he thought she'd started to become slightly manic, and at times unreasonable. It was then he decided to send her to a child psychologist. Her mother had been against it.

It was the first time she'd been disappointed in her father. She wanted to know what had happened. Why had her grandmother been sent to Berlin? What had happened to her in Germany? Why didn't anyone talk about it?

She signed all those things later in her room in front of her computer—talking to herself, as she was wont to do. A half hour later she was reading about the war in Syria. It was at that moment, reading about that new barbaric war, that she decided to become an adult and stop asking her parents about the outside world. She no longer wanted to be put off or trifled with.

Childhood was over. Her interest in free climbing grew. It was the climbing itself that made her feel connected and sane, for whatever reason.

Chapter 11

The small room had a poster of an idyllic lake—Como in Italy, O'Higgins decided, studying it. It hung on the wall directly across from where he sat. He'd been sitting alone after ingesting the drug for the first time. He'd asked the male nurse who had administered the LSD—a kind of paper that melted like a host in his mouth—where the doctor was.

The nurse, preoccupied, seemed to find it all routine. He said the doctor would be in by the time the drug had begun to take its effect.

"What should I look for?" O'Higgins asked the nurse.

"You mean when it's coming on?"

"Yes."

The man, one hand on the cubicle's doorknob, stopped to answer.

"Somewhat skewed perceptions. If you run your hand quickly in front of your eyes, it may look—have a strobe effect. Things like that. Enjoy the trip." He closed the door behind him.

The room was part of a warren created for the experiment. The room, perhaps ten by ten, was kitted out with a new couch and a throw rug—black and white squares—and nothing more except two colorful travel posters. The lake was one. The other showed the Dalai Lama walking in a wood, fall colors surrounding him, his red robe striking but at the same time fitting him into the landscape.

It seemed corny at first, but he was drawn to the magic of fall. He wondered where the photo had been taken. He wondered what kind of man the Dalai Lama was. He seemed genuinely jovial. The perfect neighbor? He turned and looked at his shoes. His daughter had helped pick them out before she'd left. She'd stepped into her mother's role, trying to be a kind of ersatz wife. He looked up... he had nothing to do but to wait. For what, exactly, he had no idea. He napped.

When he opened his eyes, the waiting room had changed somehow, slightly different in feel. It felt like some sent-down third-world clinic. He looked at his coat hanging on the back of the door. It seemed to wiggle slightly, as if the sleeves were alive. The hallucination scared him a little, as if he'd slipped in a shower but caught himself.

He gripped the arm of the couch and looked at his watch. It was an Apple watch Robin had bought him for Christmas. She'd chosen a cool face, aviator-style with a second hand at the center. He watched the sixty-second counter hand sweep, transfixed. It too seemed to waver slightly.

He closed his eyes. He was on Fillmore Street, alone, driving toward the restaurant where he met his brother. It was spectacularly clear, the colors vivid—people vivid— as if he were watching an old-school eight millimeter movie, but one where the director had found a way of jumbling the senses so that the colors were washed out at some times, and at other times multi-chromatic and rich.

**

The extra magazine to his Glock slid off the floor as he turned the corner onto Fillmore Street. He had squirreled extra magazines around his person and car since the shootout in the Mission District where he and Marvin had almost bought the farm. No place for snowflakes, gun haters or pencil-necked do-gooders. What had saved him was the trained killer in him. The Marine Corps had done a good job. It had appeared ready and able, untouched by his years as a civilian or hours of psychoanalysis. He had returned fire as he'd been taught by "some of the best killers in the world."

He parked his SFPD-issued Ford in a red zone near the hospital and headed out down Fillmore Street for a lunch date with his older brother, a brain surgeon. The air was clean and cold, with a certain eternal promise.

He passed an attractive woman, his age, in grey yoga pants dark with sweat, very blonde—her cheeks rosy, her yoga mat tucked neatly under her arm, her small breasts pushing seductively against her zippered-in-the-front Lululemon jacket. She smiled at him.

For a moment he lost himself in the pleasure of the young woman's bright smile and galvanizing figure, and forgot the rest of what he was carrying around. He realized that he was now, more than three years past his wife's sudden death, on the make. The shootout had triggered something magnetic in him. His compass overridden, it pointed toward the intoxication of sex and alcohol. He'd gotten a girlfriend and spent a lot of time fucking his brains out. A few ecstasy-laced moments of gratification, and then his angst would return like a high tide at night—unseen but making itself felt in myriad ways.

***

The doctor walked into the room. She smiled at him. She was wearing what she normally wore when he saw her, a white blouse and black pants—put together. He felt better that she looked like she normally did when they met. Official-looking.

"Michael, how are you? Everything all right so far?"

He nodded yes. He was high, and seeing things more clearly, more intensely. He held his hand up, giving the thumbs-up. She smiled. He had a horrible fear that he was getting an erection. It was shocking. He looked down to see if it was showing.

"What's wrong?" she said.

"Nothing," he said. "Nothing..." He looked across at the lake. It seemed to be real—the water real, the boats in a small harbor real... the mountain towering above it, real.

She came and sat next to him on the couch.

"What is it I'm doing?" he asked.

"Relaxing, I hope," she said.

"No, what is it I'm doing? I went back in time. Really back in time. Not just remembering, but back—with Clifford in the restaurant."

"That's okay. Go with it. Is that when he told you?"

"Yes."

He was staring at Lake Como's tiny harbor. Now a boat moved out of the harbor. Only it was his boat, the one that was the source of everything that had happened...

"This is very crazy, all this." He moved his hand in front of him and he saw it partition into several hands sweeping, and then one of them had an eye in the middle of it. It was his wife's eye. He started to cry. He felt the doctor take his hand.

"Sit back, Michael. Sit back."

"Is this my hand or your hand?" he asked. He looked down at her hand holding his.

"Does it matter?" she said.

***

O'Higgins took his butter knife and spread strawberry jam on his thick piece of rye toast.

He ate with gusto, listening to his brother beat around the bush and thinking it uncharacteristic. Clifford explained his girlfriend's plans to go to Chile and paint her father's portrait, so she would always have him with her. She was going to send a photo of her father to Kissinger, too, saying that despite it all he was alive—the CIA had failed to kill him.

"How is Marvin? I mean since the ambush?" Clifford asked. "I've always liked Marvin. We were all worried."

"He's fine. The surgeons—your team—did a good job that day. He almost bled out," Michael said. "Everyone likes Marvin, except the

Mexican gentlemen who tried to kill us."

Clifford looked at him.

"I'm honestly grateful to the medical profession. I couldn't stand getting a new partner."

"So he's back on the job?"

"Yes, thank God, three weeks ago. I had some kid to train, he was driving me crazy. He went to Cal. Can you imagine? And he's a homicide cop! You don't need to go to Cal to be a murder cop."

"You didn't like him?" Clifford asked.

"I didn't understand him, was the problem. There was nothing to like or dislike about him. He couldn't think straight—it was strange, no *dúchas*." He used the Irish word their mother used for people with no drive or native intelligence. When he thought about his mother, he thought about her speaking Gaelic on the phone to her people. "It was like he was sleepwalking. Sometimes I wanted to just reach over and slap him and see if he was really awake."

The strong Italian roast coffee was helping, but he was slightly hungover. The feeling—a mush-headed feeling—was pretty much a constant. He'd grown used to it. It was easy to hide behind it.

"It's not been easy living with this, I can tell you," Clifford said.

"Living with what?" Michael said, tucking into his lunch.

"By the way, they're torturing my girlfriend's father in the other room. Do you want to have a look?"

"What room?"

"The other room?"

"What?"

"Yeah, it's been going on all morning. Can you hear the screams?"

"Wait, I don't understand."

He looked up from the table. The chic restaurant was grey and ugly, in the bowels of a Latin American jail. He and his brother were still sitting at their table, food in front of them, but screams were coming from a tunnel-like hallway that seemed stretched out, its dimensions cock eyed.

"I don't want to be here. This isn't right," he said. His iPhone, bright red, was on the table. It rang. He picked it up

"Hello?"

"It's Emma. Emma Barre. I've been raped."

He looked at the screen and saw the girl's photo. "It hurt."

He heard a scream and stood as if some giant had hauled him up.

"Go on, then," Clifford said. "He won't mind if you watch. He's used to people watching him."

Michael walked down the hallway, but the hallway was moving and he was standing still. Cell doors passed him. He looked at his feet and saw sewage and blood running in an open gutter, covering his dress shoes in human shit. He reached an open steel doorway. He saw two men in suits standing in front of a young man, maybe twenty, a ragged beard, sweating. The young man was hooked up to a machine like a computer, and when one of the men touched the keyboard, the young man would scream, the muscles on his neck bulging.

He was back at the table looking at his brother. They could hear the screams, but Clifford didn't seem to notice them.

"More coffee? I'll get it," Clifford said. He looked around the busy restaurant and signaled to a busboy.

Michael realized his brother was used to people obeying him.

"I was supposed to wait a year until after Mom was gone," Clifford said. "And then tell you. But I postponed telling you—after Jen's accident, I couldn't. So I just didn't keep my promise. But it's been bothering me, and now I want to tell you. I think it's time."

"About what?" O'Higgins asked. He looked at the phone, which was ringing. He saw Emma Barre's face on the screen.

"She's deaf," he said to his brother.

"Yeah, I know," Clifford said. "We all are, to a point."

***

He was back from where he'd been—the high. The doctor was still sitting near him. "I don't like it," O'Higgins said. "What it does. It doesn't make any sense. It's just a bunch of—I don't know what, dreams or something. Where you go—"

"That's often the first reaction," Schneider said. "How do you feel?"

He looked at the poster of Lake Como. It seemed normal. He looked for the sailboat—his boat—to see if he were truly back from where he'd been. It looked normal now, just a travel poster. He looked around the room.

The doctor stood up.

"What time is it?" he asked.

"Three thirty. Your phone rang twice," she said. "We'll wait two days, then start again."

Chapter 12

O'Higgins spotted Cassandra Lee's new white Jeep Cherokee at the Marina Green parking lot. Her car was facing big-money yachts, sheltered by the long rock pier that protected the San Francisco yacht harbor. The bay was choppy, a wind blowing due East. Ten or more soccer teams—little leagues—were using Marina Green for practice. The youngest kids couldn't have been any more than seven or eight years old, and looked Lilliputian.

O'Higgins got out of his car and walked over to where the Jeep was parked. He slid into the passenger seat. He smelled marijuana, but didn't say anything.

"Why did you call?" O'Higgins asked. He leaned over and gave Marvin's wife a hug, which was normal for them, but he could tell something was wrong. It was the look on her face and the way her body felt tense.

On the drive from the hospital he'd been careful to test himself in case he was high. The feel of her stiff hug felt peculiar. He tried to put his finger on it. He'd had a drink at a bar on Chestnut to help him calm down after the LSD trip. Maybe that hadn't been such a good idea.

"You've been drinking, Michael?" she said.

"Yeah, I have." And he was going to say: and you've been smoking weed, but didn't.

"Has Marvin been drinking?" she asked. "He's come home lately acting strange."

"Yeah, I guess." He couldn't look her in the eye. "I'm not going to lie to you."

"He's been distant sometimes. Even with the girls," Cassie said. "What's wrong?"

"World's wrong, is what's wrong. Case has gone sideways. There is another girl missing," he said. He didn't want to talk about the girls they'd found. Cassandra had two daughters, and it seemed cruel to discuss the Seven Hills case.

"I get it."

"Well, it's been so—you want a drink."

He turned and looked at Marvin's wife. She was a beautiful woman. Even now something was classic about her. You'd expect her to be doing perfume commercials or be a movie star, maybe a Bond Girl. Men, and probably women, wanted her the way you want to drive the latest Porsche when you see it roll by on the freeway. You knew it would be fun. He looked at how the curve of her ass pushed into the car's leather seat.

"What do you see in Marvin, anyway?" he said, half-joking.

When he was high, he would follow a thought—pick at one. He'd always known she was exotic. Marvin, despite his good looks, was the boy next door, but she wasn't the girl next door. He'd guessed that the moment he'd first met her. Something in her eyes, flinty and worldly and sexual. It went beyond her sex, yet was attached to her sex all the time—ginned up by it.

He finally had the thought he never would have allowed if he'd been sober (or was it the LSD?). He wondered what she looked like without her clothes on. He finally went there and was sorry he did, immediately. He turned toward the windshield and looked out on the Bay, feeling guilty.

"Anyway, I'll try to get him to stop. If that's what you want," he said.

She didn't speak, and he turned and looked at her. She was wearing a black sweater and grey wool pants.

Again, he thought. He reached for the door and was going to leave, but she grabbed his arm.

"No, that's not why I called. I don't care about the drinking—not really. I knew after the shootout that he would be different."

He felt her hand on his arm It was warm, and he liked the touch of it. It felt different than the doctor's. Hers felt cool. She let go of him.

"You're planning a surprise party or something? Is there a reason you wanted to see me alone?"

"Yes."

Uh-oh, he thought. What was he going to do if she crossed the line—and why would she?

He was anything but handsome. His wife had once said he was big like Michael Caine, but without Caine's '60s-era good looks. He'd never forgot it. He'd been almost six feet in junior high. Kids had called him the Hulk behind his back.

"Michael, I need to—I need your help."

"What's wrong?" he said. He saw that this had nothing to do with him and was relieved, but also disappointed, if only a little.

"Where do I start?"

"Try the beginning," he said. He pulled the Jeep's door shut again.

"I lied to Marvin," she said.

"So? I lied to Jen lots of times. Said I wasn't drinking when I was. I shoved a suspect, roughed him up—I never told her. I got caught, too. Never told her. I was ashamed of what I'd done. I knew she would be too. You know what she was like. Okie straight arrow. Religious."

"No, Mike. I lied to Marvin about something important. Something about me."

"Okay—what was it? What did you do? Cheat on your taxes? Lie about your age? And are you sure you want to tell me, Cassie? I mean it's like I'm married to Marvin, too. You know that. You know. If it's something—you know, something to do with your marriage—I don't really think I should be the one . . ."

"I do want to tell you."

"Oh, shit."

"I lied about my past. What I'd done in my past."

"Is that all?" He was instantly relieved. "Who doesn't? I said all kinds of things when I started dating Robin. That I could ski like Jean-Claude Killy. That I wasn't impressed that she's got a lot of money. Shit, she's got more money than God—that stuff is normal, white-lying. I wouldn't worry about it."

"No, not like that. I lied about being a—about what I'd done before, before we met."

Michael took his hand off the door's lever. "All right," he said. "Okay."

"You heard the story—about being a model in LA. Commercial work—and lingerie…"

"Yeah." He felt himself sobering up. The fog was coming in, a thin plank of it sitting over the Marin headlands. One of those giant Chinese freighters, a big orange one, was pushing past Alcatraz going toward Albany, full of junk for Target.

"It was true for a while. I did some modeling. That part's true."

"For a while?"

"Yeah. I never told Marvin the whole story."

"So what? It doesn't matter now, does it? He loves you. You love him, that's all that matters. He never even looks at other women. He could care less. So leave it be. You guys are good." He started to get out of the car again, anxious to get away before a betrayal.

"Problem is, I can't," she said. Her blond hair fell over her face, framing it.

"Why the hell not?" he said.

"I was—an escort," she said.

He didn't say anything. Half the Chinese freighter had disappeared, bow in the fog. Twenty kinds of grey-green fragments were painted on the surface of the Bay. It was summer, so it was always unsettled like that: Alcatraz looked like the ugly rock it was. Reminded you of wrongdoing and suffering.

"Mike, I was a—prostitute. High class, but I was a—a—" She couldn't bring herself to say the ugly word. "I was a prostitute. Do you understand?"

"Cassie, why are you telling me this and not Marvin?"

"Because someone came into town, someone from my past, and he wants me to do something for him. If I don't, there'll be consequences."

"Who?"

"The guy I worked for. You know."

Michael's phone buzzed, and he heard a text hit.

"Oh shit," he said. "Oh shit. I got to go. It's probably Marvin wondering where the hell I've been, all afternoon."

"Please don't go. Please. I'm begging you," she said. "He said that I had to go see him, or there would be consequences."

"Who said that?"

"His name is Thorpe. Robert Thorpe."

"He was your—?"

"Manager." She used the euphemism for pimp. "I worked out of LA, but it was very—exclusive. The men we—dated—they were very rich men. Sometimes they were scary. I know, I've seen what they can do to people. They own you, and I—please. I need your help, Mike."

"Jesus, Cassie. We got a case that—it's bad. Really bad. I've got to go."

"Mike, these people. They don't—when they say they'll hurt you, they will hurt you. They're not like regular people. They're not afraid of anyone. I know what they can do."

"You want me to go talk to this guy. Get him straight." His anger was preternatural. He did his best to control it, but lately it was getting harder and harder. "I'll set him straight. Okay. I promise. Is that what you want?"

"Yes. Please. I knew you would. I can't ask Marvin. Marvin would— you know what would happen." She didn't have to say anything more. She wanted this guy beaten up. She wanted him to do it, and she didn't want Marvin to know a thing about it.

"He's expecting me this afternoon. But I thought if you told him, explained to him that I can't—whatever it is he wants—I can't do it. He's got to understand that. Marvin, if he found out what I'd been, he would leave me. I'm sure of it. I can't risk it. I love him and I love the girls.

"You know how he is. He believes in God. It's not a joke, all that religion stuff. Not with Marvin. He'd hate me, Mike. I'd be the last woman he'd have married. Please go talk to him."

"What time?"

"In about a half hour."

"Where?"

"At the Fairmont. Room 1443."

"What's his name again?"

"Thorpe, Robert Thorpe. You can't tell him that you're a cop, Mike. Please don't. Please don't tell him that. I'm afraid he'll only get mad. Just tell him that I love Marvin and I can't do it. I can't see him."

He nodded, turned, and opened the door and got out. The wind was blowing across the parking lot. It was cold as he walked toward his beat-up Ford. The orange freighter was completely engulfed in the fog, as was half of Berkeley. Snuffed out.

As he walked to his car, he realized he was about to lie to Marvin for the first time—and about his wife. *Fuck*. He hit his phone and leaned against his car. He watched Cassie's Jeep pull out of its spot, head along the yacht harbor and finally turn toward the exit.

"Marvin? I got a thing with Robin. She's got some kind of emergency—I can't explain. You'll have to interview them again without me. Is there anything new?"

"No. No one down there saw anything. Store owners, or the security people," Marvin said. There had been a shooting on Market Street in front of Nordstrom. A street hustler shot in the back of the head. "Hurry the fuck up, man—Jesus, Mike. Where the hell you been all fucking afternoon?"

***

The lobby of the Fairmont was full of Salesforce executives from out of town, a convention. None of the gaggle of casually dressed young people looked to be over twenty-five. He went to the elevators and realized he was getting older as the door closed behind him.

The City had taken on a two-tier look. The up-and-coming, mostly young white and Asian, or East Asian—and everyone else. It was weird and so different from the city he remembered as a child, before the Big Money time. It had been a peaceful, elegant, low-key vibe that fit with a city on the edge of the Western World. That vibe was gone.

Marvin had texted him twice, but he didn't read them. He was trying to get a grip on what all this meant. Why hadn't Cassie told Marvin the truth about something like that? What, he wondered, would he have done if the shoe was on the other foot?

He supposed—stepping out on the 14th floor—that he might not have married her. What difference would it make now, he wondered. Whatever she'd been in her past, she wasn't that now. They had a family. Two beautiful girls. But if he found out, after the fact—?

Yes, that would make a difference, he thought. He knew Marvin. It just would. The hallway was plush and quiet. He glanced at his watch. It was just 4:30.

"I was expecting Cassie," Thorpe said.

"She can't make it," O'Higgins said. He walked into the room, not waiting to be invited, pushing past the bigger man.

"I see," Thorpe said.

It was the Presidential suite, with a stunning view of the Bay and Oakland. All the Bay's August drama was exaggerated and stunning, seen from up here. It reminded him of another view, from the case that had changed him forever—he was in love with a woman and it wasn't the one he was dating. He thought of her for the thousandth time since she'd left and gone back to India.

"Nice view," O'Higgins said, turning around.

"You aren't the husband."

"No," O'Higgins said.

Some Louis Vuitton suitcases were open on folding racks, three of them lined up along the wall. An expensive wool overcoat was thrown on the bed in another room, through open French doors. The suite had to be ten grand a night, O'Higgins thought.

Thorpe was big, and despite the well-cut suit and the polished shoes and the thick smile of a car dealer, he vibed street. Creole, O'Higgins guessed. He felt the knuckle duster he'd slipped into his pocket. He carried it often, even when he was off duty. His psychiatrist had suggested that his paranoia-fueled weapons collection was a sign of PTSD. He had stopped carrying all the backup weapons for a while, but lately he'd started carrying them again, one by one. He had his regular pistol, but a fighting knife and the knuckle duster always on his person. He dug in his overcoat pocket and let his fingers find the weapon's oily holes.

"Look, I'm just a friend, but you got to understand that Cassie doesn't want to see you. And it's as simple as that, really. She isn't going to show up." He tried to sound matter of fact, not angry as he felt. He'd loathed the man from the moment he'd seen his phony smile. Pimps came in all kinds, but the executive-suit wearing types were the worst, he thought.

"I see."

"Yeah. I'm here to make it crystal clear," O'Higgins said.

"Did she tell you she used to work for me?"

"She mentioned it. So, do we have an understanding?" He put it that way to make sure the guy understood that he wasn't playing.

"Drink? We haven't been introduced. My name is Thorpe—Robert." Thorpe started to extend his hand, but saw it wasn't going to be that kind of meeting.

"My name is Al Capone," O'Higgins said. "And I don't give a fuck what your name is. For the record."

"Al Capone? Wow. Sounds familiar. Interesting. Any relation to the gangster?" Thorpe went to the minibar and opened it. "Gin and tonic?"

"Okay." He knew he shouldn't, but he might as well get a free drink out of the whole mess.

"She's beautiful, Cassandra. I've had a lot of women work for me, but some you just don't forget. She was seventeen when I found her. She was working parties in LA for a talent scout I had back then. A caterer. People would walk in and she'd be standing by the door with a drink tray. Can you imagine? Every guy had a hard-on by the time he crossed the foyer."

"Yeah," O'Higgins said. "I don't really want to hear about it."

"Are you a policeman?"

"No."

"You strike me as a policeman," Thorpe said, working on the drinks, his back to him.

"No."

Thorpe dropped the ice in his drink and brought it across the room. "Sorry, no limes."

"That's okay," O'Higgins said, taking the glass. "I'll survive."

"Aren't you curious about Cassandra's past?"

"You mean about her and you? Not in the least." O'Higgins took a pull of the drink. He wondered what this dirtbag had on her. It was obvious he did have something. He seemed typical of the breed: well-dressed, soft spoken like he was going to call a doctor for a confused old lady he'd found sitting in the lobby. Just another good-looking businessman doing the right thing.

"She was making, sometimes—I don't know, with tips, it was probably hundreds of thousands of dollars a year. That's the kind of business it is. It's not at all what you imagine. Not my business, anyway. Well, looking at you I don't think you could imagine, really. Not your crowd."

O'Higgins realized that Thorpe was looking at the stain on his shirt. He'd spilled coffee on it that morning.

"I'll take that as a compliment," O'Higgins said. "Now…" He put his drink down on the fancy glass coffee table, then wiped his hand on his coat. He was shaking slightly with anger.

"This is the deal: there's no deal. You forget about Cassandra and I won't come back here and kick your ass into the new year. That's not a threat. That's a promise. Are we clear on the concept?" He wanted to hit the man, fighting the urge to plant the knuckle duster in the center of his freckled face and take out a few teeth along the way.

"I—well. I see. I'm sorry you feel that way."

"Do we understand one another?" O'Higgins said. He shrugged, his hand in his coat pocket.

"Perfectly. Detective. You see, I know all about Cassie's new life. I thought she'd send her husband. But my guess is that you're the husband's chum. I know his name—Detective Marvin Lee—and I would bet any kind of money you're his faithful partner. She's very predictable, Cassie. In any case, threatening an honest businessman with violence is something you should be concerned about."

Thorpe took out his cell phone and turned the screen towards him. He'd been recording the conversation, the recording app displaying a pulsating red circle.

O'Higgins was stunned that he knew who Marvin was.

"You're out of your league here, my friend. Completely out of your league. Please tell Cassandra I would like to see her. I'm afraid there's no other solution to this problem."

Chapter 13

The Lees had bought a house in Bernal Heights. It was a new house at the very top of Bernal Hill, facing the East Bay. They'd been excited the day they'd moved in. It had views of Oakland. More important, it had the rooms they'd needed for their two tween girls. It was more house than they could afford, but they'd bought it anyway.

"Damn the torpedoes," their preppy English realtor had said, smiling, when they signed the offer. It was a saying Cassie had never heard before. She had to ask what it meant. She loved the house and had never been happier than the day they'd moved in.

It had all been so perfect before he'd called. *It was as if that part of my life hadn't existed*, she thought, working alone in the sparkling new kitchen.

Marvin pushed through the kitchen door. He'd showered and put on clean clothes for their eldest daughter's birthday party.

"It's a party, honey," Marvin said. "What's wrong? I'll help you. Tell me what to chop."

"They're going to be here soon— nervous. This is a new recipe, that's all."

She'd been trying not to look at her phone. She had it propped up by the stove, afraid that Thorpe would call her again and Marvin would pick it up or ask who it was.

"Did you get it?"

"iPhone XR. I made Mike wait in the car."

She'd had Marvin pick up the gift, afraid she would get the wrong model. Marvin was a techno geek and she knew he'd enjoy going into the Apple store, making sure it was just right and what their daughter wanted. He spoiled the girls because he'd grown up poor as she had.

"It's what she wants, an iPhone XR." She smiled and picked up a beef shank for osso bucco. She started to roll the ring of meat so that it would sear the outer end of the wheel.

Marvin came up behind and held her, his arms around her waist, tight. "I got to get some of this sweetness, girl." He kissed her neck.

It felt good, but she couldn't relax. She wiggled free. Everything, even his holding her, seemed confining, as if she'd been thrown into a room without enough air.

"Is it wrapped? Like I asked," she said trying to get free.

"Yeah. They give you a gift box," Marvin said, not letting her go.

"Where is it?"

He persisted in kissing her, and continued to work down her neck with his lips. "Honey, I could burn you—really." She wiggled again, but he didn't let her go.

"Burn me up then. I hid it," Marvin said, standing behind her.

"Okay, I got to cook this—they'll all be here soon!" His arms let go of her.

"What's wrong, baby?"

"I'm fine. Really. It's just I get nervous when I have to produce a dinner that's eatable. Your sister is a gourmet. She makes me nervous."

Marvin's sister ran a restaurant. She had gone to cooking school in Paris, and had worked her way up from sous chef at Boulevard to restaurant owner.

"It's just Mike and Rebecca and Mike's new girlfriend and my sister and the kids. You know she won't—you know. Ronda isn't like that."

"I know, but I want it to be good. Everything perfect," she said.

Marvin looked at her, then went to the refrigerator and slid out a bottle of tequila. He poured a shot into a blue rimmed thick-glass Mexican tumbler they'd brought back from their honeymoon.

Their daughter Matilda walked in. She was already beautiful at fourteen, tall like her father, with blue eyes like her mother. Boys would stop and look at her the way they had her mother at that age. It was becoming a problem. Cassie never said it, but she wished that her daughter wasn't as pretty as she was, or was certainly going to be. It was a horrible thought for a mother to have, but she had it again looking at her. It wasn't a gift.

"Daddy, will you please tell me what you got me. Please? I can't stand it." Matilda pulled a face. Her hair was blond and kinky and she was letting it grow out into an old-school Afro. Her skin was the color of milk with chocolate in it.

On a visit to LA a friend of Cassie's from the old days, who had made it as a casting agent, begged her to take Matilda around. She said no, in an angry tone of voice that surprised the woman. "Why in the world would I let her do that? That would be ridiculous. Being a model is ridiculous. She's going to be something—go to college."

"Not your birthday yet, girl. Another two hours, baby doll. You were born at 9:00 p.m.!" Marvin said.

His daughter came up and hung on him with a pleading look, but he shook his head in mock street anger.

"God!" Matilda flew out of the kitchen.

"She's going to love that thing. It's the—"

"Are you drinking on the job?" Cassie turned from the stove and looked at her husband.

"Not enough," Marvin said. "Not enough." His expression clouded over.

"You going to tell me why? Is that going to turn into a problem? What if—you know. It happens again and you're not sober. A shootout or a fight? Don't you need to be sober for that?" She moved the hair out of her eyes.

He walked out of the kitchen and left her to it.

She looked at the swinging service door. She heard the doorbell ring and then her daughter's squeal with delight, extreme, tween-sharp squeals, at the sight of their cousins. She was going to run out to greet everyone, as she normally would, but couldn't face her sister-in-law, or anyone. Instead she got a bottle of white wine from the refrigerator and filled a glass before they all trooped in to say hello, and she would have to put on a jovial face. She drained the glass straight away.

It was hard to look across the table at Michael. They shared a secret. She was dying to ask what had happened with Thorpe, but instead they had barely spoken.

He'd pecked her on the cheek the way he always did, but it felt different, distant. He didn't look at her.

She looked at O'Higgins' girlfriend, Robin Sparks, who hadn't touched her dessert.

Cassie saw what he liked about her. She was tall and thin, and very, very rich from what Marvin had told her. She dressed well. Cassie had seen lots of women like her when she was in LA. They had time to shop and the money to do it with. Their DNA was different. They carried a certain aura and self-assuredness that were so foreign to her kind.

She turned and looked at the girls helping Matilda with her new phone. Her daughter was beaming. Her cousins, all of them, looked so innocent, so pure, so—

If they knew what I'd been. What I'd done. Your mother was a—

"And is it hard? Being a policeman's wife?" Robin asked out of the blue, looking across the table.

Everyone seemed to stop talking. It was a question their daughters didn't like. Even amongst themselves they didn't talk about it, especially after the gunfight that had almost taken Marvin's life and was probably the cause of his drinking. She'd begged him to leave the police, but he'd refused, saying he had the girls to bring up, and what would he do if he left? He had a pension to protect.

"It's—it's—did you get enough to eat?" Cassie asked.

The phone ringing saved her. It was a number she didn't recognize, but she picked up the call and escaped to the kitchen.

It was Lana.

***

Turk Street, the heart of the Tenderloin. The dirty concrete sparkled with broken glass from wine bottles that caught passing headlights.

Cassandra crossed Jones Street. She rolled down the window and got an immediate wet-cardboard smell. The grit, the grime, the cum-stained yellow bedding of the SROs where she'd lived as a girl with her mother: it all came back to her. The smell of Vietnamese food cooked on hot plates. The parolees—poor white and black men—leaning out on a mean world, keeping their secrets, mostly violent ones, watched her drive past, hulking guardians of the demimonde. Her "father," a long-distance trucker who drove in and out of their lives in a funky tractor-trailer when they'd still lived in Las Vegas, told her once that he was as rough as a day-old beard. She remembered touching his poor white lined cracker's face. He kept a handgun by the bed.

She'd loved him and missed him still. He'd been the one man who had treated her with real care and love until she'd met Marvin. She'd never told him his brother had abused her.

"He's dead," her mother told her when she was eleven. In her mother's world, that was what you told children if someone had gone to prison for something bad and for a long time. She often thought about him, his kindness. She'd had to leave the Catholic school he'd been paying for and re-enter the sent-down public school with its bullies and morons interrupting the teachers at every turn.

He'd always been kind to her, watched out for her when he was around, a presence in her lonely, TV-constantly-on, pervert-infested world. She learned later he'd gone to Folsom Prison and died there in a fight on the yard. He'd left her mother the truck. She sold it and went on a drug bender.

It was where Cassandra would end up, her mother always told her.

Her mother had worked as a street prostitute in Vegas. When it got bad, when her looks slipped, her tits flattened and she gained weight, she'd tumbled down to "Frisco's" Tenderloin. It had been her mother's lively blue eyes Cassandra remembered, not the husk of a dope fiend she'd found half dead when she was thirteen, needle stuck in her arm. 20 years in the business.

Why she'd kept a trick's daughter, not had her aborted, Cassandra never understood. There were others she didn't keep—three of them.

"See me? I'm a billboard for everything you should run from, honey." She heard her mother's whiskey voice now, like the slide of an Albert King riff.

"Okay. Where are you, Lana?" She spoke to herself in the car. Her fear was that she wouldn't find her friend in time. She checked her phone for Lana's text:

Turk and Mason. Red coat.

It had been raining slightly, but like a lot of girls with a jones to feed she was still trying to hustle despite the cold weather. Her lipstick was on, but off the mark, so her face had a frighteningly clownish look. The once pretty girl—anyone could see she'd been a beauty once— was in patent leather knee-high boots, the heels worn. She smelled almost like the street itself, wet pavement.

They'd met in Hollywood when they were both underage, part of the hordes of runaway kids from all over the country. Lana had saved her life, been like a sister to her. Lana the protector, the knife-wielding hell's goddess when it was necessary. Fearless.

"He's here," Lana said, getting in the car. "Isn't he?" Her hair was wet. "Yeah," Cassie said. "He called."

"Fuck." Lana looked at her, then started digging in a worn big red knock-off purse. A Muni bus passed them as she dug. "Fucking rat hole of a fucking purse. Why is he here?" She found what she was looking for, a package of Lucky Strikes, and fished out a cigarette, then a black Bic lighter.

"Why do they call them Lucky? They ain't been lucky for me. Shit." She blew smoke out of her nose. "What's he want, anyway?"

"Wanted to see me," Cassie said.

"Why that man want to see you?"

"I don't know."

"Well, I don't want to see him," Lana said.

"I thought you'd know why."

"Me? No! No, doll, I don't."

"You stayed on, after I left. Why?"

"Good money."

"I took the book," Cassie said.

"Say what?"

"I took the book. His book. When I left."

"You did what?"

"I took it," Cassie said. "I wanted to—I wanted it. It was stupid, but I thought if I had the book, I had his power. I don't even know why I took it. But I wanted it. I made sure it looked like—you know. I made it look like I'd been gone on a weekend. Made up a client. Paid for myself. But I—I fucked his doorman. And I got the book."

"You took the man's book, baby?" Lana said, not believing it, wide-eyed.

"Yeah. I sure did."

"Oh, girl—shit. You got it still?"

"Yeah. On a flash drive."

"That's some crazy shit, Cassie. Crazy. He's going to beat your ass you the one that took his book. He beat people looking for that book. Let me tell you. He was one angry motherfucking player when you quit."

"I don't think he knows it was me. And it was years ago, now."

"Why you keep it?"

"Don't know. I just did. Insurance, I guess."

Lana sat back and smoked. They didn't speak. The car started to smell of the fog and concrete and the ugly smell of street depravity: a heavy fug as if all their past was filling the car with its ugliness of forty-thousand-dollar weekends on yachts with men and women who didn't give a fuck about them, but wanted their youth, the only thing they had. It was an ugly combination: their wealth, their power and the need to see her do what they paid for. The look they got when she gave it to them. It was in the car now with them both, how they felt afterwards on the ride home. Dirty and used.

When she'd taken his book—with all his important johns' phone numbers in it— it was as if she'd stolen back something that he'd taken from her, that all the rich johns had taken away from her. One by one, pieces of herself had gone missing.

"He asked about you, where you were—if I knew," Cassie said.

"Me?!"

"Yes."

"What you say?"

"I said I hadn't seen you for years. That I'd heard you were dead. That's it."

"Wish it were true," Lana said.

"Don't say that."

Lana reached for her hand and across twelve years, even further when they'd met at a do-gooder's place on Sunset. Lana so skinny that her bell bottoms kept sliding down, her hair in Jheri Curls, her eyes red. She'd sat next to Cassie in a group session— the group therapy for street kids who were suspected of turning tricks—and they'd just looked at each other that first time. An older man stopped in a yellow Caddy in front of the place on Sunset, and Lana had gotten in. Cassie had watched her go down the street, a connection made when Lana turned to glance back at her. She felt it now again.

"So now what you going to do?" Lana said.

"I had a friend go talk to him. Tell him I couldn't see him."

"Talk to Thorpe. Sheeeee—it." Lana turned and looked down her nose at her, the way they used to sometimes in London or Cannes when the clients would sit down with them. It was a funny thing she did, as if the seventeen-year-old girl couldn't believe what was happening and that it was all good. They were the two most popular yacht girls one year; they were both tall, they were both underage, and they were cool with "whatever."

"That man got a real boat, girl. Look!" She remembered that day riding in the new Chris-Craft, that first time they shot across the water at Cannes. It was so blue. Lana was excited because it was a big fucking boat—dead ahead.

"You know he's going to find out exactly where I am if he wants to."

"How could he?" Cassie said.

"Because, he hooked up with the Man. You know that. I know that. Don't kid a black girl. Baby. You know who those people were. That's the man he works for, half the time anyway. I got to go… He running with the Man. You know that."

"Lana, don't go."

"Don't go?"

"No. I don't want you out there anymore. Please, it's killing me. I want you to come with me. Home with me."

"Home with you?"

"Yeah. At least until we know he's gone."

"Home with you? You are crazy, girl. You think that man of yours wants to see me? A beat up, black as night two-dollar crack whore? Huh. Come on. Don't think so."

"I don't care. I'll explain. Somehow. You can't—I don't want you out here."

"You going to explain that I'm a junkie and a whore, too? And then what? You goin' to explain how we know each other? You going to explain LA—and you going to explain to those girls of yours what we were doing in France, in Spain? Huh? No, I don't think so."

"I love you," Cassie said. "You know I do." Lana was her family, too. It was something she couldn't deny, seeing her, being with her.

"I love you, too, but that's not going to make the difference. Is it?"

"I'm taking you home. I'll lie." She pulled out into traffic.

Lana smoked and seemed relieved that she didn't have to go back out there. "You own a house now?" she said from the darkness, putting her cigarette out.

"Yeah, I got a house now."

She took Lana to a hotel in the Mission and paid for a room. They sat together and watched "Real Housewives of Atlanta" on Bravo. They called a joint for pizza the way they had in LA when they were starting out together, taking the dirty bills they'd been paid and laying them out on the motel's bed—counting it, making one pile to pay the hotel bill, one pile for food, and one pile for Lana to send home to her grandmother.

L.A.
2006

Cassie rolled over and looked at the guy lying next to her. He was skinny with sloping shoulders, muscles non-existent, like some kind of alien. It was the body of the wealthy, mostly white men she was used to. Spending most of their youth playing video games left them this strange effeminate body. Her age, maybe younger.

She tried to remember his name and exactly where she was. She wanted to just call him John, but hadn't the balls for that. She needed to get better, that was her first thought. A hit of blow would get her going again. He had put his dope in a bowl by the bed.

It had to happen sooner or later, she knew—the johns would start to be younger. She was nineteen, and felt old.

She tried to roll over, but something stopped her. She was handcuffed to the bed, her left arm. The expensive chromed chain led from the police-style handcuff to the headboard. She bridled and pulled on the chain again. Dread came over her, like something inflated in her chest. Fear.

He woke up.

"Let me go," she said. "Not cool."

"What's wrong?"

"Let me the fuck go!" she said. She tried to sound hard and unafraid.

"If you ask me nice," he said. "The meter is still running."

"What meter?"

"It's only Saturday."

"Let me the fuck out of these."

"No, bitch." He smiled. He thought it was all part of the service.

"Not cool. Let me go." She looked at him again, drawing on all her experience, leveling a cold stare.

"How about some blow?" he said.

He rubbed his eyes and pulled himself up with his palms, leaning against the headboard.

The sun poured through the windows. She remembered where they were: in Malibu, on the beach. They had walked right out of his house onto the sand.

She'd been wearing what she always wore, yoga pants and a white blouse. Her ass in the pants, Thorpe told her, was the best advertising he'd ever had. She remembered feeling the water slipping over her feet, and liking it. The blackness of the water, the way her toes smushed into the mud-like sand, the feel of the crystal wine glass in her hand with its cut-glass edges, sharp.

She'd looked down the beach. The john was talking to her, showing the normal john's anxious-to-look-cool face. She blocked out his bullshit, so used to it. She flattened it out with a smile that promised a lot while he blathered on about how he was producing a movie with a big star. She took in the view of the houses on the beach, their inviting lights that sparkled and told of wealth and domesticity. She wished she could have brought her mother to a house like this and set her up, tell her she never had to work again now that she was bringing down the brick— 40 000 G's for a weekend and full Girlfriend Experience. Long after her mother died, she still entertained that fantasy. All the houses looked swell. She tried to pick one out of the line that looked the most exclusive, the most desirable.

She interrupted the guy's blather. "How much?"

He was taking a drink. He had a bottle of champagne in one hand, glass in the other. He put the bottle down in the wet sand. She was ankle deep in the foamy surf, the water black and glistening.

"What?"

"Your crib. How much?"

"This place?"

"Yeah," she said.

"Show me your tits and I'll tell you. Just kidding. Seven million. Like it?"

"Yeah."

She turned and looked at the huge glass walls lit up: two stories facing the Pacific Ocean, the surf white-capped, the air perfumed by the smell of honeysuckle hedge and warm, the way she remembered it in Mexico. There was a john who would fly girls in three at a time. They called him Three At A Time… She'd fucked a young US congressman from Texas in a house in Playa del Carmen. He'd told her he was going "all the way" to the White House, the next John Kennedy. He was kinky.

"Sean Connery owned it once," the john said. "The house. No shit."

"Who is he?" she said.

"Sean Connery. You know, 007. The fucking movie star."

"Yeah? No shit."

He was looking at her. She had no idea who Sean Connery was. "You're fine as shit," he said. "Really."

"Thank you." She said it every time she heard the line. It meant she would have to blow the guy before too long, as he was getting hot and bothered.

He didn't look like the kind who would fuck her in the ass and handcuff her to the bed.

But snorting the blow he offered, she thought nothing surprised her anymore.

The drug hit her brain while he was doing it to her. It felt like grabbing the handle of a car just as it started up. She'd done that once on Hollywood Blvd. The john, a businessman type, had been nervous. Having passed her twice, he'd decided at the very last minute to take off just as she'd grabbed for the door, throwing her to the ground.

Chapter 14

"Are you ready?" Dr. Schneider asked.

"I guess," O'Higgins said. "I haven't told anyone about this—this experiment. I feel like I should be wearing a space suit."

Schneider smiled. She was dressed less formally, just in jeans and a T-shirt that said Tacosaurus across the front. He saw how petite she was. She'd put her hair up in a ponytail, as if they were going to the gym and not the outer edges of consciousness travel.

She handed him the dose of LSD. It was a single square in a short paper cup. It seemed all very antiseptic and above board.

"It will take a while—about an hour for it to come on. I'll be back in 45 minutes, I promise. I'll be just down the hall in my office."

He shook his head.

She took his hand and led him to the cubicle they would use that day. It was decorated with paintings and kitted out with comfortable furniture, a little crash pad in feel. He sat down in a leather club chair.

In about thirty minutes he felt the first effect while surfing on his phone. It was queer, a kind of separation from things. He'd hadn't felt it the first time; he'd been too nervous. It was a pleasurable, soft feeling, the chair suddenly warm…

The doctor stepped into the room, holding a juice bottle and smiling. "I thought you should drink this. How are you doing? Okay?"

He shook his head and smiled. Then everything changed … He had his first hallucination: the doctor, naked. Like Venus de Milo … and he was off.

He closed his eyes and heard a riff his mother used to play on their CD player: Ten Years After's "I'm Going Home."

"Mom?" He was going through the kitchen, riding the rocking horse broomstick he'd kept in the corner of his room. His brother was sitting at the glass table, eating cereal. His mother was working on her PhD in European history. They didn't see him.

"Mom! MOM! MOM!" The music got louder—the famous rock song— and then his mother looked at him, but she was the English girl.

"Where are you from?" the girl asked.

He looked behind him and saw a dirt road in West Marin projected on some kind of movie screen. Then he turned around, and he was in bed with his wife.

"What took you so long?" Jennifer said.

He could smell her like he remembered the smell of their bedroom: soap and sandalwood oil. Her laptop ever present, with its collection of crazy stickers…

"Are you here for good?" Jen asked.

"No. What happened out there?"

"Water. Water everywhere," Jennifer said.

"Michael, are you okay?"

He thought he heard the doctor's voice and he came around. She was sitting on the floor at his feet.

"Okay," he said. He reached for the doctor's hand, and his wife took it.

"You have to find that girl," Jennifer said. "Emma Barre. She is expecting you."

"No shit. I know that! But if I can't find her? Then what?"

"Are we going to do this? The big one?"

"What do you mean?" he said.

"Screw?"

"What?"

"Screw!" Jennifer said.

"No."

"Why not?"

"I don't know. Afraid of it."

She pulled the covers off and he saw she was pregnant. He started to scream, but it wasn't his scream…

He was driving and saw in front of him that Latin kid, one of his men… just his torso where it had tumbled out of the blown-up halftrack shaking, still moving like a horrible insect, as if he wanted to get up and live after being stepped on.

***

The introduction to her two daughters had gone well. They sensed something was wrong with Lana, as they were both bright, but they'd been taught to treat people with respect. The two girls had shaken Lana's hand and accepted the explanation that Lana was their mother's long-lost high-school friend, who was visiting San Francisco and would spend a few nights with them.

The girls exchanged a look of confusion as Lana smelled bad and was obviously high, but she'd won them over with her references to their mother's past in LA. It was a topic the two girls were very much interested in. They believed their mother had been a model, and were proud of it. Modeling was the acme of female tween culture.

"You knew Mom back in the day?" asked Katie, her younger daughter. She was gangly and had her mother's "good hair."

"Yes, I did."

"Did you know any movie stars?"

"Yes. I did," Lana said. She smiled. "You're pretty, like your momma when I met her. Just like her." She reached over and touched Katie's hand. Lana's fingers looked grey.

Cassandra tried to weigh in, asking what everyone wanted for dinner.

They decided that because it was Tuesday, they would stick with the All-American Taco Tuesday menu. The girls sat down at the dining room table. Everyone was quiet for a moment, all the collected cell phones untouched, Lana a presence in the room, like a black Buddha.

"Mom was a model. That was so cool," Matilda said finally. "Were you a model, too?"

"No way," said Lana. "I was too skinny to be a model."

The girls laughed.

Lana shot Cassie a look. She had been thrown into the deep end, and she was struggling.

Cassie herded the girls up to do their homework. They were both going to private schools and they were loaded down with work every night, sometimes she thought too much. But Marvin insistent that they go to private school.

"They don't know anything," Cassandra said when she got back downstairs. She sat next to her friend in the dining room. A clock in the living room struck five. It was a clock that Marvin's grandmother had owned and brought from the island, and they'd kept it after she'd died.

"Nothing?" Lana said.

"No. I said I did some modeling and worked for a caterer. That's all." Lana shook her head slightly.

"I told them their grandparents were dead and had been doctors."

"Both of them?"

"Why not? If you're going to lie, lie big, right? You want to take a shower? I've got some things you could wear." When they were in LA, they'd often worn each other's clothes.

Lana just looked at her. "Your girls, they're beautiful. I never will have no family. You lucky girl."

"You have me," Cassie said. "The white girl." She smiled.

Lana smiled back. It was what she had called Cassie for weeks after they first met. She'd kept saying, "You a white girl, why you want to do this shit?"

"I don't want to wreck this," Lana said. "This here."

"You're not going to wreck anything."

"He going to come home and take one look at me and know."

"Know what?"

"That I have a jones. That I look nasty. One and one goin' to make two, baby girl."

"Come on, we'll see what I have for you to wear."

"Is it Thorpe? Is that why I'm here?"

"Yeah—but I was worried about you, too. I wanted you to come here. Be somewhere safe. Till we can sort you out."

"I love you, girl. I want you to know. I love those girls too." Lana nodded toward the stairs. "I could be like an auntie, right? I'll be like their auntie?"

"Okay, Auntie Lana, upstairs with your fine self."

Lana struggled to get up out of the chair, as if she were ninety and not what she was, Cassandra thought—a thirty-three-year-old woman with AIDS.

Chapter 15

They were at the Royal Cuckoo sitting perpetually lit in a red tuck-and-roll barroom light. The bar top to O'Higgins's right was wet, the varnish spotted with rings on rings on rings like some modern painting. The rings were white with age, lit by the barroom's demi light.

He was drinking tequila, which he'd grown fond of. Stewart the bartender, whom they'd gotten to know, was simpatico. They liked his quiet, methodical vibe. It was a solid, reassuring counterpoint to their inebriated imbalance. The three of them reminded O'Higgins of those perpetual-movement metal balls, knocking one way then the next.

"I need to tell you something," O'Higgins said. He looked at his partner.

Marvin's eyes were red. He had finished a gin and tonic and signaled to Stewart to hit him again. "What, man?"

O'Higgins had just spent the last half hour explaining in granular detail the walk he'd taken with Barre. Every detail that he and Emma's father had discussed. Everywhere they'd stopped to take in the view of the Bay from the Embarcadero. They'd gone out the long pedestrian Pier 14, just down from the Ferry Building, a place that O'Higgins knew well because he and Marvin had caught the Kate Steinle case, the young woman who had been shot while standing next to her father on a Sunday morning after having brunch. A random shooting by a Mexican crackhead with a long record. Drunk, the man had been firing a stolen pistol at—it still wasn't clear, as he'd been hallucinating under the influence of meth produced in Mexico by the ton.

"I don't want you to get mad," O'Higgins said.

"About what?"

"Cassie called me, two days ago. Monday."

"Okay." Marvin turned to him, his long face still handsome despite all they'd been through in the last year. He'd been in the hospital for two weeks after the shooting. He had insisted on coming back to work six weeks later. He'd been sullen that first week and barely spoke.

"She wanted me to go meet someone," O'Higgins said.

"She called you to go meet someone?" Marvin gave him a look.

"Yeah," O'Higgins said.

Marvin shook his empty glass. The ice made a sliding-around sound. "Who was it? She never mentioned it to me."

"This is the hard part," O'Higgins said. He looked down the bar. A couple of hipsters, sporting big new Samsung phones, had come in and sat down. They were drinking beer and hand-fucking their devices, obviously in love.

"Hard part. What's that mean? Who the fuck was it?"

"A dude named Thorpe," O'Higgins said. "At the Fairmont. Presidential Suite."

"Say what?"

"She wanted me to get him to stop bothering her. It was someone from her past. That's all I know. I went up there and he knew who I was and who you were. He wasn't afraid of me. Not one bit. He recorded the conversation. I left. That's it. That's what went down."

"When were you going to tell me?" Marvin said.

"I told you this was the hard part. Cassie asked me not to tell you. Made me promise. The guy was someone from her past, like I said. She asked me to go over to his hotel and tell him to leave her the fuck alone. So that's what I did."

"Told you not to tell me, that you went to the Fairmont Hotel to lean on someone that was bothering my wife?"

"Yeah. But I'm telling you now because it's the right thing to do. Okay? It's been less than three days. I needed the right time to tell you, man. Give me a fucking break—it's not like we've not been busy."

"Mother fucker." Marvin got up and left. He closed the door on the way out a little too hard, banging it shut.

The two guys at the bar with their in-style beards and full-color tats, looked up from their phones, finally.

O'Higgins paid their bill, but he didn't leave for more than an hour. Instead of thinking about Marvin being mad at him, and the can of worms he'd opened up, he went, in his mind, back to the Embarcadero. He walked it again, from the very beginning at the Gandhi statue—looking for something, anything, that he might have missed.

When he left, he drove out to Pier 39 and walked amongst the tourists, half drunk.

***

"Who the fuck is Robert Thorpe?" Marvin asked.

He was sitting in the living room of their place on Bernal Heights. He was high, and Cassandra could see that immediately. She'd noticed that his drinking was getting worse but had decided to put it aside. It was too frightening. Since the shootout, she'd worried about her husband. Anything she tried to say about his drinking he would deflect, as if she were the enemy.

She believed the case they were working on had driven both him and O'Higgins to it. She'd figured that out herself. It was a shared look the two men had exchanged when Marvin's sister had asked them about the killer, if they were any closer to catching him.

"Thorpe is someone from my past," she said.

She'd been to the Safeway on Mission Street, doing the week's shopping.

120

She put the full grocery bags on a table in the hallway and walked into the living room.

"Did Michael tell you?"

"Yes. What did you think? It was about you."

She nodded. She'd almost expected it. She'd been stupid to ask him to keep it a secret from Marvin.

"Are you going to tell me what the hell is going on?" Marvin said.

"No," she said. "You have to trust me."

"I don't have to do shit," Marvin said. He was sitting with both arms resting on a club chair they'd bought at Macy's. His suit coat was buttoned. His eyes were red.

"I'm asking you to leave this alone," she said.

She saw something in her husband's eyes she'd never seen before. It wasn't just anger; it was that volcanic look she'd seen plenty of times in other men's eyes. It always ended in violence of one kind or another.

"Who is he?" Marvin said.

"Just some guy I knew in LA—a long time ago. Before we got married."

"So some guy you used to know in LA is calling you on the phone and saying what? Why did you ask Mike to lean on him?"

"I just didn't want him to call me anymore."

"You could have just blocked his fucking number. If that's all it was about."

"Just drop it, Marvin. Please."

She turned and walked out of the living room, bent to pick up the groceries. She could feel her whole body shake. It was a kind of terror she'd never experienced, like seeing a tsunami coming and having a cliff at her back.

She came out of the kitchen in a few minutes, expecting to see him, but he'd left. She called O'Higgins.

"I think he's going over there to the Fairmont," she said.

"Did you explain?" Michael said.

"I can't explain. Okay? You shouldn't have told him—"

"He's your husband. I had to tell him. You know that. We're partners."

"He won't be my husband if he hears the truth," she said. "Please stop him, Mike. Before something crazy happens. Please."

Chapter 16

Since his grandmother died, Marvin had known he would face life alone. His grandmother had been everything to him, mother and father.

It wasn't that he had not loved his father; he had. It was that he didn't know him—not really. His father was always working at the pool hall he'd owned. And then he'd just disappeared, never to be seen again, when Marvin had still been in junior high. The older boys in the neighborhood, around 98th and MacArthur in Oakland, knew his father was in the game. Most likely he'd been murdered by the two Italians who'd taken him out of the pool hall one afternoon. News of that kind moves at lightning speed along the demimonde's street-corner newswire.

Sometimes he loved his father very much. Other times he realized he didn't know the man, and therefore couldn't love him. For whatever reason, on the way downtown, Marvin thought of him, what his father might do in this circumstance. He reasoned that, like him, his father would simply kill the motherfucker. If this Thorpe guy posed a threat to his loved ones, he had to go.

He concocted a story he could give, something about Thorpe being a suspect in the killings. How they'd gotten Thorpe's name would have to be thought through, but Marvin suspected he could come up with something plausible. O'Higgins would back him, no matter how lame the connection to the murders.

He would, if necessary, shoot the guy in "self-defense." He looked for their throw-down gun as he drove, but realized O'Higgins was carrying it. His cell phone rang, and he picked it up when he saw it was O'Higgins.

"Where are you? I don't—"

"Fuck you!" Marvin said. He threw the phone onto the passenger seat and headed down Van Ness, shackled to his seat by anger and doubts about his wife. The busy boulevard was a blur of colorful lights, like electric pinwheels.

Marvin parked his wife's Jeep in the little courtyard in front of the famous hotel. A short Filipino valet in a red vest and white shirt came trotting over to tell him he couldn't park there. Marvin flashed his badge, and the young man nodded and stepped away.

At the desk, Marvin had done essentially the same, showing his badge and asking for Thorpe's room number. He told the smartly dressed young woman not to call the room and strode across the ornate gilded lobby, passing columns painted with trompe-l'oeil gold veins. A massive chandelier hung high above the room, its crystals sparkling blue-yellow. A paneled gallery above the lobby was full of tourists and business types having cocktails, a luxe reassuring hubbub highlighted by lubricated voices talking, one over another.

He rode the elevator with a gaggle of old German ladies on a once-in-a-lifetime tour who stared at Marvin because he was so handsome and so black.

A young Latin girl, about eighteen, stood in the doorway when the hotel room door opened. She wore a short black dress, and had straight black long hair and big breasts.

Marvin walked by her, pushing her aside. He saw a bald-headed black guy sitting in the living room facing the bank of windows with views of the bay, a large cell phone pressed to his ear. The city was falling into twilight.

Thorpe started to turn when Marvin hit him with the side of his Glock, smashing it against his face, catching the cell phone and breaking its screen, so that a piece of it stuck in Thorpe's cheek—a sliver driven in an inch deep.

Marvin hit him again, this time higher up on the head, at the temple. The second strike made Thorpe go limp, just as the big pimp was trying to stand up. Thorpe slumped heavily, dazed and wobbly, back into the chair. His legs splayed in front of him, his big ass hugging the soft edge of the chair and barely holding him in place.

Marvin thought of bringing the pistol's butt down on the top of Thorpe's skull, but stopped himself at the last moment, knowing it might kill him. He turned and saw the Latin girl and O'Higgins in his peripheral vision.

Thorpe's young whore bit him in the ear, like a wild dog might.

O'Higgins had to slap the girl to get her to let go. She was ferocious. The first slap didn't do any good at all. It was then that Marvin, jacked up on adrenalin, felt her biting him.

O'Higgins' second blow—more of an open-handed punch than a slap—made the young whore let go of Marvin's ear at last. The punch sent the girl flying across the hotel room, staggering backwards in heels.

O'Higgins looked at Marvin in the eye. The girl fell over, tripped by a low coffee table and landing on her back. She stayed down for a moment, then started to get up, but slowly. She was hurting.

O'Higgins walked over, handcuffed the whore and sat her on the floor, her arms behind her. She hadn't said a word.

Thorpe was still out cold, the smashed cell phone lying on his chest, blood dripping from behind the shard of screen stuck in his face.

***

"You've only made it worse," Cassandra said. "You and Mike don't understand."

"Why didn't you tell me the truth?" Marvin said. They were looking at each other from across the room like strangers.

"Because I was afraid to. I couldn't. I fell in love with you."

"You could have told me the truth," Marvin said.

They were in the living room of their home. Both girls were still at school. The house was quiet.

Cassandra looked at her iPhone, checking the time. Lana had decided to leave. She'd taken a Yellow Cab, afraid of what Marvin would think of her and what it might do to their marriage. Cassie had pressed all the cash she had into Lana's hand. They'd hugged for a long, seemingly timeless minute, and then she was gone.

"I have to go soon. I've got to be there on time. At school. To pick them up." Both their daughters were going to the French-American School, and it took time to cross town.

"I don't want you near my girls," Marvin said.

"What?"

"You heard me," Marvin said. "I'll pick them up."

His shirt and coat were bloody, and he needed to change. His right ear had a Band-Aid on it; it looked both funny and grotesque. His ear had swollen up. He'd have to get an AIDS test, after the girl bit him. He was beyond angry. He felt exhausted and humiliated.

Thorpe's words rang in his ear as he pulled off his coat and climbed the stairs to their bedroom. Everything he'd believed in had been destroyed with a few words.

"Your wife was my bitch, like it or not." Thorpe had said matter-of-factly, holding a bloody hand towel to his face. "So, you best calm down, homeboy. You've attacked a respectable businessman in his hotel room. And before that, your boy here threatened me. I got it on tape. So what you want to do now is leave, and we'll forget this. Just tell Cassie that nothing has changed. Now let that girl out of those handcuffs."

Marvin was frozen, trying to understand what it meant, and then he knew: everything his wife had said about her past was a lie. He'd married a whore.

He heard O'Higgins unlock the girl's handcuffed wrist. She called him an asshole while he folded up the cuffs and put them up in his jacket pocket.

"Let's go, Marvin. He's right. You got to drop this. Marvin! Come on!" O'Higgins's tone was strident and had a hint of panic that Marvin remembered from the gunfight, when he was dragging him to safety.

"Marvin. Let's go. Come on!"

Marvin turned and looked back. Thorpe was comforting his girl.

***

The young woman, Mareva Marks, was SFPD's newest forensic scientist, fresh out of school—UCLA. O'Higgins didn't know her, but he'd heard she was bright and diligent. She was slight and attractive, and didn't look the part of scientist at the lab south of Market Street. It was a new facility. Half the people in it looked like freshmen in high school, the detective thought as he walked down the spotless hall that reminded him of a hospital.

He found Marks in a small lab testing a Faraday box used to keep cell phones from being electronically tampered with. He and Marvin had asked her to study the rope that had been used on the English girl. Pathology on the girl's body had not turned up any semen or genetic material that would have given them a DNA sample. They assumed she'd been raped, but the killer had used a condom. He was smart. But he'd left the rope, and they were hoping it might tell them something.

"It's nylon, of course. Very worn. And it has a lead core. Used for crab pots, so it will sink. Not uncommon. I've seen it before. Anyway, it had pressure marks. Flattening under the microscope you could see them plainly," Marks said. "My dad has a boat, and he crabs on the weekends. He uses a winch to bring up the pots."

O'Higgins nodded. He'd seen the crab pots stacked up on the docks where he'd kept his sailboat, and remembered the rope and buoys stacked alongside them.

"Crab pots?"

"Yeah. There're zillions of them out there. So I showed a photo to my dad, and we took a sample of the rope my dad uses. It's the same size rope. Same marks left from the winch."

"Your dad—his rope?"

"Yeah. Like I said, I'd seen this kind of rope before."

"Holy—" O'Higgins said.

"So it's from a winch, maybe one called Extra-Deck-Hand. But it could be another type of lift. Extra-Deck-Hand is what a lot of people use—it's the one my dad uses, because it's so beefy. The winch."

She looked at him as if he might not understand. She was only about twenty-two or so, proud of herself and confident. Her lab coat looked extraneous, as if it were a costume. He saw she had a blue/pink strip running down one side of her head, the same "unicorn" look he'd seen on his daughter that was popular with iGen.

"And of course, it had been saturated with salt water. Salt breaks down nylon. It's in a study at Virginia Tech I found online— 'The Effects of Salt Spray on Nylon 6.' Stays on the rope's fibers. Salt fatigues nylon. Yours was very fatigued. Old."

She walked him back to her glass cubicle and a laptop with stickers that meant nothing to him. He assumed they were bands; one was a photo of Taylor Swift with a the international symbol for No covering her face, meant as an obvious disrespect.

Marks played him a YouTube video of an Extra-Deck-Hand, showing how the rope was pulled through two small rubber tires used as guides. A diesel motor did the work of lifting the crab pot.

"No blood on the rope?" O'Higgins said.

"No. Nothing. Random stuff, bird shit and some gasoline, and lots and lots of salt."

"So the killer could have picked it up anywhere—the rope?"

"I guess so," Marks said.

He looked at her. She was about the age of the girl he had found. Hers was the social media generation, having grown up with smartphones and

YouTube. They owned Instagram and the rest of it.

"Where was she from?" Marks asked. "The girl?"

"London," he said.

She nodded. He noticed she had blue eyes. "She was my age, wasn't she? I read about the case in the paper."

"Yeah. She'd come here on vacation. Bad luck."

"Sick fuck," Marks said.

He saw her step out of her professional attitude, which didn't really fit her, and into something different. He caught a glimpse, he supposed, of the teenager she'd been. He didn't say anything.

"I think maybe he'd been a Boy Scout. Or is a sailor. Experienced with knots," Marks said.

"Okay, I'm listening. Why?" He'd learned long ago from his wife that women scientists tended to be even more clever than their male counterparts, if only because the competition had been so difficult on the way to a job. Not to mention the harassment.

"It's the whipping."

"Whipping?"

"The way the ends of the rope were finished."

She pulled photos she'd taken of the rope from a drawer under her desk. "Whipping is the tying of the rope's end, so it won't unravel. Most people don't do it. My dad doesn't bother with it. Sometimes he'll just burn the ends of his 6.6 ropes, but look at this. It's called a Sailmaker's Whipping. It's very involved—you unbraid the rope to do it right. It's painstaking. Old school. I looked it up online. The first thing that came up was from a book called *Knots and How to Tie Them*. It was published by the Boy Scouts."

"How do you know that it was the killer who did it and not someone else?" Marks looked at him, pushing the hair out of her face, and thought about it.

"The twine. It just looks weird. I've not been able to find any like it. But it looks new. I think he's a freak who likes to fix things correctly—nerd. Just a feeling. No science, it could have been done by anyone. You're right. Your killer could have found the rope, or stolen it—"

"Have you ever heard of the Sea Scouts?" O'Higgins said.

"No," she said.

"They're kind of like Boy Scouts, but with boats."

She smiled. "It's full of pedophiles, isn't it—the Boy Scouts? Or is that just the Catholics?"

"I wouldn't know," he said. "My mother didn't let me join. She called it the Hitler Youth." He saw her smile a second time and realized she was different. Something about her intelligence came through, and had nothing to do with any generational limitations cooked up by *Time Magazine* and Madison Avenue marketers. Something about her face was exceptionally alive.

"Do you like beer, Detective?"

"Yeah. I guess." He smiled back. "Sure. When it's cold."

"I'm having a birthday party," she said. "I'm not gay, by the way. Don't let the haircut fool you. I make my own beer—ale, really. In the basement of my place." She wrote her cell number on a yellow stick up and handed it to him.

"Ten o'clock Saturday night. Stop by. I'll look out for you."

"I'm way too old," he said. He had to admit he was intrigued by both her intelligence and her oddball, offbeat manner. But he knew it would be a bad idea.

"Don't worry," she said. "I won't hold it against you."

Chapter 17

Lana was in the hallway fumbling with the keys to her room in the SRO when she saw an extremely skinny white girl—sixteen or seventeen, tops. What the old-school pimps called a "pink toe," referring to white whores.

The girl was wearing old-school '70s era gym shorts and a man's black sleeveless T-shirt, no bra. She was crying, tears running down her baby face.

Lana stopped, leaving her room key in the dead-bolt. She smelled bad, and her white Ann Taylor blouse—picked up at the Salvation Army store—was stained where she'd spilt Southern Comfort on it. Her breath smelled of alcohol, sperm and Kool menthol cigarettes that she'd stolen from a passed-out homeless man.

The white girl stopped and looked at her, wiping the tears from her face. Her dirty blond hair was cut short.

"Cassie? What you doin' out here?" Lana said, hallucinating. She had bought a pint of Southern Comfort from her earnings, which were meager. She was too old to catch much on the streets. Because she was old, the pimps left her alone on the track—a crazy renegade whore who, judging from the look of her, wouldn't be on Turk Street for long. So she was "allowed" to work.

The crying white girl watched Lana walk toward her. The old whore was scary-looking, and she thought of running, but didn't. Her pimp, King

James, had beaten her. She had a split lip and her ears were ringing. She was hearing a kind of loud feed-back, oscillating in her head. She had been hearing it for days, since the first time he'd rammed her face into a door for being "short." Even when she was having sex, she could hear the damn ringing.

"You bleedin', girl. What the hell?" Lana walked up to her. She was unsteady on her feet, due partly to the drinking and partly to labyrinthitis in her right ear, one of several opportunistic infections she was suffering from.

The girl wiped her eyes with her fingers, making her seem even more like a Dickensian urchin.

"I been looking all over for you," Lana said.

"For me?" the white girl said.

The girl, who went by the street name X-Static, was from Seattle. She'd been born into a squat to a meth-addicted mother and father, who had once wiped shit on her legs for fun. She'd been put into foster care at the age of five but ran away when she was fourteen, tired of the Social Services shuffle. She'd started selling herself soon thereafter, helped by a mixed-raced pimp and member of the Holly Park Crips who had said he understood her, cared for her, and would be her family.

He'd bought her dinner in a Taco Bell, having spotted her on the street, and got her a room for the night at the Klose-In motel on Aurora Avenue. His bright idea was that once he had her staying near the "track," she could be turned out quickly. She was just fifteen. The pimp was young, too, and trying to make a name for himself. He called himself Batman, and was later shot in the head by a Vato Loco on Cherry Street for turning out the guy's little sister—a big mistake.

"Damn right. Where you been? We have to go to the—" Lana looked around, losing the thread. "You know, for teenagers, like us."

The girl looked at her like she was stoned crazy.

"My name is X-Static, not Cassie, and I don't know you from Adam, bitch." All her street muscles contracted at once.

Lana walked up to her and held her face, wiping the blood from her split lip with one long finger. Her other hand held a Kool cigarette. The girl didn't move, the motherly touch melting her defenses.

"What happened to you?" Lana said.

"He didn't want me to come back," the girl said. "It was too early."

It had been days since she'd spoken to anyone beside tricks, and the Palestinian guy at the liquor store, and her pimp King James from Oaktown, and the other kids working for him who were perpetually on their cell phones playing Angry Birds. She nodded toward the door, where King James was waiting for her. Three other teens were with him, a boy and two girls.

Lana looked at the door and rocked back on her Nancy Sinatra-style worn boot heels, nodding, her face ashen.

"You working for that gorilla pimp? I saw that nigger yesterday. Naw, that's not going to wash, baby girl. Come with me. Come with Lana now." She took the girl's hand and led her toward her room.

The girl held back, and Lana turned around, letting go of her hand.

"I ain't going to drag you—Cassie? What the hell is wrong with you?" She held her hand out again.

The girl, with no education and no hope, walked down the hall and followed her into her room. She couldn't explain why. It had been a horrible night, one more in a nightmare that she thought was over when she met King James who promised to be her man. The plain truth was that she was exhausted, and any kind of honest kindness was impossible for her to resist. She just wanted to sleep. She didn't care what the old whore called her.

She dreamt that she was living with the Kardashians and had been invited to the royal wedding, which she'd seen on a trick's iPad while he pounded her.

At least her man was royalty, too, she'd thought.

***

"I'm here, aren't I?"

"You sent your husband and that other cop," Thorpe said. He had a bandage on his face where he'd been cut. O'Higgins had told her that there had been a fight, and he could do no more about Thorpe, who was insisting—despite what had happened—he see Cassie.

"No, I tried to stop it. But what did you expect my husband would do?"

"I told you on the phone that I wanted to see you," Thorpe said. "You look nice. Some women just don't age."

"What the fuck do you want from me, Richard?" she said.

"Come on in, then."

She walked past him into the suite. It was late in the afternoon and the water out on the bay was changing from blue to a steel-blue, cold looking. The area near Alcatraz filled with sailboats, some of the small ones looking like bathtub toys.

"Sit down," Thorpe said.

She went into the hotel room that she remembered so well, with the killer views of the Bay. She remembered the room itself. It was from this hotel, in fact, that she'd walked out on Thorpe and the producer she'd come to San Francisco with. He'd been short and cruel, everything about him snide and insistent, as if he were constantly making up for his short stature. He had hated everyone.

"You want me to kill someone? You're joking. You're serious?"

"Yes," Thorpe said. "As a heart attack."

"Why should I do that?"

He sat back and looked at her. He didn't have to say anything. The look on his face said it all. It was supercilious and at the same time convincing.

"This is just a job. Think of it that way. The people who want it done will get rid of me and you and everyone in between. That's how they are. I don't have to tell you that. Right?"

"Who are they?" She knew who they were, but she couldn't help asking, hoping that somehow it wasn't them.

"You don't want to know. But you do know. I don't have to tell you. You were always a smart girl. I'll give you that," Thorpe said.

"No, I don't," she said.

But she did. Sometimes they were asked to steal certain things from a client's apartment. Or to steal the john's cell phone, or describe exactly, into a recording device, the nature of the security they'd seen around a john and his home or office. Thorpe made cryptic remarks about these assignments, but it was clear that someone, or some group, was using Thorpe and his stable of women to collect intelligence on important men. At the time she thought it funny, and had enjoyed the game. It all changed that morning in Malibu.

"You better think about that answer," Thorpe said.

"You're crazy," she said. "You know that—right?" He shrugged and took a sip of his drink.

She left him like that. She'd gotten up and walked out of the room. In the elevator, she leaned against the back, shaking like a leaf. She got to the lobby and tried to call Lana, but it went to voice mail. She texted:

I'll pick you up: Jones and Geary. Now.

To her relief, Lana was waiting for her. They drove in silence down Geary Street for several blocks.

"Where are we goin'?" Lana said finally. She'd put her big knock-off Gucci bag on her knees. Her coat was dirty, stained with blood. Her hair looked matted. She smelled rank.

"I don't know yet. Marvin kicked me out."

Lana looked at her, not really tracking, lost in her jones. "I got to get well first, honey. You got to go back to the Turk. I'll show you where…"

Cassandra turned to her friend. She knew what Lana meant and at first wanted to play the concerned little sister, but she knew it was a waste of time. One thing she'd learned from her mother was that junkies don't change. They couldn't, not really.

She turned left at the next corner and headed toward Turk, an open-air drug market that the police, City Hall and the powers that be left alone.

Why it got a pass, no one could say. She'd watched a SFPD patrol car pull over and arrest Lana as she was scoring. She recognized the two female officers; they'd been the women who had taken Marvin to the hospital the day of the shootout. She had thanked them both for helping save Marvin's life.

She parked her car in a red zone and ran to the cruiser, asking the officers what Lana had done. Recognizing Cassie from the hospital, they told her it was for a murder at an SRO.

Chapter 18

It had begun to rain. It rains in San Rafael in early August, half-heartedly. The rain is the traditional signal that summer is tired and over and that the fall, with its barrel-chested storms and tin-pan grey skies, isn't far off.

O'Higgins watched the rain hit the window in his dining room. The table was covered with mail and paperback books, a gun magazine, and random vitamins. The picture window had a view of the Bay and the Richardson Bay Bridge and beyond it the Oakland skyline, growing every year. The glass was rain-splashed, unable to give an accurate picture of the world. It reminded him of the ocean's spray when he was tacking in his little sailboat. The boat was gone. Lost at sea.

"I've always liked your place," Cassie Lee said. She was in his daughter's bathrobe. He'd asked her if she'd wanted to spend the night. She had slept in his daughter's room. He heard the rain pick up. The picture window began to glisten as the rain pelted it again, static drops pushed around by the wind.

"I like the rain. It never rained in Las Vegas when I was a kid. Or in LA, for that matter. It was funny watching people in LA when it rained. They would look shocked." She sat down at the table and looked out at the Bay.

They were silent, too much unsaid the night before. He'd watched her cry and tried to comfort her in an awkward way. They'd ended up drinking a bottle of wine and pretending everything was normal, when it was anything but. She had tried to call Marvin, but he wouldn't take her calls. He had asked her to leave the house. Lana was in custody for murdering a pimp in the Tenderloin, cutting his throat with a razor that she'd had in her purse when she was arrested.

"So do I," O'Higgins said. "My father loved the rain."

He turned to look at her. Even in the morning, first thing out of the chute, she looked beautiful, like a movie star who had gone astray somewhere on the set.

She looked at him carefully. "I did it for a long time. I started young. Fifteen. Marvin will never forgive me for that. Ever."

"It's really no one's business, is it?" he asked. "Coffee?" He asked. He'd put on black sweatpants and a T-shirt, careful to be respectful of his guest.

"It's Marvin's business. He married me. I lied to him," she said.

He shook his head, as if she'd asked him directions and he were a stranger with no idea what to tell her.

"Okay. You lied to him, but you've been a good wife and mother. How long have you two been married now?"

"Twelve years. I got pregnant right away." She smiled. "I love him. I never loved anyone before Marvin. That's the funny part."

"So it's all in the past. That other stuff. Whatever. He's angry—okay, but he'll get over it. I'll talk to him. Coffee?"

"Yes, please," she said.

He went to the kitchen and poured her a cup of coffee. He heard a text hit his phone, but was afraid to look at it. It might be Marvin, asking him if he'd seen his wife. What was he supposed to say: "She's here? She spent the night. You kicked her out of her home. She called me crying. Now what? Don't be ridiculous—she loves you."

He put a coffee cup in front of her. He tried to do it in a kind way, to show her something—he wasn't sure what. Maybe just that he liked her. After his wife died, he'd learnt that the smallest kindnesses meant a great deal. Any kind word, even from a stranger, meant something to him. Even now.

"No, you haven't asked about Thorpe or any of that. My past. What I did in LA. Why not? Aren't you curious?"

"It's really none of my business, Cassie. Is it?" He didn't add that he didn't talk about The Past, or dare even think about it. His past was like being followed at night by a thug who would mug him, given the chance; so he kept walking, picking up the pace, never stopping to think about it. The threat was too obvious. There was no reasoning with The Past. The only solution was to walk quickly into the future.

"In the life, at least you know the score. The rules. What to look out for. When I was a kid, I walked the streets in LA, and it was there that you had the most control. People—you had a moment to size them up before you opened the car door. You could look at them. Check out their vibe. The further up the ladder you get as a—the further you go, the less chance you have of doing that. Escorts, you go to the guy's room. There might be three guys in there when they said there was only one. You see, you have no way of knowing. Ironic, isn't it? On the streets, when you're giving blow jobs for 50 bucks, you at least could choose.

"I went to a psychiatrist, after Katie was born. I told Marvin it was for post-partum depression, but really it was because I was terrified Marvin would come across my rap sheet, somehow. I was arrested a couple times. He never did—until now. Will you talk to him, Mike? Tell him I'm sorry that I didn't tell him the truth. Tell him that I tried to tell him a thousand times. He's stubborn like that—maybe because of his dad. You see, his dad and me have a lot in common. We were both bent, and he hates his dad for abandoning him." She was talking quickly, as if she could solve her problem by pouring it all out to him.

His phone rang.

"I've got to take this," he said. She nodded. "I promise you I'll fix this."

"It's me," Marvin said. "She's there, isn't she?"

"Yeah, she's here. What was she supposed to do, Marvin?" He looked at Cassandra.

"We caught something in the Tenderloin. The Maverick Hotel," Marvin said.

***

"I know the suspect," Marvin said.

They were standing in the hall. Lana Taylor was inside the interview room. She'd been in custody for more than twenty-four hours and they were going to have to charge her or let her go.

"It's a friend of Cassie's—a whore she knew once." Marvin opened the door to the interview room without waiting for his reaction.

O'Higgins followed behind him.

"I'm Detective Marvin Lee. This is Detective Michael O'Higgins." Marvin got out his card and handed it to the black woman. She was wearing a jailhouse orange jumpsuit and looked pitiful. It was obvious to O'Higgins that the woman sitting across from them was a junkie and in withdrawal.

Marvin sat down. He obviously hated the woman. It was palpable. He ran his hand over his necktie.

"You know why we're here, Ms. Taylor—right?"

"I don't know, mister. You have to call my friend, or you can call my grandmother. She'll tell you. Have you called her?"

"We're here investigating a murder at the Maverick Hotel on Jones Street. A man called Roger Phillips was murdered. His street name was King James. A witness is saying you were in an altercation with Mr. Phillips. Is that true? Did you fight with Mr. Phillips?"

"Who dat? He a preacher. My momma knew a Mr. Phillips. Did you call my grandmother? Why don't you call Cassie? I want to talk to Cassie. She lives on Sunset. We have a place at the motel there on Sunset. Call her. Motel Six—" She looked at O'Higgins. "Why won't this negro listen to me?"

"Do you know a young woman named X-Static? That's her street

140

name. She says she saw you and Mr. Phillips have an argument. It got violent. You protected yourself—I can understand that. Why don't you tell us what happened, in your own words?"

***

THE DAY BEFORE LANA'S ARREST FOR MURDER

Lana was looking down on the young girl, who'd fallen asleep. She'd put a throw over her that she'd gotten at the Salvation Army. It was a prize; she'd stolen it. No one had said anything or called to her as she walked out of the store. She'd walked down Hayes Street with it under her hand.

What she didn't know was that the old white man behind the counter had watched her steal the afghan. He'd done twenty years in Soledad and just didn't care that the old whore had stolen a blanket. He'd developed a kind of heartfulness since being paroled. It happened the day he was left off in the Tenderloin, a felon pushing 50. It was a come-to-Jesus moment as he walked amongst the poor and the wretched with no clue as to his future, and understood something about humanity. From that moment on he'd been nice to everyone he met. The vicious young man he'd been when he'd gone to prison was no more. So he'd let the woman walk out of the store without stopping her.

Lana had sat on the bed and watched the girl sleep. Once she'd reached over and touched the girl's shoulder. In her confused state, she thought she'd found her long-lost daughter and that her daughter had become a whore because she'd not been there for her. She began to weep. It was quiet in the room otherwise. On occasion she heard loud voices in the hallway. She didn't want to wake her daughter and so she stifled the desire to cry, covering her face with her hands until her hands were wet with tears.

She got up and looked in her oversized purse. She wanted to take her daughter out to breakfast and explain to her that her father was a king. She'd seen him on TV, and she was going to write to him. She was conflating the English royal family with a man who had kept her on his boat off Corfu for a whole month. He was English and had married into the Saudi royal family. The man's wife was on board the yacht and she knew about Lana, had seen her more than once. She was convinced the Englishman was the girl's father, and that he was the king—she tried to think of what country. She'd been to many. France? Germany? She'd been to a lot of places in Europe with Cassie… but she couldn't remember now.

"Bitch are you in there?! Open the fucking door!" The man's voice was loud. It had a nasty quality that Lana understood. It would belong to the kind of man that you couldn't reason with. She stuck her hand in her purse and came out with the straight razor. It was one she'd been carrying for a long time. In fact, it was one of the few possessions she'd made sure to hang onto.

Lana looked down at her daughter, who had woken up and was looking at her. She saw the fear in the girl's eyes. The girl cowered at the sound of the pimp's voice.

"Shush, now, baby girl. Your momma is going to take care of this."

X-Static, half asleep, had been dreaming of a ride in Disneyland that didn't stop. She'd liked it at first. It was a kind of wild Teacup ride. But she'd seen King James sitting in the next cup with her father, and she was trying to figure out how the hell to get off the ride as the cup spun faster and faster. She was feeling sick. She didn't yet know she was pregnant, and this was morning sickness. It was King James's baby.

"Who the fuck is you?" King James said, standing in the doorway. "Where's my—"

Lana struck like a cobra, with the blade hitting him in the throat. She opened his windpipe. She saw that one bone in the body that is connected to nothing and is instrumental for speaking. He didn't speak again, but fell on to his knees and bled out.

Lana shut the door, turned to look at her pretend daughter, and smiled.

Chapter 19

He was sitting in the cubicle on Parnassus Street waiting for the doctor. He'd taken the micro dose of acid and was waiting for the first signs it was coming on, used to this line between out there and hard reality.

It was the cubicle with the photo of the Lake Como and the small, intimate-looking boat harbor. He turned to look for the other poster of the Dali Lama, but it was gone. It was indeed Lake Como in Italy, he'd learned. At least, that was what the male nurse had told him. He said George Clooney's house was in the photo if you looked closely.

His phone buzzed and he picked it up, seeing it was a text. The nurse was telling him that Clooney had been invited to the royal wedding, and how cool was that!

You want the French girl?

Yes.

It will cost you.

What do you mean?

I'll give her back for twelve million dollars.

What?

Twelve million dollars. Her father is some bigtime guy in the French government. Tell them I'll sell the bitch back to him.

For a moment he forgot where he was, dumbfounded by the text. He immediately called Marvin and told him what Seven Hills had asked for. It was a total change in his MO.

"You are joking, right? Twelve million?" Marvin said.

"That's what he said," Michael said.

"Motherfu…Okay. Where are you?"

"I'm at the doctor's."

"The head shrinker?"

"Yes. I have to call you back."

The nurse walked in and said that Dr. Schneider couldn't make it. One of the med students would sit with him during his session, the nurse said. A young Asian kid walked into the room behind the nurse. He seemed both preoccupied and at sea, obviously dragooned into this.

O'Higgins stood up. The semi-daft look on the student's face, one of complete and utter innocence, set him off for some reason. He couldn't share his trip with that kind of spirit. The kid's unblemished youth and innocence were too alien.

"You can't just leave," the male nurse said. "I can't let you." He blocked the door.

It was the wrong move. O'Higgins felt the old war-blood fill his veins. Ice cold. The nurse was his size, a big man too, and he must have thought that O'Higgins would be intimidated by him.

"You two going to stop me?" O'Higgins asked. He gave the man the "look." It was a look all men understood. He walked by the two astounded men, both gobsmacked that he was leaving and going to experience an LSD trip without any kind of supervision or protection.

Outside, he walked across the street from the hospital to the red zone where he'd parked.

He noticed the first wavering patterns: people's faces looked slightly mask-like, cars had light trails. The streetcar seemed to grow large as it passed him. Its familiar sound intensified. He got to 19th Ave, stopped, and looked up into the cold August sky. It seemed endless, marvelous, a kind of free limitless possession, as if he'd never seen the sky before. It was his for the taking now.

Marvin called. "I told Barre—he said—"

"What's up, doc?"

"Huh?" Marvin said. He sounded frightened.

O'Higgins, because he was stoned, could hear tones and color in Marvin's voice. They came over the phone in blocks. It had a vibe that made him feel that day still... The dragging of Marvin down the stairs, certain that they would be shot down. His body remembered the feeling of dragging Marvin, the way his feet bounced on the stairs. The sound of his heels. He heard the rattle of the AK.

"I said, what's up, doc? Can't you hear me? I think you're an asshole for charging that women with murder. She's out of her head. Why do you hate that lady? The DA won't try her, and you know it."

"You're drunk," Marvin said.

"Not really. There is a blue sky out here that would be a great place if it were indeed real. It's not real. Not real at all. Too deep to be real." O'Higgins said, looking up and trying to capture the sky's essence. Essences seemed important, practical and essential for any kind of discourse. He was tripping and didn't realize it. His eyes were pinwheels.

"Fuck. Sober—the fuck—up, Mike!" Marvin hung up.

O'Higgins looked at his cell phone and saw the harbor in Italy on its screen. A boat took off. It was not a sailboat, but a rowboat. He looked carefully at the screen and saw that Emma Barre was in the boat.

He threw the phone down, turned right on Nineteenth Avenue and headed toward San Rafael, not sure what else to do. As he approached the Golden Gate Bridge it seemed alive, a sentient cold-blooded breathing creature. The iguana-like monster that was painted as a cleverly disguised metallic reptile wrapped around the bridge—magnificently camouflaged, fooling everyone but himself. The steel reptile, he thought, was going to move at any moment. He was sure of it. He dug it and sped up.

Cassie Lee was packing the few things she'd brought with her when she heard O'Higgins come through the front door. She'd called Thorpe and begged him to get Lana an attorney. He said he would if she would do as he'd asked. She agreed.

Lana had called her from SF County jail, in tears and confused. She had been intending to visit and go on and meet Thorpe. Lana had said that a "negro man" called Marvin Lee had questioned her and hated her and she didn't understand why because he was black, too. The horror of Lana's confusion, and Marvin's role in her arrest was too much to take. She couldn't stand it. She'd been crying and packing when she heard O'Higgins's car door slam shut on the quiet street.

Cassie came out into the living room, having heard the front door open and close. The room was bright. It was only one in the afternoon and the sunshine was intense pouring into the room. O'Higgins walked to the living room windows, facing the Bay, and looked out onto San Rafael and its toy-town-like quality.

"Mike—you okay?" Cassie asked. He didn't turn around.

"Yes. I took some LSD—the doctor didn't show."

"You did what?" She thought she hadn't heard him correctly.

"I dropped some acid." He turned around. "Would you sit with me? I don't want to be alone. Do you know someone named Lana?"

"Yes," she said.

He nodded.

"Why did you take the acid?"

"Because I want to kill someone—like your pal did. For about the same reasons," he said.

She was staring at him. "Will you sit with me?"

"Of course."

"I need a glass of water." She went to get it for him.

He crossed the living room. The trip was getting intense—more intense than he'd experienced before—but he was more accustomed to its push-power, too. He had practiced out in the car how he was going to ask her for help. He sat, making sure to appear calm and in control while the drug's lava was starting to spew through him.

Cassie came across the living room. For a moment he thought it was his dead wife, and it startled him. He took the glass and drained it. The drug made him thirsty. He placed the glass on the floor. It seemed to fill with a jeweled liquid that in fact were just simple droplets . . . that became diamonds.

"You're very beautiful," he said, forcing himself to turn away from the magic glass. "But you know that—right? No. I'm not . . . you know. I just wanted to tell you. You're special. You have it. You know what guys want. What every man wants." She smiled. "Or they think they want. It's like a jewel, you see. You can't take your eyes from it. You want to hold onto it. Steal it. Take it home—then call someone and tell them you have it."

Cassie sat down next to him in the couch.

"I miss my wife." He started to cry, the tears streaming down his face. His cheeks got wet.

She was shocked.

He took her hand, and the trip started in earnest as soon as she touched him. He closed his eyes, tethered to her energy and spirit—all of it that ran into the lava and calmed it, rooting him in the experience. For a moment he just fixated on the touch of her hand. She was talking to him. He could hear her, but—as before when peaking—auditory inputs got confused. Speech sounded disjointed, coming in pieces failing to reach him.

He opened his eyes and saw that Asha was there instead... and he heard the rock song "96 Tears" start.

"Hold it hard," he said.

She squeezed his hand, afraid. She thought of calling someone, but held back.

In his mind's eye's dreamland he was standing in a muddy trench. Other soldiers were around him. An officer was blowing a whistle and waving a red flag. Someone pushed him toward a ladder. It was raining, and the ladder was slick with mud and trench shit. He climbed up—the music still going on in his head—and suddenly he was running into No-Man's Land. He heard bullets whiz by. The sound they made: a kind of percussion when they passed close to his head. Men near him were running and falling. He jumped into a shell hole and saw the Latin boy from the halftrack, legless and armless, laughing.

"Where you been, ese?" the Marine said. He started to twist his body to the music, dust-covered and bleeding.

Cry… Cry… And when the sun comes up… I'll be on top, you'll be up there looking up. "Come on, Captain—sing! What do you have to lose? Your legs and arms?"

"Too many tear drops for one heart to carry on." He sang the words. The sound of explosions was louder. He was blown up and vaporized, and yelling in pain.

He landed on Marvin and stood up, no man's land gone in the flash. He was standing in the dairy beside the dead English girl. Marvin was on his knees studying a map, his knees dirty with cow shit… He looked up at him.

"We're lost, amigo," Marvin said. "It's a cluster fuck."

Cassie watched him twitch and cry and sing while she held his hand. Something about it was beautiful, and she wasn't afraid. She hung onto him when he screamed, holding him until he stopped and got quiet. When he asked her if she was Jennifer, she said she was—for some reason that would forever be a mystery to her, she wanted to be someone else—and he smiled and held her. He touched her face and kissed her.

"Where the hell have you been?" he said. "I had this nightmare that we were out sailing and the boat lost its rudder and you died. Crazy," he said.

"It was just a dream," Cassie said. "I'm here."

The land line started to ring. It kept ringing, and she decided she should pick it up. It was Dr. Schneider, wondering what had happened. Cassie explained he was safe and at home. She hung up and turned and looked at him. The house was quiet. He was murmuring something.

When he took her hand and led her to the bedroom, calling her Jennifer, she didn't try and stop him. She felt as if she were a goddess who could make life happen for him, and her, wipe away something horrible that had started the day she'd been abused. It was the first time she felt that power—a different kind of power that was tied to her sex but had a healing quality, a life-sustaining quality. She took off his jacket and pants and put him to bed.

When he woke up, he felt calm. His cell phone was ringing. It was Marvin.

"He's asking the French government for the money," Marvin said. "Barre. Did you sober up?"

O'Higgins had to clear his head. He sat up. It was late afternoon. He could tell from the quality of the light. The hallucinations, so strong when he'd arrived, were barely perceptible. He always had the feeling of a calm after a storm when he was coming down. A sense of peace after the hiatus with reality. The afternoon light exquisitely soothing, the only telltale sign that he'd been high.

He saw his pants and jacket on the chair in the corner and remembered the dream. He and Jennifer had been making love. It had been super real and super intense. They'd talked afterwards. This was the most intense of the three trips he'd taken. But he felt changed, this time for good. The ratchets and sprockets were catching differently in his head. He remembered seeing Cassie in the living room when he'd come home.

"Yeah, sober. Okay—now what?"

"Barre wants to see us. I've not told the FBI—it's a kidnapping now."

"Right. Who have you told?"

"No one but you and Barre. He called his people. I think the French spooks are on this. His spooks. They don't want me to call anyone, Barre wants you and me to handle this. He wants their money, but wants us to handle it."

"Okay. Where are you?" O'Higgins said.

"I'm at the hotel with Barre."

"I'll be right there."

"Mike, if you talk to Cassie, tell her—tell her I—tell her to come home. She's not taking my calls or answering my texts. I fucked up."

"Okay—will do."

Chapter 20

Lana had pressed a few hundred dollars into her hand and called her honey child. The money was wet with blood, sticky. Lana had taken it from the dead pimp's front jeans pocket, which was soaked by the time she'd dug into it. The fat roll of bills had been difficult to extract; she'd had to yank his roll out. Lana had seen King James flash the roll on several occasions, making an exaggerated show of it to impress the whores in the SRO, with a mind of stealing them from their pimps. It was a common pimp tactic that Lana had seen all her working life.

Money and cars attracted whores, just like they attracted some women outside of that world.

Lana held the girl, but didn't say anything else to her. She left, opening the door to the room and stepping over King James's dead body, the carpet soaked with his blood. Her boots tracked bloody prints down the hallway.

Several prostitutes and two just-released, fresh-faced Latin felons were staring at the dead man. They rifled his pockets, looking for his cash, and came up with a small Sig Sauer as their prize. One of the whores told the desk man, an Indian who was constantly digging in his nose, that there was a body on the third floor. One of King James's whores started to yell for help.

It was the yelling that got X-Static up. And she would have made it out of the building, and to safety, if she'd not been trying to hide the wad of cash. But it was too late. The cops came and shut the hotel's main entrance down, not allowing anyone in or out, putting the entire SRO's population on lockdown. A few enterprising hoodlums left via the working fire escapes, having to jump to Jones Street from the second floor. Everyone else was pretty much stuck.

Four floors of hoodlums, prostitutes, junkies, crazy people on SSI and old women in their seventies who had worked as waitresses and barmaids downtown, back in the day, and never gotten married—living on Social Security and forced into the SRO because it was cheap—were told to line the hallways and wait to be interviewed. X-Static sat on the dirty carpet, as did most waiting to be interviewed, terrified that her stash would be found. The building was notorious for thefts of the most inconsequential things: candy, condoms (those were like cash), lipstick, junk food of any kind. The list of quotidian items that would be purloined by junkies was endless. Break-ins were common as overdoses. She couldn't keep her mind off the cash she'd hidden.

She watched as King James's body was finally hauled away by two black men using a narrow skid gurney, a sheet thrown over the dead man. One of the crazies yelled "Au revoir, motherfucker," as the gurney bounced down the stairs almost comically.

"Did you know the victim—King James?" the detective asked when it was X-Static's turn to get the two-minute interview. More than 80 people lined the hallways of the hotel, waiting to be interviewed.

"Who?" she said, playing dumb.

"That was his street name. He was staying in 302—black guy," Marvin Lee said.

"No." X-Static looked up at the detective. He handed her his card, but she didn't bother looking at it. She had put on a sweater that covered her tattoos. One was a small gold crown, tilted rakishly. James had all his women tattooed with the crown.

"My name is Detective Lee. We're investigating a murder. I'll need the card back." The cop was looking at her the way she'd seen cops look at her a hundred times. It was a typical cop-sizing-you-up look. "What's your name?"

"Anna Owens." She gave him her Christian name, not wanting to use the street name in case it led back to King James. One of his other whores was sitting across from her, a black girl around her age. They exchanged a look.

"How old are you?"

"Eighteen."

"Do you live here at the Maverick?"

"No."

"Why are you here?"

"I was visiting a friend," she said.

She looked away down the hall as if her mother were calling for her. It was a street tactic, a fatuous nonchalance used to deflect attention. She had two reasons for it: she wanted to show the others that she was not cooperating with the Man, first and foremost. And second, it was important to waste the cop's time so he would move on, frustrated.

"Can I see your phone?"

"I lost it."

Marvin gave her a look of disbelief. "You lost it?"

"Yes," she said.

"Who was your carrier?"

"It was a burner—I don't know. Some guy gave it to me in a club."

"What's your Instagram account and password?"

"I don't have one."

"You're lying."

"I am not," she said.

Another cop came and spoke to the detective, interrupting. She couldn't hear what they said. The white guy glanced at her and pointed something out, then reached down and pulled on her sweater, exposing her neck. He saw the tattoo and took a photo of it with his phone.

"Take off your sweater, please," the white cop said. "You have something on underneath?"

"Yeah."

"Okay, take it off."

The white guy was different than the tall one. He looked mean and was stocky, in his twenties.

"Take it off or I'll arrest you for being underage and out of parental control. You should be in school. Right?" the mean cop said.

She scoffed and tried to play it off. But she felt frightened of him, recognizing that he was a brute.

"Come on. Off with the sweater."

She stood up and took off the sweater. Her arms had two tattoos, the same one on each elbow—an eye. She'd seen the Indian Warli eye tattoo when she was in Seattle and wanted them immediately. They made her feel protected, the open eye watching her back.

The mean cop took a photo of both her elbows and left without saying another word.

She turned around and the black cop looked at the crown tattoo, moving her so he could see it more clearly. It was plain as day, on the right side of her neck.

"Why didn't you tell me you were working for the dead man? He was your man—right? He had your photo on his phone."

"No," she said. "I don't know what you're talking about. It's someone else. Oh, maybe I was with my friend. The one I came to visit—"

"Bullshit," Marvin Lee said. "Let me see your ID." He unbuttoned his sport coat and she saw how thin he was.

"I lost it," she said.

The detective looked at her.

One of the crazy SSI people—a Vietnam vet in filthy clothes— started to yell that he was going to piss himself if wasn't allowed to go back to his room. The detective turned and looked at him, then turned back to her. The crazy guy got up and walked down the hall. No one paid any attention to him.

The truth was she had an ID from Washington State that gave her age as seventeen. It was an ID that the state gave to wards of the court. It was with her cell phone and the cash the old whore had given her. But she was smart enough to hide her phone because of the calls and texts to King James, which she knew the Man would see immediately. Like so many street people, she'd watched "The First 48" and got schooled in police ways. Cell phones were the first to be "lost."

"You have blood on the bottom of your shoes," Marvin said.

"Yeah, so what?" she said. "So do you—I bet."

"Stay put," Marvin said. He moved on to the next person in line, a young junkie in a stolen down coat from a car smash-and-grab. He was standing, but bent over, in that weird junkie slouch, completely out of it.

***

"I don't want the DGSE2 to handle this. But unless I do, my government won't give me the money," Barre said. He looked at O'Higgins, then at Marvin.

"Why?" O'Higgins said.

"Because they might get my daughter killed. I know how they work. They're very protective of themselves, first and foremost. Their reputation inside the government is what's important. They will be afraid to lose the money. They won't care about Emma. Not really. I think you two do care." Barre said. They'd gone up to Barre's room at the Marriott. O'Higgins had finally shown up. Marvin was tired looking from interviewing so many people at the SRO.

"Do you have twelve million dollars?" Marvin asked.

"No, of course not. My only hope was the French government. They will give me the money, but only if the DGSE is involved. They assure me they will get Emma back," Barre said. "My wife wants me to agree and have them handle it."

"And you don't buy it," Marvin said.

"No, I don't," Barre said. "I don't know why, exactly—but I think you two can find her. It will take DGSE weeks to organize themselves. I don't think we have that kind of time."

"Our FBI would get involved if we report this as a kidnapping," O'Higgins said. Barre looked at him.

"Do you think they can find her? Your FBI?"

"No. I don't. They'd start from scratch, too. They would ignore Marvin and me, for the most part. They would take over the case. And you're right—we don't have that kind of time," O'Higgins said. "He doesn't keep them long. He knows it's dangerous if he does. We have to have an answer for him when he contacts us."

"So I have no choice, you see, but to trust you will find Emma." Barre said.

They were silent as the two detectives realized that Barre was going to enter their conspiracy for the sake of his daughter. They could hear the sound of traffic on Bay Street, outside. The hotel room's curtains were open. The August light was dying at 6 PM. The room's white walls were painted with a platinum-colored light, church-like.

"Marvin and I discussed it. We have an idea. We want to try and grab him, tell him we have the money. He'll have to prove to us that Emma is alive, first. Then we'll make sure he brings her with him when he picks up the money. We won't agree to anything else—only an exchange on the spot."

"But we don't have the money," Barre said. "I can get perhaps fifty thousand, but that would be all."

"No, we don't," Marvin said. "But we can get enough to fool him. Maybe."

"Do you believe you can find my daughter? That's she's still alive?"

"Yes. But we might fail," O'Higgins said. "And if you tell anyone what we're doing, we'll be fired, and you'll lose Emma. I'm sure of that. He'll kill her."

The words hung in the air. Barre had lost weight in the days since his daughter had been missing. Already thin, Barre seemed especially fragile.

The big king bed was unmade. It was obvious he'd kept the maids out. The room was all sixes and sevens.

"Maybe I could raise more, a hundred thousand Euros—but I would have to get my wife to cooperate, and she's convinced that Emma—she's convinced that it's too late. She read about the other girls. She thinks Emma is dead," Barre said. "She thinks we would pay for nothing."

"We'll get some money. Enough to make him believe we have it all. He knows who you are and will probably believe we have it. He's very smart," O'Higgins said. "Maybe this time he's too smart."

"Where will you get the money?" Barre asked, incredulous.

"I can't tell you. That's the deal. You don't ask, and you don't tell anyone what we're up to. Do we have a deal?" O'Higgins said.

"Yes. Thank you." Barre shook both their hands.

"We may fail," Marvin said. "Do you understand that? We can't promise you that—that Emma will come through that door alive. We can't."

"Yes," Barre said. "I understand." His phone rang and he looked at the screen. "I'm sorry, I have to take this—it's work. Oui, c'est Barre?" he said into his phone.

Chapter 21

She sat in the front of the *Boston Whaler* getting soaked by splash from the sea, still wearing what she wore the day he'd taken her out of the Hall of Mirrors. The man had injected her with ketamine, the infamous rape drug, bought from his heroin dealer. It was fast-acting. His dealer had explained the dosage, what would be necessary to disorient the victim but make walking still possible. The dose had been enough to make her appear drunk. People must have thought the man leading the girl out of the attraction was a helpful relation, dealing with a daytime drunk or dope fiend.

She remembered the Hall of Mirrors, the way people would stop and laugh when they found the direction blocked by a mirror. It was in a mirror that he had appeared behind her.

Nothing special, just part of the crush of people, his face hidden by the darkened weirdly lit place.

Just out of the Golden Gate, they passed other boats—all crabbers working at night, mostly Vietnamese-owned boats of various sizes, bobbing like corks. Their small portholes hung with Coleman lamps that emanated a wan yellow light, like a Van Gogh nocturne. The scene was complete with cold-looking morning stars.

She'd thought of throwing herself in what she knew could only be the ocean. But she couldn't bring herself to. The Golden Gate, lit up, loomed behind them as they plunged due west, turning finally north. The boat's outboard motor ran at full throttle, and loud. But for Emma she heard only silence and the lunging of the launch.

She looked toward the man who was destroying her, one rape at a time. He sat in front of her. She remembered a photo she'd seen of women marked with a white cross painted on the backs of their coats at Ravensbrück. The Red Cross had made the mark to identify the most severely ill.

She held up her hand and made a X in the air. The man watched her. Then she crossed herself. He'd given her an old peacoat to help hide her. It smelled of diesel fuel and sea water, but it was better than nothing. His one kindness, she'd thought, but he'd done it only to help disguise her.

She raised her hand again and gave him the finger. She felt as if she were going insane—on the edge of losing her mind, slipping into a strange land where she would be forever lost. She fantasized that she was a superhero and that soon, she would find her power—tear off the tape that covered her eyes, keeping her in the dark, and kill the man tormenting her.

Emma, haggard and cold in the over-sized coat, its sleeves too long for her, looked out from the narrow mouth of the sea cave where he'd left her. It must have been mid-day, she thought, looking out at the afternoon sky.

She had peeled the duct tape off her eyes as soon as she could. The sky seemed alien and limitless. A cold grey marine layer made a straight pencil mark over the calm teal-colored ocean. She willed herself to be strong, as she knew she had a tentative grasp on reality. She wanted to disappear into the fantasy world where she'd placed herself during the worst of the rapes.

It was a strange world, oscillating between horror and beauty. One moment she was with her family, or with friends, and at times she was reliving history: the war years she'd read about and in a sense been captured by. Then, she would imagine she was a superhero who would find her power and use it to save herself from the nightmare. Other times she was free climbing and reached a spot high above the ground, somewhere in

France, before she got stuck, unable to go forward or backward, frozen in place and tiring.

No such powers came, no matter how hard she willed it. But at least, now, she was alone.

He was gone, and he couldn't touch her. It was a blessed relief, even though she'd been—she assumed—taken to this place to die. The thought of her own death didn't affect her, one way or another. She was too exhausted to feel the impact of that expected death sentence. She had given up hope of surviving. She touched her hair and felt the dampness from the boat trip in the dark.

The tide was coming in, rushing the thin strip of beach in front of the cave. The beach had been empty only an hour ago, stretching along the cliff for half a mile, twenty feet wide at low tide. Now greenish waves were covering it.

The opening to the cave was a wide slit in the cliff face, a kind of louvre in the rocks. The cave complex had been known to the Modoc Indians since pre-history. They'd hidden here— men, women, and children—from the Spaniards who were determined to make slaves of them, forcing them to build the chain of churches running up the coast of California after the conquest. The church complexes were mini-concentration camps. The tribe was exposed to diseases and rapes, the children to conversion, and everyone worked as slave labor.

Emma, ignorant of all that, turned and saw the black stain of past campfires, coal black, on the rocks near her. The huge fires built by the tribe when they huddled here two centuries ago, their canoes having been pulled up into the cave's mouth, and out of sight. They'd been blessed with driftwood thrown into the cave during storms. Some of the tribe were able to take their families up the coast eventually, disappearing into the great Goddess of the North, now Trinity County, where they were left in peace for another two hundred years. Until the white men came again to ruin their lives for the last time, and forever. On "Red Sundays," drunken men searched the woods for Modocs to shoot, all legal and for sport. "The only good Indian is a dead Indian," the pioneers had said.

The man had brought her at a low tide and handed her a backpack. He'd raped her on the small beach. He seemed sexually insatiable, like a street dog, taking her again after he'd eaten, just inside the cave's mouth, with the sound of the ocean amplified behind them. It was the meth that fueled his appetite. She had sat on the sand, numb and cold, unable to see where he'd taken her. She only knew she'd stepped out of what she thought was a launch. The sand inside the cave had been wet. He used the peacoat as a blanket.

The sea cave was just past Bolinas, to the north, and before Point Reyes. The man had been fishing and discovered it by sheer chance one day. It was unknown and untouched since the last Modoc had slid his canoe into the ocean and left it behind. He'd been the first white man to find the cave since the conquest.

She had stopped struggling days ago. He seemed only excited by her fighting him, so she'd stopped. She stopped trying to communicate with him at all.

After he'd left, when she was able to see again, she opened the backpack. It held a store-bought sandwich tightly wrapped in plastic, the lettuce's edges dark and ugly; two large bottles of water; and a flashlight. She'd put the food aside, but drank water. She couldn't remember when she'd eaten last. She'd lost track of the days.

He'd left in the *Boston Whaler*–she'd read the famous logo on the boat's gunwale, having created a chink in the tape with her finger while he was busy starting the engine, his back to her. He'd seen the chink immediately, as soon as he'd turned around. He added to the tape, forcing her to turn her face away with his hands.

The word "whaler" made her think of whales and their calves that might be below their boat as they raced across the ocean, at times crashing over a wave. Maybe a whale would breach and tip them over and kill the man? She'd had a fantasy of watching him drown. Love the sinner, hate the sin. How absurd those words seemed to her, how she regretted believing in them. Or ever believe you could reason with Evil. The face of Evil was something she understood now. It had been an abstraction until he'd taken her. Now she'd seen it full on. It was an indifferent cold face—a chink in the tape of history. What she'd read about in history had become concrete. She had a new understanding of that awful history. What her grandmother must have felt on her way to Germany. She, too, had been a captive. She, too, had been a powerless girl. She, too, must have been cold and desperate. Had she been willing to please in order to survive?

***

They'd driven in silence, the sun coming out when they were passing San Francisco International Airport. Cassie looked out on the anonymous office parks facing the freeway heading south, most of their windows tinted dark reflecting a just-released sun.

"Do you miss it?" Thorpe asked. They were in a rental car, a white Cadillac Escalade, with the air conditioner on.

"No."

"You never told Lana the whole truth, did you?"

"No," Cassie said. She was wearing a smart-looking leather jacket he'd bought her in Sausalito and tan pants. She looked like an aging model who was on the cusp of retirement.

"Why not?"

"I don't know," Cassie said. "Just thought it was for the best."

Thorpe shook his head. "I admire that," he said. "Most people would have spilled the beans. Why did you agree? You didn't have to."

She turned and looked at him. He'd forgotten that she had had no choice in the matter. She'd killed someone, and they had proof. The fixer had come with Thorpe when Lana called them to the address in Malibu.

Lana had come to the house, and when she rang the doorbell, the kid had let her in.

Thorpe had sent Lana to check up on her. She'd been gone three days without calling. The kid was stoned and thought he'd ordered another girl. He'd taken her up to the bedroom and Lana saw what he'd done to Cassie. She'd let out a scream. He'd beaten her while still handcuffed to the bed. Lana had pulled her razor out and told him to unlock the fucking handcuffs. Frightened, the kid had. Cassie had not said a thing from the moment Lana had walked into the bedroom and seen her. It was Lana who unlocked the handcuffs and helped her out of the bed. The kid had just watched as if it were all a big joke.

"She loved it," he'd said. "She did. I fucked her, and she loved it."

Lana looked at him. Cassie took the razor out of Lana's hand and walked toward him. She backed him into his enormous paneled walk-in closet with its watch safe and black marble countertops. She was stoned, naked, her face puffy, her legs black and blue. She could hear Lana behind her.

"What you fixin' to do?" Lana said.

Cassie didn't answer. Her voice was hoarse and she tried to speak, but she'd screamed so much that she could not. She saw a clutch she'd brought sitting on the island in the middle of the closet. She tore a pistol out, an old-school five-shot Chief's Special Thorpe had given her.

He walked backwards away from her, scared. It must have been the look in her eye, which told him he was doomed. He started to beg for his life. She shot him dead as he begged, in the face, blowing out the back of his skull. The bullet lodged somewhere deep in the house.

"I'm not most people," Cassie said. "That night changed me. You got the lawyer for Lana?"

"Yeah. I got her a slick yid. She won't stand trial, he's sure of it. The worst she'll do is some time in a state hospital. Two years, if that."

"I want money for her when she gets out."

"Okay."

"Until the end. An apartment. A nice one. And a nurse. She'll need a nurse."

"Okay. I'm not an asshole. I do care what happens to her, too. They made me find you. I had no choice."

She didn't answer. They pulled off highway 101 and made their way down a wide new street. They passed the humongous Google complex. She saw a crowd of young techy types mostly East Indians, cross in front of them at the cross walk, a few women mixed in with the group. She wondered, watching them, what her life would have been like had she not agreed to work for the people they were going to meet. If she'd just had walked out that door in Malibu and not looked back. She reminded herself again that she'd had no choice.

Thorpe stopped, and let the young people—all with large ID badges around their necks—cross the boulevard. Everything seemed bright and new here: the kids, the buildings, even the cars that passed them. Everything new.

"I bought Google, back in the day," Thorpe said. "I have a couple of their top guys in my book." He sped up again. "It's my retirement. You can only ride the tiger for so long, you know."

She wasn't listening anymore.

They drove on in silence until he finally turned into an anonymous office park, all its windows tinted, reflecting the clear blue sky. It reminded her of Guatemala.

San Isidro plantation, Guatemala

Her pistol instructor had been a very short man. He was patient. He had been in Tripoli working for Gaddafi's Praetorian Guard, and before that he'd been a major in Italy's 85th Target Acquisition Regiment. He spoke English with an accent and was extremely polite and soft spoken. She never forgot him because he was both kind with her and respectful, something she'd not expected, nor was used to. She had never fired a pistol in her life before she'd shot the man in Malibu—much less the long rifles she would be trained on— before they had recruited her.

She'd lived in a barracks on a plantation in Guatemala, near Tapachula. Two other women lived with her. She was twenty and out of shape physically. She couldn't drink or smoke. The plantation where the young women were being trained was in the hills above Coatepeque, just over the Guatemala side of the Mexican border. It was about as far from American civilization as anyone could get.

They'd arrived in a Guatemalan Army Huey helicopter. The pilot, an American, set them down on the coffee-drying patios that were used after the harvest.

The barracks and the plantation were run by Guatemalan intelligence, G7, she would learn later. The people who employed her were using the facility. When they fixed the murder in LA, they had taken her in and made it all go away. As they explained to her in a new Town Car on the way to LAX, they would look after her. She would work for them, and she would no longer have to worry about any kind of legal problems. Those would be in her past. She would come back and work with Thorpe, but it would be different. She would receive "assignments." She had no idea what was in store for her.

They respected her and didn't judge her, two middle-aged men in dark suits who took her to the airport and stayed until her flight took off. At the Arora Airport in Guatemala City an older Australian met her, another man in a dark suit who walked her by customs as if he owned the place. He told her to call him Gus.

It was Gus who picked her up after her training. Even he noticed how beautiful she looked now that she was clean and sober. She looked entirely different than she had six months before. It was true she sported a black eye, given to her by the Italian instructor two days before she left. Later she was grateful for that last lesson, as what he taught her then would save her life.

"Crikey! You look great," Gus said. "What a difference a little fresh air makes."

Two day before she left for her first assignment, Cassie woke up as usual. The Italian had told her that she would be leaving—she'd been there six months. It was raining. She opened the louver doors, their paint peeling, the French paisley-blue floor tile cold under her bare feet. Her private room had a black old-school ceiling fan turning night and day to keep the mosquitoes at bay and a big door that led to a deep plantation-style veranda, like a portico. It was on that veranda, years and years before, that the Bay of Pigs invasion was discussed—clean-cut American pilots briefed before the big day that had become part of San Isidro's lore.

The rain cascaded off the tin roof like a waterfall, making for a strange netherworld seen from inside her room. She liked the room with its tile floor and armoire, a few paperback books that gave the room a sweet-old-paper smell.

It had felt strange to her the first day, an odd kind of jail. For the first two weeks she'd seen a French doctor who helped her off her heroin addiction, injecting a cocktail that got her over the worst of withdrawals. Unable to speak English, the Frenchman simply smiled and told Gus—who stayed at the plantation until she was sober—to have her drop her pants. Then he injected her in her butt cheek. She was so out of it those first few weeks that it all seemed like some long dream.

Now that she'd sobered up and gotten clean and right—for the first time since she was fifteen—the sweet-smelling room was her sanctuary, and the first real quiet place she'd ever known.

The room's old books were in various languages. One was a pulp novel about a fast-thinking English spy in Berlin after the war. She'd read it twice along with old *Look* magazines from the '60s. Some reported on the new rugged Special Forces—President Kennedy's James Bonds— perusing the Viet Gong in a strange country called Viet Nam. They had black and white photos of glamorous Madame Nhu, South Vietnam's "First Lady."

They had breakfast in the plantation's dining room every morning at seven sharp. The stiff cow-hide chairs were from Tapachula, Mexico; the huge dining table was laid with condiments of all kinds, to appeal to different cultures that passed through for training. You could choose what you liked to eat for breakfast. She always had the same thing—eggs and orange juice—because it was what her mother made for her when she was a little girl, when she was around.

As they trained harder, she found herself eating more. When she was working for Thorpe, she'd barely eaten. Men had liked her blond waif-dope-fiend look, and would request her because of it. She saw that same look, years later, on the cover of chic women's fashion magazines and laughed.

The odd tropical weather, and especially the fauna of the Guatemalan highland mountains, seemed to embrace her, protect her. When they went for hikes with the Italian, at first it had been relaxing. After living in LA and New York, to be out in nature was special and calming. It felt that way even when he'd started making them jog with old surplus packs made in France, and used by the French Army at Dien Bien Phu.

She'd cried the first time she had to run on the slick clay road with a twenty-pound pack filled with bags of sand. The German girl had cried too. At one point they'd both quit and said they couldn't go another step, refusing to move, their faces flushed, their stomachs churning with exhaustion. The Italian, instead of yelling at them as they expected, had come back down the road, his face sweaty. He looked at them and smiled and assured them they could do it, rather than yell at them. He was so encouraging the two girls got on with it, the Italian running alongside, making jokes about jungle boots being the latest fashion in Milan.

It was the right way to be with young women, he'd learned. With young men, he could yell and be the drill sergeant they expected; with young women, he tried to be patient. The Colombian girl was a good runner and seemed never to tire. Cassie and the German girl called her "big ass" behind her back. The Colombian girl, a real stunner, was in love with herself and an attention whore.

After a while Cassie had gotten in shape and was one of the fittest. She led the strange group of young women and the middle-aged man along red-rutted muddy tracks that followed the contours of the plantation, sometimes becoming exceedingly steep. In those places the plantation workers had paved the road with rocks to help the Jeeps get traction so the tires wouldn't spin. The old-school Land Rover Jeeps used to work the coffee. It was coffee harvest time. The plantation's workers, partially hidden in the bushes they were picking, would stare at the young women, but dared not say anything, as it was well known that they were training at San Isidro and you didn't ask questions about the goings on. It was infamous.

After several weeks she felt as if she'd disappeared into a spa, albeit one with automatic weapons training, hand-to-hand combat practice, and oddly, the art of disguise. At one point she'd even been told that religious garb of any kind —depending on the culture she found herself in— was always a go-to when she was trying to pass. Twice later she would be dressed as a nun. She found the training almost comical at first, but as it went along, and she was more and more fit, she began to enjoy it. She liked the Italian, who was avuncular. She liked having meals prepared for her, and she liked the German girl. But most of all she liked not having to service men. It was the first break from that she'd had since she'd walked out of her mother's apartment and gone to LA to be a movie star.

They were fed by a cook and two young Guatemalan maids, their own age. The cook was from El Salvador and was an albino in his 50s. He tried to talk to the girls when he could, hoping that he might get lucky. The girls were told to use only their first names. She'd become relaxed with the other girls. One was a striking German girl, about nineteen, who would later be infiltrated into the German Far Left. The other girl, a tall Colombian, athletic, acted as if they were on school holiday. Because the girl had Spanish, the maids treated the Colombian differently, like she was the owner.

The albino had tried to sneak into the Colombian's room late one night, and had been fired. An American ex-nun called Vivian came in and did the cooking after that. She treated the younger girls kindly. Rumor had it that she drank heavily and had been run out of the Maryknoll order because of it. In fact, she was a US Army intelligence officer who had been infiltrated to spy on the spies. One agency afraid of the other.

She and the German girl had bonded. The German girl was a lesbian who had grown up in East Germany. She tried to kiss Cassie one night in the hallway in the dim light, the sweet smell of kerosene lamps in the air. Cassie pushed her away, not shocked, but not into women. They stayed friends regardless of the girl's attempts at seduction. The German girl's English was good.

It was August, and it rained sometimes in amounts that were diluvial. After training all day, the two girls would sit in the German girl's room and talk about their lives before coming here. They could see the rain, grey sheets of it hitting the forest of banana palm trees along the gravel drive that ran for a mile before coming out on the two-lane Pan American Highway.

Sometimes workers passed the plantation house hoisting torn-down banana fronds as impromptu raincoats.

The Italian came to get her at 11:00. She'd thought training was over, as Gus had called her on the heavy black phone in the kitchen to say that he was coming to pick her up the following day. She put down the phone and felt strange about leaving the place. She realized what it meant. Her assignments would start. She could die.

She'd gone to her room and started to get ready. The knock on the door came at exactly 11:00. The Italian stood in the doorway, a pistol tucked into his pancake holster. He had another rig—a smaller Glock and clip on holster—in his hand.

"Last lesson, Cassie." He smiled. "Raincoat. *Sta piovendo duro.*"

She looked out the French door to the veranda. She could barely see the road. The tops of the banana trees were waving in the wind as the rain pelted.

They walked out of the house and onto the plantation's cobblestone road. Both wore parkas. His was a military one, camouflaged, showing his Italian regiment's insignias and campaign patches. She followed. She'd belted the pistol the way she'd been taught. They walked past the plantation's church; churches were de rigueur in the feudal landscape. Every plantation of note had one since the conquest. They walked on past the stalls that had once housed the owners' racehorses and were now empty, the line of stalls wet, the cobblestones worn smooth.

They passed the household pigsty. She heard the grunting of pigs shielded from the rain by a few pieces of tin roof, their dirty faces curious as they passed. They were heading to the range, a converted soccer field where she'd spent hours learning how to fire every kind of pistol, revolver and most of the common automatic weapons in the UN and Eastern Bloc arsenal.

It was the pistols they concentrated on most: learning how to cock an auto when you were wounded by using the heel of your boot, learning to fire using the "instinctive" method developed by the Israelis. She followed him as the rain fell in sheets, blown by a wind sometimes so intense that everything turned grey and seemed frosted. The grass was worn here and there by their exercises. Their targets hung from a muddy berm.

The Italian turned to her. He had a look in his eye she'd never seen before. "Try to take my pistol."

"What?" She almost had to shout to be heard over the downpour. The Italian's parka was greasy, with rain cascading off his shoulders.

He slapped her hard across the face. "Try and take my weapon."

She made a move toward his pistol. He slapped her again, knocking her to the ground.

She felt her knees in the mud. He pushed her down, so she was facing the sky and the rain was in her eyes. She felt him pick her up. As she started to stand, he knocked her down again.

He kicked her in the thigh, the pain electric and numbing all at once. "Stand up. Come on take it from me."

She stood up and he struck her with the back of his hand, knocking her backwards. She stumbled, nearly falling again. She was drenched, the hood of her parka having come off. Her hands were muddy.

He closed in on her and waited.

"I'm going to kill you," he said. "Are you going to let me kill you?"

Before she could answer he struck her again, this time in the solar plexus, at the vagal nerve so that she slumped and gasped for breath. He stepped toward her and stood over her. The man she'd thought was her friend seemed on the verge of murdering her.

She was stunned and angry. She stood up, swaying from having the air knocked out of her. She drew the pistol and fired at him. The pistol clicked empty. He grabbed her by the arm and half-dragged her toward one of the wooden posts usually hung with paper targets.

He took his pistol out and handed it to her.

"Now kill him, go on then… kill him. Before he can hit you again. She lifted the pistol. The shots that had been so easy before when they'd been fresh and clean and unhurt now seemed impossible. The post was fifty feet in front of her. Her hands were muddy, her right eye was closing up from his slap. She held the pistol out in front of her and saw the sight picture waver.

The rain had slowed. She fired and missed. She fired again and missed again, her hands unsteady.

"Now you understand," he said behind her. "It won't always be easy. Go on again, fire a burst."

She fired a rapid-fire burst. Two shots hit the post. She saw the wood splinter. "Now kneel," he said. "Go ahead, kneel and fire again."

She fired until the pistol was empty. He took the pistol, ejected the magazine, rammed in a fresh magazine, and handed it to her.

"When you're hurt, and there will be times you are hurt, it will all be different than shooting at paper targets. Do you understand?"

She nodded. And then she turned toward the post. On one knee it was easier to steady herself. She fired again three times in rapid succession, just her right eye open, her left swollen completely shut.

Chapter 22

"My grandfather built the building. He passed—last month, in Hawaii. He left the apartment building to me. I'm going to move in," Robin said. "I was thinking maybe you—maybe you might move in with me? If you want. I want to fix it up."

"What about your other place, at the Harrison?" O'Higgins asked. They were standing in her grandfather's apartment just down from Coit Tower, number 200 Telegraph Hill. Pioneer Park, with the famous tower, just above the apartment building. He'd never seen a view like this one. Something about it was almost overwhelming. The scope of it: The Golden Gate and Marin to the west, and the East Bay and Alcatraz directly in front of him. It was a penthouse apartment in a six-unit building, sitting on top of the world. It was worth, he thought, ten million dollars? More, probably.

"I was my grandfather's favorite. I was the only grandchild to get a degree in agriculture—well, oenology, but he loved that I'd done it. He'd started out as a farmer's son, you see—his father. They started buying up farms in the depression, and the rest as they say is history. Do you like it? Want to move in? It won't be ready for a while. I'm having the kitchen done right away, and the upstairs, all new baths—"

"There's an upstairs?" O'Higgins said.

"Yes. It's two floors. There's an elevator. Want to see it? It would be our bedroom—upstairs." She stole a look at him. It was hopeful, about a future she was plotting for them. She had a look in her eye he'd seen before. It was the look she'd had when she was laying out the new winery surrounded by architects and engineers, officials from Sonoma County's Building Department—all of them realizing that she knew exactly what she wanted and was going to get it. By the end of the meeting, they were all charmed and on the Robin Team.

"I don't care about that girl in India," Robin said. "I really don't. I think we're good together."

"I'm just a cop. I went to public school—Galileo High. Your friends think I'm a curiosity, like land lines."

"I don't care what my friends think," she said. "Do you? Let that go, Mike."

"No. I don't care. You're right."

"I'm falling in love with you. Okay? Do I have your permission? Is that okay?"

"You don't need my permission. You haven't met my daughter yet—you might change your mind. She acts like my mother now."

"We have a company jet. It's mine to use. We could go to New York tonight, if you want, and I can meet her. I want to meet her."

"Slow down," he said.

"I don't want to." She looked at him. "I really, really don't want to." Her phone rang, but she didn't bother to pick it up. It was lying on the window ledge. She always answered her phone, but not this time.

"Okay—I'll move in. If you want me to. Rebecca is coming home for her birthday in September. She'll be eighteen on the sixteenth. You can meet her then. She knows about you. I've told her we're dating. She Googled you, and was very impressed."

Her phone rang again; whoever it was didn't give up. She ignored it again.

"Okay. I'm going to kick some ass to get them to finish the place by then. We can have Rebecca's birthday party here if you'd like to. Do you think she'd like that?"

"Yes. I think you beat me, as far as real estate goes. She'll die when she sees this place. She'd love it—no doubt."

"She can stay here, too. I would like that—there's room. When she's not away at school, I mean."

"I have a favor to ask," he said.

"Ask it."

"I need to borrow fifty thousand dollars—in cash. I need you to buy Bitcoin with the money." He hadn't known how he was going to ask her, but he knew he had to as soon as Barre agreed to let them handle the ransom.

"Bitcoin? Are you in the drug business?"

"No. I'm trying to save that French girl. The guy who got her is ransoming her. I told her father I would handle it. He wants ten thousand in cash, and the rest in Bitcoin. The father doesn't have that kind of money. I could lose it, the whole thing—you could lose it. If we don't catch him."

Robin looked at him, her expression unchanged. It was as if he'd asked her for parking-meter change, not fifty thousand dollars.

"Good, you're not in the drug business. That would be hard to explain at the Christmas party. Okay." She picked up her phone and crossed the room, talking with the family's office to make the arrangements. At one point, over obvious objections, she told the person on the other end of the line to "Shut up and do it—I don't care what the issues are. Put forty thousand worth of Bitcoin on a USB stick. The rest in cash. Send them to the to my grandfather's place on Telegraph Hill."

She ended the call. "It will take a few hours. They're upset because we'll have to report a cash withdrawal to the feds. Is that okay? They'll hand deliver the USB stick and the cash here. The office is handling it, the bitcoin passwords—that crypto stuff is all Greek to them, but they'll sort it. Want to see the upstairs?"

"Yes," he said. "Thank you for trusting me. I'll get it back to you—the money. I promise. We'll catch him."

Later he drove by and picked up the thumb drive with the bitcoin wallet's password— public and private—and the cash. He got a text from Asha as he headed back out to meet Marvin. He looked at the text as he started up the car. She was inviting him to come to India for a visit.

He didn't answer. It was the first time he'd ignored her, feeling guilty about their texting. Instead he called Marvin and told him he had gotten what they needed.

* * *

The front company was called Bio Analytica. The company had a legitimate biotech business incubated at Cambridge University—high-powered young boffins involved in bio-engineering. It was also a business used by the intelligence officers waiting for her, to produce and distribute highly sensitive chemical weapons and their precursors around the globe on a when-needed basis. The company was headquartered in London, but had offices in the Silicon Valley. So many tech companies—some very famous ones— had close intelligence agency ties, of one kind or another.

A young East Indian with an English accent ushered Cassie into the slick conference room for her "eleven o'clock." He asked her if he could get her anything, his smile pasted on. Cassie shook her head, nervous. It had been years since she'd been in the game, as the spooks called it. She looked for Gus, her handler from years before, but didn't see him and it made her all the more apprehensive.

She sat across from two nondescript men, one black. The black one stood and shook her hand, calling himself Paul—no last name. She heard the conference door open behind her and thought it would be the young Indian, but it was Gus, holding a Styrofoam cup of coffee. She felt relieved. He didn't look any different. He seemed ageless: more grey hair, but his bon vivant manner alive on his big Aussie face.

"Darlin'—how the hell are you?" He wore a trim suit and tie. She felt reassured. He hugged her, and she let him. She had always thought of him as kind, and despite the bloody business they'd gotten up to—someone she felt oddly at home with since he'd picked her up at the airport in Guatemala all those years before.

"Would you leave us, old boy? And leave the laptop. I think we can take it from here."

The younger men in the requisite dark suits and ties nodded, got up and left them. Gus pulled out a chair and sat next to her. She noticed a view of a monstrous parking lot, and beyond it a private airport.

"It's the Google airport out there. They come and go. Used to be a military airport," Gus said, reaching for the laptop and sliding it over toward them. "So how have you been?"

"Married now," Cassie said. They were the first words she'd spoken since walking into the building. Thorpe had stayed in the car, saying they didn't want to see him.

"I know—a policeman. I'm not surprised, somehow," Gus said. "Opposites attract, don't they? I've always thought it true."

"What is it they want, Gus?" she said. "It's been so long."

"Well, they want you to do someone in, of course. It's what we do, isn't it?" He smiled at her. "I've missed you. Worked with other young women—other men, for that matter—and always wondered when you were coming back. You are a natural. I'm sorry, but it's true. You were good at it. Fearless. Our fearless lassie."

Since she'd shot the rich kid in Malibu, she'd grown a new skin. All of her mother's ruthless quality, which she'd seen in one city or another, had been there for her to call on. It had surprised her at first, but she began to rely on it. Even to look forward to the assignments, as if they were a kind of payback for what had been done to her and her mother by the kind of men she was sent to deal with. Wealthy, arrogant, insiders who believed the world revolved around them. They were always shocked when a twenty-year old ex-prostitute put them down like cattle in a slaughterhouse, if they had time to realize it.

"The colonel—the Italian. Is he—?" Cassie asked.

"Dead. Died in Tripoli—he was with Gaddafi when they caught up to him. Ugly business. We saw the video. He was loyal to Gaddafi. I never understood that. But he was— loyal. It was his nature."

"I'm sorry," Cassie said.

"He was a soldier of fortune, after all. It's to be expected—for all of us. Our line of work."

"Did you ever tell your husband?"

"No. I've told no one."

"Right. Didn't think you would. I wouldn't have told them if you had. I happen to like you. You have that quality—somehow, the others, I never cared whether they came back or not. Not really."

She smiled. She felt it was true. She remembered the way he'd prepared her the first time. He'd spent a week with her in London; a dissident Saudi, a member of the royal family had been the target. Gus had been granular with her. They had the plans for the man's house on Regent Square. She'd memorized the entire floor plan. A maid from the Congo had been hired to leave a gun in the man's bathroom.

She'd shot the target in the back of the head while he was pulling on his pants. He'd simply disappeared on the other side of the huge bed, the shot silenced. The bullet had kept going and she saw the neat hole in the plaster. She dropped the pistol on the big unmade bed. She'd dressed and walked out onto the street and into a waiting London cab. She saw she was shaking while they drove toward Piccadilly, a silly advert on the small screen facing her for Victoria's Secret. She'd been wearing similar lingerie when she'd shot the man.

Gus was waiting for her at a cafe. They had coffee while she debriefed him, still in shock that she was able to be so callous and cold-blooded.

"I always came back."

"Yes. Thank God," Gus said.

"What is it—who is it?" Cassie asked.

"Russian oligarch. Staying on his yacht off Sausalito." Gus launched into the business at hand as if they'd not been apart for more than ten years. He flipped up the laptop's screen to show a photo of an ultra-modern, sleek super yacht. "He's having a party this Saturday, called Thorpe for some girls. Likes them young—very young. Has a special room in the

176

place for his goings-on."

"Then why call me? Don't you have someone else? I'm not that young kid anymore."

"We sent your photo, and—one supposes—he couldn't resist. They never could."

"Saturday?"

"Yes. He's to send a launch to pick you and two other girls up."

"How?"

"Well, now, that's the tricky part."

Normally she would dispatch the man—sometimes it was a woman—in fairly conventional ways. Most often it was made to look like a suicide, a drug overdose being the most common ruse. Not difficult, as many wealthy tricks were drug abusers of one kind or another. She'd be given a "hot shot." She'd wait for the man to doze off, then stab him with the specially designed pneumatic syringe she kept in her elegant clutch.

On other occasions she had to shoot her target in the most cold-blooded manner to make it look like a robbery gone bad, the second most common cover for an intelligence-agency assassination. She would be assigned things to steal and told where to find them. Most often, household employees had already been infiltrated and put on the payroll, or threatened with death, to help her open safes or find jewelry caches. She wasn't allowed to keep anything she stole, as those items would later be "found" in the possession of some second-rate criminal who would be accused of the robbery and murder.

The spate of high-level bankers who'd been throwing themselves from buildings of late—and were very much in the press—were probably assassinations, she knew. Gus had once let it slip that even the head of one of Germany's most important banks was a target, with her friend the German girl among the hit team.

"Do you remember a Russian dissident in London a few years back? Poisoned?"

"Yes. I saw his photos," Cassie said.

"Well, they want the same show here—polonium 210."

"What is it?"

"Doesn't matter, really. Madam Curie discovered it. It's a radioactive substance, found in ground water. It is harmless, unless you ingest it."

She looked at him. She recalled the press reports of the Russian in his hospital bed. How miserable he looked—his head bald, his expression one of resignation, and even an odd detachment, as if he'd expected it all along. And now, there he was, on the verge of a horrible death. His insides turned to shit. The polonium delivered in a cup of tea, the press claimed. She doubted the cover story, as the footprints left by the polonium—traces of it at the time found all over London—were obviously meant to misdirect. They would never be that sloppy.

"I've got kids, Gus," Cassie said. "Two girls."

She studied his face. It was a little fuller, and she realized he must be in his sixties.

"I know," he said. "Two little girls…" He gave her a penetrating look, as if perhaps he'd tried to avoid using her. "I said it's not dangerous to you, if you don't ingest it. You'll have to bring the stuff on board. We've got a hot shot for you to take. You can inject him or something he's going to ingest. He's a Diet Coke fiend, apparently drinks the stuff all day long. He has it with him when he has sex, part of his ritual. He's got a special sex pod on the yacht. Big bed, no windows—James Bond stuff. He'll take you in there You'll have to find a way to spike his drink. Or simply inject him directly. It's up to you. Just get it in him."

"I won't be alone with him?"

"No. There'll be other girls, but they'll not be ours. And we don't have anyone on the inside. Our person was fired two days ago, and there's no time to get someone inside now. You'll be on your own."

"It has to be like this? It has to be now? Here?"

"Yes," Gus said. He turned an electronic page on the laptop and showed her a floor plan of the yacht.

It had three levels. The pod was on the deck, near a hot tub at the very bow. He showed her photos someone had taken of the pod and the surrounding area. The pod was strange: a low- hatchway door, a giant bed and bathroom. No one could see inside once the lid was closed. She had an instinctual bad feeling about it—the cloistered bedroom felt sinister— but it was too late. She couldn't go back. They would kill her if she didn't do as they asked. It was one of their ugly rules.

"He has security?" Cassie asked, studying the bow of the super yacht.

"Yes. Former FSB people running it, men and women. Very professional. They'll be there on the yacht. At least three."

She didn't like the odds.

Gus hoisted a briefcase, left by the other men, and opened it. A foam insert cradled an expensive-looking black pen. She'd used one before.

"This is the device. You've used it—looks like a Mont Blanc pen." He pointed out the gold clip. "Depress this and hold it against the skin. Simple as that—right?" He closed the lid and handed her the pen.

"I didn't ask for you," Gus said. "I want you to know that. It's just the way things worked out. It's part of the game. No one is ever really free."

"Unless you die," Cassie said. She put the pen in her purse. "I want a pistol. A hammerless revolver. Five shot. .357. Can I shoot him, if it goes bad?"

"No, but you can have it. They'll probably take it away from you when you arrive."

"They might—and they might not. I was a yacht girl a long time ago. These yacht parties, they're chaotic. Lots of people to vet."

He nodded, then surprised her with a hug when she stood up to leave. "I won't ever see you again. I'm retiring. When I heard it was going to be you, I insisted I be the one to brief you.

"That last day in Guatemala, when I picked you up—what happened? You were in bad shape. I always wondered. The black eye?"

"Oh, well—I got my diploma, you see. Goodbye, Gus." She hugged him and remembered his cologne. He'd been a bizarre kind of father figure to her, one she'd never had.

Gus stood by the window and waited for Cassie to emerge from the building. He could feel the air-conditioning blown down from the ceiling. As he watched her get into Thorpe's car, he supposed she might well not make it.

The car pulled out of the lot. He followed it as long as he could, until it just disappeared.

He felt old, and was glad he would soon be out of it. Turning from the window, he wondered what he'd done with his life. It seemed shabby, all the places and people—his grim back-alley existence starting in Vietnam, when he was only a kid. And for exactly what? He would retire with a pension and an empty house near a secluded beach in Australia a few kilometers from where he'd been born. He'd never married. That girl in Guatemala—she'd gotten through his spy's thick skin.

He sat at the conference table, feeling exhausted. The damn pen had been with him for a week. The possibility that it could leak had been nerve-shattering.

He closed his briefcase and remembered seeing the girl for the first time in the airport in Guatemala. She'd looked ill and was terribly thin, a waif. It was impossible to believe she'd been a whore since the age of fifteen. They'd given her a cheap old-fashioned flight bag. It had seemed too big for her that afternoon.

He'd walked up to her, and saw those blue eyes. They weren't the eyes of a burnt-out drug addict. They'd held onto an innocence that shocked him as he took the bag off her shoulder, immediately acting the role of her protector. He'd felt oddly fatherly toward her, as he looked at her. She got through to something he'd thought had died years before, a feeling of tenderness. He never forgot it. His humanity had been rescued. He'd felt like a convict reprieved after years in solitary—the cell door thrown open to the light. Someone he could love, even.

"My name is Gus," he'd said. "I'm with them."

"Hello," she said. "Where am I, again? I've been asleep."

"Oh, it's Central America. It will take some getting used to, I'm afraid."

For a long time he stared at his cell phone, wanting to delay the rest of his life—a yawning, miserable future. Finally he sent the text: **Passenger on board**. Then he went to the airport, just an older-looking businessman, rather nondescript, and flew home.

She felt sick. It was warm outside. Thorpe's car, as soon as she pulled the door closed, was cool. They didn't speak until they were well past the airport heading back to the city.

"I want to flip their script, or I'm not going to make it. Will you help me?"

"Sure," Thorpe said. "We're just bitches to them."

Chapter 23

He had a voice mail from Marvin. Someone had confessed to killing the Russian on Gold Mine Drive. It turned out to be his girlfriend. She was coming into Bryant Street with her lawyer to turn herself in that afternoon. It was unexpected. He texted back:

Meeting SH in park at 3PM.

Seven Hills had sent him a text, ordering O'Higgins to meet him at the Arboretum in Golden Gate Park and bring the ten-thousand dollar good-faith payment. He was to go to the famous Redwood Grove, sit on a bench, and wait. If Seven Hills suspected that O'Higgins wasn't alone, or it was any kind of trap, he'd kill the girl, he threatened.

O'Higgins had gone back to his place in San Rafael and began counting out the cash on the dining room table. As he was counting it out, Cassie came through the door with Thorpe, surprising him.

"Retirement fund?" Thorpe asked, looking at the table strewn with bills. The big man had a smirk on his freckled face. He was dressed well. Very put together, still sporting a bandage on his face.

"None of your damn business." O'Higgins said. He was angry that Cassie had brought the pimp to his house. Now Thorpe knew where he lived.

"What do you want, Cassie? You should go home."

A UPS driver rang the bell, and Cassie darted for the door. She returned to the living room with a small package, and opened it on the table next to the piles of hundred-dollar bills.

"I needed an address, and I couldn't—well, you know. I didn't want the package going home."

"Marvin told me to tell you to go home," O'Higgins said. "He's over it. He's sorry for what happened. He said you should come home. Your girls miss you, Cassie."

"What are you and Marvin up to?" Cassie asked, looking at the cash.

"I'm going to get the French girl back. That's what we're doing. Now you get the fuck out of my house." O'Higgins said, looking at Thorpe. "I'm not going to tell you a second time."

"Right. You got a problem with black people, boss?"

"Go on," Cassie said. "I'll be out in a second. Robert, please—leave." Thorpe walked out, leaving the front door ajar.

O'Higgins watched her tear open the cardboard box. Cassie, the mother he thought he knew, pulled out a snub-nose hammerless revolver and a fresh box of ammunition. He watched her spin the revolver's barrel and load the pistol, taking the rimmed cartridges out from their white foam seats until the old-school revolver was loaded and she closed the cylinder. He saw nothing amateurish about the way she'd done it, all the movements oddly masculine.

"You know how to use that?" He asked.

"Yes, I do," she said. "Tell Marvin I've got something I've got to do, then I'm coming home for good. Tell him I love him. Will you do that? Don't tell him you saw me with Thorpe, Michael—okay? Friends can have secrets—right?"

He nodded finally.

"Cassie—why?" he asked. "I don't get it. You got a family. What's with the bullshit?"

"I was never what you assumed. People assume things. You know. I hope you find the girl and get her back to her people. I really do." She took his hand. "Maybe it will change things for all of us."

"So do I," he said.

She took the revolver and the rest of the ammunition, put them in her coat pocket, and left.

He went back to counting the dirty bills into stacks of hundreds. He thought about killing Seven Hills in the Arboretum. Right then and there. Part of him was moving to a cold, out-of-control place... was it the LSD?

He saw the grove in his mind's eye, its beauty—the sunlight-dappled place he remembered from childhood. The Redwood needles golden, the collection of benches nestled under the redwoods. A special light filtered through the giant ancient trees. He knew the place. They took his daughter to the Arboretum when she was a toddler because she loved the big grassy places. The Japanese pond, with its romantic quiet teahouse and a small pier.

He imagined Seven Hills there—waiting for him, a dark outline, sitting, facing away from him as he entered the idyllic crepuscular sun-dappled glen, his Glock drawn, the slippery-feeling safety on the trigger depressed. He walked deliberately through the shadows, the English girl watching him. Standing naked nearby, her arms bruised, urging him on, pleading with him to shoot the man. He walked on, his footsteps cushioned by the orange redwood-needle carpet, the barrel of his pistol going up to the back of the man's head... the bang of the round going off... the light above him in the trees. He looked up to see a vortex of boughs and tree limbs, darkness and light, running up into the maze, a fantastic web of sunlight and shadows. He looked down, and the figure on the bench was gone—escaped.

He snapped out of the daydream and finished counting the money, wondering where Emma was. Was she even alive? Was he going to win? How had Seven Hills eluded them and been able to do what he'd done, again and again? *Maybe he's just plain smarter than we are.*

Dr. Schneider rang his cell as he was driving back into the city. She scolded him for missing an appointment. She was disappointed in him, she said, and hoped it wouldn't happen again. He promised her it wouldn't. She had a knack of making him feel sixteen again.

***

X-Static was waiting at SFPD's Tenderloin Station on Eddy Street, technically under protective custody as an at-risk minor. She felt antsy because she couldn't smoke. They'd discovered "Anna Owens" after running her name through the system of at-risk youth. She'd used a welter of aliases since leaving the last foster care home. The sound of her real name—the name her teachers called her in the second grade when she had been a promising student, although troubled, as one teacher said to her aunt who had come for Parent-Teacher night.

The black detective had told her to sit and wait. He had gotten nicer, telling her that he had two daughters and that he didn't want her on the streets. That social services could help her. It had been one of the boys at the foster care home who really got her to hate men. He had raped her in a closet and then pissed on her for fun. She'd just turned fifteen. After that it was a long slide downhill. The skids were any kind of drug she could get her hands on.

She was passing into adulthood in the familiar surroundings and care of the state. She was eighteen as of 7:00 a.m., when her drug-smashed mother gave birth to her tiny preemie reddish-blue body. Her mother had been too drug-addled and out of it to be allowed to hold her.

A nurse had held her and prayed to her God that something, anything, good would come of the birth and of the child. After all, wasn't the baby Jesus at risk the night he was born?

Weren't the Romans after him? Or perhaps just poverty? She was a black nurse who believed that by holding the child and praying to her God that it would make a difference. She begged her God, rooted in the south of Georgia and the horror of slavery, a God that she honestly and truly believed had been there for her and for all the slaves.

But God had been missing in the closet when the sixteen-year-old soon-to-be serial sex offender ended any chance of a normal life for her. Anna Owens was born unlucky, God or no God.

Her phone buzzed. She'd gone back into the room after telling the black cop that she was having her period and needed to use the bathroom.

"Yes."

"I am a friend of Lana Turner's," the voice on the phone said. "She wants me to look after you. Help you out."

"Who?"

"Lana. She was staying at the Maverick with you. The black—"

"The old crazy lady?" Anna said.

"I think I can help you," the man said.

She heard something in his voice, maybe a kindness she'd been looking for her whole life. A man who could or might protect her.

"Yeah, I'm listening."

"Yes. A better job. Real money. You won't have to be out there on those streets. Where are you?"

"I'm in the fucking cop shop. Central Station. I'm yours—if you can get me the fuck out of here." She saw the black detective walking toward her.

"I'll be in touch," the man said and hung up.

"What's up, officer?" she said as Marvin approached.

"Happy birthday," he said. He looked disappointed. "I thought you'd lost your phone."

"I found it," she said.

She got up and slipped her phone into the back pocket of her dirty jeans. She heard a text ping, but didn't bother to look at it.

"Where are you going? There's nothing for you out there but trouble. Do you have any people? Mom or dad? I'll buy you a ticket back to Bellingham," Marvin said. "I'll take you to the airport, myself. Right now."

It was just more Do-Gooder talk. She'd heard it all before, a thousand times. There was no back there to think about, only memories that hurt. Why did the Do-Gooders always assume there was a back there?

"No one I want to see. But thanks," she said. "Have a nice day, officer."

She read a text from Thorpe as she pulled her stash from inside the toilet tank at King James's deserted room at the Maverick, still having her key. The other kids had already been picked up by other pimps, and in a hurry, too. A working girl in Bellingham had taught her how to turn off the water to the toilet's tank and use it as a stash. It had worked. The money the old whore had given her, wrapped in a condom to keep it dry, was sitting in the toilet tank where she'd left it.

She slipped the wad of cash into a Mickey Mouse backpack she found in the room, along with a few of her things the others had not been pilfered, and left. The carpet where King James had bled out was still stained, and would remain that way for years.

Thorpe called an hour later. He told her to walk to the Hotel Nikko on Mason Street and give the doorman her name, and he would call a cab for her.

A day later she was glad she had rolled with the old whore's man. Thorpe had paid for a hotel room at the Clift—a hotel she'd been in more than once to work—and a new wardrobe, and she hadn't had to blow anyone, yet. She posted a photo of herself on Instagram in her new clothes sitting in the famous Redwood Room, wearing bunny ears with a caption that read "X- Static to be here."

***

The Pacific Ocean was less than a mile away. O'Higgins could feel that as he stepped out of the parking structure under the aquarium—the cold. The fog had been pouring over the Great Highway moving in brutal strips, ocean swells dotted with surfers, like bits of black flotsam, as he drove toward the Panhandle. The Sunset, the city's most western neighborhood, drab and cold. The weird foggy neighborhood hiding the facades of houses, set cheek to jowl, facing the dark grey ocean. All of it needing a fresh coat of paint.

A thick, late-summer fog-like rain was leaving windshields caked. He crossed Tea Garden Drive, walking up and behind its famous bandstand and music concourse. Visitors to the park, heading to the aquarium or the De Young Museum, were wearing winter clothes. Some even held umbrellas. Tourists were easy to spot by their summer clothes, caught-out thinking that San Francisco had a summer at all. That was a lie—it was always winter in August. They wore shorts and tank tops and looked miserable, their knees pink from the cold.

He knew he was acting improperly, but it was part of the nightmare that had no limits and certainly not any rules. All he cared about as he climbed out of the car, carrying his wife's old briefcase, was not failing. His job, and everything he had built over the years—career, family—didn't matter. It all seemed ephemeral and not worth worrying about, a dream past and gone.

Emma could be dead, he thought as he hustled across the concourse, and yet he was acting as if she were alive. He had to, for his own sake.

Marvin called as he climbed along the bandstand and passed the food trucks lined up in the no-man's land— a service road closed to traffic.

"You there?"

"Yeah. Are you sure, Marvin? We're fucked if—if they find out. You know what will happen."

"Fuck it. Do it. I'm on Bryant Street. Call when it's done."

He'd gotten a photo with Seven Hill's text message. The photo showed a collection of benches surrounded by redwood trees, a stock photo pulled from somewhere of a specific place in the Arboretum. He showed it to the ticket taker at the Arboretum's entrance, an old woman with a fey smile buried in old sweaters and an Inca-style wool hat. She told him the photo was the new Redwood Grove picnic area, and unfolded a map of the Arboretum to explain how to find it.

"I used to come here as a kid," he said. "I don't remember it."

She drew on the map with a green highlighter. "The picnic area is new—the redwood trees aren't." She smiled.

He nodded and took the map with the women's highlighted direction.

She called after him: "Are you meeting someone?"

He didn't answer. His gaze fixed on the entrance. The idea that he would finally face his nemesis was all he could think of.

"We're closing in an hour, young man. You mustn't dawdle—but you have time to see it. I'm sure the young lady will love it," she said. "People like to propose there. It's a good choice, very popular for that. Proposals." She'd assumed his refusal to answer was a case of suitor's nerves. "Good luck—I'm sure she'll say yes!"

He turned and smiled weakly at her, holding the map she'd marked. He went through the gate and followed the path she'd outlined. It was just as beautiful as he remembered, even now in the mist of summer's winter. He'd come with his mother as a kid. She'd take them all here to play in October—San Francisco's October, when the weather was perfect—while she studied, finally getting a PhD in Irish History when he was in high school. The park and the Arboretum, especially, were some of the best memories he had of his childhood. The special freedom he had felt to run endlessly, his sisters left behind playing dolls near their mother.

He and his brother would play cowboys and Indians, and no corner of the place was unknown to them. Their mother, unlike so many American mothers, was not at all concerned or paranoid. She'd grown up in an Irish country village that had allowed children free rein—their safety guaranteed and unquestioned by a thousand years of village life. Paranoia, about molesters or worse, was something his mother didn't seem to know or acknowledge. Her children had sensed this and felt protected by it. Children, she believed, were safe in this place. So she'd let them run wild, be boys, while she studied.

That sense of freedom for children was gone, parents and children tethered together by fear. He felt his mother's presence as he walked through the iron gate, as if she might be around the corner waiting for him. It was overwhelming. He realized how much he missed her, and how angry he was with her for not telling him the truth about who he was.

The garden's paths were wide at the outset, great swaths of grass made grim by fog tendrils sweeping across them. The generous walkways gave way to more cloistered tunnel-trails as he went further into the green cantonment. He passed exotic Dr. Seuss trees—some of them bizarre, even frightening-looking, a sign giving their genus and Latin names. They were from South Africa. He passed a silent Japanese pier with an overlook and green pond that he'd pushed his brother into years before.

He saw the redwood grove to his right, a darker shaded place, slightly hostile looking. He moved the briefcase from his gun hand to his left— and for the first time since he'd been back from Iraq with the tremendous guilt of having survived, he felt oddly free of himself, of his past and his future, as if he had been dropped in from outer space, a death angel.

As he walked into the grove, the temperature seemed to drop. The air felt dank—an alive-feeling shrouded in gloom. The hulking redwood trees obscured each other, silent yet present, part past, part future. It was a kind of netherworld, where nature barred its door to any lie about life's meaning. There was a cold truth about mankind, if you could only sit long enough to glean it. No doubt the Indians had, he thought, and were stronger because of it.

Was the new paranoia everyone felt a kind of horrible fiction fronting for something else, something they couldn't understand? All the lies twisting them with their 5G-streaming power, day-and-night, an Orwellian power to mint fear passed on to their children, in a hundred ways.

The path narrowed, and was littered with a thick orange carpet of redwood needles. His dress shoes sank into the them, just as they had in his dream/hallucination. The damp cold got to him. It came through his light sport coat, biting into him.

He stopped and looked up into the redwoods trees that towered above him. He saw streamlined dark boughs wet with fog—light and dark places. He touched his weapon, the bulk of it under his coat. In a moment he would have the chance to put a bullet into the man they'd been chasing for months. He doubted the French girl was alive. This monster was simply having them on, and wanted to get paid on top of it.

The cold gripped him. He would have to fight the desire to shoot the man in cold blood, there and then. Everything was pushing him toward that … he had no governor.

Ahead were the huddled benches, looking wet and forlorn. A drop of fog-rain hit his hand, running between his fingers and down onto the briefcase. He thought he felt Emma's presence—that she was alive, that she was trying to speak to him, assure him that she was alive and that she was waiting for him to find her. That there was a chance. One chance.

He walked into the clearing. It was empty. His phone pinged, and he put down the briefcase and looked at the screen.

Leave the money and go … Instructions to follow.

He hesitated. He scanned the deserted gloomy picnic area, everything grey and mottled. He wanted to move, but felt unable to. He strained to see anything in the deserted place—then did as he'd been instructed and walked out the way he'd come, knowing that the killer was watching, and that he was close by.

He left the money in that gloomy wet theater of redwood trees for Emma's sake.

Chapter 24

"Why the girl, Lana?"

"She reminds me of you. She reminds me of us in LA."

"But you asked Thorpe to take her in—why?"

"Because it was him, or the streets. It's gotten worse—you've been gone. It's worse. The tricks are meaner," Lana said. "Hold my hand."

Cassie had come to SF General. Lana had developed a serious lung infection, and was moved from the county jail to the hospital. She looked horrible and frail. The young doctor Cassie had met weeks before was on duty, and vouched for her with the sheriff's deputy standing guard at the door that Cassie was family.

"Close the door, honey child—please."

Cassie went to the door and closed it. The guard had gone somewhere. "That man knows I can't run," Lana said. "You look good."

"I'm back at work," Cassie said. She'd lied to Gus. She'd told Lana the whole story the morning she'd returned from Central America. It had been their secret.

"For them? Those people?"

"Yeah."

"Did you tell your husband?"

"He threw me out. He found out about—about our past. He doesn't think I should be around our girls."

"He'll get over it." Lana started to cough and gripped her hand tightly. "I'm scared, baby girl. I should have—you know, gone with the church like my grandmother told me to. But I didn't. I went to LA instead."

They were silent, all those years pressing down on them. It seemed impossible, Cassie thought, that she could be looking at the same beautiful girl she'd met that first day on Sunset Boulevard.

"I'm glad you did," Cassie said finally. She sat on the edge of the bed. The fluorescent lights made everything look ugly and cheap. The oxygen device Lana had in her nose was coming out after the coughing spell, and she reached over and tried to adjust it.

Lana grabbed her hand before she could, surprising her. "Do you remember, back then, when I came to the house—in Malibu?"

"Of course I remember," Cassie said.

"You said when we were in the car, after we left—you said that if I ever needed you, you would be there for me."

Cassie nodded.

"I need you to do something for me, now." "

"Okay," Cassie said. "What?"

"It won't be easy," Lana said.

"Okay." She stroked Lana's hair. Lana had "good" hair, and had always been proud of it, part of the exotic beauty given to her by some European ancestor.

"The girl came here today—she left something. In the robe, in the bathroom. I asked her to bring it."

"What girl?"

"X-Static. She's a good girl. I want you to go and bring me the thing she left. I want you to bring it here, Cassie."

"What is it?"

"It's my ticket back to Chicago."

"What?"

"Yeah, I want to visit my people." She let go of Cassie's hand. "Go get it. You know I have people there. Go on. Get it."

Cassie went into the bathroom. She looked into the pocket of a hospital robe hanging on the door. She saw the drugstore red-capped syringe; she'd seen them ever since she was a child, and knew what it was. She looked out into the room.

Lana was trying to sit up in the bed. "Go on, now—you're all I got— out here in LA. I want to go home now. You can have the room, and my clothes."

Cassie looked at the syringe, its plunger brutal looking. The red cap over the needle. She understood what her friend wanted, and froze.

"You promised me." Lana was coughing again. The sound was ugly.

When Cassie had asked the doctor when Lana could leave, he'd just looked at her. She was never going to leave, he said. She'd had to wait a while after she'd heard the news, unable to go into Lana's room. She dug in the robe, pulled out the syringe and came to the bedside.

"I love you," Lana said. "Do you know that?"

"I know that." Tears rolled down her face. She remembered the drive back to their apartment on the 405. It had been early morning, the sun coming up. She was terrified and hurting, her wrists swollen. She'd wanted to die after he'd beaten her, and she'd realized that she was completely powerless to stop him. She'd begged the trick to stop. He'd laughed in her face and said that's what he'd paid all the god-damn money for. She still had nightmares that she was handcuffed to that bed, and just waiting for him to come back.

"That's the ticket," Lana said.

"Are you sure, Lana?"

"Only way I'm getting back to my grandma's—that ticket, right there, in your hand. I want you to do it. I want it to be you, honey child. And I want you to tell me we're going to the bus station, and that you'll visit, and that we're sisters … That's what I want to hear."

Cassie sat on the edge of the bed and knew she would do it. It was always there, that kind of love between them. She was shocked at how powerful and clean it was. It had never been touched by anything, never once. Even her children and husband were beyond it. It was a sacred love, like between soldiers.

"You gonna do it?"

Cassie nodded, wiping the tears away with her fingers. But they kept coming. Lana held out her arm, looked at her, and closed her eyes.

"Where are we?"

"We're in the car, and we're going to the bus station. We're on La Cienega."

"You going to come visit—when I get settled?"

"Yes. I'll come visit." Cassie leaned over and kissed her.

"I'm glad we went shopping—I want to look good…"

"You'll look pretty."

"How long does it take, the bus? I bet you a long time, huh. You got to go through Texas—Oklahoma…"

"It takes time, baby. You call when—" Cassie shoved the needle into the flesh, the way she'd seen her mother do so many times. For a moment she held back, her thumb on the plunger.

"I'll call," Lana said. "I promise."

"You see we're at the station," Cassie said. "I love you." She felt her thumb push the drug.

"I see it…"

"You'll call me when you—when you get there."

But Lana didn't answer. She was gone.

Cassie got up off the bed. For the first time in a long time, she felt alone. She put the syringe in her coat, then went and got the doctor. And then she left. In the car, she broke down sobbing.

***

It was cold. Emma moved back, away from the incoming tide. She thought she would drown, as indeed the first Indian families thought they might. But a Modoc boy, about the same age as Emma, wouldn't accept death. He kept looking for a way back and finally found it. It was a cleft, a separation in the dark igneous rock that he slipped though and saw that the cave was only part of a larger complex. The boy long ago, as Emma did now, saw the water coming from above—a rill of fresh water. Emma, too, slipped by the rock gate, her hands on the plastic bag the man had left her. She turned on the flashlight.

The path she saw led up, away from the ocean, the rill moving to the right. She bent and tasted the water. It was sweet and she cupped a handful and drank it. Her fingers were red from the cold.

She followed the path into the cave's interior, glad to be away from the tide that had moved in violently, bringing with it flotsam from the ocean. In just a short time she'd been forced back against the cave wall, watching the ocean move toward her, platinum at dusk.

It was then that she thought of the women she'd read about. She thought she heard their voices, of the women on the train she'd read about. French women, young women, some her age, who had been caught by the Nazis, women of the resistance who were heading for the camps in Germany. They had held hands, rich women and poor women who'd joined the French Resistance in university and peasant women angered that the Germans stole everything from their farms. They had been women who in normal times would never have spoken out, and who now rode a train in winter toward the death camps…

She'd watched the cold ocean move inexorably toward her, back against the rocks, no escape, no help, no one. She'd screamed in despair, and it was when she thought her fear would swamp her that the sounds of the women, their whispers, took hold of her like a force and she didn't accept her fear or the ocean coming for her. She would not accept death.

The scream went into the mouth of the cave, its sharp report mixing with the sound of the tide beating into the cave, the foam and flotsam rocking to some internal ocean rhythm that was timeless, dumb and smart all at once. The earth's heartbeat was a warning that despair was not the way to live. Life filled her lungs where the air of fear had built up and exploded. She'd turned and against all logic, searched for some way out—and found it just as the Indian boy had found it. He had done it at night, without light, in the pitch dark. He'd turned to his people and in his language called to his mother. Driftwood was lit and they'd escaped as Emma now escaped, into mother earth—into a womb of darkness and fluids, a few yellowish shards of light sent out by her flashlight. Womb-comfort was in the air… the family with the boy in the lead had all sensed it that night, two centuries before. Mother earth, our first and foremost memory: the push-pulse of life as we lie in the womb waiting, aware.

"I am with you now," Emma said aloud. Instead of the walls of the cave, she could see the women riding toward Ravensbrück. She saw their faces projected on the cave wall like scenes from a movie. She had not eaten for days, and it was having its effect on her mind.

She walked up the path, around her the visions of the women as they huddled tired and hungry on the way to the death camp, the train car ice cold.

"Aren't you frightened?" Emma said. She stopped the flashlight's beam, catching driftwood dragged into the cave by the Modoc family. A place lay ahead. It was all too much, these two worlds coming together, here in this lost place. She knew she was losing her mind, but there was nothing for it. She shone the beam of her light ahead and moved on.

She felt something else, a male presence. She'd felt it before, a sense that someone out there was looking for her. She stopped again and let the presence grow. She held up her hand like an antenna, trying to bring it in closer.

***

He was tripping. The session had started normally. The nurse had given him his dose and closed the door. A resident, a young Jewish kid, had sat across from him. He seemed impossibly young.

"Good afternoon, Detective," the kid said.

O'Higgins nodded. He watched the kid make a note on his clipboard. The kid reminded him of the young men under his command, with his untainted, impossibly fresh-faced youth.

He closed his eyes and saw the airplane that had brought them to Iraq. He felt its vibrations the way he had that day. He was twenty-two. He had not yet taken anyone's life, so it was a different feeling as they flew toward a war that they had not been prepared for. They had arrived clean and left dirty-minded and slightly sinister, because it was a war against fear and loathing—with the pretense of anything higher gone on the quiet flight home.

Oddly it was not a war so much as an occupation, with its loathsome endless missions to nowhere of real importance, no signal that victory was even the point. A soldier at the edge of his fear had once sung in the halftrack: *I know a place—I'll take you there.*

They were following a convoy, its rear guard, and expected to be the target of some IED. It was constant, the pressure-fear, and the boy had just busted out singing to calm himself.

All right now come on come on I'll take you there... I know a place you all... nobody crying, Ain't nobody worrying... I'll take you there. Mercy now I'm calling...

They got through that day. A female sniper had shot the boy two days later as he was pulling his helmet on. The helmet rolled out into the road and lay there as the medics tried in vain to save him.

O'Higgins started to sing without realizing it, his knee moving to the song, the boy singing it in the halftrack... all the men taking comfort like slaves on a plantation must have, and he had understood that day that they were working for the Man, the same asshole that had taught him nothing about the eternal lessons of war. The old men who sat in Washington laughing and drinking fine wine while they rode on into a bloody eternity, forced to kill the innocent and the guilty.

The Jewish kid, a third-year med student who would end up leaving the profession and following in his father's footsteps in LA as a movie producer, was a little frightened by the big Irishman rocking to a song he'd never heard. He'd grown up with the simple minded and profoundly empty rap music. In his protected, privileged world, the old songs from the '60s had failed to get to his generation. The songs that had lifted people up once. The lyrics were literally non-sensical to him. Let me take you where? He had no idea, and that scared him. He would never see war, but he would write two war movies about cool ultra-elite troops, the new gods, all of it a pack of lies pulled out of his ass when he was high on coke.

Ain't nobody worrying... I'll take you there... That's right. O'Higgins, high, was moving his big body to some terrible rhythm that was a mixture of red dust and sudden death, the sight of the helmet. He'd picked it up and it was the first and last time he had cried in Iraq. No glory here, no bands to strike up the stirring music of a false patriotism.

"Are you okay?" The Jewish kid turned and looked at the door. He was afraid to ask the attending nurse for help. He'd never made decisions for himself. His was a generation of play dates and helicopter mothers and wipe-your-ass nannies.

O'Higgins was tripping and almost two generations away from his infantile expression. He was in Iraq. He was in that death alley, red and dusty, and he was dancing and singing—the black kid, and him. They were learning steps as if they were to star in a musical called "It's All Fucked Up and Nothing Makes Sense." He and the kid were looking at each other, their sand googles on, their combat boots kicking up dust... Now other soldiers were joining them, the dead and alive.

"Hit it," O'Higgins yelled at the top of his voice. "Come on, hit it!"

"*I'll take you there... Let me take you there. Ain't nobody crazy I'll take you there.*"

The Jewish kid got up and went to get help. He was scared. He'd never seen a man as big as O'Higgins dancing in a small room, tears of joy rolling down his face as he and his comrades danced.

I know a place you all... I'll take you there... Ain't nobody crying, I'll take you there.

The kid never came back. It was all too much for him. They called Dr. Schneider from her office. She came into the room, saw O'Higgins, and smiled. She'd never been afraid of anything, even the absurd— much less the wonderful. She stayed with him, watching him finally go to the corner of the small room and sit, his back to the wall.

"You're beautiful," he said, looking at her. "You know, in that way. You know that way? Men like—that way you women have. It's special. I like you."

"What way is that, Detective?" Schneider said.

"Well… it's on the tip of my tongue. That way. You know—that men like."

"Can I leave you alone? Are you all right? The guide—"

"The kid?"

"You freaked him out. Upset him."

"I upset him?" He saw the doctor move, and the acid flash was of her moving like those first moving pictures, motion as a flipped-through deck of cards. "I came because you expected me. I shouldn't have today," he said. "Not today of all days."

"Thank you. I know," she said. "But this is important, too."

"I feel different."

"You're high. You should feel different."

"No. Really, truly, different."

"Come see me next week, okay? We'll have a session. Okay?"

He nodded, and she left. He thought of getting up, but he was still high. He had a sense of floating. The sense that the floor under him was undulating. The window seemed strange, the curtain mottled.

He closed his eyes, and it was then that he had the first vision. He saw Emma Barre. She was standing in a passage. She was alive.

He opened his eyes, the room's walls darker and seemingly in some kind of 3D transition. He looked around the room and saw the walls of a cave. He could hear the roar of the ocean. He saw Emma again, on the walls, as if he were seeing a film.

He stood up, unsteady, and walked to the wall where her image was. She turned and looked up at him. She was wearing a peacoat and jeans.

The coat was too large for her. She held her hand up, fingers spread.

"Emma?" She turned away and walked further into the cave. The walls went dark, but there was a tremendous crashing sound of surf.

He slid down the wall, hyperventilating. For the first time since he'd started the trial, he felt frightened.

"It was her. You have to find her."

He looked up and saw the dead English girl. She was as they'd found her: her panties dirty, her wrists marked and blue, her hair greasy and matted.

"Go away," he said. "You're not real! Are you real?"

He looked at her.

"You have to find her, or you aren't real. You're a fiction, an adopted fiction that belongs to no one. Is that what you want to be— a failure? You failed your wife, didn't you? You intend to fail again? Is that what makes you feel better? So, you can feel sorry for yourself? You failed me, didn't you? Didn't you? You aren't that smart, Detective. Face it for once in your life. Look at me."

He opened his eyes. He had hoped the English girl would go away. He knew, or thought he knew, that she wasn't real.

"You aren't real," he said. "You aren't!"

"I am as real as you are," she said.

Chapter 25

"Let's get something straight. I don't like you," Cassie said. "But Lana did. She cared about you."

"The old whore?" the girl said.

"Yeah. So I'm going to help you. But if you screw with me, it will be a different story. Now we're going to go to a party … You got two days to learn some shit. If you don't learn it, we both may be in trouble with Thorpe. Is that clear? You got that straight, little girl?"

"How did you know her—the old whore?" X-static said.

"Her name was Lana," Cassie said. "If you call her that again, I'll beat you until you can't stand up."

"Yeah— okay. Lana."

"We came up in the business together. She was my sister." "

"You some old bitches," the girl said.

Cassie nodded her head and broke a cold smile. It was true, she realized, looking at the girl. Everything about the young woman standing in front of her seemed fresh, except her eyes. They told a story much the same as her own. They were dirt people. The phrase came to her: Dirt People. Pathetic, Walmart-quality whores built in America's destroyed narco-neighborhoods. Her mother, and her mother, and her mother before her— no doubt crashed through the womb without a prayer, bloody and new. In America, money talked, and Dirt People walked. They were the cum-stained, the drug-addicted, the helpless. They were the dregs, and no matter how far she'd climbed the social ladder, it would always be written in her heart.

Perhaps Marvin was right, she thought. After all, she was a killer and a whore, and that was the true story. The soccer mother had been a well-intended lie. Look how quickly she'd agreed to go back to her old life. Lana was dead, and she was back to what she'd once been.

Why?

The fact was that she had a sense of power that she'd never had before meeting Gus. It was a simple-minded power reserved usually for men, and she'd missed it. That was the horrible truth. No turning away now.

Thorpe had put X-Static in some designer skinny jeans, taking the girl to Nordstrom on Market Street. The three of them had gone together, and it reminded Cassie of the first time Thorpe had taken Lana and her shopping on Rodeo Drive. She'd remembered the way the "old" women on that famous street had smirked at the three of them, sensing that they didn't belong to their Beverly Hills club. The club that she'd learned about later, in a hundred different mansions from London to Madrid—it was the club that ran the world and relished its power over the Dirt People.

She was the wild card, the avenger who had crawled out from under some tub of lard who'd pawed her over dinner and then fucked her. She had turned over his ace of spades and put a bullet in his face. It was a bullet that none of her ancestors had been able to fire. But she had. And it felt good. That was the truth. She realized it all at once, standing in front of what she must have looked like, years before. Young, ambitious, and dead inside.

The girl had cleaned up nice. She was the kind of girl Cassie knew the old rich guys would drool over. It was the schoolgirl ponytail and the skinny ass. Thorpe knew his business.

"Yeah, well, old or not, honey, you're going to be working with me. And that's the name of that tune. School's in session."

"Are you trying to scare me? I'm not scared of you. I came up on the street, bitch."

Cassie crossed the living room. The Latin girl and Thorpe had gone back to LA. It would just be the two of them, they'd decided. The Latin girl was a dope fiend, and Cassie wasn't having it.

"How old are you?"

"Eighteen."

"You want to see nineteen?"

"Yeah."

"You ever kill anybody?"

"No."

"It was Lana who did it, right? Your man?" The girl nodded.

Cassie could tell it had scared her. Lana's cold-bloodedness had frightened her, and it showed on her face "She cut him?" Cassie asked.

"Yeah—straight up, cut the man's throat. Bitch wasn't playing. He dropped, just like that. Lights out."

"You're going to start by dropping the street talk. Cursing. You got to talk like they do. The rich guys. That's got to change if you want to make it off the street. You want to make the brick, don't you? Forty G's, maybe more, for a fuck? Right?"

"Yeah. Why not."

"Yes—yes. Why not. Don't say 'yeah.' Go ahead, say it." "Yes. Yes. Why not."

"And your Christian name—what is it?"

"What do you mean?"

"The name your momma and daddy gave you. What is it?"

"Anna. Anna Owens."

"Okay. Lose the Owens. We'll make it Anna Harley. Got it?"

"Yeah—yes. Anna Harley. Cool," X-Static said.

"Tilt your head when you say it. Look them in the eye. They love that. You're just as good as they are—that's the first lesson. They pay more if they think you're just like their daughter's best friend. You need a legend."

"What's that?"

"A personal history. One you talk about after you're done fucking them and they ask for it. They all will want to know why you're a whore and not in school studying Italian. You want to tell them a good, sad story. They'll pay more for that. I used to tell them my mother was a missionary and she disappeared saving children in Africa, and that we came over on the Mayflower. Don't worry, we'll come up with something good."

The girl looked at her. It was starting to sink in she was, at last, going to get off the streets. It scared her, because the street was what she knew.

***

"So who is going to do it?" Marvin asked. "Me or you?"

They were waiting for a prisoner to be brought down for an interview. It was the Russian's girlfriend. She was going to confess to shooting the Russian on Gold Mine Drive, and they could put the murder down as solved. "It won't be long now, right? He's going to call. About Emma? That's what he said?"

"Yeah, that's what he wrote," O'Higgins said.

"So—me or you?"

O'Higgins looked at him. Marvin looked angry. It was because of Cassie, O'Higgins knew. She hadn't come home, and Marvin was angry, probably at himself for having thrown her out in the first place.

"How are the girls doing?" O'Higgins asked.

"How do you think they're doing? They want to know where their mother is," Marvin said. "Are you going to answer my question or not? I want to know."

"Does it matter, really?"

"Yeah, it does."

"We don't know how this is going to come down. He said nothing, only that he was going to text and he would give us the girl and we would give him the Bitcoin."

"You know she's probably dead," Marvin said. "Right? Emma."

"No. We don't know that, Marvin. I think he wants the rest of the money. He knows we won't give it to him if we don't see the girl. He knows that."

"Why won't Cassie come home?" Marvin said.

He was high, O'Higgins realized. He must have had a couple at lunch while O'Higgins had been at the hospital.

"She's angry." He couldn't bring himself to tell Marvin that he'd seen Cassie and Thorpe together, and only God knew what they were up to.

"Is she still staying at your place?"

"No."

"Her friend died, the one who—that woman she knew in LA," Marvin said. "The one we banged up for killing the pimp."

"I heard," O'Higgins said.

"She OD'ed at SF General. I heard that Cassie was the one who found her," Marvin said. "I don't get any of it. That's the truth. It was all normal before her friend showed up. And then it all changed."

"She's still your wife, man. She's still the same woman you married."

"I forgave her. But she won't come back home. Why?"

"I don't know."

"Why are your eyes dilated all the time, Mike? Is that part of this? Is there something going on between you two, you want to tell me about? Are you taking drugs? Is that it? Are the two of you on drugs?"

"Don't talk crazy, Marvin."

The Russian girl, a Ukrainian national, came down from the county jail and changed her story. She said she'd been threatened. She had nothing to do with it, she told them. She'd just hired one of the best criminal lawyers in San Francisco. They had to let her go, as she gave them an alibi that turned out to be airtight. She'd been in LA.

Seven Hills texted as they were heading out for a required "sensitivity" training class.

I'll give her to you in the park... half hour... do not. I repeat, do not fuck with me. Location to follow.

"We promised Barre we'd tell him," O'Higgins said, watching Marvin

206

read the text.

"Well call him the fuck up, then." Marvin said.

Marvin, driving, swung the Ford out into traffic and hit a left on Sixth Street, sliding the car so O' Higgins thought they'd flip. It was the first acid flashback. The doctors had failed to mention that after several sessions he might have them. Maybe they just hadn't thought it was important to tell him.

"Oh, stand by me," Marvin sang. "Whenever you're in trouble, stand by me. And when the land is dark... I won't be afraid ... Right, white boy?"

"You're driving too fast," O'Higgins said. "Yeah, well I'm the man, aren't I?"

"You're drunk," O'Higgins said. *And I'm seeing things*, he thought. They ran the light at Mission Street.

Chapter 26

Seven Hills had texted them a photo of the bandstand in Golden Gate Park while they'd driven up Market Street. At times the Ford seemed to be flexing, the car's dashboard looking more like a face of some plastic creature, its dials like a video game. The flashes— hallucinations—were coming and going. It had never happened before with this intensity. The Ford seemed to sway as if their car were a trolley… Pedestrians on the street became holographic blurs, then snapped into clear view, but grey and dismal. His vision was turbulent: some things went too fast, others moved too slow. He'd said nothing to Marvin, who was driving. They rode in silence, just the sound of traffic and the police radio breaking in.

Seven Hills texted as they came up by the Juvenile Hall at Twin Peaks in heavy traffic:.

Send your partner up to the top of the De Young museum—the Observation Deck. He can see the girl. I'll give you 30 minutes to get up here. He hands the flash drive over. I take the elevator down with the drive and the girl. Your pal stays up there. I let the girl go in the sculpture garden, behind the De Young's café. Do you know it? The lawn?

O'Higgins texted back: **Yeah, I know it.**

It had been almost a year since the first girl had gone missing. Seven Hills was no longer a stranger. He had become part of their lives, day in and day out. Perhaps he'd driven them mad. It occurred to O'Higgins that they were confronting not only a superior intelligence, but an influence of the worst kind. Had he managed to scar them, change them? Had they allowed the killer to force them to become instruments of his mindless cruelty?

O'Higgins had never granted him that corrupting moral influence, but he felt it now. It was so obvious. He'd beaten them before, so he was cocky, and for good reason. He was in possession of the girl, and he was sure of himself. Confident. That very confidence was a strange catalyst, destroying O'Higgins's own sense of right and wrong.

"The De Young. The observation deck. He wants you. He'll leave Emma in the sculpture garden after he gets the thumb drive." O'Higgins looked at Marvin. He realized Marvin was not just high, but was losing it. It unnerved him.

His phone pinged again.

I want to see you, O'Higgins, standing on the bandstand. I want you to handcuff yourself to the railing. I'll see you from the Observation Deck. If I see that you don't lock the cuff and throw the key, I shoot the girl. Text me a photo of your handcuffed wrist. You got that?

OK, O'Higgins wrote. He read the text to Marvin.

"So it's up to me," Marvin said. "Good. Motherfucker."

"You can't shoot him up there," O'Higgins said. "There's too many people. No way can you risk it. And he knows it. It's pretty smart, to exchange there in a crowd."

"Why the fuck not?"

"Because—Jesus, Marvin. What the fuck? What's wrong with you, man? That observation deck is always full of people—kids and mothers— and he knows it."

They rode in silence down Ninth Avenue, Marvin still driving too fast. They entered Golden Gate Park, Marvin going through the red light at Lincoln Way and just missing a Muni Bus going west. The bus looked gigantic as it barreled toward them, blaring its horn extra loud.

O'Higgins grabbed the arm rest and quailed, thinking they might be T-boned. He turned and looked up at the bus driver. The man's Fu Manchu mustache was ridiculous, but he could see the driver's frightened paralyzed expression. They just made it by the bus as the driver lay on his horn, the sound of it chasing them as they nosed down onto Martin Luther King Drive.

Marvin glanced over at him, slowing, realizing that O'Higgins was not right in the head. It wasn't like him to show that kind of fear. O'Higgins was acting like a child, and not the ex-Marine who had pulled him down the stairs to safety that morning in the Mission.

"Why your eyes always dilated, man? Huh? You ever going to tell me the truth, Mike? Or do I have to sit here and guess about what the fuck is going on with you?"

"You have to calm down, Marvin. That's what you have to do," O'Higgins said in almost a whisper. He could see the wide tree-studded concourse opposite the museum and the aquarium, anchored by the bandstand between them. He'd played here as a boy, and knew it intimately; his parents' house was only a few blocks away.

It all seemed out of control: the manic drive, their near accident, symbolic of lives that were falling apart. Because of that, they could not succeed. The monster was going to beat them again. Emma would die because they were not up to it anymore. Something was wrong with them that he'd failed to see or understand until now, something terribly wrong since the shootout. Marvin had not been the same since… O'Higgins saw them for what they'd become: two middle-aged men who were battling demons that were winning. Too much had gone wrong in their lives, each year, slowly weighing them down until they were sinking, trammeled by their failures.

Marvin pulled the Ford off Martin Luther King Drive and into the service road behind the famous bandstand to their right, passing the queue of food trucks parked along the service road. To their left was the new De Young Museum, a dark several-story monolith; to their right the Academy of Science, its white marble facade a positive to the De Young's black-walled negative charge.

"You'll be alone," O'Higgins said. "He might not be. Have you thought

210

of that? That maybe it was never one guy."

"I don't give a shit. I'll stop him if I see the girl. I just need to see Emma, and his ass is mine." Marvin glanced at his watch. "We're ten minutes down. Come on, Mike! He's up there counting."

O'Higgins got out of the Ford and handed Marvin the thumb drive. As soon as he walked out on the bandstand, Seven Hills would be able to see him from the museum's observation deck. He took out his handcuffs, slipped one over his wrist and emerged onto the stage.

It was a brilliant day, the fog having cleared. He looked up at the black tower jutting above the Museum's top floor that marked the museum's observation deck—a separate, smaller story, almost as if the architect had blundered.

He'd been there for his daughter's fifteenth birthday with a gaggle of young girls, his daughter's mates from the dance school. He saw his daughter laughing, looking at him, her chestnut hair brilliant, dazzling. His wife taking photos…

He took his eyes off the tower and found the railing that followed the steps up to the bandstand from the concourse. He walked halfway down the steps and locked the other end of the handcuffs to the iron railing. A couple of tourists, standing on the bandstand, watched him do it and decided to move on. He heard the metal ratchet of the lock.

A gaggle of tourists crossing the concourse seemed to shimmer, as if they wore special clothes. He heard the click of the cuffs again, and then again—auditory hallucination. He realized that he might have people nearby and he looked, but everyone passing seemed uninterested, not noticing what he'd done.

He spotted Marvin disappearing into the front of the museum. He held the cuff's key in his fingers—he had a spare, would Seven Hills know that? Probably not, he decided. He finally tossed the key down the stairs and raised his hand, so the monster could see him. He took a photo of his manacled wrist with his iPhone and texted it to him.

He had a sense at that precise moment of Emma, of her person, a physical sense of her being alive. It was the strangest feeling he'd ever had. It was as if they were in a house together and he'd heard some quiet cue, the way he heard his daughter in her room. He could always tell when his daughter was in the house. It was that feeling. "Emma, I'm here. Don't give up. Please. For both of us. Don't you dare give up. We'll find you. I swear it."

***

Marvin pushed open the museum's fourteen-foot door, the entrance to the hulking new museum so out of character with the rest of the Belle Epoque style that once marked the city's public buildings. It was giving way to the brutally modern, encapsulating the city's speed-of-greed changes, the brave new skyline its out-of-control manifesto. The military-industrial-information juggernaut that had razed the former city was building a dystopian perfection from the ground up, each moment shared on Facebook and captured in countless tourist selfies. The streets were full of starry-eyed wannabe Mark Zuckerbergs, all in the archetypal hoodies, and all in penury. The young had no idea what they were part of. They had no memory of anything but their glowing know-it-all screens, constantly cueing them for their next thought—electronically groomed by their masters.

People noticed the crazy look in Marvin's eye. The alcohol was wearing off. He'd started to sweat, his shirt sticking to his skin. He felt his gun hand pulsate—throb, in fact, as if all his hate were lodged there waiting its chance. *I'll kill him.*

He thought of the missing girl's father as he approached the security guard just inside the massive lobby-cum-gallery. The tone of Barre's voice over the phone when they'd called him from the car. "Please, bring Emma back to us."

The words had had a galvanizing effect on them both. The helpless father's voice, so reminiscent of the other father's, had sealed the monster's fate: He'd never live to see the inside of any jail. He'd never live to sit in front of a jury of his "peers" who might decide he was simply mentally ill and therefore needed to be pitied. No jury would ever find the English girl on that terrible morning in February, her body fog-wet and stiff; her eyes cold, no life in them—horrible milky eyes. No jury would see the look on her parents' face when they'd heard the news of her brutal murder. No jury would hear the ululations from the mother who had driven her daughter to Heathrow, both women crying as mother and daughter said goodbye for the last time. She was going to America, after all. What could happen to her?

"The Observation Deck?" Marvin said to the guard.

The man pointed across the enormous lobby. "Elevator, at the rear," he said.

Everything seemed normal as Marvin Lee crossed the lobby of the De Young Museum at noon and disappeared. The earth spun on its axis as it always had, evil or no evil. The noontime sun was, as expected, directly overhead as the elevator doors closed in front of him. He felt the slightly sticky polymer-plastic of his pistol's grip. He tipped the Glock out of its holster.

He felt himself being dragged down the stairs in the Mission, heard the sound of automatic weapons fire, saw the stark blue sky—the way it looked as he thought he was going to die, so blue.

But not today. Not today.

He remembered how O'Higgins returned fire and dragged him by the collar, chin tucked down.

The elevator doors opened behind him, and he had to turn to exit into the bright light from the room's ceiling-to-floor windows, blinding. It was a savage light—a real force.

Outside, the De Young's fortress-like, high-polished marble walls, east facing, reflected the few clouds drifting in the August sky. No one noticed the handcuffed white man at the foot of the bandstand across the road. Something about the noontime sun obscured details, swallowed them whole. What you got was the full fleet of humanity: tourists, homeless, dog walkers, college students—cut moments. Their images moved by in bits of old-school film— grainy color-coded life vivisections, saying whatever was going to happen, it was happening now. Look!

***

Emma Barre had been talking to herself. She looked behind her. The waves pressed the cave's entrance, shattering in white billows of spray that overwhelmed the cave's entrance, crashing as if Neptune might walk out of them holding his trident.

She'd gone on. Her flashlight was the guide. She had no other light. But she'd pressed on, partly out of boredom, and partly to travel to the end of her known world. The images of the train and the women inside its carriage—silent faces, frightened faces of women on the way to certain death. Confusion in the carriage. Germany at night... Water was passed in a wine bottle to what must have been a woman who had simply given up and collapsed.

Snippets of French came to Emma, as if she was writing captions for the scenes she was seeing. Why these scenes? Why? The women—from all walks of French life, Emma had read. Resistence fighters gathered up by the French police, first in Paris, sent on finally to Germany... They huddled with faces bathed in a strange light, filling up the darkness, and she would stop and watch them as if she were in a theater.

When you starve, you gain a sharpness... nothing between you and existence, none of the entropy of normal life's digestion. All the meaningless bits disappear, Emma thought. She heard the rumble of the train, heard its cold whistle as it made for the Fatherland. Flashing lights— perhaps a crossing, or road, that showed through the slates of the cattle-car; the train slowing, swaying. A wealthy Parisian socialite, still wearing the fox fur she'd been arrested in, pushed a note out the slates of the cattle car. Emma, facing the cave wall, saw the note, projected and large, as it floated to the ground. The train's caboose's sole red light rushed on, finally swallowed by the night. The note would be found by some sympathetic French peasant and sent on to Paris…

My name is Nora and I am the daughter of Jack and Louise. I am being taken perhaps to Germany on a train for being a member of the resistance. Tell my parents. They live in the 15th arrondissement at 14, rue Stanislas. God bless you…. Vive la Resistance! Vive la France!

Emma turned away from the images and went down the cave's sandy trail, which got wider as she headed uphill. The cave's walls got higher. It was another world here. She saw driftwood that had been washed up on some King Tide, perhaps, left bone-like, smooth. The sand was dry, so she it would be safe from the tide.

She looked in the bag the Monster had given her and saw that he'd put in a gas-fired match gun. She'd missed it before. It produced a single flame when the trigger was pulled. Her parents had one sitting in a basket by their fireplace at their ski house in Val Thorens.

She built a fire, enjoying the work. At least for now, she was free of him. She walked about collecting the right bits of driftwood, and after making a beehive shape, she lit a fire, the smallest twigs at the base. It sprung to life. The sound of the wood being bitten by the flames unheard. She squatted by the growing fire. The heavy peacoat seemed to weigh her down.

She stared at her boots. So clean the day she'd pulled them from her suitcase, they were filthy now. She'd not bathed in days. She didn't dare look up, too afraid that the images that had hounded her would appear again, and she would have to explain them to herself again. If she couldn't explain them, she would have to admit, that perhaps she was mad, and incapable of any kind of rational thought. If so, she might as well be dead.

Would he come back for her? The gold-blue tones of the flames rose as she added more of the sentient-looking driftwood. The smoke trailed up, and she realized that there was a natural vent above. It was the same discovery that the Indian family had made two hundred years before, smiling, taking it as a good sign. She watched the smoke climb like white fingers into the dark.

If she could become smoke for just as long as it took to climb to the top and escape? The light from the fire exposed the enormity of the cavern. Each log she brought amplified the huge space above her.

Why haven't I cried? she wondered, staring into the blue flames. At one point after he'd touched her, she'd wanted to cry and wash herself.

She looked at her dirty hands. The life line on her right palm was dark, the line dirty; it looked like an ink stain. Her father, when she was small, would tell her stories about her future using the life line as a map. She would go to university, he told her. She would marry, he told her. She'd hoped it would be a boy like her father, with glasses and a quick smile.

Had her father seen the cave? Had he seen the Monster? No, of course not. No one sees Evil until it's too late and too big to fight.

That was the problem with evil: it appeared out of nowhere. Her head was not right. It couldn't be. How could it be? She felt the Monster inside her. The way it felt. Every time she thought of that physical feeling, she wanted to die. Could she be pregnant? No one could have believed it. Her parents had kept from her the truth of life . . . Love the sinner, hate the sin. What if she was pregnant with the unthinkable?

How stupid she'd been. She wanted to kill the Monster, blot him out, free herself. And what of the child? She would have to hate it—but it was innocent? That was the impossible truth. It would be innocent...

She looked up at the cave wall, expecting to see the frightening image of the train car and the women's wan faces as they rushed through time, keeping their horrible appointment with history. Instead she saw a park, a shimmering park, as if she were a bird flying above it. And she heard a voice, so clear that it startled her—a man's voice, as if the cave were hiding someone.

"Emma, I'm here. Don't give up. Please. For both of us. Don't you dare give up. I'll find you. I promise."

***

Hallucinating … The food trucks on the service road behind the bandstand became one long truck with various colors, then a monstrous snake-like thing. What good could he be to Marvin?

Can I kill him like this?

The drug was still having its way with him. The idea of pulling his pistol and killing their enemy was fantastical. He touched his weapon; it felt strange, alien.

His phone rang. He looked at the screen. It was Asha; he saw her name. He thought of answering it, but let it go to voice mail.

"Hey mister, what's wrong? Why are you chained to that?" A Chinese-American kid, about ten, was looking at him. His parents were staring at O'Higgins. They called the boy away in Mandarin. He smiled at O'Higgins before he turned and ran toward his mother.

His phone rang again. It was Asha, calling again from India—or was it? He looked at the screen and saw the image of Ganesh riding a mouse. He dropped his phone, saw it tumble down the concrete stairs—and with it, his extra key to the handcuffs that bound him.

He pulled on the cuffs. Looking at the museum across the way— it was reflecting the summer sky—he froze. He saw a line of elephants crossing the concourse, a canopy on one of them, gold cloth, shimmering. At his feet he saw a ring of cobras, their heads bobbing, their grey hoods puffed up, ready to strike at him.

He screamed. He didn't realize he'd screamed. Across the noontime his voice, so masculine and so frightened, rang around the trees and hit the ears of strangers. Some ignored it. Some stopped and looked out toward the bandstand, but because of the sunlight, they couldn't make anything out. It was too intense. But then the scream issued again, and a few people instinctually turned toward it. Something was so horrible, and so human, in that cry, that even the coldest, most alienated, couldn't help but respond in some way. For a moment the people in the park, tourists and native, were back ten thousand years and part of a tribe with tribal instincts.

Someone was hurt.

***

"Thumb drive," a woman's voice said.

Marvin, having looked carefully for Emma amongst the crowd of people, studying each face carefully, his sport coat unbuttoned, his hand on his Glock, had not seen her anywhere. He walked finally to the huge windows. Below he could see the aquarium and the bandstand. He could clearly make out O'Higgins.

Whoever had spoken to him was directly behind him. He pulled the Glock, heard it clear the plastic holster.

"Thumb drive," the voice repeated.

He felt something poke him in the small of his back. It was him, and he was armed. He dropped the thumb drive. He heard it hit the floor. He looked in the reflection of the glass and saw a woman, a blonde, with long hair stoop and pick it up. She was shorter, so he could make out only the top of her head as she bent down. When she stood up, he saw she was wearing dark glasses with large lenses, helping hide her face. She held a pistol in her left hand. She prodded him in the back with it a second time.

He dropped the Glock, heard it hit the floor. Someone must have seen it, as he heard a woman scream.

The blonde fired a round. He thought, when it went off, that she'd shot him. The shot caused a panic in the crowd: people screaming, running, trying to find cover.

He turned, and the blonde was gone. He bent down and picked up his weapon. He pushed people out of the way, heading back toward the elevator. He caught a glimpse of the woman a few yards ahead of him. But he couldn't move quickly because of the crush of people, and certainly couldn't fire his weapon. He saw the face of a child and slowed down, realizing what the woman might do. He started off again more deliberately, careful.

218

The blonde had a random tall Asian girl by the neck, and stood with her back to the elevator door. She had to wait for the doors to open. He was sure the hostage was a random tourist, as it clearly wasn't Emma Barre.

Marvin had a good look at the blonde. She was young, with long hair and dark glasses, black yoga pants. She had a revolver, its barrel shoved up under the girl's jaw, so that it forced her captive's face up.

He ignored the screaming. An elderly female docent came forward as if the blonde were simply a naughty child. The women pulled the gun from the girl's chin and shot the docent. The second shot created an even greater panic.

The elevator door opened behind the blonde. She backed into the elevator still holding the Asian girl, looking straight at Marvin. The two of the them locked eyes. He thought he might have a clear shot, but she drew the girl in front of her and the elevator door closed.

The docent would bleed out if nothing were done. Marvin knelt next to the woman, who was writhing in pain. The bullet had passed all the way through her upper arm.

He pulled out his phone, called 911, and asked for an ambulance. He told the woman to hang on. She was in shock, her face white. Marvin pressed as hard as he could directly on the entrance wound, but it was arterial bleeding and came in spurts. The blood pushed out around his fingers, an oily feel to it. He pressed harder and looked for help.

"Any doctors?" he shouted. No one came forward.

He placed his left hand on top of his right, pressing as hard as he could. It helped. The people around him were still crouching down, some mothers lying on top of their kids, all of them watching him. Several people had gotten on their phones and were calling for help. All of it played out in the incredibly intense sunlight, pouring through the floor-to-ceiling windows at noon.

He realized, to his horror, that if he called O'Higgins to warn him, he would have to lift his hands away from the woman's wound and she would surely die.

Chapter 27

"So—she escaped?" Schneider said. "This accomplice?"

"Yes," O'Higgins said.

He'd come to Dr. Schneider's office on California Street to tell her he was going to leave the experiment. He was suffering from flashbacks, and he'd not been warned he might experience them. He'd tried to be calm, but he felt anything but calm. He was angry and blamed the treatment for the shitshow at the museum.

"It was our chance and we failed. I'm sure the girl—Emma—is dead now. And it's our fault. He's not working alone."

"You're sure you were—you're sure you were impaired because of the drug?"

"Yes. Of course, I'm sure," he said.

The doctor looked away. She heard the hostility in his voice.

"We've not had any reports of this kind of after-session experience. I don't know what to say. I'll look into it. I promise. I'll get to the bottom of it, Michael. But please don't leave the trial, yet. I think it was doing you good—that it has been therapeutic. Am I right?"

"I can sleep for long stretches. And the dream—the one that—the one about the English girl, I've stopped having it lately."

"Since you started the trial?"

"Yes."

"What else did you notice?"

"I don't fly off the handle—not like before. I don't feel the—that feeling of being pushed into a corner emotionally. It's hard to describe, but—it's like I feel a distance now. Space. Between me and it. It's still small—the space—but it's there."

He hadn't told her about losing the money. They'd told no one about the money. They simply told their boss that Seven Hills had called them and wanted to meet; that he had Emma, and wanted to turn himself in. It was all a bold-faced lie, but the department powers had believed them.

Marvin had been credited with saving the docent's life. The front-page story had run in the *Chronicle*. The newspaper had declared Marvin a hero and responsible for saving the woman's life. Their bosses asked why O'Higgins had not been there to back Marvin up. They'd lied and said that O'Higgins was in the museum's lobby in order to arrest Seven Hills when he came down from the observatory, but that they'd not expected him to have an accomplice and weren't looking for a woman. It seemed, they'd said, that Seven Hills never intended to give up Emma Barre but simply wanted to have at the two detectives, who'd been chasing him for a year. The story sounded wrong, but the powers that be had bought it, especially after Marvin had been named a hero.

A gutter punk had fetched one of the dropped handcuff keys and handed it to O'Higgins. He'd not come forward to tell the cops what he'd done. It was unlikely he ever would. The whole farrago had been neatly disposed of—all because a docent had been shot. The irony hadn't escaped them.

"Thank you."

"For what?" O'Higgins said.

"For telling me the truth. I know you're upset about what happened," Schneider said.

He had not expected to tell her anything. It had all spilt out of him. He'd not been able to sleep well since he'd come back from Iraq. When his wife was alive, she would hold him, and only in her arms could he sleep, albeit fitfully. But since she died he'd had days when he barely slept at all. It was the lack of sleep that had started him drinking. Only when he was inebriated did he finally fall asleep. LSD had changed that. He had to admit it.

"Okay, but do something about the dosage or whatever." Schneider nodded.

***

"They're coming for us in an hour," Cassie said. "A car service." They were using Thorpe's room at the Fairmont.

"We have to pick out what you'll wear." She was in a bathrobe.

Anna was watching cartoons in the huge living room with views, sitting on the couch.

She looked like any teenager: sullen, pretty, innocent.

"You pick," Anna said, not bothering to turn around. "I don't know what you want, anyway."

"I said an hour. Take a shower. I'll pick then."

"Okay—shit." Anna turned around and gave her a look. She was frightened, but putting on a hard face as if she weren't.

"It's going to be all right," Cassie said. "I won't let anything happen to you."

"So, we're the roadrunners—right?"

The girl was watching the American cartoon. The roadrunner had just freed himself from some train tracks, so the train hit the coyote . . .

Cassie watched the cartoon and wondered if she'd make it out the other end of their assignment. When she'd been younger, she'd never much cared. It was what Gus and the others had liked about her: her sangfroid, attached to that killer body. She never once explained that she was, if not enjoying the job, getting something out of having power over the men she would dispatch.

That had been wrong, she realized. Empty. She had killed people, and it was wrong to have reveled in it. But she had. It was payback— not just for what that man had taken from her in Malibu that night, but for her mother, too. Payback for all the times she'd seen her mother come home in the wee hours beaten by some trick who thought he had the right because she was just a girl, and who gives a shit about that kind of human garbage.

"They like the Daisy Dukes and no bra," Anna said.

"Not tonight."

"And you're going to make sure we win?"

"I am," Cassie said.

"Have you done this before?" Anna said. "Fuck bigshots?"

"Yes."

"So—you're like John Wick's girlfriend, in the movies? Never a dull moment. Fuck."

"No," Cassie said. "This won't be like the movies. If you do a good job, no more Turk Street, no more sixty-dollar blow jobs. And you're not on Turk Street tonight, so it will be a dress." Cassie went into the bedroom.

"I want to be Ginny. My name—Ginny Weasley. Like in Harry Potter. It's funny. Don't you think? Tonight."

"Okay, Ginny. Now go take a shower."

Anna got up, gave her a look, and headed into the bathroom and shut the door.

Clothes were sorted on the bed. Cassie had bought several things for the girl and herself at Nordstrom and Macy's. She looked at the assortment and tried to decide what she'd put the girl in.

She remembered the caterer who had first tried to turn her out, her first week in LA. She'd been just sixteen, with twenty dollars to her name. He'd hired her and put her in a short black Armani dress with black pumps. Her first straight job had been for the head of the Electricians' Union, who was being feted by one of the secondary studios. It was where Thorpe had spotted her. Even she realized the power that dress had had when she put it on.

Armani still sold the same dress, more or less. She went to the bed and picked it up. It had an open back with sheer sleeves. It would do for the girl. She dropped a Vince Camuto four- hundred-dollar faux fur blue coat onto it. It would be cold on the bay, as it was always winter in August here. She decided on a bomber jacket, perfect for the weapon, and skinny jeans and a white blouse. She would play the older woman to the hilt.

She turned and looked at the clutch she'd put the polonium 210 in. They might search it, so they'd hidden the shot mechanism in a pen. But if they x-rayed her purse? She tried not to think about it, and instead got their makeup together.

They could be wanded with a metal detector once they were on board the yacht, that was to be expected. The brief had said it was more than likely they would be wanded. The pistol she'd had them send would be detected; it would be impossible to get it by them.

The first lesson in tactics the Italian had given her was to, when necessary, improvise and take what she needed. But now? She decided to leave the pistol behind.

"Okay, I'm ready," Anna said from the doorway. She was naked from the waist up, a towel around her hips.

"Makeup first," Cassie said. "I'm sorry I've been a bitch." The two looked at each other.

"Okay," Anna said. "No problem."

"There's something I've not told you about tonight."

"What?"

"There's some kind of pod they'll put us in. It's where he takes the girls."

"What's that?"

"I don't know for sure, but there's no windows and he'll have the control. We'll be in there, just us and the john."

Anna shrugged and picked up a bra from several on the bed. "I am going to buy some tits—when I get ahead, you know," she said, not getting it.

Chapter 28

O'Higgins had gotten a text from Marvin:

He made a mistake. Call me. Now.

He had turned around just before the Golden Gate Bridge, right at the toll plaza in front of the bridge restaurant. He'd been trying to call Barre, leaving messages since they'd lost the ransom money. But Barre wasn't returning his calls, which he found strange. He'd gone to the Marriott on the way home and stopped at the desk and called again from the house phone, thinking that perhaps Barre's phone had been lost. The desk clerk put him through to Barre's room, but there was no answer. He left a message with the desk clerk. He'd texted Barre's wife's number and she'd just texted back—which was why he'd pulled over. She said that there was an emergency at one of the reactors in France and that Barre had been taken to the French embassy to work on the problem. He would call O'Higgins back as soon as he could.

Marvin's text came in as he was reading Mrs. Barre's message. He headed back downtown to Bryant Street.

She was a German girl—Julia Weber, only seventeen, a striking blond girl, tall for her age and willow thin. She had come to San Francisco to visit her older sister, who was working for Google. They had her in an interview room at Bryant Street.

"You rented a bicycle this afternoon?" Marvin said.

"Yes." She was wearing the clothes she'd been wearing when she'd gotten away from her would-be abductor. Her hoodie was ripped, torn at the shoulder during the struggle.

"On—street? I don't know the name."

"But it was near Pier 39?"

"Yes. I wanted to ride to the Bridge and Fort Point. My sister said she'd rented there, so I went there. I had the address on my phone."

"Was your sister with you?" Marvin asked

"No," the girl said. "she was at work."

"Google?"

"Yes—here in San Francisco. I came in with her in the morning."

"You rented the bike from the man—from the man that you fought off?"

"Yes."

"What happened?" Marvin asked. "Exactly. From the moment you rented the bike."

"Nothing. I just rented the bicycle. The shop was crowded. The man—"

"How old is he?"

"About thirty? I don't know. He had a beard. He seemed nice. He spoke a little German." "

"You paid, how?" Marvin asked.

"With a credit card."

"And you left the shop?" Marvin said.

She nodded. "He came out and gave me the shop's number, and said if there was a problem, to call that number."

"And you did?" Marvin said.

"Yes—at Fort Point."

"What happened?" Marvin said.

"The chain—I don't know, I couldn't pedal. Something happened to it."

"So you called the number?" Marvin asked.

"Yes. The man I spoke to, he asked me where I was exactly and I explained. He said he would send someone with a van and to wait. That they would bring a new bike."

"You explained you were at Fort Point?"

She nodded. "I stood with the bike out in front of the Fort. I wanted to make sure the driver would see me."

"And—it was the same man from the shop, he came?" Marvin said.

"Yes. I didn't have to wait very long."

Marvin looked at O'Higgins, who hadn't said a thing. They were talking to a victim, who, miraculously, had gotten away. He was still in a kind of shock that Seven Hills had finally made a mistake. One that might be his last.

"Okay. I understand, this is difficult," Marvin said. "But it's important. What did he do next? The man, when he picked you up."

"He parked and I walked the bike over to the van."

"It was the same man who was working at the store? You're positive?" O'Higgins said.

"Yes. The same man," the girl said.

"Go on," Marvin said.

"I had to pick up the bike and walk with it. He got out of the van and took the bike, and we walked to the van. I thought he would have the new bike with him. There in the van."

"But he didn't?"

"No. He said we would have to drive over to pick up the new bike. That it was very close—he would take me in the van."

"Then what happened?"

"I thought I would ride with him up front, but there was no seat. It seemed strange. He said I would have to ride in the back, with the bike. I do not know—I had read about the French girl in the newspaper when I came. I looked at the back. It had no windows. And he was—in my *Raum*, my space, close to me, and he took my arm. I didn't like that he touched me. I pulled away. He grabbed my arm and tried to push me into the van," the girl said.

"That's when I hit him."

"You hit him?" Marvin said.

"Yes. With a side punch."

"I don't understand," Marvin said.

"*Ellbogenschlag.*" The girl brought up her arm and swung her elbow. "I spun. It was instinct."

"Instinct?"

"Karate. My father has a dojo in Berlin. I have been studying since I was five, all of us in the family—all girls. We can fight," she said.

"You hit him, then?" Marvin said.

"Yes, of course!"

The two men looked at each other. It was the first time she showed the strain of what had happened to her.

"And he let go."

"No. I hit him in the nose with my elbow—but he did not let go, he held on. I slipped my arm out of the jacket and ran toward the Fort. There was a Ranger there, inside—I told him what happened. He called on his radio."

"And when you came out?"

"We came to the doors of the Fort and the van was gone," she said.

The interview room was quiet. They knew they were looking at a miracle. "You saved your life—because you fought," O'Higgins said.

The girl just nodded. She understood.

"It was the van," she said. "You hear so many stories. Was it the man who took the French girl?"

"Yes," O' Higgins said. "We think so, yes."

"Can I go? My sister is waiting for me."

"Why didn't we see anything about that bike shop on the other girl's credit card transactions?" Marvin said.

"I don't know," O'Higgins said. "My guess is that he didn't ever run their cards. The ones he'd chosen."

They were in the Ford, parked in front of the bike shop a few blocks away from Pier 39. The street was crowded with tourists. They finally had his name: Jesse Porter-Scott. It seemed impossible after all these months. They were waiting for a call back, having run his name. No one in the shop knew where he lived. The store had half a dozen part-time employees and three full-time. Porter-Scott was part-time, according to the manager. He had been in that morning, working his regular shift from seven a.m. to one. She said he'd failed to come back from his lunch break, and hadn't called back. She assumed that he was sick and would call in soon.

"It's him. I'm sure of it now." O'Higgins looked out at the street. The fog was lying just under the bridge, a dark grey wedge.

"So, our girls, all of them, came to rent a bike," Marvin said.

"He gives them one he knows will break down, and knows they'll call."

"The card has his cell number on it," Marvin said.

"Right. The van's his van—the manager confirmed that."

"So, he just has to pick them up. He tells them to get into the back, and—"

"It's over for them. And there's no record of them ever having come into the store. They just disappear."

"What about Emma?" Marvin asked. "Her father said she was at the Pier. Nothing about the shop."

"I don't know," O'Higgins said. "Maybe he changes it up somehow."

"Why would he? It was working."

They got a call over the radio. Porter-Scott was from South Africa, in the US on a student visa that had expired. His last known address was Bodega Bay. O'Higgins got a text with his California drivers' license. Porter-Scott was white, good-looking—a surfer type, twenty-nine years old.

"Six three. Two hundred pounds—the German girl has got balls, all right." O'Higgins read Porter-Scott's details from his license.

"White?" Marvin said.

"That's what it says. His hair looks straight. Brown." It was surreal that they were sitting in the car with this, after a year without a clue as to who their man was. Now they had IDed him.

"I thought everybody in South Africa was black," Marvin said.

"Bodega Bay," O'Higgins said.

"Bodega? Where the English girl—"

"Joanne Taylor—her mother called her Joe. She had saved money for two years to come here. She wanted a job with one of the tech companies. She had an interview at Facebook," O'Higgins said. "Her mother calls me from time to time to see—to see if we have caught him."

"We should call the Sonoma County Sheriff," Marvin said. "Have the asshole picked up."

"Yeah. I should stop drinking and start exercising more, too. Let's go."

"Nobody is going to like it, Mike—downtown."

"We'll call on the way. Tell them that we couldn't wait. That he might have Emma Barre there at his place. She could be alive."

Marvin pulled out into traffic.

They rode in silence all the way past Mill Valley. He wanted to be the one to arrest him. It was existential. He owed it to the women who had died.

"Do you have the Sig?" Marvin asked. "The one from the shootout on Alabama?"

"Yeah. It's in the trunk."

"Good," Marvin said. "Good."

O'Higgins turned and looked at him. "Don't do it, Marvin. It will fuck up everything. Let's just arrest him."

"Everything is already fucked up—isn't it? He's got the money. He will get away—with that kind of money it would be easy. He can go to Mexico. It's seven hours away."

"I didn't give him the thumb drive with the Bitcoin. I don't know why. I thought we'd catch him at the museum. There was nothing on that thumb drive I gave you at the museum. It was blank."

"What?"

"I didn't. I thought he would kill Emma, if he got all the money. He only got the money I gave him at the arboretum. Ten G's."

"Why is he still at the bike shop? That doesn't make sense. He had the ten Gs."

"Because that's where he gets off—isn't it? Maybe the money doesn't matter that much to him."

"You don't think Emma is still alive. She can't be."

O'Higgins didn't answer. Instead, he said, "I've been taking acid. I didn't want to freak you out. The psychiatrist's giving it to vets with PTSD—that's why I was fucked up at the Museum. I had a flashback. I'm sorry."

"You could have told me, Mike. Shit. LSD?"

"The address—his address. It's Joy Road. I dreamed it—the address. I never thought it would be—" He turned and looked at Marvin. "It was in the dream, Marvin, swear to God. I had it every night, and didn't think anything of it."

Marvin turned off the road at Petaluma. They'd called the Sonoma County Sheriff. They were sending a deputy out to the location.

Chapter 29

It was obvious that the man who had brought her wasn't coming back. No one would find her here, Emma thought. The idea that she was going to die in his wretched cave, never to be seen again, was sinking in. Her parents would never know what became of her, or hear from her ever again.

She shared something with those women she'd read about who had been sent to Germany, she thought. They had gone to their death without their loved ones knowing anything about them. They had faced a horrible death—most starved to death—without ever feeling the touch of a loved one. How different it was to feel that yourself, to face it yourself. She wanted to cry, but no tears came.

Her peacoat had dried out. She touched it. The fire had died down. It was early morning. She'd slept by the fire and gone out to see that the ocean had calmed down. The heavy fog had lifted. She could make out two small islands in the far distance. Shore birds were sweeping over the cliffs—hawks, she decided. She thought of swimming along the coast until she could reach the shore. But the way the waves slammed the black rock cliff, she knew it would be impossible. She would drown.

For a long time she sat looking out to sea as the morning turned to early afternoon.

Finally, she turned back. Turning away from the mouth of the cave, from the ocean, and the open blue sky. She understood she would die here in this strange place. Alone.

The idea of death started to wind its way through her consciousness. The profundity of that. What it meant to die—the unimaginable finality of it. Infinity in front of her. Would it be painful? She turned over the small fire with her boot in frustration. She was out of fresh water. It would be the lack of water that would kill her.

She'd got up and searched for water in the cave. The flashlight's batteries were low, its light wan. She found none. The rill she'd seen the first day had dried up. She made her way back toward the fire. She was tired from the lack of food, but had a new clarity, too. Three days without eating and she felt as if a veil had been lifted, everything clear and concise looking. She looked in the water bottle the man had left. It was almost empty, just a few inches of water left at the bottom. She threw another piece of driftwood on the fire, which had burnt down to embers grey and yellow, like some sleeping creature. A single ember kindled. She followed the reddish glow with her eyes as it headed up—and saw it the small chink in the roof and a shaft of sunlight at noon.

There was a way out?

She stood up. She could see the blue patch clearly—the size of her thumb when she held her hand up. It was why the smoke had gone up.

Her first rock-climbing class at school had a climbing wall and an instructor who was young and handsome. All the girls had fallen for him. She had loved climbing the wall—the way she could find a toe hold, the way it felt to pull herself up to the next level. It had all been done with a safety harness at first, so that when she fell, it was only a moment of merriment and laughter from the smiling faces of her schoolmates below.

Now it would be something else. She could fall, or she could starve to death—or she could escape.

***

The sun was low, but still light at seven. They were going to be picked up at the Embarcadero behind the Waterfront restaurant, which had a dock for private boats.

She remembered the beach at Juan les Pins. As yacht girls that first summer in France, they were living in Juan les Pins, she and Lana. Thorpe had rented a condo for them near the beach. Some days, if they had no dates, they would simply be free to shop and stroll on the beach. The sound of children's voices, the elegance of it all. French kids her own age—seventeen—with their parents on holiday, the way the families seemed so self-assured— little tribes with their two leaders. The beach bags, bright umbrellas, cell phones. The daughters so innocent looking and fresh-faced. Mothers and daughters sat together, sharing the mother-daughter bond.

She'd never been on a vacation with her mother.

Once she'd gone to the pool with her mom and her pimp. The pimp had an apartment in a nice building in Las Vegas, the kind that had BMWs parked out in front and palm trees and manicured fronts, and sparkling glass windows. She'd been around ten. She and her mom, who was only twenty-four then, had sat on the steps of the shallow end of the huge pool. She'd never done anything like that. There was a momentary sense of holiday. Her mother wore a new bathing suit they'd bought at Walmart that morning.

She noticed the needle marks on her mother's arm as she took her hand and asked if they could move there. She'd understood something that day, something profound about their situation: they would never live in a place like that, or have a nice car, or not move from one cheap room to the next, sometimes shared with other working girls.

It was a short vacation, lasting perhaps all of two hours. Her mom had gone with some old man after lunch who had spotted her for what she was. The pimp had kept an eye on her, making sure she stayed in the shallow end—playing the ersatz father. But she had kept looking for her mother.

It was while she'd been in France that she got the news that her mother had died of an overdose. Her aunt, a blackjack dealer, had called her and they'd said a few words after her aunt told her what had happened. Her mother had OD'd in a truck stop near I-5 and Panoche, near Fresno. Truck stops were the last rung on a working girl's ladder. The older women, the most drug-addicted and hopeless, worked them—a kind of asphalted hell.

She'd gone down to the pool where she and Lana were staying, sat in the shallow end and waited for something to happen—some emotional response or memory of a bit of fleeting happiness, a conversation the two might have had, but all she could remember was looking for her mother up there in the apartments that afternoon. Each floor had a gallery facing the pool.

The pimp had taken her home later that afternoon in his Cadillac and dropped her off. Her mother came home two days later and gave her ten dollars.

"You can put your phone away now," Cassie said.

They rolled into a VIP parking place. Anna—Ginny—looked the part, her youth carrying the day. The dress she'd chosen ramped her up, erasing the streets. She could have been some rich man's daughter on a night out. It was hard for Cassie to look at her, as she was in a sense looking at herself, the way she'd been years before.

"Remember, let me do the talking. Okay?" She reached over and pulled the girl's hair back. It was a strange thing to do, motherly.

Anna looked at her. She had pretty blue eyes that told nothing about her hard road, or that she was a Dirt Person, Cassie thought

The Bay ran grey-blue in the twilight, fog free and calm. She caught a glimpse of the super yacht. It was the biggest one she'd ever seen, and she had a real sense of dread. The yacht's hyper-modern design made it look more like a battleship in some futurist movie.

She grabbed her clutch and slid out of the town car. A launch waited with two crew in the uniform she remembered so well: white pants and white polo shirts. The young, good-looking men were one more layer of ornamentation. These uniforms looked tailored, lacking the studied carelessness she was used to on the Côte d'Azur. Someone had wanted that kind of control, right down to the crew's designer uniforms. The yacht's sail number and name were embroidered on their shirts in black.

A text hit her phone. She looked down at her screen as she and the girl headed down the dock.

No wands for the princess, sorry. We have a new friend at the castle— Gus

The ride across the bay was smooth—the launch's motor reassuring, the wake it kicked up white, a smooth-looking plume. She almost expected to look across and see Lana alive and young and full of girlish bonhomie. For Lana the men she would meet were like gods, whom she wanted very much to please.

She watched the Embarcadero recede behind them, the Bay Bridge to their right. The launch turned toward Sausalito.

***

They heard a shot as they were driving up the mountain.

They waited, feeling that something wasn't right. They'd taken Joy Road out a few miles east from Bodega. The famous movie town hadn't changed much since the Hitchcock movie: a gas station and a few restaurants. The hills immediately east were brown in summer, the air cool because they were so close to the ocean. They had come this way once before, but the English girl had been found further west, in sight of the ocean.

They could see the Sheriff's car, its driver side door left open. It seemed wrong as they wound their way up the hill on the dirt road. The view of the house on the hill got closer after each switchback—sometimes disappearing altogether, then coming back into view.

"Where is the officer?" Marvin said.

"Slow down," O'Higgins said. He slid his Glock out and laid it on his lap. The Ford slowed to a crawl, with the familiar sound of popping tires on gravel—the sound he remembered so well from his dream.

They passed a ravine filled with blackberry bushes laced with fruit, the leaves caked with dust from passing cars. They came around another switchback. They'd climbed high enough to see the famous church spire in Bodega, and beyond that the ocean directly behind them.

"The officer's car—it's too far from the house. Right?" Marvin said.

"Yeah," O'Higgins said. He calculated the distance to the farmhouse, its metallic roof brilliant. A thousand yards, maybe less. "He could have a long rifle. We've only got the AR in the trunk and pistols."

"He's got Emma up in there, too. Probably," Marvin said.

"She's probably already dead," O'Higgins said.

"You don't know that," Marvin said.

"He's got the high ground, the open field of fire. It will be like Alabama Street all over again, but worse. He'll have about three hundred yards on us."

"Maybe the officer is inside with him, has it under control."

"We'd have gotten a call."

O'Higgins called the Sonoma Sheriff's and waited as they checked. The officer had called in, and that was the last they'd heard. They were sending a backup, but they were a half-hour out. He ended the call and looked up at the white farmhouse in the distance.

"A female officer. She hasn't answered her radio."

"Mother fucker," Marvin said.

O'Higgins looked at him. It seemed all too real again. He wanted to back the car up and take Marvin home to his daughters. He couldn't stand the idea that they could be killed by this animal, so far down the road.

"She needs our help. That officer—" Marvin said.

"Yeah, if the officer is still alive—but I doubt that. You heard the shot? I did."

"You think I'm scared? Because of what happened?" Marvin said.

"No, I don't. I think it's crazy to go up on someone who's got that kind of open field of fire. That's what I think. A long rifle and a good scope, and we're fucked. Period. It's a bald mountain. No cover, man." He saw Marvin undo his seat belt and thought that he might get out of the car for a more careful look, but he simply pulled his pistol and stuck it in the seat between them, barrel first.

"Get out the AR. Go on, then," Marvin said.

"You're serious?" O'Higgins said.

"Yeah. There are people up there who need us, okay? That motherfucker doesn't scare me."

"He should," O'Higgins said. "It's suicide."

"Well, he doesn't. Now get the goddamn rifle, Mike, because I'm going the fuck up there—with your ass or without you."

O'Higgins opened the door, slid out of the seat and went to the trunk. He unclipped the AR from the gun rack. They had not been able to use the weapon that day on Alabama Street because it had been too far away.

He broke the magazine open, checked it, and looked up at the house. It was quiet on the road, the kind of stillness he remembered when he'd been hunting quail—a soft imperceptible hum of nature in summer, super real blue sky scattered with aimless flat clouds dwelling over the ocean.

He thought of his daughter, where she might be. In class? He thought of simply putting the rifle in the car, and leaving it at that. No shame in wanting to live.

He came back around and opened the door. He peered inside and saw Marvin, both hands on the wheel, his eyes peering at the white farmhouse in the distance, resolute. O'Higgins slid into the seat, the long rifle held between his legs and a sense of obligation overwhelming him. Or was it something else?

"Okay, Let's do this," Marvin said. He punched the accelerator and they sped up, the gravel kicked out from their tires. The Ford headed toward the turn that would expose them for a few seconds.

It's Wooly-Bully time again, O'Higgins thought. It was a song they used to play in Iraq before going on patrol. *Matty told Hatty about a thing she saw... had two big horns and a wooly jaw...*

From above, it was a simple scene: dirty brown summer grass cut by a red road that had been plowed into the hillside years ago; a dirty grey Ford moving fast like a toy car, heading toward a bone-white farmhouse from the 1920s sitting alone on a bald mountaintop; a Sheriff's car parked fifty yards out from the house. Before the shooting started, while the Ford picked up speed, sliding into turns, he felt a familiar sense of the chaos to come.

O'Higgins had missed it—combat. In those moments of combat, ordinary existence was left behind and he entered this special timeless place, hung on Fate's door hook... He felt truly alive. Fighting was what the Irish were built for.

Chapter 30

Emma turned off the flashlight. She couldn't take it on the climb. The opening above was no longer lit by the sun. It was past noon, she guessed. She stood and thought about the climb.

The idea of falling frightened her, that moment when she would feel herself slip. She remembered those moments well from the climbing wall.

She looked up again. It was a foggy grey, where the dime-sized patch of blue sky had been only moments before.

She slid off the peacoat and let it fall to the ground. It was fate, she thought. All of her life had led to this moment. It was like her deafness: a mark that had made her life so different. She thought of her mother and father. If she was successful, she would live to see them again. And, if she fell…

She turned around toward the mouth of the cave. What if he came back? Or if the police came, if she only waited? She believed they were looking for her, but—if they came too late?

She turned away from the sound of the waves and walked to the wall. It was crenulated sedimentary rock, reddish grey. The chimney that she intended to climb—five feet wide—was inclined, especially near the top, toward the opening, a good fifty feet above. It looked impossible. The last part she would have to do almost in the dark.

She put her hands to her face on the edge of a horrible panic, but stopped herself. She'd felt a rubber band on the seat of the man's launch and had put into her pocket. It had been a mindless act. She found the rubber band now, tied her hair into a ponytail, and started the climb.

***

She'd forgotten the odd dreariness of the super wealthy, the Forbes 100 types. They had a special indifference, mixed with superiority of the worst kind, and with it a studied fatuousness, too. It could be ginned up with any manner of fronts: folksiness, red-carpet glamour, cunning businessman, depending on the PR people employed. But however it was portrayed, it still lurked: a shapeless, not-so-subtle sense of moral decay, that if you stood close to it—or in her case, slept with it—no PR varnish could hide.

It was there that evening, as they came aboard through the ultra-cool landing built into the side of the Russian's super yacht. The pilot of the launch had only to head into a special dock/opening in the yacht's side; then, motor cut, slide effortlessly inside and against a padded landing. They were onboard. The bay lapped quietly in this metallic, well-lit metal cocoon.

A young woman with a wireless earpiece for communicating on an open channel was waiting for them. She wore the same crew's uniform, but her blouse was sheer so that you could get a hint of her bra. She said nothing, but by her cold demeanor Cassie understood. The young woman obviously knew why they were there. She had done this crude business before, her look said. They took an elevator to the top deck. The three women rode in an uncomfortable silence.

"Bar—please," the girl said, pointing the way. She was about twenty. All the crew had been selected, like the furnishings, to be sleek and beautiful.

The main deck was larger than any yacht Cassie had ever been on. In the time she'd been out of the game, she realized, a kind of arms race had been waged. The super yachts she'd been on had seemed like just that— yachts, with their peculiar boat-ness. But this had the feeling of a hotel lobby.

They were taken to a bar on the aft deck. The bartender looked at them and smiled, also obviously in the know.

"Ladies, good evening. What can I get you?" he said.

"Jameson. On the rocks," Cassie said. She felt the clutch and put it on the bar. She wondered how many people it would kill if, somehow, she got it wrong.

"And for you, miss?" The bartender gave Anna a feral look, a micro expression. "She'll have a white wine," Cassie said.

A few others were on a deck above them, speaking Russian. She glanced up and saw a row of windows and a row of exercise bikes... inside. The bartender slid a glass in front of her. She lifted it and took a drink, glancing back toward Sausalito, all lit up.

"Come on. Shall we?" She nodded to Anna and they made their way to the extreme end of the bow, past a huge hot tub surrounded by a circular couch...

"Now what?" Anna said.

Cassie was going to answer but heard a commotion behind her. She recognized the owner from his photo—only in his forties, balding, in designer jeans, coming toward them with two other young women. "Ah... more friends," the man said and smiled. It was the kind of smile she understood.

She smiled back, putting on an expression that she had learnt years before.

But the man was looking at Anna. He took her by the hand and kissed it as if she were a member of the royal family.

"I thought we'd hot tub? There are bathing suits in the cabana... Please find one you like," the man said. He turned to a crew member. It was someone Cassie hadn't seen, short and stocky, a weightlifter type. He led them to a set of cabana doors behind the bar to "change." The cabana was stocked with bathrobes with the yacht's name, T1. She slipped her shoes off.

"Gus sends his regards," the man whispered from the other side of the louvre door. She froze. They had gotten someone on board. She pulled her leather jacket off, then began to take her pants off.

Black and white photos hung on the walls, of the T1 standing off Juan les Pins and Cannes. She recognized the beach at Juan Les Pins. She stared at the photo, then got on with it, choosing a black bikini from several on a shelf. She felt too old for this show, but finally stepped out onto the deck and headed toward the tub.

A helicopter passed overhead, heading toward San Francisco. She looked for the weightlifter but didn't see him. The lights around the hot tub had been dimmed so that only the hot tub's colored lights shone, bathing the women in a kind of psychedelic old-school strobe effect. The two other women she'd seen with the Russian, moments before, were sitting inside the tub drinking from fluted glasses.

"What's your name? You're beautiful!" a very young, maybe seventeen-year-old, asked as she walked to the edge of the built-for-twenty hot tub. It had a strobe light in the bottom that projected colors up into the faces of the girls: pink, blue, red.

"Mike Tyson. What's yours?" Cassie said, looking for Anna.

The girl gave her a look. "Well, I like older girls, Mike—so that doesn't, you know, turn me off."

***

Their windshield on the Ford was partially shot out. The shooter had a long rifle and was placing his shots carefully. The first one had smashed their windshield. The bullet's sonic imprint passed right by O'Higgins's ear. Marvin at the last turn, two hundred yards from the farmhouse, had pulled out into the field and headed toward the Sheriff's car, whose driver's door was open. The noontime sun painted the cruiser bright green and white.

Marvin was trying to put the abandoned patrol car between them and the farmhouse. The next bullet hit the rear-view mirror and tore it off, smashing the safety glass, puckering it in a way that the safety glass became a grey-green web, partially torn loose. It showed a ragged hole that grew bigger after the second bullet struck them, again missing Marvin.

The bullet was loud, its sound familiar to O'Higgins. It had passed close, a second time. The shooter had to have a scope of some kind and was dialing them in, adjusting each time to his right… O'Higgins reached over and turned the wheel to the left. They heard the third shot, but it missed completely. The car fishtailed across the open field.

Marvin grabbed the wheel again and sped up, turning left, then right, understanding that it would throw the shooter's aim off.

O'Higgins ran his window down and held the AR out from the side. He let go a burst, the hundred-round drum rattling, spewing brass. He hit the farmhouse's big picture window with the intention of interfering with the shooter's field of fire. The Ford was hitting rocks that were slamming the underside of the car. The tall golden Johnson grass folded down in front of them in a swelling green wave. The Ford's bumper bent it down perfectly, as if the car were a piece of farm equipment that had gone out of control.

The shooter's window, shot out and gone, forced a change in his tactic. He fired at their tire and caught the front passenger side. The Ford, at 40 miles an hour, sank violently, the noise of the tire's rim on the dirt. The front end bounced, slowing them down to a crawl. The Ford started to spin to the left, the front tire completely flat. They rammed the back of the sheriff's car, moving it, bounced and came to a stop. The Ford's engine raced. The front air bags deployed, releasing talcum-like motes of powder into the cab.

"Bail!" O'Higgins yelled.

He'd faceplanted into the bag and had to push it away from his face. They fell out on each side of the car and into the shoulder-high Johnson grass. It was a good idea. Lying in it they had a lacuna and were out of direct sight, but they had no visibility either.

He looked for Marvin, but didn't see him. They were a good fifty yards from the farmhouse. The last 25 had been cut with a lawn mower and were clean, no cover.

He heard a pistol shot to his right and crawled toward it. The grass pushed down with the AR. He saw the Ford's punctured front tire, still turning slowly. The car's engine was in Drive, but it was caught in a deep ditch that had trapped it.

He stopped crawling. The sheriff's officer, too, must have pulled off the road after the suspect had opened fire.

He saw Marvin's pant leg. Finally, getting up and leaning against the sheriff's car, he stood up enough to see Marvin leaning on the Ford, shooting through its broken-out windshield.

The car was hit with a withering full-automatic gun fire that demolished what was left of the glass and slammed into the airbags, deflating them. O'Higgins pulled Marvin down. They were face to face in the shadows, the Johnson grass hiding them. The firing stopped.

Marvin looked at him. He got out his spare magazine. "Well?"

"He has more than the long rifle," O'Higgins said.

"No shit."

"They will come for us. The Sheriffs," O'Higgins said.

The automatic weapons fire started again, hitting the sheriff's car a few yards in front of them. The bullets made a crazy metal-punctured music.

O'Higgins took off his coat and checked his pistol. He put the two spare magazines he'd taken that morning and laid them down in the dirt.

"We have fifty rounds left in the drum, maybe, and—" He did the math. "About 18—27 rounds here. Not enough. Did you see the body anywhere? The officer?"

"No," Marvin said. His shirt was wet, sticking to his skin. "I think she's near the patrol car. He can't see us."

The firing started again. The sound of the bullets had changed, their smashing sound gone. O'Higgins guessed they were hitting the interior of the car. Another long blast swept the side of the Ford, loud.

They got down on their faces, the bullets hitting the Ford low on the door panel. The car had turned to the side when they'd hit the ditch, so that it was almost parallel to the farmhouse. He's trying to get a down angle. It had changed… He's trying to hit the gas tank?

"He's moved—higher—up in the house?"

"What?"

O'Higgins crawled around to the Ford's passenger door. The seat where he'd been sitting moments before was pock-marked with bullet holes. He looked under the car. The gas tank was bleeding gas onto the dirt. If the vapors built—and he knew they would—a single spark would ignite the vapors, as happened so often in Iraq.

He crawled back to Marvin. "He's firing, maybe full metal—the spark will ignite the vapors. Smell it?"

They could smell the gasoline fumes.

"I'm going to check the officer's trunk, see if maybe it's open and has a long rifle," O'Higgins said. He crawled in the grass, seeing almost nothing until he almost crawled into the back of the patrol car. He reached up and felt for the trunk lid. It was open; she'd unlocked it, before she got out of the car and was hit.

He stood up. Everything was brilliant. He glanced at the white farmhouse. He could see the shot-out picture window, a dark room behind it. He looked down into the trunk and saw the officer's AR was gone. The automatic weapons started firing, smashing into the Sheriff's car.

Seven Hills had seen him, and clearly. He was six four and impossible to miss. He ducked back down. Fear and panic began to climb through him. The killer could have thousands of rounds, and they were down to almost nothing.

He crawled back; the grass was matted down and easier to get through. "We have to move. He knows that the vapors will build. He's smart." Marvin looked at him. "The officer had an AR, but she took it."

"Ideas?" Marvin said, his face close to the dirt.

"Let's see if we can crawl that way out to the right, find her body—get her weapons. We need them." He handed Marvin the two spare magazines.

Marvin took one and shoved it in his back pants pocket.

"You might as well put in the fresh one now."

Marvin nodded and put the fresh magazine in. The gasoline smell was getting stronger, the air thick with it.

"She's probably out there, not too far from the patrol car."

Marvin took off crawling, his thin body moving easily, creating a tunnel in the tall Johnson grass. O'Higgins followed, glad to get away from the Ford, the stench of the gasoline vapors overwhelming. He's waiting to see them in the sun… the vapors? He's smart. When they've built up enough, he'll fire.

They crawled to the right. Marvin stopped, and O'Higgins came up behind him. "Blood," Marvin said, nodding. O'Higgins saw the drops of blood, thick looking, on the Johnson grass. Marvin was pointing with his pistol now to beyond them. It was a tunnel the wounded deputy had made heading toward the side of the farmhouse.

"Plan?" Marvin whispered.

The firing started again. They heard the shots hit the car, then the explosion he'd expected.

"Keep moving. He can't see us, or he would fire. We'll put the side of the house between us. I think he's on the roof or in the attic, higher up." O'Higgins could feel the sun on his back. The sheriffs were only twenty minutes out; another ten minutes and they would be there.

He'd left his phones in the car, he realized. "Hey, your phone," O'Higgins said. "You got it?"

Marvin tossed it back to him and it landed in the grass to his left. He looked: there was no signal this far out in the country. He put his face down and tried to think of a way to cross the open space where the grass had been cut. His mind was racing, but found no solution to those thirty feet.

"If we don't attack him, he'll come out and kill us."

"Where the fuck are the sheriffs?" Marvin said in a whisper.

They heard a shot—a single shot coming from somewhere in front of them. It was a pistol shot.

O'Higgins jumped up. He saw Seven Hills in a white t-shirt, his brown hair in the sun, pistol pointed toward the ground. He was aiming at the deputy. The man fired again and was just starting to turn when O'Higgins caught him across the chest with a burst from the AR, fired instinctively. He crouched, then charged the spot, adrenalin full, leaning forward, the tall grass hitting him in the face as he trotted.

Chapter 31

"She's dead!" O'Higgins shouted, wiping the sweat from his eyes. The temperature had gone up, the cool marine layer burnt off.

He knew it as soon as he saw the officer. She had crawled to the edge of the cleared grass, wounded but alive. Her face was obliterated by the rounds the killer had put in her face.

He heard Marvin trot up behind him. Seven Hills was lying with his eyes open behind her, cradled in the grass. His chest leaked blood from the massive wounds.

O'Higgins knelt beside him. "Where's Emma? Where? It's over. Tell me."

"Who?" He died.

O'Higgins stood up. "Shit!" he said. He ran his hand over his hair, and sharp spurs from the Johnson grass stuck here and there.

Marvin ran toward the farmhouse.

O'Higgins turned and saw the lacuna the deputy had made. She was brave. That was his first thought. She'd saved their lives, probably, because Seven Hills had to come looking for her, not sure where she was. He'd gotten scared that she could get behind him—or he knew that more police would be coming.

"She's not here," Marvin called from the porch.

He bent down, pulled the pistol out of Seven Hills' hand, and tossed it aside. Everything had gotten quiet. A yellow jacket landed on his hand drawn by the sweat. He swatted it away and walked toward the farmhouse.

"You sure? Look again," he called.

"What about him?" Marvin yelled.

"Dead. He's dead."

They heard the sirens coming up the hill. O'Higgins looked at his watch; it was twenty-five minutes after one. He set the AR down at the foot of the stairs and went up the paint-worn steps, feeling weak. Marvin turned and walked back inside.

The living room was in shadows. Seven Hills had set up a table with two sandbags to stabilize his rifle. He had an expensive-looking long rifle with scope resting on a sandbag. An empty box had held 30.06 shells.

O'Higgins looked for the automatic weapon, but didn't see it. He turned and looked out at the Ford. The fire, about 50 yards away, had died down. It looked strange, the bright sunlight. He looked across toward the '20s-era kitchen—white and black tile, a farm sink, a black pan on the stove.

Marvin came out from one of the bedrooms. "It's just two bedrooms. She's not here."

The sirens were getting closer. They both turned and watched through the broken-out picture window as two Sonoma County Sheriff's cars came and went from view, exposed by the switchbacks.

"Why?" Marvin asked. "Why did he fight?"

"He knew it was all over. My guess is that he had been a soldier— instinct in the end."

"Fuck. Where is she, Mike?"

"I don't know. And he wouldn't say." He felt empty, sure the girl was dead somewhere, left to rot in the sun. He'd held out a stupid hope that they would find her here, alive. But that was destroyed. He looked around at the brass on the floor, scores of empty cartridges.

He checked the sheriff's cars, which had slowed. They were calling for backup, he imagined, not going to make the same mistake as the deputy.

He turned and walked out of the house, his hands in the air, the sun

250

in his face, walking toward the stopped sheriff's cars. The only reason they had survived, he realized, was that he'd run out of ammunition for the AR. They found it on the back porch—two taped-together magazines, both empty.

The yellow jackets buzzed his face as he made his way toward the patrol cars. They had a nest somewhere, close. They had been riled up by the fire, leaving the nest in a swarm, and were looking to attack.

When he came back, driven in the back of one of the patrol cars, Marvin had found a root cellar. It was where Seven Hills had held his victims. They found passports and clothing, even cell phones that had belonged to the other girls, but nothing of Emma Barre's.

One of the Sonoma County detectives drove them back to San Francisco. The female officer who died had been a veteran, they learned, and had been on their force less than a year. She'd grown up in Sonoma, not too far from where she'd died. Somehow that was telling. How many times had she seen that white farmhouse growing up, O'Higgins wondered, as they pulled out onto the asphalt two lane road.

He turned around. He could make out the farmhouse high on the hill, a bit of white. They asked to be taken to Bryant Street. They spoke to their boss, then left for a drink at the Royal Cuckoo, neither wanting to go home yet.

"So if Emma's things aren't there, now what? Doesn't make any sense." Marvin said. They'd both ordered tequilas. It was late and the bar was crowded with twenty-somethings, mostly young men, dressed similarly, like actors lining up for the same part. The two older men stood out like sore thumbs, their clothes dirty from the shootout.

"Maybe he had another way—not the bicycle ruse," O'Higgins said. "Something else?" He took a drink, emptying his glass, and got the bartender's attention, signaling for another round.

"He obviously was collecting mementos, phones, passports—but not Emma's," Marvin said.

"How the fuck do I know what some fucking lunatic thinks?"

O'Higgins said. He was tired, exhausted. He kept seeing Seven Hills in the sunshine, firing down on the wounded officer—the greasy-looking fire, the smell of the burning Ford.

"I'm glad you're safe," O'Higgins said. "That's what counts. I can't stand the idea of training someone else."

Marvin smiled at him. His face was dirty, and he looked exhausted, too. It was the first time O'Higgins had seen him smile in days. He realized how much he cared for him, but would never admit it. Marvin was like his daughter, a constant in his life—someone he could count on.

"I've got to go home. My sister is taking care of the girls," Marvin said, looking down at his phone. "What do I say when she asks me how my day was?"

"Eventful. No word from Cassie?"

"Nothing."

"You better call Barre—tell him we didn't find her," O'Higgins said. He watched Marvin get up and step out of the bar to make the call. O'Higgins turned toward the old-school mirror behind the myriad bottles of booze. *I look old*, he thought. *Fucking job.*

***

Cassie had waited, thinking that Anna was still changing, but she'd not come down to the hot tub. The red-headed girl who had made a pass at her had been sent for, taken by one of the female crew. Skinny, the redhead had turned, looked at her, and winked.

Cassie turned and looked for the weightlifter. She saw him standing by the bar where they'd first landed, hoping to see Anna.

She'd hidden the device in her vagina. She'd had no choice. If it leaked, she would die a horrible death. She looked down the long deck toward the bow of the boat, a row of lights illuminating the polished brass railing, but didn't see anyone. She glanced above, to the upper deck, but didn't see the Russian—or Anna.

She headed off quickly when she saw Anna step out of an elevator at last. She walked away from the hot tub and toward the bar, catching the weightlifter's eye as she did.

"He's asked me to stay," Anna said, approaching her.

"What?"

"His guy just asked me to stay. Wanted to see if I would go on with them to LA tomorrow."

Cassie froze. "What did you say?"

"I said how much?"

"And?"

"Fifty Gs a month." She smiled as if she'd won the lottery.

"You can't stay. That's impossible."

"Why the fuck not!?"

Cassie looked at the girl. They'd given her a thin wrap, sheer. She looked beautiful. It was hard to believe, but the idea of the job had given her a certain look, a kind of wide-eyed beauty. She was excited at the prospect of big money.

"Because I'm going to kill him," Cassie said.

"What?"

"You can't stay. Do you understand?"

Anna looked at her. "Fuck that." She walked off toward the bar and spoke to the weightlifter, turning to point to her. He nodded and walked toward Cassie.

"She's going to send up a flare," he said. "I'll take care of her." Cassie nodded. She knew what it would mean.

She saw two girls get out of the hot tub, led by the same female crew member. She followed behind the two women; they'd been given robes, because it was getting colder. She turned once to look back at the girl, then followed the two women who were high and giggling.

She poisoned the Russian while he was fucking. Four girls were in the "pod." They were too stoned on coke to notice what she'd done, or when she'd done it. At just before 4 in the morning, Cassie and several other girls were taken back on the launch they'd come in. Anna wasn't with them.

Cassie threw the pen overboard.

***

O'Higgins looked at the Marriott's clerk. He'd stopped in first thing on the way down from Robin's new place, where he'd spent the night. He still didn't have a phone, and thought this would be the quickest way to get in touch with Barre and explain that they'd caught Seven Hills, but found no sign of Emma.

"Mr. Barre must have checked out," the clerk said.

"That's impossible. Check again."

The clerk looked at him, then again at his screen with a peeved expression. "The room was vacated two days ago. It's occupied," the woman said.

"By whom?"

"They appear to be a Chinese couple."

"I want to see the room," O'Higgins said.

"I'm sorry, sir."

He showed the clerk his badge. "Now," he said.

The manager had come along with him. They had to explain to a man in his fifties, who only spoke Mandarin, that he had to get out of the room, that the police needed the room.

O'Higgins walked through the door, pushing the man away. A good-looking girl was with him, Chinese, in a sheer robe, about twenty. She was too young for the man, and he got the picture.

"Get out," he said.

The girl slid out of bed and ran to the door.

"This is unacceptable," the manager said. "Really, these are paying guests, officer."

"Detective," he said. "Shut the fuck up. All right! Now get out. No one comes in—is that understood?"

He'd yelled at the man for no good reason, he realized. It wasn't a good sign. He'd had a dream he was running toward Seven Hills through the Johnson grass. He'd been holding a pistol to Emma Barre's head and she was watching him. As he approached, Seven Hills shot her in the head.

"I'm at the Marriott," he said to Marvin. "Get over here." He'd bought a "burner" in the hotel lobby, and had to leave a voice mail. It was a cheap old-school phone, impossible to text with. All his contacts were gone with his phone, burnt up in the fire. He would have to get a propeller-head on Bryant Street to help him get his backup off the cloud.

He looked around the room. The Chinese guy had left his suitcase on a stand. A bottle of OS Glenlivet stood on one of the night tables with two dirty glasses. A room service dish had been used as an impromptu ashtray. He recognized nothing of Barre's. He went to the closet and opened it. Empty, except for a few hangers and a laundry bag. Nothing else.

He walked to the window that looked out on Bay Street. It was busy. He watched a family of tourists hop in an Uber, clueless as to where Barre was.

***

At the last minute, Cassie had decided to simply go home. She used her key. The limo driver waited to make sure she got in safely. It was a kind gesture, but odd, given where she'd been and what she'd done.

The house was quiet, one light left on in the kitchen. It felt strange to be home again. She'd missed it. She slipped off her high heels and walked toward the kitchen, pushing through the swinging door. She went to the liquor cabinet, pulled down the gin, and poured herself a glass. She'd always drunk gin when she was single. It was what her mother would drink when she could afford it.

She sat at the kitchen table. They had a small view over the rooftops of the East Bay. She saw the lights twinkle, she looked at her phone. It was 5 AM almost exactly. She wondered if Marvin would really let her stay, or if she was destined to be alone.

She drank in silence. She wanted to take a shower and get the Russian's stink off her. She had found him fucking the redhead. He had her handcuffed to the bed, her face down, when Cassie walked in. She'd injected him in the right butt cheek, and he never felt it. He was too busy enjoying himself.

She kept replaying that moment. When he turned and grabbed her arm and brought her around to him, his sweating face near orgasm, wanting her to join in…

"They're with my sister," Marvin said. He'd come down early in the morning and had seen her sitting at the table, the gin bottle in front of her. "Where have you been?" he said. He was wearing a robe she'd given him for Christmas.

"I missed you," she said.

"Why didn't you call me? The girls have been crazy wondering where the hell you've been."

"I had a job to do."

"A job? What job?"

She got up and made coffee. A crepuscular light was growing in the East Bay, Mt. Diablo painted by it, pale and weak at first. She made a pot of coffee and told him who she really was, starting out the first time she'd been paid for sex. Who Lana was, and what they'd been through together all those years before.

"You said you—had a job. You don't mean—?"

"No," Cassie said. "Something else, but I can't tell you."

"Why?" Marvin asked.

"Because you have to trust me now—or not. It's up to you, Marvin. I'll leave and never come back—but I can't tell you. And they won't let me stop now. I'm sure of that." She took the revolver out from her purse and put it carefully on the table between them.

"Are you a criminal?"

"I don't know. In some ways. Maybe? I'm not really sure," she said. They sat in silence. The pale light had grown, the dawn's filaments brighter, like a far-off room that had had a single light switched on.

"I don't care. You're my wife. You're the girls' mother," Marvin said. "That's all I care about." He glanced at the pistol, then put down his cup and left the room.

She got up and tidied the kitchen, taking dishes and putting them in the dishwasher just as she always had.

Chapter 32

"I called the embassy," O'Higgins said. "They didn't know what I was talking about." They were standing in Barre's room at the Marriott. The manager had arranged for the Chinese couple to move to another room. A bellman had taken the couple's things. The bed was still unmade, and the room stank of illicit cigarette smoke.

"I don't get it," Marvin said. "None of it—since yesterday." He'd shaven and was wearing a clean suit but looked exhausted, as if he'd not slept at all. "I spoke with the Sonoma Sheriff's, and they haven't found anything else. Asshole had a storage locker in Petaluma."

"They're going to toss it today and they'll call us. The guns were bought legally. He was a soldier, they said—they found some photos of him in uniform in South Africa. You were right. He'd served in Iraq."

"Barre can't just disappear," O'Higgins said. "Why would he?"

"If he were—"

"The French Embassy wouldn't lie—right? Why would they?" O'Higgins said.

"Maybe he couldn't say. Because of his job. Maybe the embassy had to lie for good reason. He's too important, or—"

"I don't have my phone. We had their contact stuff on my phone, texts, all of it," O'Higgins said. "I found this on the floor of the closet."

"What is it?"

"Ticket stub—Air France with the date and flight number. They'll have a record.

"Homeland Security will have their contact info. We can start there.

And we have to stop at an Apple store," O'Higgins said.

"Mike—are we about to look for Emma's parents now, too?"

"You have a better idea?"

"What if it was all bullshit? Or the kid came back and the two simply went back to France, afraid what would happen to them if they told us she'd just was a runaway? Because that's what it's starting to look like to me. It was all bullshit," Marvin said.

"I heard her voice on the phone. That first day. She didn't sound like a runaway to me."

"Why would she call me? That doesn't make any sense."

"We aren't sure Seven Hills even took Emma, now. Right?"

They heard a knock on the door and Marvin went to open it. A tiny Latin woman, with no English, wanted to come in and clean the room.

***

She'd fallen once at the very beginning of the climb, and it had made her stop and rethink it. Her shoes, a kind of fashion boot, had leather soles and were too slick. She finally slipped them off. The idea of climbing the rock wall in her bare feet seemed desperate, but it was all desperate now. As soon as she started again, it went better. The soles of her feet had a super tactile quality, a kind of intelligence that helped her sense what would work and what might not. If it felt too sharp, she waited until it was easier. The first twenty feet went well. At one point she looked down at where she'd been prisoner, the fire still smoking.

The Week Before

On the plane six hours from San Francisco, Emma turned on the reading light above her head. She had liked feeling cocooned with just the light from her Kindle, her dinner tray in front of her.

Her mother had been working on her laptop with her earbuds in, sitting in the aisle seat in front of them. Her father had been watching the map on a screen showing their route to San Francisco. He too had been working, but had strayed after dinner, watching *Black Panther* but switching it off halfway through, telling her it was a ridiculous movie.

"What happened to Grandmother?" Emma asked.

"She was taken to Germany," her father signed. It was obvious from the way his hands moved that he was being forced to speak about a subject he would rather avoid. Signing, as a physical act, had all the nuances of gesture, the way the face tells as much as the voice.

"Why?" she signed back quickly.

"She was arrested by the French police. She was fourteen, a lycée student, working in the Resistance."

"What happened to her?" Emma signed.

The steward came by, poured her father another cup of coffee, and asked if they were enjoying the flight. He looked at Emma and she'd read his lips. She smiled back and nodded. He was young and handsome and obviously flirting with her. She was getting used to the attention of men. At the climbing gym, boys were always chatting her up. The climbing had made her more self-assured and physically stronger, and the two seemed to have gone together.

"Why this interest? It's morbid, Emma," her father signed. "It's nothing to do with your generation, for God's sake." He had turned and

260

was speaking as well as signing. Her mother glanced at them and smiled, unable to follow the conversation. She went back to her work.

"She was sent to Ravensbrück concentration camp."

The plane was dark. They were in the business section; the seats were huge and comfortable. She had been reading her Kindle and had finished *A Train in Winter* with no idea that her own grandmother had witnessed the unthinkable there. She was stunned and felt alarmed, as if it were yesterday.

She looked across at her father's wine glass; he'd husbanded it after their dinner service. The red wine was vibrating slightly.

JULY 1945, GERMANY SOUTH EAST OF HANOVER

Civilization— and with it any kind of decency— had been destroyed and lay in a charred ruin from Stalingrad to Berlin. Hanover had been bombed to a cinder. It was apparent on the roads south of Berlin as the two teenage girls, one pregnant, saw on the road after their liberation from Ravensbrück concentration camp. They were attempting to get home, to get back to Paris. They had survived the unsurvivable. They had seen firsthand the destruction of the human spirit. Seen it go out of women's eyes… seen the babies of Gypsy prisoners bashed to death and thrown in the snow by female guards. Germany that morning, the country that had nurtured Kant and Beethoven, had been reduced to cannibalism — European Fascism's final high-water mark.

In another, unexpected irony, German-speaking people were being sent to concentration camps in the Soviet Union, or simply gunned down from Hungary to Poland, although many had lived there for generations. What had been the greater Germany was dead, and being ripped into pieces by the Allies. Near Hanover they were selling meatballs containing human flesh, the great city flattened.

The two teenage girls, having walked through the fire-gutted city early that morning before they were picked up, could see block after block, whole blocks razed by the bombing. Cigarettes were money, as was sex; the detritus of the greatest war Europe had seen was everywhere, as were the decomposed bodies of those who had fallen in the last hours, glum reminders, half burnt, forever nameless and horrible.

Guns were plentiful. People of every stripe had them, including wizened concentration camp victims, wearing their frightening camp uniforms, French prisoners of war, women of unknown origins, cutthroats, lunatics, German soldiers, Russian prisoners of war in mufti with their dark beards, all part of the mass of humanity called the Wanderers by the American MPs who had picked up the two French girls outside the city. They had stopped not far from the town of Mindin in a forest beautiful in July, as if the whole bloody business had never happened. That is the irony of Nature's face; it will never reflect human agony no matter how great. Rivers and mountains are beautifully indifferent to man's fate.

The two young soldiers were from New York. Both were to form the nucleus of a successful gang that would be headquartered in Berlin, would make a fortune in the chaos, and go on to build housing for GIs back home. Both would become prominent business tycoons, the Nazi aftermath becoming a road to riches for so many in the dirty world born in May 1945.

The two French girls were raped repeatedly, and were left like so much garbage under a beautiful oak tree, its great limbs silent protection from the July sun. One of the girls finally made it back to Paris, but pregnant. Her son would become a famous French scientist. The other girl disappeared in a summer rainstorm amongst the mass of people waiting for food at a Red Cross DP camp. She would work later in a brothel in Argentina.

The two had been friends before and lived through it all, as the older women died off, even the strong ones. The two girls had stood in the snow together during those terrible roll calls, often in a blizzard, as, one by one, women fell.

Emma Barre's grandmother Celeste never saw her friend again. She left messages later with the Red Cross in Paris, but there was never any news.

A few years later a lover told her to forget the past, that it must be forgotten, or one would go mad. He'd been a policeman and had helped round up Jews in Paris. He'd lied to her about his past—so many lies would be told. They were commonplace. The Cold War came and helped remodel the truth. The Wanderers disappeared into history. The oak tree and the beautiful field remained.

"I don't know who my father was," Barre signed. He had waited, deciding whether to tell his daughter the truth.

"Why not? I don't understand," Emma signed.

"Because your grandmother—she came back pregnant," her father said. "I don't understand?" Emma said again.

"She was raped, on the way home," he signed. He reached up and turned on his reading light. He picked up his book, a history of physics in the 20th century.

"We're on vacation," her father said, not bothering to sign. "I don't want to talk about it anymore."

***

They stood in the Homeland offices at SFO and reviewed the tapes. They had replayed them four times before they were convinced.

"It's not them. … The Barres we met." Marvin said. They had watched Emma and her parents go through customs with all the foreigners arriving on Air France flight #2013 from Charles De Gaulle airport that day. The duty officer, a woman, had been energetic in getting the video. The department of Customs and Border Protection had, she told them proudly, an extraordinarily "robust" database, cross-referenced in a multitude of ways. They had simply needed to type in the date and airline and flight number. The cameras were HD, the video quality high.

Emma's mother and father were clearly seen at one point, in closeup, as they showed their passports. They were not the two people the detectives had met at the hotel—physically close in many ways, but not the two people caught on the video. It was obvious. They'd been duped from the beginning. They were given the passport photos of the Barres along with their contact info. They immediately called the two numbers and heard a recording in French that they didn't understand. They learned later, from one of the French-speaking translators at the SFO help desk, that the message simply said the mailbox was full. It was the case with both cell numbers given by Emma's parents listed on their passports.

Confused and shocked, they walked through the international arrivals. The breezeway was chock-full of mostly tourists, from all over the world, eager to get on with their vacations and get into what the Chinese still called "Golden Mountain."

On the way back into the city, O'Higgins got a text.

You'll have one more chance, or Emma dies. Nothing's changed.

Chapter 33

The last ten feet of the rock chimney, composed of fire-blackened chert, seemed impossible. Her feet were bleeding from the climb. Smoke from the embers was still wafting up, with ash flakes, and collecting at the top of the chimney. The updraft would take them out the vent. The smoke made her eyes burn.

She would have to step over and across the chimney. She would have to use one leg to hold her while she found some kind of purchase on the other side, for a final pivot. The wall's inclination was getting more pronounced. If she failed to find a foothold across the dark space, she would die. It was that simple, and she knew it.

Her fingers and calves were cramping, made worse by the lack of food. She was tempted to look down, but it would only hurt her eyes. She thought of her grandmother. She, too, must have suffered, yet somehow a girl of fourteen made it back home to Paris.

It was fall, or not. One gesture, one decision. She looked across the chimney, tried to see how she might manage a pivot on the other side. The darkness and smoke made the rock chimney's opposite face difficult to judge. She swung out with her right foot. It slipped down, but held. But she was cockeyed, her hands and feet in a cross, her weight on the lower side. Her right arm screamed in pain. Her knee trembled with the strain. She screamed and brought the right foot up, so she was balanced. It stuck. The X her body made was strong and even. Her mouth full of smoke, she used her upper body—both arms at her waist — to shimmy toward the opening.

Something hit her leg. She looked down and saw a man through the smoke. She started to cough.

Her heart seemed to stop. At first, she thought she was dreaming or seeing things, the way she'd seen things on the cave's wall.

It was the first time she'd seen the man who had abducted her clearly. She recognized the man who'd picked them up that day at the airport, their Uber driver. He was speaking to her. She could tell by his gestures. In fact, he was speaking in French. "Don't be stupid. Come down."

She stopped climbing. She looked up and saw the three-foot vent in the rock, and was sure she could climb through it. She glanced down the fifty feet and saw the top of the man's head and then his face again. He was bending down doing something. She looked up again and all pain stopped. She shimmied closer to the vent, moving like a mechanical doll that had been wound very tight, and once released, was unwinding quickly.

"I've lit the fire," he said. "It won't be long, and you'll feel the heat. You won't make it. You'll be burnt. I guarantee it."

Almost immediately she smelled the acrid smoke. She could see it gathering around her. She fought for breath and kept moving. The heat started, but she didn't give up. It was the sweat from her face and arms sliding onto on her fingers that made her lose her grip and almost fall.

She realized she would die if she didn't stop, go back—"down climbing" the way she'd been taught.

Later, in the man's Boston Whaler, heading toward the Golden Gate Bridge, her body and mind exhausted, she fell asleep and had a dream that was super real. She thought she was stuck, unable to force her lower body through the vent. But then it happened, as if she were being delivered by the earth, born on a grassy wind-blown hillside overlooking the Pacific Ocean. She lay face down in the grass, wearing just her panties and bra. She could feel the grass against her stomach. She finally stood up. She looked at her hands. They'd been cut in several places, her fingers cramping still. She had lost all track of time, but she could tell from the sun that it was afternoon. She turned and looked inland. She saw a herd of Tule elk. An alpha buck raised his head and stared at her. Something strange passed between them, some precious bit of instruction about life.

Chapter 34

"So—you're a badass? Is that it?" Marvin said.

Cassie didn't answer. "I have to pick the girls up," she said.

She was getting things ready for dinner. The girls were at ballet class. O'Higgins's daughter had been an inspiration, and they were going to the same dance school in Mill Valley. The commute was difficult, but worth it. Cassie would pick them up at the south end of the bridge, at the Marin Transit stop twice a week. They'd missed their mother and had had to stop going to the school while she'd been gone. It was the first thing she'd made sure went back on track, as the girls loved the school. They were spending less time on social media as a result, something they noticed right away.

"Is that pimp part of it, then?"

"Yes," she said.

They were standing in the kitchen, Marvin in a suit and tie. She was de-veining shrimp, planning to make scampi that night. She looked entirely different again. The look of his wife the night she'd come back was gone. She was wearing yoga pants and a sweater with her hair up, no makeup—the pretty girl next door again. The night she'd come back was the first time he'd seen her in makeup in years.

"I need to know what it is you do. You have to tell me, or I don't know if this is going to work. I'm a cop, Cassie. You knew that when you married me. I can't be married to someone who—to someone who is a criminal. I can't—I don't care about the past. But I have to know the truth."

"I'm not a criminal." She didn't stop working on the shrimp. She cut along its bottom, withdrew the thin vein of mucky intestine, and wiped the knife on a dish towel.

"And how is that? Thorpe is a pimp. That's an illegal business."

She turned and looked at him, touching her cheek with the back of her free hand. She had a moment of crisis. If he knew, he'd be part of it, by default.

"It's a world you don't understand, Marvin. That's all. Let's leave it at that."

"What don't I understand? I want to know."

"The way things really get done at the top—there's a top normal people, regular people, don't ever see."

"Top of what?"

"It's not like on CNN, or on the nightly news. Those are all—like the movies."

"What top, Cassie?"

"The top of all this. Look around you, for Christ's sake! The men who own us."

"Nobody owns me."

"That's what you think," she said. "What everybody thinks." She looked at her watch.

She would have to leave soon, or the girls would be wondering where she was.

"I need an answer—now," Marvin said. "What is it you do? Why do you need a pistol? Why do you need to see Thorpe? Where were you the other night?"

"I work for them—the top. The people who own us. They owned my mother, and they own me, and they own you, whether you think so or not." She tried to make a joke of it. "Just ask Alexa." She'd understood what the Amazon device represented the moment she'd seen her husband set it up.

"You're not making any sense," he said.

She looked at him. "Why can't you see it? It's right in front of everyone, but no one sees it. Sees them. They don't go to the supermarket. They don't live in the neighborhood. They don't send their kids to your school. Do you understand? They don't intersect with us—ever. Never.

"You see them sometimes on TV, okay? You see them with their suits on, very sober, talking about disarmament, or the interest rates, and not the way I saw them—naked. All right? Is that what you wanted to hear? I used to fuck them while their wives were on the plane. Okay? You feel better now? I used to fuck them for money—so, you see I really saw them. I heard them talk about people like you and me.

"Dirt People—that's what they think of us. You think it's just black people? Well, I got news for you, Marvin. It's not. They hate us all, the same way, believe me. We're just here to make them richer. Okay? You get it now? They don't give a fuck about us."

"Rich people—is that what you're talking about?"

"No, it's not. You still don't get it. It's not about the rich—some john at the country club with a Mercedes. It's about power—over people, over a country. Because they're all the same people. It's a club."

"What is it you do for them?"

"I fix problems. Problems that need my attention. That's what I do for them, all right?"

"Problems?"

"Yes. You see, I'm not a criminal. No laws apply to the top, and I work for them. You understand? I can't be a criminal. I'm something else. I don't know what, exactly. But no cop will ever knock on the door and take me away. I'm sure of that. If that's what you're worried about—is that it?"

"Yes. Of course. I don't want our daughters' mother to—to be arrested one night. What the hell."

"Won't happen. So, I'm going to pick up the girls. Should I come back in the house when I get back, or not? I don't want to have this conversation again. I can't take it. This is my home, Marvin. I love you and the girls. That has to be good enough, or not. Now, I want to finish this before I go. You let me know."

Marvin said nothing. She was afraid to look up, but finally did.

"I like lots of lemon," Marvin said. "You know, with the scampi."

"I'm not—not your father, Marvin. I'm not going to disappear. If that's what you're worried about."

Marvin nodded and walked out.

***

O'Higgins had a drink at the bar at the Marriott on Bay Street. He couldn't go home. He had nothing to go home to. He'd called Robin to see if he could stay the night with her, but it had gone to voice mail. Lonely, he'd called his daughter and spoken for a few minutes, moving to a booth at the back of the bar. Rebecca was in her boyfriend's car. They were on their way to his parents' summer place in the Hamptons. It would be the first time she would meet his parents, and she was nervous. He told her she had nothing to worry about, and to just be nice, and it would all take care of herself.

"It's the Hamptons, dad."

"So what? Just another beach town."

"Did Mom's people like you?" she asked. "I mean, when you first met?"

"Yeah. They were nervous, because of your uncle being—"

"A Hell's Angel?"

"Yeah, and me being a cop. But it was fine."

"Uncle Jimmy isn't bad, really. I've only met him a few times, but he seems cool," his daughter said.

"Uncle Jimmy is okay, for an outlaw biker. Anyway, they liked me. We got along right away."

"But Noah's parents are—you know. His dad is a big-time banker."

"So what?" he'd said again.

His daughter had not gotten any of the Irish resentment of their supposed social betters, hating their English masters who thought them inferior and treated them as such. It was natural to the race, like breathing. His daughter had instead gotten her mother's working-class Okie insecurity, assuming that money was the determining factor. If you had it, it made you better— and smarter—than those who didn't.

"How's Robin?" his daughter had asked.

"Fine. She wants me to move in with her."

"And?"

"I'm thinking about it. I just might. I'm tired of San Rafael. Too many memories there. I'm just keeping it for you. So you'll have a place here, if you want it. I won't sell it."

The barmaid came as he ended the call. He ordered a second gin and tonic. She flirted with him. She was his age. A redhead with very white skin. Her hair dyed and braided "unicorn" style. Buxom and vibing louche.

"I've seen you around," she said. "You and the tall guy. You kicked some Hong Kong high roller out of his room yesterday. That guy doesn't tip. Zero."

"My partner," O'Higgins said. "The good looking one. Yeah."

"Are you staying here ?" she asked.

"No. Just business, I guess you could call it."

"You're a cop, right?"

"Yeah. How did you know?"

"My dad was twenty-five years with the LAPD. It's easy to tell the difference between you guys and civilians. You stick out. Sorry."

He laughed, and she smiled at him. There was an attraction. Instant sexual chemistry. The kind that happens between human beings and can't be denied. He felt it.

"Hey," he said. "Can you help me with something?"

"Sure. But I would just give you my number—if you want it," she said.

He smiled. "I'm flattered, but no—it's this. This guy. Have you seen him in here?" He picked up his phone and showed her the photos of the Barres he had gotten that first day. "Here at the hotel—maybe you've seen him."

She took his phone. "No. Maybe an Uber driver, but there are so many of them."

'What about her?" He showed her Mrs. Barre's passport photo.

"You're kidding, right?"

"No."

"That's Zoe Gille. She was our night manager until she was fired a few months ago— dope fiend. Was nodding out in the office all the time," she said. "I'll just punch in my number, so you have it. Just in case? I'll get that drink."

He stood up. She was inputting her number and calling herself. The woman didn't notice the anxious look on his face.

"No. I've changed my mind—thank you." He showed her Mr. Barre's passport photo again. "You sure you don't recognize him?"

"Maybe . . . not sure. He looks familiar, but—"

"Was she married? Gille?"

"To a needle and spoon, maybe," the barmaid said.

***

"Is Cassie back home, then?" O'Higgins asked.

"Yeah, she's back. It's all good now," Marvin said. He was looking out the window, O'Higgins driving. They were on Market Street at Seventh. Pedestrians huddled on the meridian, waiting for the next streetcar. O'Higgins punched it and they raced through a yellow light.

"Good. Glad to hear it. Are we going to find Emma there—at Gille's place?"

"I doubt it. I doubt they're still there. Why would they stick around? They have the money," Marvin said.

"And he wants more. Seems stupid. Desperate. I don't get it," O'Higgins said.

"You said she's a dope fiend, right? They do strange shit. All I know is that we got a problem. We could lose our jobs. She tells everyone downtown what we did."

"Tells them we gave her man ten thousand dollars. How do we fix that?" O'Higgins said.

"Are you done with the acid bullshit?" Marvin said.

"I don't know. Haven't thought about it," O'Higgins said.

"Do you like it?"

"No. Not really."

"It must be freaky-deaky, man. You going to grow your hair long now and shit?"

"It's kind of a mind fuck, really," O'Higgins said. They both laughed. "I think Emma is alive. I believe it."

Marvin didn't answer.

***

"Slap her again," Marvin said.

O'Higgins looked at him. "We should call an ambulance."

"Slap her again," Marvin said.

They were on Potrero Hill at the address the DMV had given up for Zoe Gille. They hadn't expected her to be there still. O'Higgins had kicked the door open and they'd gone up the long stairway to the flat on the second floor. Zoe Gille was sitting at a dirty kitchen table, two cockroaches on her hand. She had nodded out. Her works were on the table: spoon and syringe.

O'Higgins slapped her again. "Is she dead?" O'Higgins said.

"No. Again. Go on."

Instead of slapping her, O'Higgins stood her up and started to walk her around the apartment. She mumbled something, then opened her eyes.

"I told you she wasn't dead," Marvin said. "Where's Emma?" he got in her face.

Gille looked at him and recoiled slightly, the heroin in complete possession of her. Her eyes were dull, her skin thick looking. Drool came from between her lips. It was hard to believe she was the same woman who had posed as Emma's mother at the Marriott only a few days before. She'd been on a bender, it was obvious.

"Look for Emma," O'Higgins said. He half dragged the woman back across the kitchen and out to the living room. The apartment—once probably chic, judging from the furniture—was filthy, fast food containers everywhere with half-eaten food. He sat her on a couch by a window looking out on Kansas Street.

"She not here. No trace," Marvin said, walking into the living room.

"She's pissed herself." As soon as he'd sat her down, Gille had urinated. The urine ran into the couch and onto the floor. "Shit." O'Higgins said.

"It's normal for junkies to piss themselves," Marvin said. "You got to keep her moving. Get her up and walk her around. I'll go get some Red Bull." He walked out and O'Higgins could hear him going down the stairs. For a moment he thought he would leave her on the couch, disgusted. But he fought that, yanked her up and walked her back toward the kitchen. The stench of the urine was strong. It was like walking a foul-smelling rag doll.

He walked her to the sink in the kitchen and looked out the window toward the Bay. Everything was steel grey, the street half hidden in the fog.

"*Frederic… Frédéric, c'est toi? Merci d'être venu, mon cher,*" Gille said, her chin down. She looked up. Marvin came back and made her drink two cans of Red Bull, one right after the other. She tossed the first can, but kept down the second, finally sobering up.

"Where is Emma?" Marvin said. They had sat her back down at the kitchen table after letting her change out of her urine-soaked jeans, in front of them. She was wearing a robe, with no underwear.

"I don't know," she said. "I'm sick. You have to understand."

"I don't have to understand shit," Marvin said. "Tell us where Emma and your friend are."

"I don't know." She looked up at them. Her matted hair looked damp. She ran her hand over her face. A cockroach ran across the table, hiding in a half-eaten box of chicken nuggets.

"Where are Emma's parents?" O'Higgins said.

"I don't know."

"You're lying," Marvin said. "Where are they?"

"I'm not lying. I don't know."

"But you helped take Emma? Didn't you? And you know where she is?"

"No. Frederic came to me after he had the girl. He needed someone to play the mother. Someone who spoke French and looked enough like her mother. He promised me money—I went to the hotel and acted like the girl's mother."

"You never asked him what he'd done with the parents?" O'Higgins said.

"No. I didn't want to know."

"But it was you at the museum?"

"Yes. I gave Frederic the memory stick with the bitcoin. He never paid me. I haven't seen him since. He cheated me."

"He's a heroin addict? What's his name?"

"Yes. It's how we met," she said. "Frederic Desper. He drives for Uber... It's how he met the parents. He's French. He offered to show them the city. They paid him to be a guide."

"Tell him you have to speak to him," O'Higgins said.

"He won't believe me."

"Tell him you have the thumb drive with the bitcoin. That you kept the one with the money—and you're sorry. You want to give it to him."

She looked at O'Higgins and rubbed her face. "He never got the bitcoin. There was nothing on that thumb drive you gave him."

"You have his number?" Marvin said.

"He changes phones constantly—borrows them from street people. I don't know how to contact him. I have no number for him."

"You two have a dealer?"

"Yes," she said.

"A dealer he might still use?" O'Higgins said.

"Yes, maybe," she said. "I feel sick. Please, I need to lie down."

"How do you think Emma Barre feels?" Marvin said. He went and found her cell phone. "What's his name, your connection?"

"George," she said. "George. He works at a bar…"

"What bar?" O'Higgins said.

"A bar on Harrison. Buddies, something."

"The gay bar on Harrison? Blow Buddies?"

"Yes… He tends bar there. Frederick might go there to score."

"How did Desper know the Barres?" O'Higgins said.

"Uber. I told you. He picked them up at the airport their first day. He offered to be a kind of guide. He is from Lyon—he came back and told me he looked like the father. We're both French… He came up with the plan to kidnap the girl and to make it seem like it was like the other foreign girls who had been murdered. That we could make big money if we took the girl. That the Barres were wealthy… I didn't want to do it. He threatened me."

"What about the parents?"

"They came to the boat. He had a slip at the yacht harbor behind pier 39."

Frederic had taken them to Pier 39. Had met the family at the Ferry Building that morning for a walking tour and left them at the Pier. He suggested Emma would like the Hall of Mirrors. He had expected the parents to go with her. It made it that much easier when he saw she had gone in alone. After he'd taken the girl to the boat, he called the Barres who were waiting, not sure what had happened to Emma. They'd texted her phone, but she hadn't answered.

Frederic found her parents and said that Emma had been attacked—that he'd happened on her behind the pier, and that she'd been attacked by a homeless man, but that she was okay. He said the man had stolen Emma's phone. That he'd taken her to his boat to rest, and that he'd called the police to report the robbery already. Emma had asked him to go find them.

"He took the Barres out to the boat," Gille said. "They were grateful—believing the girl was okay."

"He killed them? Emma's parents?" O'Higgins said.

"Yes. He threw their bodies overboard, outside the Golden Gate Bridge. The girl was asleep—he'd drugged her. She didn't see what he'd done. She didn't recognize him inside the attraction, either."

"What about the passports?" O'Higgins said.

"We had their passports and their phones. Room keys at the Marriott... Frederic doctored their passports. He had a junkie friend who is a lithographer. He took our photos and used them on the Barres' passports."

"If you're lying, we'll come back. You understand? You're going to disappear now."

"We'll look for you, but we won't be able to find you because you left the country. Is that clear?" Marvin said. He glanced at O'Higgins. They had no choice. If they arrested her, she could implicate them in the ransom plot.

"Yes. Yes." Gille was shocked and grateful. She fell on her knees and grabbed Marvin's hand and kissed it.

O'Higgins looked at Marvin. He was digging them a bigger hole, but they had no choice.

They couldn't afford to arrest her.

Chapter 35

Exhausted, Emma had watched as the Boston Whaler passed the Golden Gate, the excursion boat only a few hundred yards away. It was there, as she watched the people on the deck from every country on earth, she knew that her parents were dead. It was the first time she allowed the obvious to make itself felt physically. Because she was so exhausted, the realization was a strange one: horror and disbelief at once.

She'd woken up cold and sore from her climb, her feet lacerated. The Boston Whaler's outboard engine droned on in the twilight.

She had had another dream. In the dream she was sitting at breakfast, talking with her parents. It was in the kitchen at their home in Lyon. The windows were dark, as if they were living during a war where a blackout was being imposed. She could hear the sound of protesters outside chanting "Fake News! … Fake News! … Macron, resign! Macron, resign!"

"*Casseurs*," her mother said, looking at her and taking her hand. "The right wing is back."

"No," her father said. "They are not the same. This is different. Can't you hear?"

"My father is right. It's different."

"Don't listen to your father, dear. He lives in the future, and I live in the past, her mother said. "I read history."

They had passed under the Richmond Bridge and were heading toward the Sacramento Delta. Car headlights lined the bridge.

The man was sitting in the bow, shooting up his bare foot up on his opposite knee. He was looking for a place to inject and was oblivious. His arm still guided the outboard as he found the spot. She noticed a scab on his ankle.

"They're dead—my parents," she said in French.

The man looked up at her, the drug making its way to his nervous system and doing its work. His eyes moving queerly, he started to nod. If her parents were dead, she realized that in a real way, she too was dead. The girl who had belonged to them was gone.

He put on his filthy white sock slowly, like a sick man. He pointed his pistol at her. He fired, the bullet going over her head. She saw the flash from the pistol's barrel. He smiled at her, his eyes half-shut.

"I'm going to kill you," she said, looking at the man.

He straightened himself, coming out from behind his dope-addled indifference, and looked at her.

"Why? What did they ever do to you?"

"*Ferme ta bouche*," he said. Shut your trap.

"You'll see," she said in English. "I'll watch you die." He smiled.

"They're looking for me—I know they are. The police."

"And how's that working so far?" he said.

Night fell as they headed into the Sacramento Delta's brackish water. They passed shoddy-looking houseboats. Forlorn boat docks attached to lit up one-story houses, set back from the water, their dull lights hovering over the dark marshy landscape like smudge pots.

"What did you do with them?" she said. "They trusted you." He nodded toward the opaque water.

"Do you even realize what you've done?" She stared at him. All the belief in mankind and any goodness died in her. She no longer loved the sinner. She understood, finally, why her grandmother had fought, and why she'd suffered. There were the antichrists destroying everything they touched, killing those who opposed them and their hell on earth. It was as simple as that. She hated the sinner. She stared at the pistol in the man's

280

belt and longed to kill him with it.

***

Cassie had read that the Russian oligarch had checked into a clinic in Basel, Switzerland. The English tabloid the *Daily Mail* ran a photo. The English newspapers were almost always the first to carry news about her work.

The man looked completely changed. His hair had fallen out, and he looked ghastly. The headline under the photo was simple: PUTIN RIVAL POISONED BY RUSSIA'S FSB. There was a comparison to Alexander Litvinenko in London, including Litvinenko's now famous hospital-bed photo, in case there was any mistake about who was responsible. It was done, and she knew why it had been done. Like all the times before, she put it aside.

Cassie was starting to get back to what had been her life. It was different now. She was carrying with her the weight of her husband's knowing exactly what she'd been, and that had engendered a fear that was not going away. She had a nagging feeling that he must think less of her now, despite his saying otherwise. The truth had also brought a humiliation. They'd not made love since she'd gotten back. It was as if some unseen person was pushing them apart, and she didn't know what to do about it.

Her phone rang when she was on the way into yoga class on 24th Street. Her friends from the class stood around with her, all women her age and younger who had gotten to know each other there. They'd been planning a birthday party for one of the women in the class who'd lost her job and had been distraught, afraid she would lose her home.

She saw the number and moved away from the group, giving them a weak smile.

"It's me. Your uncle Gus," the familiar voice said.

"Yes," Cassie said. The sound of his voice was both frightening and reassuring. It had always been that way.

"There is someone we'd like you to meet—seems she knows your husband, thought you'd like to meet her. Details to follow. Tell Marvin hello from the family, that we are always thinking of him, too. He has friends. Cheerio, dear."

She got a text a minute later with an address on Potrero Hill on Kansas Street and a photo of a woman.

She picked up her yoga mat and begged off from her friends, saying that one of her girls had felt ill and she was going to pick her up at school. She walked to her car, slid behind the wheel and studied the photo she'd been sent.

We are always thinking of him.

She played Gus's words back in her head. They were listening to Marvin, intercepting his calls—had they been worried he would pose a threat to her? And this woman in the photo? It was clear what they wanted.

Nothing was going to be normal again, she thought as she started the Jeep and pulled out onto 24th Street. She'd been lying to herself. She was part of the game again. And now, it seemed, so was Marvin. Like herself, he'd become an asset. One day, sooner or later, they would ask her to involve him.

"Who is this woman?" Cassie said when he got home.

Marvin said he was only in for a shower and something to eat, and he was going out again. O'Higgins was waiting for him downstairs. She'd come into the bedroom and watched her husband undress and wrap a towel around his waist. He looked thinner than before she left.

When she'd first met him, he seemed to eat rarely. She saw the scar on his thigh from the shootout on Alabama Street. It looked like an ugly worm, the skin having scarred, the scar tissue smooth.

He looked at the photo on her phone.

"How did you get this?" he said shocked. It was Zoe Gille's photo.

"It doesn't matter. Who is she?"

"Dope fiend. Part of the Emma Barre case—she and her boyfriend are the ones that took Emma. They pretended to be her parents. Fooled everyone. Now how in the hell did you get this?"

282

"Is she a threat—to us?"

"What do you mean?"

"Marvin, I'm not asking you for the hell of it. Is she a threat to you? To our family?"

"Yes. In a way."

"Why?"

"We paid her the ransom—for Emma. We didn't tell anyone. It's been a secret. We should have—well, it doesn't matter now, it's done. We kept it a secret, Mike and I. We're both fucked if she tells anyone we paid a ransom. We didn't arrest her. We could have today, but didn't. We should have. But we want her out of the picture. She's helping us find Emma."

"Why?"

"Why what?"

"Why are you and Mike doing all this?"

"Because we want to find Emma. That's why."

"And you had to break the law?" Cassie said. "You're a policeman."

"Yeah. We lost the rule book on this one. So what? Do you know what it's like to find these girls—out there? What it does to you, because you failed them, and they died? You don't understand. How could you? You think fucking for money was a big deal—well guess what, it wasn't. Okay? You're alive. Those girls aren't. And it was our fault."

"It's not your fault. You did your best." She ignored the remark about her past. She'd been expecting some sign of resentment, and was almost grateful. It meant he was still emotionally involved, she hoped. Maybe he'd not given up on her—he was hurt. "Marvin, I'm sorry. I didn't mean—"

"What if it were one of our girls? Huh, would you care about the fucking rule book then? Are you going to tell me how you got this photo?"

"No."

"Fuck, Cassie—what the hell?! This shit has got to stop!"

"It can't stop—don't you see? It will never stop, now." She threw her arms around him and held him and started to cry. "I love you and the girls so much. That's all I know. Okay?"

"Okay," Marvin said. "All right. Jesus. All right."

***

They had decided not to play Desper's game anymore. When he contacted them this time—and they were positive he would—they were going to ignore any requests for ransom. They'd concluded he would kill Emma as soon as he got what he wanted. Their only hope was to find him before he could. It was risky, they knew, but they had no choice. They concluded too that Emma's parents were most likely dead. There was little point in searching for them until Emma had been found.

"Are you George?" Marvin said.

The bouncer-cum-doorman at Blow Buddies—a muscle twink, in gay parlance—was trying to stop them until O'Higgins had simply pushed him out of the way.

"Who are you, doll?" the bartender asked.

"Homicide, SFPD," O'Higgins said curtly.

"Fuck you," Marvin said. "I asked you a question."

George was in a black leather vest with nipple piercings. He and another short man in leather gear were sorting lubes on the bar, given out free, along with condoms. The place was a sex club, masquerading as a bar. The name said everything.

"I'm your worst nightmare," Marvin said. "And he's your second." Marvin nodded toward O'Higgins. "We found your phone number in the address book of a man who was murdered on Gold Mine Drive. We believe you were selling him drugs."

"Do you have some ID?" George said.

He was, O'Higgins thought, looking at the man behind the bar, the last San Francisco cliché: the gay "leather boy." He'd learned all about their subculture on another case. It was more than just a fetish, or even a bizarre semi-naked look. It was a complex knotting of sadomasochism and gay identity, attached to a fantasy masculinity that seemed to live exclusively for sex and drugs. They were some of the first to go in the AIDS epidemic. The disease had cut a wide and cruel stretch across the city, thirty years before. The bathhouse scene bookmarked by drugs and pedestrian sex was making a comeback now that the antivirals were keeping people alive. It was 1980 all over again on Harrison Street.

"You're coming with us," Marvin said. "So get the fuck out from behind there."

"I don't know anybody on Gold Mine Drive," George said. He had been all attitude, feeling safe, but having seen Marvin's other violent self, he was afraid. What he didn't know was that Marvin's best childhood pal had died of an overdose. It had had given him a pathological hatred for heroin dealers.

"You're lying," Marvin said. "I will pull you the fuck out of there!"

The muscle twink came in, looked at O'Higgins, then walked back through the door, not wanting any piece of it.

"Do you have some ID, if you're the police?" George said.

Marvin punched him in the face, knocking the butt lube and condoms off the bar with his free hand. He jumped over the bar, dragged the bigger man out and cuffed him, making him kneel.

O'Higgins looked on in dread. Their lives were being torn apart by Emma Barre.

Everything the case touched— including them—was turning to shit, like some ugly virus. It was an official nightmare, he thought, with no good outcome.

"Okay," O'Higgins said. "Calm the fuck down, Marvin. Fuck."

Chapter 36

Cassie picked Lana's ashes up from the Neptune Society in the Richmond District at 11:30 in the morning. It felt good to have her near again. She'd tried to find Lana's people, but failed. She found no trace of the grandmother who had raised her. There had been no one else to collect her friend, she thought, pulling onto Geary Blvd.

The box was plain. The old man at the Neptune Society had been quiet when he handed her friend over. Had he realized what she was going through? It was hard to believe the young girl she'd known all those years ago, silly and beautiful, was reduced to ashes. The girls who had ridden out across the bay in Monte Carlo, the hot smell of the boat's leather seats in the air. The two of them holding hands—how young they were, how brave they were, how truly innocent they'd been that afternoon.

She thought of where she could scatter Lana's ashes as she drove along. She remembered Lana leaving in the trick's Cadillac, the first day they'd met. The way she'd turned around and looked at her as if she knew their lives would, from that moment on, be forever intertwined. No one would ever, she realized, understand her, the way Lana had. No one would get her and what she'd been running from her whole life again.

"You had to be a Dirt Person," she said out loud. Only the Dirt People understood what it was like to be chased by all those devils, or to be hated the way they were. She pulled over and touched the box.

"I love you," she said. "Why did it have to end like this?"

A moment of sunshine emerged, those quick ones that come in late summer when the fog finally gives way.

"Tell me where you want to go. Where would be the right place, girl? Huh? Where is that place, Lana?"

She got no answer. She thought something would come to her, just the right place.

And then it hit her. She turned the corner and went back west toward the beach. As soon as she had guessed right, she saw Lana sitting next to her, the eighteen-year old, bellbottoms and a dashiki, her "good" hair shiny and beautiful.

They talked all the way to the great highway, just young women, about who they might marry someday. Lana said she would marry a guy from the neighborhood called Tyrone. She said they would have four kids and live in Europe, somewhere—probably France, because she liked it. And they had black people there, too.

Cassie pulled the car over on the Great Highway and left it there. She carried the box down the wide stretch of empty cold beach, the Pacific Ocean great and powerful in front of her. The beach was empty because it was cold in August. She held the box, Lana walking next to her.

"Good," Lana said "Good. That makes it all right then. No one understands us, do they?"

"No, they don't. It doesn't matter."

"This isn't goodbye—right?" Lana said. She stopped and smiled. "Is it? I don't want to say goodbye."

"No, it's not." They hugged alone on the deserted cold wind-swept beach. It miraculously turned warm, and they were in Cannes again, walking on that happy beach, families around them—summertime happiness. Colors. Noise—not Dirt People, just two young women.

Cassie walked out into the waves, the churning surf cold, the wood box in her hand.

When she couldn't walk anymore, she let her sister go free. The foamy water took her away. She felt her going back to mother earth.

When Cassie got back into the car, wet and cold, she pulled out onto the Great Highway and turned on the radio. An old pop song came on, one that had played when she and Lana were driving back from Malibu that morning so long ago now:

All the leaves are brown, and the sky is grey... I've been for a walk on a winter's day... I couldn't take the walk if I was in LA... California Dreaming...

***

They drove the dealer out, in their spanking new SFPD Ford, to the Bayshore, the industrial area and then down Quint Street to a desolate spot they'd once found a body. It was directly across from the Southern Pacific Railway tracks where the asphalt turned to dirt. It was a scary place. A few homeless had a Hooverville under the railway bridge across the way. They could see their tents in the distance. The railroad tracks formed a kind of no-man's land. The tracks ran down into a tunnel further north. The trains came out at Townsend Street.

"Okay, George. You know a guy named Desper? French guy, drives for Uber. We want his number. How do you get hold of him?"

"I don't know anyone. All my—clients—are numbers. That's all they are. Just cell phone numbers. They drop a pin on their phone's map and text it to me. I send a runner. That's it."

"You sell fentanyl?" Marvin said. "Why? You know they'll die."

"It's what people want. I'm just a businessman."

"Get out of the car," Marvin said. George looked at O'Higgins. "You heard me."

He climbed out of the back seat. Marvin had him kneel in the dirt. O'Higgins jumped out of the car. Marvin was resting his Glock's barrel on the back of the guy's head by the time O'Higgins got around to the front of the car.

"Don't do it, man!" O'Higgins said.

"Why not?" Marvin said. "I'm tired of people like him. We can make something up. No one will care." He was looking down at the man, his bare arms hairy.

"I don't know," O'Higgins said. "But don't. We can't come back from that."

"I can get his number—the Frenchman," George said. "He lives on a boat." His face was pushed into the dirt so he could barely talk.

O'Higgins phone binged. He pulled it out of his back pocket.

100,000 Bitcoin. To this public Key— 34566WERT45001. Tomorrow. Emma's location to follow money.

He looked up. Marvin was putting the Glock back in his holster.

"Motherfucker knew I would have done it, too," Marvin said. They'd rehearsed the scene on the way to Harrison Street, figuring it that someone who cared so little for human life might assume they wouldn't, either. But O'Higgins thought Marvin might not have been playacting.

***

"Who are you?" Zoe said.

"Are you Zoe?" Cassie asked. "Zoe Gille?"

"Yes."

"We need to talk. Can I come in?" Cassie said.

"I was just leaving." The woman had a backpack over one shoulder. She looked terrible. Cassie recognized the runny nose for what it was. "I see that. It won't take long. Promise," Cassie said. She stepped through the door and closed it behind her. "I really must go," Gille said. She looked toward the door.

"Do you know where the girl is? Emma Barre?"

"No. I told the police—I don't know."

"I think we should go upstairs and talk," Cassie said.

Gille turned and went back up the stairs slowly. She dropped her backpack and whirled. Cassie leaned back as the knife blade passed close to her throat.

She fell backwards, catching herself on the handrail, all her weight on her one arm. She tried to reach for her pistol stuck in the back of her jeans at the small of her back. She heard the pistol fall on the stairs behind her. Gille planted the knife in her chest, taking it to the hilt. She held her wrist. The pain of the blade was excruciating, but Cassie didn't let go, knowing if she did, she would die.

The two women struggled, Gille trying desperately to pull the blade free and strike again.

Cassie held onto to her wrist, keeping it locked. The woman looked at her, wild-eyed.

Cassie stuck her thumb in Gille's eye, pushing it in, the nail cutting the eyeball. Gille screamed and finally let go of the knife. Cassie kept digging her thumb in Gille's eye until she was sure she'd reached what the Italian had called the kill point, where the eyeball could be separated from the socket.

Cassie pulled the knife out of her shoulder and immediately rammed the blade into the woman's throat, at the windpipe. She backed Gille up, pivoting hard off the step to drive her back, using the handle of the knife. Gille fell backwards and onto the stairs, the knife in her throat. The fight was over as quickly as it had started.

Cassie heard the door open behind her and saw Marvin staring at her.

"What did you do?" He didn't see that she was bleeding at first. She crumpled onto the stairs knees up as if she'd meant to sit down, her blood pressure zeroing out. She lifted her head and saw Marvin coming up the stairs, two at a time, toward her.

"You were unconscious," the doctor said. It was the doctor who had taken care of Lana.

She recognized him.

"Where am I?"

"SF General," the doctor said. He was looking down at Cassie, one hand taking her blood pressure with an old-fashioned cuff wrapped around her upper arm. "You're lucky. Another inch or so, and it would have been your heart."

"Mine is hard to find," she said.

The doctor looked at her, then let the pressure go out of the cuff. "Normal. Good shape. One-twenty over seventy. Textbook.

"There is a policeman here. He wants to speak to you. Wants to know what happened. Do you feel up to it?"

"What day is it?"

"Thursday."

"What time?"

"Eight o'clock."

"Is one of them black?"

"The officers? Yes. Do you know them?"

"Give me a moment. Okay."

"Sure," the doctor said. "You and I keep crossing paths." The public address system started paging Dr. Tucker. "That's me. I'll tell them to give you a moment."

"Thanks," Cassie said. She pushed herself up higher in the bed and looked around the room. There was another patient in the bed next to her asleep, the privacy curtain pulled. She tried to think of what to say, but her mind was a blank. The pain medication made her feel woozy. She stared at the door.

Marvin and O'Higgins walked through the door. They had a moment of complete silence that seemed to last forever.

Marvin reached for her hand and held it. "How are you feeling?"

"Tired," she said.

"They're looking for the man who assaulted you," Marvin said. "He killed a woman on Kansas Street. You said he was a street person."

She was silent again.

"You answered the door at home and he attacked you. Understand?"

She nodded.

"Does he look like this?" Marvin said. He held out his phone, showing a picture of man she'd never seen before. "He's a sexual predator. We think it was him. There was a call from the FBI saying he was spotted in San Francisco." Marvin looked at her. "I think the agent's name was Gus," he said.

She took the photo. "Yes," Cassie said. "That was him. I'm sure of it. He stabbed me."

Chapter 37

"You keep looking at your watch," Robin said.

They were eating breakfast at her place in the Harrison. Her kitchen had a view of the Bay Bridge, looking down on it. All the commuter traffic looked slightly menacing.

"She'll be all right? Marvin's wife?" Robin asked.

He looked up. He'd barely spoken since he and Marvin had pulled up to Kansas Street. Marvin had been in first. O'Higgins had come in behind him, saw the pistol lying at the foot of the stairs, and had bent down immediately to pick it up.

He'd seen Cassie, Marvin picking her up, and then the dead woman. It all seemed surreal and out of place.

"She's hurt." Marvin looked back down the stairs at him. She collapsed in his arms and he was trying to make sense of it—her being there at all.

"Yeah, she's going to be fine."

"That's awful," Robin said. "It was on the news last night."

"Yeah," he said. He looked at his watch again.

"Did they catch him yet?"

"No," he said. "Not yet."

"He's been all over attacking women."

He looked up and nodded. The incredible lie about what had happened to Cassie Lee was something he couldn't explain. Marvin said in the Emergency room that there was a way out of the mess. He had gotten up and made a call. O'Higgins noticed that it was Cassie's phone, and he thought Marvin was calling his sister, or maybe the kids—but he'd gone down the corridor, and when he got back he told him it was all good. They didn't have to worry. To say nothing.

"What do you mean?" O'Higgins said

"She was attacked at the house. She was leaving, and the man attacked her."

"What the hell are you talking about?" O'Higgins had said.

"I'm saying she wasn't at Gille's place. Never there."

"I don't follow," O'Higgins said.

He had been trying to figure out how they were going to explain it all. Or if they could simply lie about it all. But he'd worked out none of it. They'd driven to SF General and taken Cassie into the ER and showed their badges. She'd been put on a gurney and wheeled away by two nurses who rushed her down a hallway.

"Can I go visit her?" Robin said.

"Yeah, of course," O'Higgins said.

"Maybe this afternoon?" Robin said. She reached over and touched his hand. "Don't you want to eat?"

He looked down at the breakfast she'd cooked. She was a good cook, something that had surprised him because he'd thought someone like her wouldn't be.

"Not hungry, I guess," he said.

"You guys, the three of you are close. I've noticed. She's really beautiful, Cassie." She looked at him—maybe, he thought, wondering if something more was going on. "Guys must fall for her all the time."

He looked up; he was thinking about the next few hours. He'd been remembering Zoe Gille lying in the stairs, dead. Someone would find her, and then what?

"Cassie," he said.

"Yeah, she's a looker all right."

"She was a model—in LA? Before she met Marvin?"

"Something like that," he said.

She got quiet, and started on her breakfast.

"I'm sorry about the ten grand," he said, getting up. "But here is the fifty Gs." He put the thumb drive she'd given him with the Bitcoin on the table. "I don't have the ten thousand. We may have lost it."

"Don't be," she said. "Doesn't matter." He nodded.

"The new place—they've started tearing it up. My grandfather's place on Telegraph Hill. I'll be with the architect, around four, if you want to weigh in?" she said.

"Okay," he said. His phone buzzed.

Pier 36... Chocolate Heaven. Front. 11 AM.

"Sorry... I've got to go," he said.

She must have seen the look on his face. "Is it Emma Barre?"

"Yeah," he said.

He was alone in the Ford on the Embarcadero, and glad of it. The silence. The City breathing in and out that morning. It seemed like the old San Francisco that he remembered as a kid, beautiful, mysterious, feminine. Maybe because nothing in his life right now made any sense, he was grateful for the surcease.

He was jealous of Marvin, but not because he was in love with his wife. He wasn't. He was jealous of Marvin because Marvin was in love, and nothing else seemed to matter but the two of them. They had that thing. He'd seen it in the Ford, when he was driving crazy to get them to the hospital. They were in the back and he thought Cassie was conscious because she had buried her face in his neck, Marvin's hand pressing on her wound. It was what he'd once had. You couldn't explain it to someone who had never had it. And when they take it away, it's all different. You're alone on the outside of life, everything pedestrian and lonely. He hated that feeling—the coldness of it. It was a kind of prison, with guards. The prisoner hearing the noises of life outside the prison walls.

He looked at his phone and thought about calling Marvin, but didn't. Whatever happened now, it was best if Marvin wasn't part of it. He wanted to do this alone.

Why, he wondered? Was he simply going to kill him? He surprised himself. It wasn't Marvin he was afraid would go off, it was himself. And if he did?

He parked the Ford in front of Pier 39, in the yellow zone, and looked at his watch. It was 10:45. He rubbed the back of his neck. Would Emma be nearby? He didn't know. This was far as he'd gotten. His plan seemed incomplete and frail.

He pulled his Glock and checked the magazine. He'd gotten a see-through magazine since the shootout on Alabama Street, so he could make no mistake about the number of rounds he had. He counted ten. He touched his jacket pocket and felt the spare magazine, examined it once and put it back. Twenty-two rounds. Since Alabama Street, he'd been obsessed with the number of rounds he was carrying. Each one carried that afternoon had been important—a counter-weight to death. Tools of the trade.

He got out of the car and looked at his phone one last time, checking Emma's photo. It was the one Gille had given them that first afternoon. They must have been using the parents' phones—gotten their codes before killing them? They'd been so stupid. He looked out toward Pier 39. The crowds were building already. It was summer and all the colorful flags were flying, crisp and clean in the wind. There was something about August and its singular weather.

Something in the mornings in the air. When he was over in Iraq, he would fantasize about mornings at home, so cool, a kind of confidence brought by the sea air.

He pushed off at 10:50 a.m., exactly. As he walked toward the chocolate store, he got a text.

Cassie going home and ok. Day off.

***

It was a Pierce Seiner Desper had bought at auction. It had belonged to an old Italian guy who had owned her for years, so she was known around Fisherman's Wharf. She was called Adriana, after the Italian's first daughter. He'd died and the family didn't want the boat anymore. All his kids were eager to sell it.

Emma had found a photo of the family in the galley on the way out from the Delta. Desper had handcuffed her left arm to a hatch ring. She'd pulled on the hatch door, but it weighed as much as she did, and there was no point. She'd stopped struggling. She was tired and didn't care, one way or the other. She'd seen him twice, when he checked on her, since they'd left the delta. He was sober, it seemed.

She'd heard the boat's big Cummings engine start up. It was early in the morning. She'd been able to watch the sky from the porthole. She'd seen the old steak knife, its tip broken, and kept on a ledge. Had he overlooked it? It was small, the handle black and worn. It would do the job, she thought. She had to try and get to it, lift the heavy hatch door and reach it. She'd tried several times, but each time the weight of the hatch door was too much. She had to lift it several inches to clear the pocket it was resting in. Her wrist was getting raw. Each attempt failed.

It wasn't until they got to Raccoon Strait, when the chop helped. Realizing she could time her pulling with the swells, she caught it at the right moment and the lid popped beyond the rim. She just managed to reach the knife, lifting it with her thumb and forefinger. The blade was rusted and dirty. It fell on the floor, and she was afraid the pitching would send it out of reach again.

***

If he didn't kill him, then what? They would be caught, and everything they'd done for the good of Emma Barre would look shabby and self-serving. He understood that as he walked along the pier. The faces of the crowd came toward him in a surreal mix. The near-noon sunlight was harsh, so that no one's face seemed entirely normal, all the nuances washed away. What you got was eyes and mouths, young and old, black, white, brown. Nothing solid, really.

Did he want to go down and be ruined, so that his daughter and Marvin's family would be ruined? No—that was why he'd come alone. He touched the Sig Sauer he'd picked up on Alabama Street. He'd left two rounds in. Enough.

He stood across from the store and glanced at his watch. It was 11:00 a.m., exactly.

Hundreds of people walked by. He looked for Emma, hoping Desper might bring her, doubting it was possible. Then what? How would he find her? *You don't have the answers, and you never did.* Now it was about something else. He thought he saw the English girl, and he was brought up sharp: she was with a boy. It startled him. No. It was someone else.

Then he saw him. He simply appeared, walking out of the crowd, and stood by the store's door. Desper looked smaller, somehow. He was wearing black skinny jeans and a white T-shirt. They looked at each other. It must have been the way he looked at Desper that made the Frenchman realize he should run. There would be no exchange.

He'd been standing in a shadow by the arcade. A family speaking German, all of them tall, passed between them. When they'd passed, Desper was gone. It was as if he'd not been there at all. He looked to his left toward the Embarcadero, thinking he would run in that direction, and not toward the pier. He turned and saw him running up the stairs toward the Hall of Mirrors.

O'Higgins took off running straight down the pier. He felt people hitting him, yelling out.

A man grabbed him, thinking him rude, and spun him around. O'Higgins had to get by him, finally elbowing the man in the face to make him let go. But the time he'd made it to the stairs, Desper had disappeared.

He took the outdoor staircase, two stairs at a time. At the top he ran toward the Hall of Mirrors.

Chapter 38

"Close it down. Now!" O'Higgins said.

The attendant at the entrance to the Hall of Mirrors looked at him like he was crazy. He showed him his badge, his Glock out and held against his thigh. The long line of people waiting to buy tickets to the attraction started to scatter. Someone yelled something in a foreign language.

"*Waffe! Waffe!*"

He pulled the door closed behind him. The lights were dim, the colors inside psychedelic.

It was crowded. He looked for Desper's white T-shirt, not knowing for certain whether he had come in or not. He'd thought he'd seen him come toward the attraction.

The lights and music were overwhelming. He saw himself in the first mirror, and it happened, a quick hallucination: Desper was standing behind him. He turned and realized the adrenalin had kicked in, inducing an acid flashback.

He held his Glock in both hands and went to his right. He saw a Chinese family. They were touching the mirrors with their hands. They became a kind of lotus of faces and colored lights. He pushed by them and ran into a mirror, smashing it. He turned. He saw the attendant, but he seemed extremely tall and ugly.

"Turn it off!"

The attendant didn't seem to understand. He pushed off the mirror and went on, the tunnels marked by an Alhambra of columns, designed to confuse. He kept moving, passing a fat girl who was holding a drink. She looked at him and screamed when she saw his weapon. He pushed past her and stood at what seemed like a fork in the passage. He thought he saw Desper—he wasn't sure. He raised his weapon, but lowered it almost immediately. He was pointing at himself. He ran again to the right, thinking an emergency exit must be somewhere in front of him, and the way Desper had exited the day he'd taken Emma.

Someone tackled him from behind. A man was throttling his neck, making him fall backwards. The man was hanging on him; he thought it was Desper, and rolled to see that it was a tourist, a big man who was shouting at him in a language he didn't understand, punching him in the face. He felt the first blow and then a second. They were on the floor, the man dogged, holding him around the neck in a kind of headlock. He smashed the barrel into the man's teeth, full on, then kneed him in the balls, as hard as he could—then again, then again. The man let go. He stood up and smashed the man in the face with the flat of his pistol as he tried to stand.

His head was spinning from the punches. The music stopped, but the strobe lights, whirling pink, purple, blue still masked the emergency exit. He ran forward and struck another mirror, bounced off, breaking it.

Something was wrong with his foot. It was dragging, not quite right. A little girl came toward him screaming. He saw the English girl in one of the mirrors—naked, staring at him.

He stopped, looking for the way out. He tried to master the hallucinations, making himself see, but they were getting worse. The Alice In Wonderland feel and look of the place grew. The voices sounded weird. The lights went off. What had been a monstrous kaleidoscope of passages and mirrors turned into something discernable. He saw the emergency exit to his left, the door ajar. He ran toward it, the pain in his ankle spiking.

The bright sun light outside was overwhelming at first. He looked down the steel staircase and saw Desper running toward the boat harbor.

He went down the stairs unable to run, hobbling. Desper turned back and looked at him and broke out into a dead run. He ran across the service road behind the pier, and toward the yacht harbor and docks.

Desper had to stop at the locked harbor gate. He made it through, using a key, slamming the steel gate behind him. He hobbled after him losing ground. He thought about taking a shot but when he raised his weapon, there was only the gate, no clear shot.

He hobbled on and faced the gate. He shook it, but it was locked. He stood back and fired a round straight into the lock. He heard the bullet ricochet. He stood there; the gate started to move. He closed his eyes and opened them. The water and boats were vibrating. He jumped off the dock and into the water, his right ankle too weak to help him navigate the rocks. He had to guide himself along the dock. At one point he was shoulder deep. He bypassed the gate and pushed himself up onto the dock on the other side. He stood up and hobbled down the narrow dock. His shoes filled with water, making it hard to walk at first. He tried to focus and force himself to see things clearly, but the wavy patterns made everything seem to run together and obscure—just watery lines, running across a sheet of glass.

He heard a motor, the diesel engine loud. He saw a sudden puff of black exhaust fifty yards away. He forced himself into a pathetic run, the pain overwhelming him. His body listed to the left, favoring his good ankle.

He stood at the boat's empty slip, watching the Pierce Seiner pulling away... thirty yards now. He saw Desper at the wheel.

He raised the Glock. The saltwater dripped from his forehead into his eyes. He lined up his front sight on the white T-shirt. He fired—missed. Forty yards... it would be too late at fifty.

He sat and held the pistol against a box for stowing gear, lining up the sights again. He calculated the fall of the bullet at that distance and fired. At first he thought he'd missed, but in a minute he could see the boat going straight on, crashing into the rock breakwater.

He stood. He could hear the boat's motor, loud. Desper had fallen on the throttle. He searched for his iPhone, but it was gone.

He turned around and hobbled down the deck as fast as he could. People working on their boats were staring as he passed, the Glock still at his side.

He got someone from the yacht harbor to run along the breakwater and bring the boat around to the dock the Red and White fleet used. He watched it come in and get tied off. The man had yanked Desper's body off the wheel. He was dead. The bullet had passed through the heart and lodged in the boat's dash—a kill shot. He stared, then climbed aboard. His twisted ankle made it painful to step down onto the deck.

He looked down into the bottom deck, but didn't see her. He sat on his butt and managed to get down the ladder, his ankle rebelling each time he put any weight on it. He came down that silly way and saw her.

"Emma?"

She was holding a knife and looking at him. She was crying. He made his way through the galley and held her. He heard the knife drop. He started to cry himself.

He found the key to Emma's handcuff on Desper's body. After finding it, he stood and looked down at the dead man. Desper seemed surprised in death. O'Higgins turned away, hearing the ambulance in the distance.

He rode in the ambulance with Emma. She was sitting up, the attendant checking her vitals. She looked at him and signed, then stopped.

"You. I felt you—you were the one looking?" she said.

"Yeah. Me and another guy—Marvin."

She nodded, sat back, and let the paramedic work on her.

Chapter 39
Six Weeks Later

It was that last week in October when the Bay Area gets its summer, finally. All the tourists who come in short pants aren't disappointed. That morning on the way to California Street he enjoyed the view: the way the Bay looked, the new Bay Bridge happily indifferent but still spanning the water in that bold way.

He'd gotten up early, rolling out of bed, and stood in the kitchen surveying the kingdom. Robin's new place made it all seem that way: The City, the East Bay, all of it, as if he were its king and it all belonged to him. It was a crazy feeling. He sat with a cup of coffee. the grand view in front of him.

Asha... Sorry I've not written...

He looked at the partial text and deleted it. It wasn't fair. He'd gotten drunk and told Robin he loved her. It was the way she'd taken Emma Barre into her life. She'd been the one to help her sort out the issues with MIT. It had been Robin who had spoken to the girl's people. She had explained to Emma's aunt, a lawyer in Paris, that Emma had no interest in going home to France. That she would go to school in the States, when she was ready.

He was learning to sign. Just a few words. When Emma finally came down to the new kitchen, he signed "good morning". She signed back "Good morning."

"Today we see the doctor?" she asked.

"Yes."

"Okay." He'd gotten used to the sound of her voice, the quality of it. He'd grown to like it, something about it, always hopeful. The struggle in her life that it represented. The struggle over what's handed to us in life and what we do with it.

Later on the Embarcadero, both of them looked at the tourists who were walking along the Embarcadero. He glanced at Emma. She looked at the crowds, studying them, it seemed. Was she looking for her parents?

They had not talked about her parents in weeks. She'd asked to stay with him. When he went to work, she would stay in her bedroom and read. She'd bought books from Amazon on climbing, some on the basics of marksmanship, some on San Francisco and its history. When she'd asked to stay with him, he'd been surprised. He'd thought she would have gone back to France. She had made friends with Robin. The two women had become inseparable, like sisters.

***

He opened the door to Dr. Schneider's waiting room and led Emma in. They sat down.

Robin had bought Emma new clothes. She looked beautiful that morning. A translator stepped in almost immediately and introduced herself. She and Emma started signing and Emma smiled.

Schneider stepped into the anteroom and the three women went into the office.

He sat down and waited. He got a text from Marvin.

731 Fell Street…. Caught one white boy.

Ok…

Emma sat in the chair across from the two women and rested her palms on the knees of her new jeans.

"I'm Doctor Schneider," the doctor said, smiling. She waited for the translation. "I know," Emma signed.

There was a pause.

The doctor leaned in and looked at her kindly. "How are you, Emma?"

Emma looked at the translator, then at the doctor. She didn't know how to answer.

"I want to climb the route. It a E7 route at Céüse. There are key places in the cliff you must reach. Each hand hold is important and signals the next," she signed carefully. "When I go back."

The doctor heard the translation. She looked at Emma. She wanted to nod, but didn't. *We both like to climb*, the doctor thought. *Even if it means dying.*

About the Author

Kent Harrington is the author of numerous acclaimed novels, including *Last Ferry Home*, *The Good Physician*, which was named as one of the best novels of the last ten years by *Booklist*, *Dark Ride*, *Dia de los Muertos*, and *The American Boys*. Of *Dark Ride*, Michael Connelly said, "It reads like Jim Thompson interpreted by Quentin Tarantino."

Visit him at www.kentharrington.com.